John A. Steuart

Wine on the Lees

John A. Steuart

Wine on the Lees

ISBN/EAN: 9783337324414

Printed in Europe, USA, Canada, Australia, Japan

Cover: Foto ©Andreas Hilbeck / pixelio.de

More available books at **www.hansebooks.com**

WINE ON THE LEES.

By JOHN A. STEUART. Author of
"THE MINISTER OF STATE"
"IN THE DAY OF BATTLE"
&c

LONDON
HUTCHINSON & CO
PATERNOSTER ROW   MDCCCXCIX

PRINTED BY
HAZELL, WATSON, AND VINEY, LD.,
LONDON AND AYLESBURY

WINE ON THE LEES

PROLOGUE

TWICKHAM declared he would treat Capel Court and its purlieus to a sensation they were likely to remember as long as they had foundations to shake; and it was generally admitted he kept his word. Sated, hardened operators owned that the Twickham flotation gave them a new and very delectable thrill; and to this day the raptures of that glorious time are recalled with tinglings and yearnings for a return of the old delirium. For to Capel Court sensation is the breath of life. Its ways are the ways of the tempest and the whirlpool, and nothing short of a million gives it an extra heart-throb. Twickham gratified it with a seething excitement; wherefore it comes that in times of petty speculation, when the frivolous block hats to prevent yawning, the more adventurous sigh and say: "Oh for one hour of Twickham!" So the Old Guard sighed for the Little Corporal.

When after many rumours, sent forth one day to be contradicted the next, it was definitely announced that Messrs. Twickham & Son, the famous brewers of St. Edmund-upon-Stare, had decided to share the profits of their liquid gold-mine with the public, the high priests of Mammon promptly made arrangements for "rigging" the market. Lean patrons of the "bucket shop," and fat dealers in "gilt-edge," were alike in a state of ecstasy. A prescient and enterprising press burst forth dazzlingly on the chances of investors, gratuitously adding tips. The passion for gambling well kindled spread like an epidemic, making a million sober heads giddy. Everybody with cash or credit, and multitudes with no pretensions to either, swarmed and scrambled for the spoil. Mayfair, forgetting its antipathy to trade, blocked the city thoroughfares with its carriages. Great ladies, bewitching beauties, amateur and professional, who had never before been east of Chancery Lane, peers and parsons, lawyers, doctors, generals, admirals, gay sparks and grave Members of Parliament, the Church, the Law, Medicine, the Army, the Navy, Fashion in all its branches, besieged the city offices of Messrs. Twickham, jostling for a word in the ear of the shining dispenser of riches. The Twickham fever raged like a plague. The talk was Twickham, Twickham, and nothing but Twickham. Before the appearance of the prospectus the shares were quoted at 250 per cent, premium.

It was an intoxicating tribute to commercial genius. For a little, Twickham the brewer had the emotions of Napoleon the Emperor at Austerlitz. The great, the rich, the beautiful sued at his feet. By a word, or a stroke of the pen he could make crowds jubilant or wretched. His figure for solicited favours was five millions sterling, with 25 per cent added as fillip, and it was offered ten times over. Touched by this flattering evidence of popularity he was in danger of yielding to feminine wiles ; and indeed, if the saints themselves have fallen when beauty cajoled, what is to be expected of a mere man of the world ? Yet even in that trying hour Twickham saw his duty and clung to it. He was a man and disposed to gladden the hearts of fair creatures who though not understanding the game would " dearly love to try their luck." But Commerce has no gallantry. The licensed victuallers had first right and were claiming it. Then came the heterogeneous outer rings of the trade, a company hard to humour. There might possibly remain a few crumbs for Mayfair, but even so much could not be promised.

Particular friends alone received special allotments, and these were generous ; for Twickham knew how to confer a favour. To the vulture-speculator his subscriptions were returned ; whereupon a cry arose that " Old Bung was putting on side." Here it is sufficient to remark that Old Bung and his advisers understood very well what they were about.

The Twickhams had long been famous makers of ale. For three generations it was their proud boast that in slaking the thirsty throats of their countrymen they had beaten all rivals, a Herculean feat seeing what gallant topers Britons are. By dint of invincible spirit and matchless resource the brewery on the banks of the Stare grew till the fame of it filled the land. Its ale became the staple of half the taprooms from Dover to the Tweed ; nay it disputed sovereignty with the national drink across the border, while abroad it kept pace with the English language and the Christian religion. In consequence the Twickhams flourished as that green bay tree which is the eternal emblem of well-deserved prosperity. A family tree so well cultivated naturally bore good fruit. Two baronets came in succession, and one fine morning the world awoke to find it had produced in consummation of its efforts, a lord, a visible indubitable peer of the realm. Viscount Twickham instantly became the cynosure of a nation's eyes.

"See what beer does," said the country, with its nose in the foam of Twickham's best. "See what beer does." And the enthusiastic shouted, "Good for Old Bung. He gives us ale ; and the Queen, she makes him a lord. Quite right o' she to mind the beer."

It is not to be assumed that beer alone sent Sir Vincent Twickham to the House of Lords. The tools to him who can handle them. The great brewer counted princes and premiers among his familiar friends. The scale of his entertainments was regal ; and in the House of Commons, which he adorned for several years, he proved the most complaisant voter in an assembly of zealous puppets. He rarely made speeches ; they were not "in his line." He had no ambition to shine as a windbag ; to tell the truth he heartily despised the species. It was his pride to serve—first the people, by giving them something to drink ; second his friends in Parliament, by voting as they wished. Political scruples he had none, and chatter about principles he left to faddists. Moreover, as the wire-pullers were well aware, he understood the delicate art of giving. No man indeed ever gave with a nicer judgment or a shrewder eye to results.

It is the privilege of statesmen to keep a jealous eye on their country's honour, but it is their duty to keep the other, and generally the alerter, on the con- tributors to the party funds. Never mind what the Twickham colours were. Enough that their owner was in due time remembered for the double grace of liberality and docility. Nor was any one bold enough to whisper he was honoured unfairly. He was rich, bountiful, pliant ; that was enough for his friends— he made super-excellent ale ; that was more than enough for such as might have been his enemies. England, heaven be praised, knows how to honour her benefactors.

It was soon after his elevation that he played nine-pins with the pillars of the Stock Exchange. When the game was over Viscount Twickham found more gold awaiting his pleasure with Messrs. Solomons, the Hebrew bankers, than dazzled Monte Cristo in the magic cavern. How to deal with it was a question which presented difficulties. As a beginning the family estates in England were enlarged—a provident stroke, for it happened that land was cheap—and Scotland was laid under contribution for one of her choicest deer-forests, a stroke of social policy. At the same time his lordship took up the duties of a peer of the realm with all the ardour of his character. He was not six months ennobled when his horse won the Derby amid unparalled enthusiasm. If his yacht was beaten at Cowes, the fault was another's. He encouraged all manly amusements, patronised benevolent and charitable institutions, and generously gave the Church a hand when she wanted a bazaar opened or a foundation stone laid ; and for the rest remembered that money is made to be spent and honours conferred to be enjoyed.

He had soared into the genial region of nobility, but he never forgot the fair fat land of cent. per cent. wherein his roots were nourished. A genuine Englishman he was proud of his race, proud of its energy, pluck, solidity, material progress and accumulated gold. Above all he gloried in its love of beer.

"My countrymen," he said once, " know what agrees with them best. On beer they have conquered the world ; by beer they will maintain their conquests. They love beer, and while it pleases Heaven to spare me they shall have it. Let who will make their laws so long as I am allowed to brew their ale."

It was observed that Old Bung knew a thing or two. At any rate he did not neglect the firm of

Twickham & Son, Limited, whose interests were still inextricably entwined with his own. He continued to give the shareholders the benefit of his ripe judgment and unique experience, a circumstance on which they dwelt feelingly once a year—at the great annual meeting when accounts were presented and passed and thumping dividends confirmed ; when also my lord made a speech felicitating all concerned, and setting forth in the most agreeable manner the ever-extending appreciation of the Twickham brew. Excellent reason they had to speak with moist eyes of his services. Under his able direction the fame of the firm, as an eloquent shareholder remarked, was every day rising higher and higher and spreading further and further till it outran the map-makers. Twickham's ale was indeed in all men's mouths. You entered city taverns to find glass and tankard frothing with Twickham ; you scoured the country with a like result. Twickham drays blocked the streets, Twickham casks overflowed railway stations and filled foreign bound ships. You could as little escape Twickham as fate. If you took the wings of the morning and flew to the uttermost ends of the earth, lo ! there was Twickham before you. It was the boast of Twickham & Son, Limited, that they were among the most successful pioneers of British civilisation. Where the sword and the Bible were to-day there the Twickhams were to-morrow with all the blessings of ale. The foremost missionaries in the world, they had veritably the earth for an inheritance, and the fulness thereof they converted in true Christian fashion to dividends, payable half-yearly at the banking-house of Messrs Solomons, of Lombard Street in the City of London. Is it any wonder that Viscount Twickham was one of the most popular men in the empire ?

It was perfectly well understood among his friends

that his lordship made no mistake about the scource
or foundation of his unique power. As a man of the
world he knew that success meant money, and money
success. To him every person, place, and thing had
a price. When it suited him he paid that price;
when it didn't he allowed the bargain to pass on.
"Money," he declared confidentially, "is your true
magician. It will accomplish anything—for him
who can use it. Fanatics, who fancy themselves
philosophers, prate about the root of all evil. Give
those pietists a chance to nibble, and see what happens.
You may like it or not, but gold rules the world,
gold is omnipotent. Preachers pretend to deplore
the fact. I take the world as I find it. God has
not made me responsible for the tastes of my fellow
men. I'm a practical man; my business is with
facts; and I tell you I wouldn't give a crack of my
thumb for all the theories ever evolved by idle or
foolish brains. If you doubt the truth of what I
say, cast your virtues into one scale and let me load
the other with gold."

He spoke from experience. Once, indeed, his
magician failed him. One day, nay, rather one black
night, there fell upon him and his an enemy never
yet foiled or overcome by power of gold. It was
a bitter fight and the scars of it he carried to his
dying day. But of that the reader shall hear at the
proper time.

Book I

Book I

CHAPTER I

TWICKHAM TOWERS, lifting a majestic front in the midst of costly exotics, looks down over a grassy slope upon a beech wood, which affords enchanted peeps of the clustered chimney-pots and rust-red roofs of the ancient town of St. Edmund-upon-Stare and of its gleaming homely river. Nowhere could a lover of sylvan landscape delight his soul with softer, more exquisitely alluring glimpses and vistas ; nowhere would the critical foreigner versed in "the holy writ of beauty" be likelier to glow in admiration of the unmatched loveliness of English woods and meadows, the quaint warm cosiness of English towns, and the luxurious repose of English mansions. For over and about St. Edmund are blended the charms which make rural England a new and better Eden ; a place of streams and gardens and orchards and blossomy bowers, of pastures rich with browsing cattle, and woodlands alive with game. A poet looking forth from the altitude of Twickham Towers on a golden summer afternoon, his senses steeped in manifold incense of flower and foliage, might dream of eternal lotus-eating ; but the peptic native is apt to find his mind running on mellow drinks and savoury fleshpots. And indeed the St. Edmund country suggests above all else the solid joys of good living.

For centuries the town had dozed beside its murmurous river, paying little heed to the vanities of the noisy outer world, drinking its home-brewed, eating its juicy roast, dancing about the Maypole, growing its corn, fattening its beeves, courting and taking provident care that the population did not run down. Slaves of ambition toiled and bled, dynasties were demolished, empires rose and fell, Cromwell decapitated a king that he might play for a while with the sceptre; Blake and Nelson made the sea England's chief highway; Clive gained India; Cornwallis lost America; Wellington trounced Napoleon; and all the while St. Edmund-upon-Stare drowsed beside its sleepy river.

It might have drowsed till doomsday; it might have crumbled and died of inanition, but for the advent of one Ebenezer Twickham, with a seething brain and an outfit of mash tuns and fermenting vats. To his energy and foresight the world owes the Twickham Brewery, which practical intellects have long reckoned one of the memorable achievements of the age. St. Edmund-upon-Stare has fittingly honoured him with a statue, in which the great man appears with uplifted arm, as if solemnly admonishing all whom it might concern to mind what they were about. He took excellent care what he was about himself, as his neighbours knew and his heirs found to their lasting happiness. Nearly half a century after he quitted the scene of his triumphs some one, sacrilegiously emboldened by liquor, knocked the forefinger from the raised hand with an oath that they were having too much Twickham; and the folly jeopardised his life. The finger was reverently restored by an artist from the metropolis, and to-day the circumstances of the loss and restoration, as well as the fate of the culprit, may be read in the town records. Since then no one, even in liquor, has ventured an assault upon Twickham.

This Ebenezer, the founder of the family, was the grandfather of our viscount. Gossip, which is ever spiced with malice, affirmed he left the paternal roof in the capacity of tailor's apprentice. Why that should be a cause of sneering let the charitable imagine. Were a king your grandfather some people would jeer, and when kings are turned to scorn what are you to expect for tailors? But of vastly more importance than the jeers of the rabble is the fact that the tailor's apprentice, turned brewer, speedily became the first man in St. Edmund-upon-Stare. Napoleons do not always lead troops to battle. The House of Hanover reigns, but so far as St. Edmund is concerned the House of Twickham rules. The power has descended as power should, from father to son, so that when Sir Vincent Twickham succeeded to the family vats it was to find himself invested with the magic qualities of an idol. *Noblesse oblige.* Viscount Twickham was not the man to forget the town which sheltered like a confiding chicken under the Twickham wing. As county magnate he directed its affairs ; as county magistrate he guarded its morals. Here and there a cynic smiled privily in his sleeve, or referred sarcastically to reformed tastes and habits, as though it were forbidden to drop the ginger that becomes hot in the mouth. That trick of recalling the past is one of the most disconcerting devices of Satan. But, if the naked truth must be told, there was a time when Viscount Twickham did not fête Sunday Schools nor applaud homilies from the magisterial bench. Once, at a fashionable public school, it was nearly being a case of expulsion. Nothing but his father's position and his own admirable nerve saved him. At the University the story of his deeds inspired a succeeding generation, though you will search the calendar in vain for a list of his honours. When in the fulness of time another

Twickham was ready for the University, the youth was sent, not to the seat of learning at which his father had shone, but to the sister University, lest he should give ear to idle tales.

"There's no use putting nonsense in a boy's head," Sir Vincent explained to his friend and old college chum, the Earl of Wegron, "that will come soon enough, God knows."

"Where ignorance is bliss," snickered the earl.

Sir Vincent shrugged his shoulders comically.

"The moralists will spare me," he said.

"As you will," responded the earl genially. "Let poets and proverb-makers slide, only I must remark they are often amazingly shrewd fellows. And some of them were masters in the art of conviviality, which I fear we are losing."

"Well, well," rejoined Sir Vincent, "let's be content with such flings as we've had. You and I have not missed our share of cakes and ale."

"Philosophic as usual," remarked the earl. "My sole regret is that you are obliged to use the past tense. Yes, we've had our bite and sup, and the flavour lingers on the palate. For which and divers other reasons, as the lawyers say, I commend the wisdom of giving Vin a perfectly fresh field. The boy should not be handicapped by the paternal virtues."

CHAPTER II

IT chanced one day while Lord Twickham sat sternly in his place as Chairman of the local Bench that a man, a stranger to the town, appeared in the dock to answer a charge of drunken and riotous conduct. The culprit was still young, under thirty probably, though it would have been futile to search his inflamed and defeatured face for a single line of youth. For the present the lines of youth were obliterated. The countenance he turned upon the magistrates expressed in equal degrees a hardened contempt for respectability and a love of unlawful diversion. Yet a physiognomist would have hesitated to condemn him off hand. The red eye which gleamed from beneath a grotesque roll of bandages suggested sociality and good humour. And indeed his instincts were wholly sociable. On arriving in St. Edmund he began genially by drinking healths, but, getting over-heated, ended illogically by breaking heads. It was always his luck he declared on regaining his wits to make "a bloomin' hass" of himself. In the present instance he added incapacity to crime, by allowing his own head to suffer in the *mêlée*. Glancing at it as seen above the dock rail, you might have mistaken it for a caricature clumsily executed out of dirty linen. It was only when the right eye winked slily and coolly below the grimy bandages that the onlooker appreciated the situation.

The left eye couldn't wink; it was closed, apparently for an indefinite period.

The available optic gazed curiously at the Bench, as if magistrates were freaks of nature, exhibited for the public entertainment. It was especially bent on the central figure, Viscount Twickham. Even while the clerk read the charge and the constable gave damning evidence, the prisoner studiously and stead-fastly regarded the chairman—naturally as the greatest of the freaks. When he was stripped of character and the Bench was ready with its sentence the prisoner was formally asked if he had anything to say for himself; for the law indulges in the pleasantry of first making up its mind and then pretending to listen to the victim.

Smiling as urbanely as was possible with his condition of face, he gave his waist-belt a hitch and cleared a raucous alcoholic throat. Then, having thanked his judges for their courtesy, he proceeded to explain that he was down from London, in search of health; no—he begged their pardon—he meant in search of work, and quite contrary to intentions, which were excellent, had got "barmy" at the "Jolly Friar." He assured their worships he "didn't want to do no 'arm to no one." Yet he had been ignominiously "chucked." He put it to their worships as gentleman, Was that fair on a bloke? The chairman remarked their worships would answer the question presently. Meantime, had he any more valid reason to give for trampling on the laws of his country? Giving his waist-belt another hitch he replied he "didn't know as he had," since he rather fancied they had heard the whole story from the "copper." He wouldn't say a word against the copper who was "only a-doin' of his dooty," though it was "cruel 'ard on poor coves a-lookin' for work," and trying to be pleasant. For the rest if their worships would only show a fellow feeling this time, "S'elp him Gawd" he'd never trouble them again.

"You've given all the trouble you could this time," retorted the Bench. "You resisted arrest, and refused both name and address."

"S'elp him Bob," he was distressed to hear that. He "hadn't no recollection, being a bit breezy atop." However, his name, he hastened to add, was Richard Goodman. "Dick Goody, they calls me, your worships," he volunteered.

"Who call you?" demanded the Bench.

"The blokes 'bout Shoreditch," he answered.

"And your address?" enquired the Bench.

That was harder to settle. To-day it was St. Edmund-upon-Stare; to-morrow it might be "Gawd alone knew wot."

The Bench had an idea what it was likely to be. Well! they knew best. Mr. Goodman was not going to "argify." "Them as gets barmy must expect to face the beak," he admitted.

Touched by the reasonableness of the sentiment the Chairman asked if this were the first offence. The man in the dock paused a moment, as if stunned by the shocking innocence of the question; then he leaned forward, smiling confidentially. He wouldn't deceive their worships; they had asked him a straight question; he would give them a straight answer. "No, it wasn't the first offence."

"How does the number run then?" cooed the Bench, leaning forward in turn. Goodman was captivated. Had it been worth while he could have lied as deftly as any diplomat and stuck to the falsehood like a man. But simpletons had put him on his honour, and he publicly announced he would be shot before deceiving them. They listened to the declaration with contracted eyelids, nodding their heads in appreciation! "First offence!—he reckoned it was somewhere about the twentieth."

A dead silence fell on the Bench at this awful admission. Mr. Goodman shifted from the right foot to the left, put his elbows on the dock-rail and waited, with a bland accommodating expression, which seemed to say there was no need to hurry. Presently the chairman's strong voice filled the room.

"I commend your honesty," he said, looking hard at the prisoner. "But yours is a case in which a seeming virtue points to deplorable vice."

Be it so. Mr. Goodman would not presume to contradict. His worship knew best. Besides his worship understood more clearly than most people the temptation of the drop o' drink. Lord Twickham drew himself up, flashing rebuke. Why, what possible temptation was drink to a properly conducted person? Mr. Goodman disavowed all knowledge of that "kind o' pusson," but reiterated the opinion that his worship must know what a sore temptation the drop o' drink is to a poor cove down on his luck. His worship knew nothing of the sort; but what had the prisoner been drinking? Whiskey?

"No, 'tweren't whiskey."

"Gin then?"

"No, 'tweren't gin. 'Twere just Twickham's ale."

It was said his lordship winced visibly; but he wasn't the man to be embarrassed.

"Nonsense," he said severely. "Nonsense. Men don't get tipsy on beer."

The man in the dock feeling sure of his ground hitched up for an argument.

"Beggin' pardon," he ventured, "but——"

"Nonsense," repeated his lordship, with increased severity. "Nonsense!"

The prisoner delicately suggested a bet.

"If I was to get a tanner for every man as I've

seed fuddled an' fightin' on beer," he said, " I shouldn't do no more work."

" You don't appear to do any work as it is,"·retorted his lordship, ending the colloquy. " Five shillings, or seven days."

" Going to pay ? " enquired the clerk.

Instead of answering Mr. Goodman turned to the back of the Court and, raising his hand, beckoned a woman who sat in the remotest corner, hiding a child in the folds of a ragged shawl.

. "Got the oof, Jen ? " he called. " Got five bob ? "

Jen rose and shuffled forward, wrapping the shawl about the child. At sight of Goodman the child held out a pair of scraggy arms ; then looking round the room began to whimper. Tears were also in the mother's eyes, and the man frowned savagely.

" There now," he said gruffly, " don't you be a turnin' on them water-works ; their worships mightn't like it."

" Silence, sir," cried the chairman suddenly. " Another word and you go to jail without option."

There was a singular thrill in his voice. His brother magistrates glancing up noted an expression of mingled surprise and anger in his face. His eyes were fast on the woman, though ·it was observed she did not once look up at him. But she was trembling violently. The shawl that held the child fluttered and her hand shook uncontrollably as she unrolled first a piece of cloth and then a piece of paper and handed out five shillings. His lordship bending forward saw that nothing remained. Jen had, in fact, paid down her last farthing. By prodigious sacrifice she had saved the little sum, hiding it from her husband, and now it was all gone—to pay for a drunken spree. Unable to control herself she turned away sobbing.

CHAPTER III

AT Twickham Towers that day Mr. Goodman's illicit gaieties furnished a distinguished luncheon-party with an occasion for some exhilarating wit and many appropriate reflections on the depravity of the poor. A few of the guests had seen and heard Dick in court ; one pronounced him a typical true-blue ruffian, a second thought him amusing, while a third, to wit young Lord Tapley, heir apparent to the Earldom of Wegron, expressly admired his nerve. The company thus agreeably diversified in opinion included Lord Tapley's father, the renowned Earl of Wegron himself, his daughter Lady Gwendoline Tibbits, ordained as the reader will find, for a splendid destiny, the Right Rev. Josiah Tinkle, D.D., Lord Bishop of Blockley, a divine famous for his social graces and the piety of his published works, Mr. Duncan MacTor, the Scottish whiskey king, for the present a missionary to the Sassenach in the interests of Usqubeagh, and the Rev. Dichory Bird, rector of the parish. The Hon. Vincent Twickham, prospective viscount, and his younger brother Reginald, then home from Harrow for the holidays, were also there. Having nothing to do but enjoy itself, the company talked with the easy good-humour which promotes digestion, lightly settling questions which have vexed the race ever since the days of Job. Lord Twickham alone seemed to feel there are things in heaven and earth not dreamed of in luncheon-table philosophy,

and this feeling presently intruded itself in conversation.

"It must be a very curious thing," he observed in
the tone of one musing aloud, "it must be a very
curious thing to part with one's last ha'penny, absolutely one's last."

All eyes were turned on him in quick surprise. Why,
what an extraordinary idea for a multi-millionaire!

"It must be a very curious thing," repeated Lord
Twickham deliberately; "I never thought of it
before."

"Visions of the poor-house," said MacTor jocularly;
"alarming!"

The Earl of Wegron grinned as he looked at his
old friend.

"Getting sentimental?" he said. "You'll have to
be careful or you'll be concerned about your soul next."
He nodded at the Bishop of Blockley as if to say:
"Look out shepherd, you'll have a sick sheep on your
hands presently." The bishop coughed discreetly
over a chicken-salad, thereby intimating the Twickham
soul was in no danger.

"I suppose it's that wretched woman in Court to-
day who put the idea in your head," concluded the
Earl of Wegron.

For himself he would not have thought twice of
the incident of a wretched wife paying out her last
farthing for a profligate husband. With ten generations of noble blood in his veins he had never given
way to sentiment, not even in his love affairs, which
were conducted on strictly business principles.
Though chronically impecunious, he despised and
ground the poor, held vulgar poverty and vice to be
one and the same thing, and hated democracy with
the quenchless hatred of a lean-pursed, long-pedigreed
peer, who hotly and persistently resents any conces-
sion to plebeianism. Firmly convinced that the

world was made for the nobility, he could not forgive Providence for permitting common folk to prosper.

For the rest, he conducted himself as an impoverished peer should—gambled judiciously, raised the wind as often and as high as was possible with his resources, did his utmost to procure pleasure at the expense of friends and heirs, and as a hereditary legislator voted against every measure intended for the benefit of the people.

"The people be hanged," was his reply to the expostulations of a party Whip once. "Are we to be for ever enriching the people at the cost of their betters? Here am I with falling rents and establishments to maintain. Do you bring in a bill for my relief? Let the people go to ——." And the Whip went off to report to the Prime Minister, who was also a peer and rather envied Wegron his freedom of speech.

When Dick came up for discussion his lordship made no pretence of sympathising either with the man or his tearful wife. So far as he could make out they deserved what they got; and the Right Rev. the Lord Bishop of Blockley, knowing that an earl's opinions are not to be treated lightly, made haste to confirm them. Dr. Tinkle was bound to say it became Christians to feel for those to whom an Inscrutable Wisdom had denied wealth or station. At the same time he was sorry to say the poor had themselves too often to blame for their hardships. They squandered their time, their money, their opportunities; they were incontinent, spendthrift, drunken, and, he had to confess, frequently dishonest. It was the old, old story.

"By the bane their own bad lives instil, they suffer all the miseries of their states."

"I was touched to-day," responded Lord Twickham

'because I know the woman. You remember Jenks?"
he asked, looking at his wife.

"Jenks?" repeated her ladyship; "not the pretty
Jenny Jenks?"

"The pretty Jenny Jenks," said his lordship. "An
old servant," he explained to the company, "and a
good one, I believe—the daughter of respectable
people in the town here. But it was London,
London ; she had that paradise of the ignorant on
the brain. So to London she went. Now she turns
up suddenly, haggard, ragged and wretched, to empty
a poor purse for that fellow—presumably her husband.
Why such a girl should marry such a man I don't
pretend to understand."

"Ah!" put in the Rev. Dichory Bird with an
unctuous smile, "your lordship can have no idea how
eager some girls are to be married. I mean girls in
her position," he added quickly, lest he might offend
an earl's daughter and the *fiancée* of the Hon.
Vincent Twickham.

"After to-day I can form some idea how eager
many of them must be to get unmarried," returned
his lordship.

"Ay indeed, you might think that," remarked the
MacTor, with a chuckle, "if it wasn't that human
nature's so queer. You can never account for a
woman's taste. It's just as wonderful, my lord,"
glancing at the bishop, "as the mysteries of Providence, and a great deal more erratic. Now there's
Glasgow and Edinburgh ; you go into the Salt
Market and the Cowgate and you find a man knocking his wife down just as fast as she can rise. You
interfere in her behalf and, by George! before you
know where you are they're both knocking you down.
In East London it's just the same. I think it must
be true that a woman has a sneaking fondness for a
scamp."

"They're only half civilised," said the Bishop of Blockley. "It's the pagan idea——"

An exclamation from Lady Gwendoline brought him to a sudden pause.

"I meant in the slums," he explained bowing with the gallantry of a Don Quixote; "with the lower orders the pagan idea that the man owns the woman body and soul still prevails."

"And the woman acquiesces, nay rejoices," put in MacTor.

The Earl of Wegron shook his head.

"Don't be too sure," he said. "One of the gamest fights I ever saw was a little chit in petticoats in the Drury Lane region, trying to close her lord's 'peepers' as she called them. I put two to one on her and I'd have won too if the police hadn't stopped her. In justice to my friend MacTor's views, however, I must express my belief that had I attempted to get between the pair they'd both have turned on me. Indeed, I rather fancy they turned on the police."

"It's very sad," said Lady Twickham, with a sigh; "very sad."

Her ladyship, a valetudinarian and a permanent blessing to the medical profession, was greatly oppressed by the general wickedness of the world. In the country she kept the Rev. Dichory Bird busy, and in town she had bishops, deans, and archdeacons on the track of Satan. At times she was unreasonably dejected, because, as Lord Wegron put it, her huntsman failed to bag the quarry. But she went on paying handsomely, and was the object of much official sympathy on the part of the Church.

"Ah! if the rich and great were all like your ladyship," eminent divines would write ecstatically, in acknowledging her cheques, "how much it would mean to us!"

Naturally she was distressed by the story of Jenks'

downfall and misery. In general, his wife's sentiments did not affect Lord Twickham, who had a will and a way and opinions of his own. But in this instance he looked at her wistfully, as with a secret fellow-feeling. Then, having in his rapid and masterful fashion come to a decision, he turned to his son and heir.

"Vin," he said abruptly, "I want you to do a little business for me this afternoon."

The business was to seek out Jenny and her husband, enquire cautiously into ways and means, and give such aid in cash as might be charitable and prudent. Vincent was ready in a jiffy, his alacrity being due partly to filial devotion, partly to Lord Tapley's meaning looks and whispers of adventure, but chiefly (if the truth must be told) to the chance thus opportunely presented by the Providence of lovers, of getting Lady Gwendoline's opinion of a new horse. At the proposition Lady Gwendoline's eyes glowed and a transporting flush overspread her piquant face. She would be delighted to judge. The astute fancied they divined other delights; and as the party drove off in a high dogcart most of the elderly people thought youth and love very touching things. Only the two grisled lords viewed the tender relations of Vincent and the Lady Gwendoline with perfectly clear and unromantic eyes.

Lord Twickham had cash and, other considerations being satisfactory, a leaning to blue blood; Lord Wegron had blue blood, and, irrespective of other considerations, wanted cash. He was therefore entirely satisfied with the state of affairs. Indeed it was due principally to his own admirable tact; for he had taken pains to school his daughter in the intricacies of the matrimonial question. A widower for twelve years, the earl had several times during that period considered the policy of ennobling the daughter, or widow (it was immaterial which) of an American millionaire. When it came to terms, however, he rated blood above current prices. So the twelve years passed and he was still in the market.

When he noticed the leaning of the House of Twickham to the House of Wegron he loyally laid his own love affairs aside to attend to those of his daughter. At first Lady Gwendoline spoke contemptuously of beer, but as a man of the world her father speedily corrected her false notions.

"My child," he said impressively, one day when they were alone, "the Wegrons have always been distinguished for a nice taste in pleasure. That taste, I am gratified to observe, continues. Believe me, I love to see my daughter make a figure among the great and the gay. A niggardly economy is the sure mark of a low mind. Some people hoard riches after the manner of the ant, a grain at a time. That has never been our way. In truth the credit of the house has been rather an expensive thing to maintain all these centuries. I am not making any reflection on my ancestors—they did well; they even did nobly. Wherever you find a Wegron there you find England's best. But the expense of being princes and social leaders is enormous. To be quite candid, the estates, as you may have guessed, are embarrassed. Exercise your good sense. Your fortune is in your own hands, and to a considerable extent mine as well."

"You wouldn't have me make a mercenary marriage," cried Lady Gwendoline. "Oh! papa, that were a fall for pride."

"Pooh, pooh," said the earl. "Don't be foolish. Pride, my dear, must have something to stand on. It prospers best on money. You remember the proverb: 'If money go before, all ways do lie open.' Not an elevated sentiment, but true. On the score of lineage, compared with the Wegrons, I grant you the

Twickhams are of yesterday, or rather of this morning. I have heard, too, that the founder of the family
wielded the shears—sartorially, not tonsorially ; a
tailor, not a barber."

" Shocking ! " ejaculated Lady Gwendoline.

" Not so shocking as it seems," responded the earl,
" We all start somewhere. If they don't lie, the best
of us are descended from a gardener, not too reput-
able a character either, by Jove. And Twickham the
tailor-brewer must have been a clever fellow. The
Twickhams deal in an article for the rabble—that's
disagreeable ; but they're rich, incredibly rich, and
they might have worse faults. If your sainted
mother were alive, Gwen, she'd put matters more
lucidly, more convincingly. As it pleased God to
deprive me of her counsel and guidance, I am charged
with a double duty towards you. I wish heaven
had spared me your mother. Be wise, my child.
Vincent Twickham has £10,000 a year of pocket-
money."

He ended with such emotion in his voice that Lady
Gwendoline was overcome on the spot. So when
the crisis came she dutifully conferred her young
affections on Vincent, thinking of the £10,000 a year
of pocket-money. For his part he adored her without
thought of her empty purse, and the world saw no
reason whatever to doubt that beer and blue blood
would make an excellent mixture.

" She is lucky," was the general verdict of her
friends. " A good fellow, and illimitable cash. Yes,
Gwen is lucky."

Somehow Vincent's luck was less remarked.

"THE Jolly Friar, I suppose," Vincent called over his shoulder, as they entered St. Edmund.

"Likeliest place of worship for one of his faith," answered Tapley. "Sure to be there or thereabouts, unless old Lobes has had him chucked or run in again."

Old Lobes was kind, or had not been provoked. At the Jolly Friar they found Mr. Goodman holding a sort of levée, and to all appearance gloriously in his element. On catching sight of them Mr. Lobes, who happened to be in his little private office and shirt sleeves, slung on his best bar-coat, and hastened with fit emotion and demeanour to welcome his distinguished visitors. He was a man with a bald head, shaped like a pear, heavy end down, a watery eye, a pasty complexion, and a most excellent nose, the nose of the favourite of fortune, the nose which is not easily put out of joint. You find precisely the same style of organ leading cabinets, directing religion on the episcopal bench, meting out justice in law courts, creating sensations on the Stock Exchange, planning and winning victories for armies and navies. A fantastical logician has plausibly held that great men's brains must lodge in their noses ; for what, he asks, are shrewdness and foresight but the power of scenting the prize afar off ? Mr. Lobes had the very best of noses for smelling out good business. He had in addition a cultivated taste in cigars, and unfailing geniality in drinking with important customers. Endowed with abundant self-esteem only one thing really awed him—the presence of a Twickham. For the Jolly Friar was one of the multitude of Twickham tied-houses. The visit of Vincent was therefore an event for the red-letter calendar.

" How d'ye do, Lobes ? " said Vincent affably taking the landlord's puffy hand.

" Putty well, sir, putty well, a' thank you," answered Lobes gratefully, making a double genuflexion.

" Humming, by Jove," remarked Tapley, fixing his eyeglass very deliberately and surveying the room. " I say, Lobes, you know, dem me if there's anything like a rattling pub. You just sit comfortably smoking at the receipt of custom, and watch the beer pouring out and the cash pouring in. I've a good mind to start an opposition shop."

Mr. Lobes grinned deferentially.

" Things is putty well, my lord, putty well a-considerin'; he admitted. " It's the Twickham ale as does it, my lord," he pursued, putting his oozy lips uncomfortably close to Tapley's ear. " Three-and-thirty year I've been a 'andling that beer—three an' thirty year come noon o' Michaelmas ; an' I tell you wot it is, my lord, it's a gettin' more popilar every day. Rema'kable, but it's trewth. 'Pon my honour."

" Swear not by your honour, Lobes," returned Tapley, moving beyond range of Lobes's perfumed breath. " The stuff's good. Lobes, tell me ; is beer made for the Englishman or the Englishman for beer ? "

" Made for one another like man an' wife," replied Lobes gleefully.

" Good, Lobes," cried Tapley. " First rate. If you hadn't been born for higher things you'd have made your mark as a wit. Interesting company today, Lobes."

"Your lordship may say so," responded Lobes, with a meaning bow.

They were approaching the bar at which Mr. Goodman held court, and at the sound of new voices he turned, eyeing the intruders suspiciously.

"Oo's the bloomin' swells?" he asked gruffly.

Some one whispered in his ear; he snorted like a wild beast and his single eye glowed viciously.

"Son of the beak," he muttered from between set teeth. "The bloomin' skunk has robbed me this morning and insulted me to the bargain."

He took a step forward, his livid right eye fixed on Vincent, his body gathered as for a spring, his fists clenching automatically. Tapley dropped his eye-glass in some excitement.

"Vin," he said, in a hurried aside. "Get in the first right-hander, on the jaw if you can. Everything depends on being first. Plaster him against the wall —or wait, let me do it."

But Mr. Lobes had stepped to the front, outraged authority in his mien, his hand raised imperatively for peace.

"Since I knowed it the Jolly Friar has allus bin rema'kable for good horder," he said, drawing himself up in his most imposing manner, "and we ain't agoin' to stand no row from you. Take that es settled. Behive like a gentleman—pay your money and take your liquor decently and according to rules, and you're welcome—distub the peace and hout you go though you was made of gold and stamped at 'er Majesty's mint. That's the motto of this 'ouse. Take note, so as to prevent mistakes."

Dick, who was a good half-foot taller than Mr. Lobes, though somewhat slimmer in the waist, looked down half savagely, half disdainfully.

"Chuck me out, will yer?" he sneered. "I knows the gime of public-'ouses right through, top to bottom.

I tell you wot, I've been a chucker-out where ye'd be took with the ague at the bare idea of showin' yer pie-crust phiz. Chuck me out! I've pitched 'undreds of gents, better'n your father ever thought of makin' you, on their 'eads, right on their nuts an' heard him crack. Get out'n my way."

Though fearing nothing in human form, Mr. Goodman nevertheless realised the folly of knocking down the landlord of a public-house on his own floor. So he dodged. Mr. Lobes also dodged, and with such amazing vigour and agility that the two collided violently. It was Mr. Lobes who recoiled groaning, both hands clasped on an injured and protesting paunch. Behind arose a tumultuous murmur and rustle of excited feet. A barman valiantly leaped the counter to cope with the aggressor ; but, luckily for himself, was too late to get in the way. Dick made straight at his enemy ; and Vincent, who had graduated in the noblest of arts, promptly put himself into an attitude of defence. A thrill in every nerve, and lithely poised to strike or evade, he awaited the onset. But almost in the instant of action he was gripped by the shoulder and jerked aside.

"Leave him to me, I'll pepper him," said Tapley coolly fronting the infuriated Goodman.

At this unexpected manœuvre Dick paused, holding his breath in astonishment. Then, in spite of himself, he smiled, and the whole room instinctively stood still and watched. He honoured pluck, and here was audacity of the most captivating kind. For Tapley, though " prime " of his inches, was to his antagonist as a leopard to a lion : one stroke of the great paw and he should be senseless or writhing. Mr. Goodman looked down upon the boyish figure before him as Goliath might have looked down on the stripling David. Tapley was but a soft youth, while Mr. Goodman was a man of war from his childhood up ; a man, moreover, little accustomed to stick at trifles. The odds in his own favour both cooled and amused him.

"You oughter be in the army, Tottie," he said, almost genially. "I've followed worse men, 'eaps an' 'eaps of 'em."

The landlord who was getting over his pain, suddenly set up a cry of "police"; but Vincent begged him to forbear, since he and his friend had really come to look after this breaker of the peace. Saying that he made to get in front of Tapley.

"The quarrel's mine," he said with a quick retightening of the muscles.

But Tapley was not to be displaced.

"*J'y suis, j'y reste*," he answered, nodding at Vincent, He was not angry nor aggressive ; he was not even defiant. He was merely cool and good-humoured.

"Mumps old man," he remarked glancing at Dick's swollen jaws. "Might hurt you know. I call a truce. My friend and I didn't come here to put you to the trouble of fighting us. Honour me by intimating what you'll have to drink."

"An' let you have first lick, eh," responded Dick smelling treachery. "Bloomin' likely."

"I ask you," rejoined Tapley unabashed, "if you'll do us the honour of drinking with us. We're all gentlemen, I think. If you insist on a fight why conditions can be arranged according to the laws which govern the conduct of gentlemen. If this isn't honest Abraham, you'll pepper me hands down. How d'ye feel?"

"Well ! you're a prime little cove, an' no mistake," returned Mr. Goodman, softening perceptibly. "Since ye arsk me, I'm dry and a bit peckish."

"Just so," said Tapley with the air of a physician prescribing for a patient. "Just so. Well ! what do you say to a plate of good old roast, the roast beef of old England, to keep the liquid from slipping down too fast? Mr. Lobes, roast beef for one, if you please."

"If you wants it, my lord," responded Lobes doubtfully.

"I said for one, Lobes," rejoined Tapley. "Look here, mine host of the Jolly Friar, make it for three, and add a private room."

And he began to hum :

    "'O Crikey, Bill,' ses she to me, she ses,
     'Look sharp,' ses she, 'with them there sossiges.
     Yes! sharp with them there bags of mysteree!
     For lo!' she ses, 'for lo! old pal,' ses she,
     'I'm blooming peckish, neither more nor less.'"

"Mr. Lobes, lead the way; Mr Goodman the honour of your company," bowing and smiling.

Mr. Goodman's single eye opened still wider in wonder and a smile lit the corners of his mouth,

"'Scuse me, sir," he said, "but I can see as you've been down our way."

"And what way is that?" asked Tapley.

"Mile-End, Whitechapel, down heast generally."

"Bless you," answered Tapley, "I've heaps of friends there. Know Velvet Chick—does a little of the scientific and is the best judge of a bull-pup in the British Isles, or anywhere else. You know him?"

"Lor', sir, you don't mean Chick, as knocked Cock Robin out twenty-third round and broke his arm."

"I mean Chick, as knocked Cock Robin out twenty-third round and broke his arm."

"Crickey," cried Dick, "ain't me an' him just the biggest pals. See that eye, sir. Couldn't count the times it's been bunged up by Velvet Chick. Don't 'appen to know Tommy Binks, sir?"

"Binks!" repeated Tapley, gripping his chin to think the better.

"Tommy Binks of the Ruggler Den," added Dick.

"Binks of the Ruggler Den," said Tapley. "Let me see. Does he sing 'The Chickaleary Cove' when he's merry?"

"The very man," cried Dick rapturously. "'Eavens above! how did you find your way here, sir? Blest if it ain't a special Providence."

"Come and I'll tell you," replied Tapley.

"What about Gwendoline?" asked Vincent.

"Oh! by Jove, I had forgotten Gwen. Vin, you shouldn't have brought her. In affairs of this sort women are always in the way. Let me see. You can trust your man with that horse? Yes? very well. Gwen's the best hand in the world at filling in odd half-hours with shopping. Let's send her the round of the milliners."

The proposal was submitted to Lady Gwendoline who was all graciousness and assent.

"Only," she stipulated, addressing her brother, "you foot the bills, you know."

He made a wry mouth.

"If I must, I must," he said, "only for God's sake, Gwen, be moderate. It gives me the shivers to think how far I'm over my allowance already."

Instead of replying she smiled down upon Vincent.

"And I'm to have this high stepper for a whole hour. Well! I drive you know; and, by the way, you don't mind a little white on the flank."

Vincent didn't mind if flanks dripped foam. So Lady Gwendoline drove off joyously, leaving the gentlemen free to entertain Dick.

DESPITE his little burst of confidence Mr. Goodman did not immediately take his new friends to his heart. The meeting was singular and unexpected. Not that the unexpected any longer caused Dick surprise. With him it was usually the expected which didn't come to pass. Consequently there was no occasion to gape. Still in a world of guile one must be on one's guard and, as a matter of principle, Goodman trusted no one. When innocent people spoke of the underlying goodness of the race he could not help bursting into hoarse laughter of ridicule. Yes! he knew all about the goodness of the race. Would to God he possessed in hard cash all that the knowledge had cost him.! Yet he made no moan over the expense of his education. He had his strokes of luck like others ; when reverses came they were accepted as part of the game. As for the good that is done by stealth, of that he had no experience.

He had no reason to suppose that his present companions dropped from heaven on a special errand of mercy. So far as could be judged they were extremely human, as human as most of the other serpents that had stung him in his progress through the jungles of this world. With a fierce beat of the pulse it came back to him, that one of them, apparently the chief, though the less demonstrative, was the son of the" beak," the smug oppressor who had taken his last penny for a mere frolic. The other might be a gilded rip, no better than himself. He had heard dough-faced Lobes address him as " my lord " : but titles are cheap—ay, often cheap and nasty. What was the motive for all this display of philanthropy? Another deception? By the gods of the desperate, let him take care!

On entering the room reserved for the trio by the puzzled Lobes, he slouched into a corner, and instead of cramming his cap into a pocket, according to habit on great occasions, he drew it defiantly over his brows. Thus he sat lowering and watching, fox and wolf in one, his solitary eye expressing avid hate and distrust. What little game were these tailor-made things playing? They were very fine and gracious, oh! mighty kind to a poor bloke who couldn't as much as stand his turn of the drinks. Did they imagine he was blind because for the present he had but one eye? If so, they might awaken suddenly to a sense of their error.

It amused him to watch their manœuvring. He even admired their cunning, their easy supple movements, as of serpents noiselessly coiling and gliding: Then, at the recurring thought of his empty pockets, the tide of his anger rose afresh. His face burned, his fingers itched. What he wanted, what he meant to have, was revenge, a thing sweeter than all the beef and ale in England. With passion gurgling in his throat and throbbing along his veins, he got to his feet, vaguely intent on mischief—and encountered the persuasive eye of Tapley.

" Getting impatient? " smiled the viscount; "and no wonder. Our friend Lobes doesn't know the meaning of haste. If he doesn't look out, the great Peter will bang the door in his face some day. Serve him jolly well right too, say I. But here comes the stuff at last. Goodman, on my right here, if you please," seating himself as president of the feast. " Vin, we'll relegate you to the left. Sheep and goats, by Jove! quite Scriptural. Pray, Goodman, no re-moving of headgear. We know what bandages are."

Goodman flopped into the chair set for him by the obsequious waiter, wondering within himself why he was giving way. To be sure, the odours were savoury and the calls of his stomach peremptory. Besides, it would be a delightful stroke of irony to dine at the expense of those whom he intended to knock to jelly afterwards. It was like making them provide the weapons for their own execution.

"Don't mind a cove that's peckish settin' to work without grace?" he said, seizing a knife and fork.

Tapley lay back in his chair, laughing aloud. "A wag of the first water," he cried. "Said so the instant I clapped eyes on you—something in your looks, you know. Grace! fall to, dear boy, fall to. And what's to be the liquid?"

"Reckon there ain't nothin' 'ere but Twickham," growled Dick, with a glance at Vincent. "Had a sickenin' dose of him this morning—cleared me out —he did. But we'll have some more of 'im."

"Waiter, three glasses of your best ale, please," Tapley called, managing at the same time to wink at his friend. "And Goodman, my boy, what about pickles?"

"Pickles?" echoed Goodman, lifting his head and staying operations with his jaws.

"Pickles," repeated his host. "For myself as I'm a little off my feed, I'll indulge in an olive. Tickles the appetite you know."

"H'm!" snorted Goodman. "Needs a power of ticklin', don't it? If you was 'long o' me for a month, t'wouldn't be the happetite as ye'd be troublin' 'bout. Got an onion?" he demanded, so sharply that the obsequious, red-haired waiter started.

"Yes—sir."

Dick looked up contemptuously.

"Oh, you needn't be makin' yerself tired with no bloomin' 'sirs,'" he said caustically. "An' it ain't in the least necessary to be crookin' yer backbone to me," as the waiter, not knowing what else to do, bowed profoundly. "We'll hexcuse ceremony in the canteen department. Let's 'ave the onion."

He had his jar of pickled onions, and for a while ate desperately and in silence, the others merely winking and looking on. He seemed to be making up for six months' arrears, and it might be impolitic to interrupt. At length he laid down an empty glass, drew the back of his hand across his mouth, and lay back with a grunt of satisfaction. At that sign of content Tapley called for cigars.

"Eating's too serious a business to be interrupted," he observed, holding out the open box to Dick. "Over these we can talk."

The features under the cap and bandages expanded in a sudden grin.

"I say, matey," cried their owner, "am I dreamin' or is this 'eaven? More'n one?"

"A fistful, by all means," was the cordial response. "Or, wait, accept the box as it stands. I can see you're a connoisseur."

"Eh! The whole bloomin' lot! Tottie you're agoin' it," taking possession of the box. "You're adoin' it 'ot, an' no mistake. Well! 'ere's to yer 'ealth," striking a match. "Ye might be bigger, Tottie, ye might be bigger, but ye could 'ardly be better."

"No flattery," returned Tapley modestly.

"Oh, Lor'!" laughed Goodman. "I'm a born flatterer, I am—meets a cove by chance in a public-'ouse, an' butters him till he shines—that's me. Tottie, I've cracked 'eads for less. Have a cigar," holding out the box in turn. "I've 'eard as how the weed makes you feel 'eavenly arter a good tuck in."

When Tapley had helped himself, the box was passed on to Vincent.

"'Ave one of Mr. Lobes' cigars, sir," said Dick, "considerin' the circumstances reckon it's good. Don't you be a-taking it to 'art as you're a Twickham. You ain't sponsible for that. The best of us must 'ave an old man ; and Twickham's good, though the guv'nor won't believe as a poor peckish bloke, down on his luck, can get fuddled on it. If he was to try same as me, he'd find out. Yes, sir, Twickham's dam good."

Vincent thanked him for the testimonial, and the three lay back each behind a coiling cloud of smoke. By-and-by Tapley adjusted his eye-glass, and looked quizzically at the guest.

"Goodman," he drawled. "I think you've a history."

"Shouldn't be 'sprised, Tottie," returned Dick pleasantly, being greatly mollified by the improvement in the inner man. "Ain't you got one ? "

"I ? Oh, mine is commonplace—the story of the herd, you know. We haven't all equal chances. Fate's limited my range ; but you—I'll wager you've been up and down the world, as the parson says, like the very devil himself."

"Passon knows a 'eap 'bout the devil," chuckled Dick. "When I was in the army our Scotch chaplain told us things 'bout 'eaven an' 'ell an' old Nick as 'ud make you sweat to hear 'em, though I 'spicioned chaplain was just kiddin', to keep us straight."

"So you've worn the Queen's steel on your left hip," said Vincent, sitting up. "Please tell us the story. We love adventure."

"So does most folks sittin' in easy chairs suckin' cigars arter dinner," responded Dick. "Well, I done my seven year in 'er Majesty's togs, an' a bit of foreign to the bargain. Reckon I'm brown yet, if you was to look well. Know the 42nd Royal 'Ighlanders, Black Watch?—that was my regiment, an' though I ain't no 'Ighlander, I'll say this for 'em : started proper, they'd chaw up any other thousand men out of perdition, they would, an' smack their gobs when the job was done! Oh Lor'! they are gluttons for blood!" he pursued, reminiscently. "Start 'em with prayer an' prime 'em with grog, give 'em pipes an' bayonets an' let 'em go !—'Ighlanders at the charge, 'Ighlanders a-cheerin' an' goin' for the enemy,—it's 'ell, sir, roarin', glorious 'ell!" He gave two or three vigorous pulls at his cigar and sat erect, the old excitement of battle shining in his eye.

"I can hear the dam pipes now!" he cried, "an' the serjeant's Scotch accent a-keepin' us steady, an' the colonel telling us the general said we was to take the position, an' he needn't be informin' any man in 42nd tartan wot was expected of him. And then the roar as drowned everything, an' we was off straight for the belchin' guns. Ay, sir, an' the position was took arter a dandy English regiment had run, tail down! I hear them bullets a-whizzin' yet !"

"Bully!" cried Tapley, "go on."

"I've 'eard," continued Goodman, "I've 'eard Lord Wolseley makin' a speech 'bout the red 'eckle of the 'Ighlanders, an' how he felt safe when he saw it. It was at Cairo, arter a little holiday trip up the Nile to have a skite at the Devrishes. I tell you wot, the red 'eckle's made 'im and many like 'im."

"I shall respect the red heckle for ever," said Vincent. "But I judge you're a cockney? Isn't it rare for cockneys to enlist in Highland regiments?"

"Yes, pretty rare," admitted Goodman. "It was like this, you see. Bob McCrae comes up to London the 'ope of his family, at 'ome in Scotland, wot was prayin' for 'im an' sendin' directions 'bout goin' to church. Bob thought the other place suited his constitution best. Well, me an' 'im drinks, fights, chums it, an' eventooaly gets through all our loose change. One night, when we was stone-broke an' was chucked out of three public-'ouses, we went to 'ave a snooze beside the lions in Trafalgar Square—bein' in that neighbourhood. Dessay you know the place? Well, our blinkers was just a-closin' comfortable when up comes a copper an' turns his bull's-eye on us. 'No sleepin' 'ere,' says he. 'Move on!' We tried another pub, an' got chucked again.

"'No go,' says Bob; ''ere's for the Embankment'; an' as we was goin' down White'all, we sees the 'Oss Guards' 'elmet, breastplate, an' all a-shinin'. Bob draws himself up before the hequestrian statoo at the sentry-box an' studies it.

"'Do you know wot it is?' says he. 'I'm sick of this: I'm cold, I'm sleepy, I'm hungry, I'm thirsty, I'm out at heel, an' I've no cash. I've a good mind to 'list.'

"'Don't be a moke,' says I.

"'Yes,' says he, 'an' it'll be a regiment of the line an' none o' yer fancy-work 'bout White'all,' says he. 'I want 'bout as bad as possible to stick somebody. A 'Ighland regiment; an' Dicky,' says he, 'Dicky, you'll come with me?'

"'Don't be a moke,' says I again. 'Come on, or every blessed seat on the Embankment'll be took!'

"'Man, I'm hardly fit,' says he. 'O God! for one square feed of 'aggis, an' vengeance, vengeance!' An' he walked on, his chin in his breast, a-mutterin' the word. 'Dicky,' says he, as he was a-settling himself on the Embankment, 'Dicky, if I'm disturbed, it'll be murder or 'listin'! I wish I had never seen your dam London! Did you ever hear of the porch of 'ell?' says he.

"'No,' says I, never.'

"'Oh, you blazing idiot! you're in it,' says he.

This is it,—this great city, Dicky, with all the food an' drink an' money that you an' me mustn't touch. This is it—this is purgatory,' says he. ' Dicky, you'll stand by me ? '

"We 'adn't begun to nod when up comes the copper with his ' No sleepin' 'ere. Move on ! ' Bob rose an' shook himself. The moon was shinin' on the river an' the roofs of S'uthwark, an' the gas-lamp beside us lighted Bob's face. You should 'ave seen the look on it !

" ' I don't want to be messed up with no coroner's inquest,' says I. ' Come 'ome.'

" ' Come 'ome ? ' says he. ' Dicky, none o' yer chaff ? ' An' then, suddint as lightnin', ' You know the bargain ? ' says he.

" ' Come on,' says I, ' regiment o' the line or any other dam thing you like ! I'm sick of this, too.' So Bob an' me was made 'Ighlanders. Afore we knowed wot was 'appenin' we was doin' the goose-step at Aldershot with other rookies, an' four months arter had our first swing on the troop-ship. He's a sergeant-major now, an' I'm—I'm back in the porch of 'ell."

CHAPTER VI

HE ended with such passionate resentment of tone and mien that Tapley hurriedly ordered a liqueur. While the cordial was diffusing its mellow glow, Vincent delicately enquired for Mrs. Goodman. Dick turned upon him as if struck. So this was their game,—corrupting the husband to get at the wife. He pulled himself together for action.

"My wife!" he said, the note of murder in his voice, "my wife!" and he demanded with a lurid oath what they wanted with his wife. Vincent answered meekly that, having chanced to hear of her unpleasant experiences in court that morning, they were interested in her welfare. Goodman made a noise, half growl, half gurgle, like a baited beast of prey. A little more presumption, a little more provocation, and he would twist their heads off their bodies.

"The beak's your guv'nor," he said, bending with a menace towards Vincent.

"My father is chairman of the local bench of magistrates," was the answer.

Goodman slid furthur forward, crouched as if for a spring.

"Curse him!" he cried, his face glowing malignantly. "Damn him! curse him from head to foot—him and everything that's his!"

"Old man, that's getting personal," put in Tapley in his suavest manner. "Have another liqueur."

"Lor,' that I had 'im just for five minutes!" hissed

Goodman, grinding teeth and heels in the fury of his hate. "He robbed me—'im that has so much money, 'im that makes the drink as sends us poor blokes out'n our senses. He robbed me—and now you come arter my wife! Think I got her for your convenience? Dessay you'd like that. I know you, an' the sort of you, an' you shan't have her, not if you was to pay down a thousand pound in gold. This morning your father took her last farthin', and——"

"There!" cried Tapley joyfully. "There! that's the point, that's business. Here, tumble off this liqueur, and you may hear of something to your advantage, as the lawyers say."

There was a brotherly quality in Tapley which was irresistible. Goodman took the liqueur mechanically, swallowed it at a gulp, and waited. Tapley made haste to present their case.

" That's worth having, isn't it ? " he asked cordially. "Give me a man who knows good stuff when he tastes it. Well! now to business, as the monk said when he kissed the nun ; and, Goodman, my boy, pray lend me your best ear. If you had no objections, mark you, no objections, for of course, as you have so justly indicated, a wife is private property, as sacred to her lord as law can make her—well, if you had no objections, believed in our integrity as gentlemen, and all that, we thought we might possibly be allowed to express our sympathy with Mrs. Goodman. You quite understand me ? "

"Dunno," growled Goodman.

"Well," explained Tapley, "with your assent—mark you, not without—our sympathy would naturally take the most fitting form. Twig ? "

"In coin ?" asked Goodman.

"Let us say in coin."

"Then," said the lord and master, planting himself

more firmly in his chair, "you can express it to me. Save trouble."

Fox and wolf were again alert in him.

"We thought perhaps you would do us the honour of introducing us," said Vincent. "The truth is, we have discovered that Mrs. Goodman is an old ser—an old friend of my mother's, and, naturally, we're all interested in her."

"Ah! very likely," said Dick. "Well, I knows all about her. Fire away!"

Vincent had recourse to something more potent than words. Putting his hand in his pocket he drew forth some silver.

"The best of us may be caught short," he observed. "Favour me by accepting this," and without counting it he held out the money.

Goodman's involuntary smirk was as the sudden breaking of the sun through thunder clouds.

"By Jupiter, ten bob!" he cried, clutching and counting his wealth. He yelled at the red-haired waiter. "Three mugs of yer A 1 ale, Mr. Foxy," he called. "An' look skinny. Don't waste time a-beckin' an' a-bowin', an' ye needn't pretend as ye've got to brew it. Come, double, if you know 'ow. This suits me proper, sir," casting a comic, half-defiant, half-apologetic look at Vincent; "the five bob wot the guv'nor took, an' five for a extra booze."

"A trump," murmured Tapley; and when the grimacing waiter had set down the ale

> "I drink this cup to one made up
> Of loveliness alone."

Goodman, my boy, give me leave to pledge Mrs. G.? There, let's tumble off and go."

Dick promptly "tumbled off," but declined to go.

"Tottie," he said gravely, "don't you be a-trying

to insult me, for fear you might succeed. That's a-playing with a powder-magazine—dangerous. Put it down, fair an' square, so as all may read that I ain't goin' to budge till we 'ave another swill."

Another "swill" got him on his feet, and much adroit persuasion induced him to walk outside—after bidding Mr. Lobes an ostentatious farewell. His gait was wavering and his speech huskily disputatious. He had a monstrous grievance against his kind, at which he hinted in words of awful significance. He railed on "beaks," but, remembering the silver, contradicted scripture by affirming that the sins of the fathers ought not to be visited on the children. The quick beat of a horse's hoofs caught his ear, and, wheeling, he spied a high dog-cart, with a lady driving. He struck an attitude of admiration.

"That's my style, now," he remarked, as she approached at a spanking pace. "O Lor'! if I had just the 'oof! She 'andles them ribbons pretty, don't she? Ain't I seen the kernel's wife a-doin' the same 'undreds an' 'undreds of times."

Lady Gwendoline advanced in a style which made her brother and lover also stand and admire. They spoke of the horse; Goodman eulogised the lady. "Give me the 'oof," he remarked at large, "an' I tell ye straight that's the kind of gel for me."

Vincent stepped out to meet her, Tapley followed, and Mr. Goodman drew himself up rigidly to the salute.

Lady Gwendoline pulled up, enquiring where they had been and what they were about. She might have bought all that was worth buying in St. Edmund since leaving them. They answered briefly that they had been engaged with the martial figure on the side-walk, explained they might be detained for a little while longer, and begged her to drive to Twickham Towers and report.

She blithely nodded assent, tapping the horse with her whip-handle.

"He'll do," she commented, "carriage good, and easy on the bit. You see his flanks ; I'll confess they might be whiter. We've had a spin."

As Vincent acknowledged the compliment to his skill in choosing a horse, Dick involuntarily saluted, the military habit being still strong upon him in gallant or admiring moods. When she turned, showing them clean hoofs, he launched into direct encomium.

"She's a dandy, she is ! " he remarked ardently, if with a suspicion of thickness, gazing after the retreating vehicle. " I tell you, the 'oss as she's behind ain't likely to fall asleep. That's wot the 'oof does. Gawd in 'eaven, if I had just lots of chink ! "

They gently reminded him of the business in hand and asked for the address. He had forgotten it. S'elp him, Jupiter, if he could remember either street or number. Another offering of silver stimulated his memory to the right pitch. Then a cab was hailed, and they were driven to an outlying street in the poorer quarter of the town. The place named by Dick was the house in which Jenny Jenks was born, the house whence, one shining May-day, she went forth, dewy-eyed and radiantly hopeful, to take the train to London—the city of dreams and marvels. Strangers were now in possession ; but in the hour of desolation she turned instinctively to the old home, and pitying hearts gave shelter.

At the head of the street the cab was dismissed on Vincent's suggestion that they should approach on foot. On reaching the little gate in the trellised fence erected by Jenny's father in summer evenings long ago, they heard a sweet, low crooning, such as mothers in every land use in putting their children to sleep. Tapley looked queerly at Vincent, and, by a common impulse, the two paused an instant with bent ear, listening. Then they went softly up the green-bordered path, followed not so softly by Dick. As they drew near the door the crooning rose, fell, stopped, began again and suddenly ceased. Then the voice within was raised plaintively, and the words of an old hymn floated to the ears of those outside.

> " Had I the wings of a dove I would fly
>   Far, far away, far, far away ;
> Where not a cloud ever darkens the sky,
>   Far, far away, far, far away."

With an oath Dick leaped forward and struck the door with his clenched fist. The singing stopped, and a little girl, answering the thunderous summons, peered timidly from behind the half-open door. Recognising Goodman she made way, and he strode fiercely into the little room off the passage, in which his wife sat, calling on his companions to follow. By way of asserting authority, he banged the door violently behind them. His wife rose, with the child in her arms, looking at him appealingly.

" Oh, Dick, where have you been ? " she asked. " I have been worryin' so about you."

" Where have I been ? " he roared, "a-listenin' to your dam doxologies ! 'Ell, but you make me sick. You've been singin' 'bout flyin' away on the wings of a dove. I wish to Gawd ye had 'em—I wish ye had 'em !"

" Oh, Dick ! " she said ; the agony of heart-break in her voice.

" That's it," he cried, with a fiercer note. " It's ' Oh, Dick ! ' an' ' Oh, Dick ! ' wotever I does. I tell you, I ain't goin' to stand it."

She looked at him mutely out of big, pleading eyes. Would he not have pity on her in the presence of others ? He had been better pleased had she hit out in the manner of spirited East-end wives, so that he might have an excuse for retributive measures. Her very meekness was an exasperation.

The exquisite misery of her looks would have touched harder, less gallant hearts than her visitors'. Her eyes were red, and tracks of recent tears were on her thin cheeks. Her dress, to the masculine eye, was mere rags, yet there was the distinct impression of personal cleanliness and neatness, as of one in love with soap and water, and deft with her needle. Studying the white, pathetic face it was easy to understand why Lady Twickham had called her the pretty Jenny Jenks; she had still a subdued comeliness of feature. It was less easy to make out why, with her soft ways and fawn-like timidity of manner, she ever came to be the mate of Richard Goodman.

The child, frightened into wakefulness, strove to hide in its mother's bosom, crying fretfully. Its whimpering fanned the fires of Mr. Goodman's anger to a blaze.

"Why ain't that kid sleepin'?" he demanded. "Is a man allus to be comin' in to yellin' kids? Choke her off, I say."

"I was just tryin' to put her to sleep when you came, Dick."

"Tryin'!" he repeated furiously. "Yer allus tryin'. 'Bout time you was doin' something. Here, give her to me."

"She'll go to sleep," returned his wife, swinging half round, and pressing the clinging child tighter to her breast. "Won't ye, Loo? There, daddy, she's goin' to sleep."

"Give me the kid!" roared Dick, clutching Jenny by the shoulder so that she reeled.

"Dick, Dick, don't hurt her!" cried Jenny, her eyes starting in sudden terror.

"Give her up, or, by thunder, I'll hurt you," was the response.

"Yes, Dick, yes," and she obediently delivered up Loo, smothering a plea for mercy lest it should incite to vengeance.

As he seized the child he felt the gentle, but firm, pressure of a hand on his arm.

"It is part of the religion of a gentleman not to abuse women and children," Vincent said quietly in his ear.

Mr. Goodman dumped the child on the bed to deal with the interloper.

"Who the blazes sent you to teach me manners?" he retorted with a more terrible suffusion of purple. "Is the kid yours, or mine? If it's yours, there it is, take it; if it ain't yours, wot bloomin' right have you to be stickin' in yer tongue an' jawin' me?"

Jenny involuntarily stepped forward to intervene, but remembering herself in the nick of time stepped back again in a flutter at her own audacity. Her lord would have knocked her senseless had she presumed to interfere.

Loo now sat on the bed silently watching; fear and wonder in her wide, wet eyes. She was already trained to keep still when her father desired to have all the attention to himself. Tapley pretended to be lost in admiration.

"I say, Goodman," he cried, as if wakening from a reverie, "what a pretty child! And she's your image, your very image."

"Tottie, you glue your gob," was the reply. "I ain't denied she's mine as I knows on, an' wot I want to know is, why he," jerking a thumb at Vincent, "comes here an' insults me?"

"I assure you nothing was farther from my mind than to insult you," put in Vincent quickly.

"But you done it all the same," responded Goodman, getting hotter as he perceived the righteousness of his cause. "You done it. An', by Gawd, ye oughter be chucked out'n a five-storey window," he pursued, flaring up. "Ye oughter be chucked ; a-nosin' arter honest men's wives. The Thames is the place for you."

He drew himself up in the middle of the floor, his legs apart, his head thrown back, and looked down on Vincent who seemed, in contrast, miserably weak and insignificant.

"The Thames, an' twenty pound of lead at yer 'eels, that's the thing for you—an' take care as ye don't 'ave it."

Thereupon he turned to his wife.

"Jen, them swells is arter you. Look at 'em ; ain't ye proud of 'em? Ain't they a credit to one as preaches at her 'usband, an' sings 'bout the wings of a dove an' flyin' away? Ain't ye wild at the idear of takin' up along of sich toffs?"

He surveyed the three malignantly.

"Gawd alive, ain't ye pretty?" he went on in the tone of one who has discovered an abominable intrigue. "Thought I was luny, or, maybe too boozed to twig. I should be a-doin' my dooty in knockin' spots out'n the lot of ye."

Not daring to question her outraged husband, Jenny turned in despair to Vincent, whom she recognised, though hiding the fact.

"Oh, sir, what does this mean?" she asked, acute terror working in every feature of her face. Mr. Goodman himself hastened to enlighten her.

"I'll tell you wot it means," he said, in a thick, alcoholic voice. He took Vincent's silver from his pocket, spread it elaborately on his palm, and held it out to her.

"That's wot it means," he added, gloating over her evident distress. "A fistful of silver—the price of you. That's 'ow toffs does business. Lor', there's a fortin' in ye if ye'd just keep yer blinkers dry an' look 'appy, 'peck an' lush, hot an' reg'lar, an' no questions arsked."

At the beginning of this speech Tapley had slipped out, put half a crown into the litttle girl's hand and despatched her round the corner for beer. He returned jubilantly carrying a huge jug.

"Dry work arranging these family matters," he observed, as if speaking to himself.

Goodman turned, and his eye caught sight of the familiar and enticing froth.

"A drink, old man?" enquired Tapley.

Goodman clutched at the jug, and the next moment was gulping as if for a wager. While he cooled himself Vincent managed to deliver a message from his mother to Jenny. Catching the tail of a sentence Dick lifted his head with a challenge.

"Eh, wot's that?" he cried, spluttering and panting.

"Good beer," said Tapley.

"Mighty cute, Tottie," rejoined Dick; "but ye shan't have her—ye shan't 'ave her—not s' long's a fist's left on me to bash——"

The truculency of spirit was in no wise abated, but Tapley's practised eye noted a swift decline in bodily power. Not all Dick's ferocity could fend the lapping stupor of big draughts and unaccustomed feeding. His tongue slid thickly in his mouth, he was beginning to hiccough, and a solemn idiocy took possession of his countenance. Tapley and Vincent exchanged meaning looks, and, with hurried apologies and expressions of goodwill, retired.

CHAPTER VII

AS the door closed behind them Dick, rolling his head and hiccoughing, leered fatuously at his wife. She knew the symptom and, by pretending to fathom the joke he must have somewhere among the clouds of his mind, induced him to lie down. Hardly was his head on the pillow when he was snoring might and main. At that grateful sound Jenny whipped out Loo to the landlady, begging, as a particular favour, that the two children might be allowed to play together for an hour or so. The excuse offered for being troublesome was the call to go out upon an urgent errand. Then, hastening back to her own room, she began with eager and tremulous fingers to make herself fit to appear at the great house. Little toilet she had to make, but that tremour of the hand hindered her sadly. Her head, too, swam in a tumult of nameless emotion; for the past was knocking at her heart, making it flutter and beat cruelly. As if in a dream of the night her old self rose before her. She saw a fair young face in a mirror, its owner turning this way and that, twisting and looking over her shoulder lest so much as a strand of hair should be out of place or a ribbon knot awry. Gracious God, what were ribbons now! It was bread she had to think of, bare bread for her famishing child. Often and often in the times gone by she had adorned herself in that very room, and, fresh as the bud at her breast, had gone forth to incite rivalry among the lads of St. Edmund. And there stood one by who never failed to remark how well she looked. What would that mother say to this tagging of rags? God be merciful to unfortunate women! Who would now give a word of admiration, who so much as a kindly look?

Tears dimmed her eyes, making it necessary to wash her face a second time. With a smart rebuke she told herself she must be strong. This weakness disfigured her, and, besides, was waste of time. Dick might wake before she got back, and if he did——She shut her eyes, shuddering. A movement on the bed made her start. Her nerves were quivering. She felt as if a fatal sickness were coming upon her. This return to her native place instead of bracing, as she hoped it would, only broke her down. She must get away again; yes, yes, she must get away. The place was full of ghosts.

Then she began to wonder what Lady Twickham wanted with her, and, wondering, found her scant toilet complete. With a look to see that Dick slept comfortably she hurried out, closing the door very softly.

Outside, the brisk April air freshened her, and she walked with a quick step, the need of haste being vividly in her mind. It was reckoned half-an-hour's walk to Twickham Towers, although by extra exertion she might reduce the time to twenty minutes. But the old strength was gone; she was soon breathing hard, and presently was forced to pause, a hand pressed against her palpitating side. A sudden pain in the heart made her blench. If she were taken away what would become of little Loo? who look after Dick? A cold sweat broke on her at the thought of leaving them, for both needed her care, the one as much as the other.

Her breath returning, she went on again, with lowered face, quaking for fear of being recognised. But though she knew many, none saw pretty Jenny Jenks in the forlorn, poverty-stricken woman who hurried by as if dreading contact with her kind. Most of the town veterans whom she met were not a jot changed. As a child she had known them every one, and lo! here she was among them again and not a countenance lit in welcome or pleasure at seeing her. " Best so, best so," she told herself, with the chill of desolation at her vitals. Let her be to them an utter stranger ; let her name and memory be blotted out. She would see Lady Twickham, and fly the way she came. London would hide her ; London would give no heed to her shame. In London she could be miserable without notice ; for London is hardened to the sight of calamity and wretchedness.

Coming to a turn-stile which led to the cemetery, she swerved as if to pass through, but instantly was back in the road again. No, she could not trust herself there. Let father and mother sleep in peace, if it pleased God, in happy ignorance of her lot. A few minutes later she stood by the sculptured pillars at the main entrance to Twickham Towers. Awed and faint, she looked up at the griffins surmounting them and at the richly-wrought iron gate swung between. A thousand times she had passed through that gate with light step and bounding heart ; now it oppressed her with a kind of shivering horror. Unconsciously she walked past along the high-road, a vague resolution to run away working upon her. But, thinking of her baby girl and her husband, she wheeled and entered, a sort of burning determination hurrying her to the meeting she dreaded.

Passing the lodge unobserved, she ran up the avenue under the elms like a culprit fleeing from justice. The thought of encountering old servants began to trouble her ; but, on reaching the rear of the mansion, she was relieved to find none whom she knew. A pert maid who was flirting with a groom asked her saucily what she wanted. When she answered that she had come to see Lady Twickham, the pert maid laughed ironically, remarking, " How good of you! but Lady Twickham don't see beggars."

The blood rushed to Jenny's face.

" I am not a beggar," she said, wounded pride coming to her aid. " And if Lady Twickham is told that Mrs. Goodman is here, I think she will see me."

With a meaning look at the groom the maid went off, tossing her head, but returned more meekly to deliver the visitor to another servant, who, in turn, handed her over to a magnificent creature in livery, whose stare was a triumph of insolent contempt.

" My lady is in her budoor," said the godlike. " Foller me."

On entering the presence, it took all Jenny's power of will to keep from swooning. As it was, the air was dim and the room unsteady. Lady Twickham lay in a gorgeous easy-chair, lapped in cushions and laces. A volume of sermons by the Rev. Josiah Tinkle, D.D., Lord Bishop of Blockley, lay face down on her lap. She had been enjoying a homily on " The Perfection of the Human Spirit," done in the best drawing-room style, and proving beyond question that the kingdom of Heaven is exclusively for the refined and the cultured. Her manner towards her visitor was subdued, but kind, the manner of the valetudinarian on whom the doctors sit heavily. Rustling gently among her silks and laces, she murmured a welcome, bidding Jenny be seated. Then, adjusting her gold lorgnette. she surveyed her old servant with some deliberation. A burning glass seemed to have been turned on the unhappy Jenny ;

she felt scorched through and through, and sat quivering. At length the sad, languid voice began to ask
questions.

"I shouldn't have known you," it said after some
preliminaries. "You are greatly altered ; it grieves
me to see you looking so ill. You have been living
in London ?

"Yes, my lady."

"And it does not agree with you?" came plaintively.

"No, my lady ; at least, not very well."

Jenny was wringing her fingers and fighting the
tears. Lady Twickham, laying aside the homily on
"The Perfection of the Human Spirit," sat up, the
better to see her visitor.

"Lord Twickham told us at luncheon of your
unpleasant experience in court this morning," she
went on. "An unhappy marriage?"

"Oh no, my lady," blurted Jenny, shame and confusion hot in her face. "Leastways, not generally, my
lady. The drop o' drink do upset Dick. But he don't
behave like some 'usbands. No—my lady ; and—
and he's good when he's sober—yes, my lady."

But in the attempt to controvert the too palpable
evidence of Dick's delinquencies, Jenny broke down.
Lady Twickham had no nerve for "scenes," and,
shaken by Jenny's pitiful sobbing, was herself nearly
overcome. To avert a catastrophe, she kept repeating,
"Poor child, poor child. There, there, you'll be better
in a moment—there, you'll be better in a moment."

When the paroxysm was past and Jenny was wiping
her eyes and trying to apologise, Lady Twickham
touched a bell. A minute later her maid appeared
and was instructed to ask the functionary in gorgeous
raiment for a glass of port. When it was brought,
Lady Twickham had it set on a table beside her.
Then at a nod the maid vanished.

"You'll take this," said my lady soothingly. " It will help you."

Jenny's impulse was to decline, but what she said was, " Thank you, my lady," and, scarcely knowing what she was about, emptied the glass. Instantly she was aghast with a sense of bad manners, but the motherly voice of Lady Twickham reassured her.

"Yes, that's right—that will help you," she said.

Already Jenny felt a comforting warmth, and a minute later had a light head, for, beyond a dry crust early in the morning, she had eaten nothing that day.

"Now," she thought in dismay, " I shall make a fool of myself, and her ladyship will think I drink, too." But the lightness passed off without any symptom of foolishness.

The conversation turned pointedly on her life in London ; and Jenny, after sore hesitation for Dick's sake, told a woeful tale.

"Oh, my lady ! " she cried, the tears coming afresh, " you can never understand what it is to be poor and live in the East-end of London. My lady, you say it is horrible—it's worse, it's worse ! "

" You'll make yourself ill," said Lady Twickham in alarm. " You'll positively make yourself ill."

Feeling herself choking, Jenny dried her eyes.

" Your husband perhaps ill-treats you," suggested Lady Twickham. That gave Jenny back her tongue.

" Oh ! no," she answered quickly. " Leastways, not always—but—but—— Oh, my lady, it's the women, it's them as kills me ! It's from them I ran away. And I thought if Dick and me was to come back to St. Edmund we could find work and be happy. And now it's worse than ever."

In spite of her languor, Lady Twickham was a woman of penetration. Understanding Jenny's case, she forbore to pursue the line of questioning.

"Yes," she said, " I know how you are disappointed

in coming back to your native place. I daresay your husband wants to return to London."

"Yes, my lady. But we'll go to another part, away from the horrible women. We'll begin again, my lady, we'll begin again."

Lady Twickham quietly produced her purse.

"You'll take this from me," she said, holding out some pieces of gold. "There, don't trouble about thanks. I'm interested in you because I found you a good servant and I think you are a good wife. You'll go back with your husband, of course. The woman must stick to the man—so much I understand. Ah! it's a strange world! When you know it you'll give me your address, and when I'm in London I'll call to see you. There, now—there!"

Jenny was on her knees, sobbing out her heart and kissing the hand of her benefactress.

Book II

CHAPTER I

JENNY might propose, but Dick took excellent care to dispose. So they returned to the precise rookery in London, whence Jenny had fled with the wistful hope of a new life in the country at her sunk and aching heart. She made a fervid appeal for a change of locality. It was best, she made haste to own, it was best to return to London where alone Dick felt at home and in his element. As an experiment in domestic economy the flight to sunshine and green lanes was a dismal failure. She was now as vehemently eager to fly from the scent of budding woods and hedges, and the songs of birds and winds and running waters, as she had been to get away from the foul odours and fouler deeds and words of the Paradise of her dreams. So much she told Dick with chokings of heart. But could they not choose a new quarter where the brutishness of the people would not be a constant threat and terror? Dick was too strong to understand the feelings of a poor weak woman, but he loved her—she knew he loved her, and he might do this little thing for her sake. Perhaps, too, and here she could not help shivering at her own temerity ; perhaps, too, it would be better for Dick himself to be away from his old companions. She did not plead for herself ; she was ready to face anything with him, but would he not think of little Loo? They three, father, mother, and child might begin life anew, and cling together and be happy.

Let them cast the past from them, let them begin again, and God would help them. Wouldn't Dick do this?" she asked, tears of appeal shining in her eyes.

Dick scrutinised her for a moment, a smile, not of sympathy, on his purple face.

"Jen—ye should 'a' been a parson," he said. "Best sermon I've heard since listenin' to the old Scotch chaplain bummin' 'bout 'ell fire. I have just one remark to make, an' it's this—a woman don't look well in her 'usband's breeches. Chuck 'em."

Jenny gazed at him an instant blankly—then turned away, speechless, wounded where wounds are incurable. As obediently as a whipped slave, she returned to the jeers and affronts which had so often made her wish the solid street would open and swallow her. The men she could make shift to endure, in spite of their lawlessness and blasphemy; but the women— it made her sick and giddy to think of the persecution she suffered because she had her own ideas of decency.

"You jest do like yer neighbours, my dear," a gin-soaked crone had said to her early in her career. "You jest take wot ye can get, an' no bones 'bout it, an' ye'll live 'appier, my dear. 'Tain't no use puttin' on fine airs, an' a-purtendin' as yer better'n others. Don't pay," and the ancient sinner grinned and winked knowingly.

Stung by the senile depravity, Jenny gave a sharp answer. The old crone promptly showed her teeth.

"Oh! you go 'long," she hissed, " nice bit o' muslin you are! Shop-soiled ain't the word. You a-purtendin'! Ugh! You ain't no good, 'cept for wallopin'. 'Ope some bloke 'll bash yer 'ead in." And she went off mouthing and breathing elements of blue flame.

Jenny knew the hobbling, venomous creature was

a grandmother; and in morality her daughter was like unto her, and her daughter's daughter, save that the younger generation played the game in better style. The old woman instantly undertook a missionary tour through Paradise Court, spreading news of Jenny's airs and pretensions, and from that moment the young wife's fate was sealed. Thenceforward she was the chosen butt of dames and damsels who took "Wot they got," with relish, and searing irons are nothing to their derision and abuse.

To be sure Dick was at pains to school her in local ways and manners. It no longer paralysed her to come upon groups of muscular sluts whooping and clawing each other's faces, tearing rags from grimy shoulders and dancing jigs on them in the gutter. Marks of death on stair and pavement ceased to make her sick. Even when in great orgies wives tucked and bled over their fallen men she did not swoon or feel faint. Once, indeed, during the process of education her nerve failed her sadly. The misfortune befell one night when she was out among the small fry of belated costers foraging, with a threepenny bit, for Dick's supper. At a street corner a furious noise of scuffling arrested her. As she turned to look what the fray might be, a knife flashed redly in the glare of a naphtha torch. For the tenth part of a second all seemed hushed; then went up a frantic, piercing cry of "Murder!" A policeman was down. Above the hoarse roar of the startled multitude she heard vicious shouts of "Boot him! Boot him!" Almost at her feet a human wave rose and surged wildly forward, overturning and smashing stall and barrow. With a screech she wheeled about and ran home, laughing maniacally, the threepenny bit locked fast in her hand.

"Murder," she gasped, in reply to Dick's question. "Policeman down—stabbed—killed!"

Thereupon he admonished her.

"Makin' a bloomin' row 'bout a stuck copper," he said indignantly. "Off, an' get me fried fish an' 'alf a pint."

Thereafter she never yielded to hysteria.

But the thought of her persecutors gave her a secret ague; and she was returning to them without option.

For when Dick discovered, after some hedging on Jenny's part, which nearly won her the marital badge of a black eye, how his virtues had opened to him a charitable gold mine he instantly made arrangements for firing the envy of old associates. He knew as well as if the fact stared him on every hoarding that he was regarded as a person who, for reasons undivulged, had found it expedient to "clear out." An artist in sensation he chuckled over the mode of retort.

"You just milk the old cow," was his injunction to Jenny. "See you milk her proper, too—and I'll attend to the rest."

"The old cow" was Mr. Goodman's delicate way of alluding to Lady Twickham.

His vanity was gratified by the eager curiosity of friends. Where had he been? What had he been about? since taking himself off unbeknown to his dearest pal. The sly dog was up to some fine game. He answered innocently that he had taken a run into the country with his family.

"Kids must have fresh air," he added, with unmoved countenance, "an' women ain't none the worse of it."

Had he been an ordinary man the response would have been a derisive guffaw. As none had nerve or muscle enough to risk a laugh or refer to swag, the general incredulity was deftly veiled in remarks on the "bleedin'" luck of some people.

It pleased him to receive these expressions graciously; and when he had been envied to the top of his bent he gallantly led the way to the Bear and Cubs, a noted public-house sacred to Twickham's ale and MacTor's Scotch whiskey. By day a huge sign set forth the unequalled merits of the one, and by night the virtues of the other were brilliantly illuminated in white and red.

Entering with the easy air of the *habitué* Dick advanced to the head of the bar, affably greeting, first the barmaid and then the landlord, Mr. Wragg, who was busy among crystals and mellow, odorous casks.

He was a big, heavy-boned, black-browed man who might be Dick's match in a tussle, one would have said, but for an undue rotundity, which suggested diminished wind, and a flabbiness of face which meant degenerated muscle. In his prime he had been the terror of the disorderly, and for that and other good reasons was put by Messrs. Twickham into their tied-house the Bear and Cubs. From that happy day he knew prosperity as a boon companion, with the result that he had now, in addition to one of the best public-houses in East London, diamond studs for his shirt, diamond rings for his fat fingers, a name on the turf, a fast horse, and a flash wife. Multitudes of flourishing men envied Mr. Wragg, and multitudes more were proud to call him friend.

Dick sniffed the delicious fragrance of the place as the war-horse sniffs battle. He felt exhilarated, his pulses beat a bounding measure. This was life as it should be—troops of friends and hogsheads of liquor.

"Mr. Wragg," he cried, "I ain't seen ye since my 'oliday. Glad to be back, I tell ye. Wot's yer tipple?"

Mr. Wragg declared he had been drinking healths all day; the conviviality of his patrons was really becoming too much for him.

" Might 'ave worse things to complain of," rejoined Dick, whereat the company laughed knowingly. " Don't matter if ye couldn't bite a finger," he went on, planking down half a crown, "yer goin' to have a wet with me." And Mr. Wragg, overcome by the sight of the coin from so dubious a customer, named his drink.

The conversation took a surprising turn. For of the great expedition to the country Dick gave a wondrous and ravishing account. Tapley, "a game cock, he could tell them," was mentioned as a bosom friend and brother sportsman, and Vincent Twickham was described as "a right down good sort; no airs, and free of his cash," ended Dick. The company drew a long breath of excitement and admiration. Dick had been doing it, and no mistake.

" 'Stonishin'!" murmured Wragg, and ordered the glasses to be replenished. At that sign of grace the most incredulous believed the amazing narrative. Dick on his part was mightily stimulated.

" Ye should have seed us dinin' together like three lords!" he cried, his eyes bright with elation. " Three bloomin' peers o' the realm. Me 'ere, Tottie, that's Tapley, there, an' Twickham round 'ere. 'Eavens! don't talk to me of drink and victuals. Ye don't know nothin' about 'em."

It was added that he had arranged to meet Tapley and Twickham in London, and possibly,—he wouldn't promise, knowing that lords and toffs are fickle,—but possibly there might be introductions. Then—well, they could picture the rest for themselves. As for himself, he declared over the third glass he was staunch for old friends.

CHAPTER II

DICK lost no time in calling on Tommy Binks at the Ruggler Den. The visit was one of ceremony and meant to be impressive ; for there had sprung up a coolness between the two, due, so far as Dick was concerned, to that frequent defect of good men—a temporary lack of cash. Binks had been insulting over the matter. High words passed, and some hastily laid bets, forgetting in their ardour for sport how masters of the noble art respect each other. There was no bloodshed ; but the coolness was decided—with a tendency to disdain on the part of Mr. Binks. Wherefore it was necessary to confound him.

Dick dressed with elaborate care. His boots shone like mirrors, his neckerchief had the ineffable touch of the man of taste, and in his vest pocket were arranged, with a fine suggestion of affluence, half a dozen of Tapley's cigars. His toilet satisfactorily accomplished, he descended upon Jenny for cash, and she submissively gave what she had. Part of it was the remains of Lady Twickham's charity ; but most of it was the reward of sore toil, for Jenny chared and washed indefatigably. Dick expressed disgust with his allowance, giving an admonition likely to strike a wife with terror. If she meant to keep a husband she must show a little more resource in raising the wind. He wasn't going to stand this barrenness much longer.

" It's all I've got, Dick," she said, thinking woefully
of the manner in which Lady Twickham's charity
was going. " It's every penny—and I was anxious
to get Loo something out of it. She's—look at her,
Dick—a shame to be seen on the stair—not to speak
of being cold—an'—an' the rent's due. We don't
want to be turned into the street again, do we,
Dick ?"

At sound of her name Loo had lifted her wan
face and looked at both parents with preternaturally
big eyes, then solemnly resumed operations on a
bare mutton bone. She was content to be naked
so long as she had something to eat. Dick took the
air of the ill-used husband. Could he never have
a moment's peace or pleasure ? What was the fuss
about ? Didn't the dispensary doctor recommend
fresh air for Loo, and wouldn't she get it all the better
for being lightly clad ? As for the rent-collector,
Dick would kick him downstairs if he showed his
phiz for a month to come. These sentiments duly
impressed on his wife, he renewed his demand for
more money ; and Jenny, being unable to coin bare
walls, was told what her husband thought of her
abilities. She didn't deserve a man, she didn't ; and
s'elp him, Gawd, she'd mend, or he'd take up 'long
of some other woman who could forage to more
purpose ! Jenny quivered as if struck to the heart,
which indeed she was. A beating she could take
like any other wife ; but to be superseded—cast aside
for another—the asylum or the mortuary were
better than that.

As Dick adjusted his cap, grimacing at the frame-
less mirror stuck against the wall, she timidly enquired
where he was going and when she might expect
him back. He answered that he wouldn't burden
her limited faculties with his affairs, but that he
wanted fried fish and hot potatoes for supper. The

Billingsgate chicken * her thoughtfulness had provided she could have for herself. With which intimation he strode away, banging the door behind him.

Coming forth on a reeking court, in which a single gas lamp made the gloom dismally visible, he passed clusters of squalid humanity lounging about doors for a whiff of such air as cent. per cent. landlords and sanitary authorities vouchsafe. He flung them a lofty "good-night," and they sang after him, enquiring when he had come into his estate. Comments and speculations were prudently deferred till he was out of earshot. Not that his critics were censorious; but they knew he was "flush," and had their own explanations. They noted that he rather sought than avoided the police; but that was wiliness, pure wiliness; for Dick could break the ten commandments and sidle innocently up to a copper, asking if anything were wrong.

From the hum of the court he passed to the clamorous'tumult of the street, feeling that for a man who relishes existence London is the place. It was Saturday night, and the East End was marketing. On pavement and roadway seethed and surged the rank lees of half the nations of the earth—eagle-beaked, many-hatted Hebrews, greasy, black-bearded Poles, crafty-eyed Italians, gesticulating French, stodgy Germans, with a sprinkling of Turks, Lascars, and niggers. For the grubbing foreigner Dick had the contempt of a true-born Briton. But he enjoyed the sense of exuberant life in the strident and variegated crowd. Even the thousand dissonances of rival stall-keepers, pressing their wares on passers-by at ruinously low prices, were not disagreeable.

Pausing under a lamp-post he lighted a cigar, and leisurely noted particular incidents in the roaring

* Red herring.

fair. Immediately in front of him a hot-potato man and the driver of a dray were exchanging civilities, to the merriment of a knot of youths, who encouraged them with boisterous chaff. Close by, a tipsy kipper vendor carried on a double argument with his wife and ass. The poor fellow seemed to be getting the worst of it, but he vowed by the 'Eavens above to take it out of them both a little later. Further on, a bear was balancing a pole to the chanting of an Italian air; and a compatriot of the bear-master ground music out of a hurdy-gurdy to a bevy of girls rendering the latest skirt dance. Finally, two boys in blue passed along, conducting a lady of ultra-convivial habits to a night's free lodging. As she protested with the full vigour of mind and body, she had an interested audience, who followed with a running commentary on the performance. These things amused Mr. Goodman.

"A dam funny world!" he said to himself; and took his way westward, smoking complacently.

Finding the Bear and Cubs extraordinarily inviting he looked in, saluting the great Wragg with easy familiarity. Mr. Wragg returned the greeting with marked civility, and half the company suspended their jabber to stare at Dick. For the tale of his adventures having gone abroad, as he knew it would, a halo of romance was about him. He had just one glass of ale with the landlord, which he tumbled off with the remark that, after all, there was nothing to beat Twickham. Mr. Wragg responded that he found himself "remarkably well on Twickham, as did his customers likewise." Twickham was more popular than ever; Twickham, in fact, was going like steam. "An' I must say," continued Mr. Wragg, "as MacTor's Scotch whiskey is comin' to the front. MacTor knows how to spend money—that's the secret. Ha, ha! knowing old dog, MacTor! Great for the ladies. Barmaids' balls done tip-top style ; presents all round ; diamond rings for the missis an' silk dresses for the girl behind the bar : that's good enough," and Mr. Wragg grinned, looking exceedingly wise.

Mr. Goodman expressed himself gratified by the tidings, and with a condescending " S'long all," pursued his journey, musing upon many things.

The Ruggler Den, whither he was bound, lay cosily under the protection of the Law, as represented by Lincoln's Inn Fields and the Royal Courts of Justice. Its career had been chequered since the malice of the police and the spirit of improvement cleared it out of Seven Dials. It had steered a round-about course by Drury Lane, the Mint, Commercial Street, and Clerkenwell, till it found settlement in the purlieus of Clare Market. There, under the sheltering caves of the Law, it felt comfortable. Its directing spirit—its patron saint, one might say—was Mr. Thomas Binks, a gentleman whose talent and unique knowledge would have been invaluable to Scotland Yard. Had Mr. Binks been made Commissioner of Police, or even head detective, the world would have seen a fine revolution in criminal procedure. What the Law lost, the Ruggler Den gained. Untold gold would not have induced a constable to intrude upon its charmed circle. The approach was such as would have pleased the leader of the immortal Forty, had Providence cast his lot in London. You went round the corner of the Baited Bull, a down-at-heel public-house, redolent of crime, into a court that was like a pit ; then up a stair, and along passages, intricate as a rabbit-warren, and awful with suggestions of ambushes and trap-doors, till you came to a collection of spittoons embedded in sawdust. Below the solitary window of this inner sanctuary was a yard into which you could drop in case of emergency. This yard had, in fact, witnessed

scenes of which Christian England never heard—
because such things might shock the devout people,
who fondly believe that the heathen live somewhere
beyond seas, and subscribe liberally to have them
converted. Once, in the old Seven Dial days, the
Ruggler had been raided. Shortly afterwards, the
leader of the expedition came to an untimely end. A
Coroner's jury, having viewed the body and heard
the evidence, found that the deceased had un-
doubtedly died an unnatural death, and left the
matter to the dead man's comrades. Mr. Binks,
watching the funeral *cortège*, hoped that such might
be the fate of all interlopers ; but expressed pity at
the evident grief of the widow.

"Didn't think she'd 'ave took it so much to 'art,"
he said.

At Dick's "Open Sesame !" all the doors flew wide,
and, without let or hindrance, he advanced straight
upon the high-priest himself. That meeting is still
remembered. Mr. Binks, who was seated on an
empty soap-box set on end, rose impresssively at
Mr. Goodman's entrance. A deep hush fell on the
room ; the two looked at each other ; then Mr. Binks
held out a hand which Mr. Goodman took and wrung
like a brother.

"Ain't bin scragged," said Tommy, smiling.

"'Tweren't a scraggin' job," returned Dick, smiling
in turn. "Suck that," he added, holding out a cigar ;
"an' as we haven't met for some time," looking round
upon his fellow Rugglers, "wot's to be the wet ?"

Dick's luck was a matter of congratulation and
envy, but the discussion was briefer than he expected,
for more important business was on hand.

WITH the air of one unbottling a sensation, Mr. Binks took a piece of printed paper from his pocket, carefully unfolded it, and handing it to Dick, asked him to be good enough to read aloud. As the feat was likely to prove troublesome, Dick passed it on to a brother Ruggler, who was once a city clerk, but for competent reasons had abruptly abandoned a commercial career. This gentleman and scholar, peering close to penetrate the dirt and grease contracted in Mr. Binks's vest pocket, read once again the intelligence which had that evening thrilled so many manly hearts all over England. An event, compared with which the fall of empires was nothing (provided Britain were safe), was passing to a happy consummation. Not to trifle, Tufty Slogget, the American heavy-weight, was crossing the Atlantic to fight Tom Crinch, the British hero, for a thousand pounds a side and the glory of the championship.

" 'Ad it straight from Velvet Chick it's to be the event of the century," said Mr. Binks gleefully. "Swells 'owlin' mad. Every man as knows a fish from a mutton pie's egsited an' lookin' out his spare cash. Oh, you mark me, it's to be rippin', rippin', that's wot it's to be!"

"Who's managin' the show?" asked Dick.

"Natrilly, the Royal Olympian," answered Binks. "But everybody's in it, everybody as is anybody— dooks an' hearls an' lords an' barynites—ye couldn't count 'em. Kemittee's a-dancin' on their 'eads. Velvet Chick ses it'll beat anythink ever knowed in the hannils of the ring, that's 'ow 'e puts it ; an' a b'lieve 'e's 'bout right. Some ses as Tom Crinch'll make pulp o' t'other chap; an' some ses as t'other chap'll make pulp of Tom Crinch. Enyway, it'll be a big thing. The money as'll be put on's intoxicatin' to think of, fair intoxicatin', that's wot I calls it."

"An' the question afore the meetin's 'ow we're to 'ave a share," put in another Ruggler.

That was a point to be thought out, and to enable them to think it out effectively Dick ordered a round of Twickham. While they drank he seemed uncommonly thoughtful.

"Distinguished patrinige," he said, breaking the silence. "Don't 'appen to know names ? "

"Well !" replied Binks, "ye knows yerself wot the Royal Olympian is."

"Aristocracy, the 'ole bloomin' lot !" said Dick. "But don't 'appen to 'ave names. Tapley, for hexample,—Lord Tapley, son of old Wegron—a rare old dicky-bird. Don't 'appen to know if he's in the show ; or young Twickham—that's his pal, an' sweet on his sister—goin' to splice, I hear—son of old Bung—that's Twickham's ale as yer drinkin'. 'Appen to know if they're in it ? "

"Tapley," repeated Binks. "B'lieve Velvet Chick did mention 'im—yes, a b'lieve 'e did. A disremember Twickham."

"If Tapley's there, Twickham's there," thought Dick. "Wouldn't be fool enough to let the honeymoon interfere."

And with that he devoted himself to the hospitality of his brother Rugglers. He left them elated and rather excited ; and elated and rather excited he returned to the Bear and Cubs to discuss events with

Mr. Wragg. Wragg, who had just been reading the momentous news in an evening paper, dilated volubly on the prospects of the fight. In the throng that filled the bar, there. was scarcely a man without ambition as a " bruiser," nor a woman who did not listen with intent ear. Sometimes a feminine voice joined in the discussion. One stout lady, who had reached the maudlin stage, shed tears over the opportunities missed by her dead spouse.

" You knowed 'm, Mr. Wragg, dear," she said, taking her gin neat. " You knowed Jim, sir, an' you'll bear me hout as 'ow 'e could bruise. 'E bashed—but then I won't tell no tales on the dead. An' you knows, Mr. Wragg, I gave 'im a bootiful funri'l—plumes an' mutes, an' never thought of egspense. Oh ! if my Jim wur only 'ere this night——"

And the good creature dissolved in tears, which must have been pure old Tom.

Mr. Wragg owned that Jim had been a very fine man in his day.

" Thank ye for that, Mr. Wragg, dear," sighed the disconsolate, wiping her eyes. " Three pen'orth more, sir, if you please. Mrs. Leary," turning to a companion, whose bonnet was suspiciously askew—" Mrs. Leary, another drop to 'eat ye. Me an' Mrs. Leary 'ave the cramps bad sometimes, an' the drop o' gin do ease 'em, it do, indeed, sir. Mrs. Leary, she thinks Irish whiskey's the thing——"

Mrs. Leary rolled her head, putting her bonnet further askew, and snickered.

" Oh ! ye needn't be a-denyin' on it, Mrs. Leary," said the stout lady. " You 'ave said to me as nuthin' outn' 'Eaven could be sweeter'n Dublin whiskey, if it warn't Dublin stout ; but I ses to 'er, sir, ' Try the gin as ye gets at the Bear and Cubs,' ses I. 'Ere Mrs. Leary, don't you be a-troublin' 'bout yer man, my dear ; 'e's boozin' on 'is own 'ook—take that from me, 'e's boozin' on 'is own 'ook. I knows wot men be."

Remarking she was a woman of wisdom, Mr. Wragg tacked for the original subject of conversation. The fight was going to be the greatest thing of its kind within the memory of living man.

"Of course, you'll be there?" said Dick.

"Wot do you expect?" demanded Mr. Wragg. He went on to say it was every man's dooty to support grand old British sports; and, though he was rather out of practice himself, he'd like to see the man who'd say the ring was not an ornament to Society. A chorus of applause greeting him, he proceeded to state that the best people in England, which is to say, the best in the world, patronised the ring. The nobility and aristocracy, from princes down, were in it.

Dick observed that young Twickham was sure to be at the Royal Olympian, and Mr. Wragg responded proudly that young Twickham was a sportsman, as his father was before him. "And is now, thank Gawd!" added Mr. Wragg fervently.

The hour of closing came, and Dick reeled into the street, shouting pæans in honour of Wragg. His heart being merry within him he ran into a policeman, singing "What the Henry Melville do you think you're doing there?" and instantly broke into profuse apologies to the Law. "Just gettin' 'ome from a temp'rince meetin'," he explained, laughing aloud, "an' I ain't used to it, guv'nor. S'elp me Bob!"

The Law warned him to mind "wot he was about," and allowed him to proceed, drunks being too rife on a Saturday night to be worth arresting, except under extreme provocation. The next minute he was pirouetting with a Hebrew gentleman, who had a bag on his back and a dozen hats on his head, one above another.

"'Ullo, ole clo'!" cried Dick hilariously, knocking half of them off. "Ye oughter know as it ain't becomin' for a son of Abra'm to go 'bout with a steeple on 'is 'cad."

The Hebrew called for a constable; but none answering, he cursed his tormentor by the twelve tribes of Israel and picked up his hats. Hardly was Dick clear of the Jew when he was into a meat-stall; and there his frolic nearly ended in disaster. But having still a trifle in his pocket, he compromised matters by investing in a string of sausages, which he hung gracefully about his neck.

"Lor' Mayor's chain," he said, grinning fearfully in the face of the stall-keeper's wife. "All we wants now, m'm, is turtle an' cham, an' lots of 'em. Lor' Mayor's ticket is gorge an' swill; an' we 'ave the pleasure of payin', m'm, you an' me, an' his nabs yer 'usband there, we 'ave the pleasure of payin'— that's our share of the peck an' lush. There's suthin' there as calls aloud for reform; ain't there, m'm?"

"There's suthin' 'ere as calls louder," replied the woman, looking him over. "You go 'ome till yer wife combs yer hair."

"I'm marchin' along, m'm," says Dick. "Glory Alleluiah, marchin' along. Ta, ta."

From that point until he reached Paradise Court he was the object of loud and varied attention, some asking where he got the beautiful fur boa, and others begging for a "sosige." One woman clung to him so desperately that he was obliged to knock her down. It might have been a police-court affair had she been able to rise. As it was, she lay kicking till a constable set her on her feet, demanding to be told what she was making a row about.

"Knocked down," she hiccoughed. "Man—sosiges —s'elp me Bob."

"Go on," retorted the constable, shaking her.

"Sosiges," she repeated—"sosiges," and went her way, shouting.

By this time Dick was into Paradise Court and toiling up the black stair.

"There, Jen," he cried, stumbling in on his wife, "see wot I've brought you—sosiges, old gel, sosiges. We ain't to be livin' no longer on cat's meat. 'Owlin' Jericho, you've bin an' got fried fish! Sosiges an' fried fish."

"You said you wanted it," answered Jenny.

"Wanted it," repeated Dick. "Wot d'ye take me for? 'Ere, let's tuck in, old gel. Ain't I a good 'usband? 'Ere, Jen, give me a kiss or ye'll forget how. Never kiss yer own darlin' Dick now. Ain't his breath as sweet as it uster be?"

Jenny obediently kissed him, and his breath forced from her the exclamation, "Oh! Dick, been drinking again!"

"There ye go!" cried Dick. "Sorry I arsked ye to kiss me. Wot if I have been drinkin'? Ain't my mouth my own? Ain't my throat my own? Ain't my stowin' box my own?"

He regarded her as if considering whether she were worth walloping.

"Times is changed," he pursued. "When you was a-courtin' of me an' my lips tasted o' beer, ye'd say, Dick, dear, when we're married ye'll not drink no more, cos I'll cure ye of that bad 'abit. This is how ye've cured me."

He laughed savagely.

"Ain't ye proud of yerself an' yer cure?" he asked. "Drink! I'm only a-beginnin'."

She made no reply, but set out the fried fish and hot potatoes. He began to eat like a famished beast, muttering inarticulately between the mouthfuls. Suddenly he called out, "Where's the kid—where's Loo?"

"In bed, asleep," answered Jenny.

Dick turned to the rickety bed, pulled back the ragged counterpane, and plucked out the child, who first stared wildly and then whimpered.

"No 'owlin', Loo—no 'owlin'," said Dick. "It's a feed, my gel—a feed from daddy."

He sat down, taking her on his knee, and began to cram fish upon her.

She was eager enough to eat, God knows; but mouth and gullet were small. Wherefore Dick crammed the more, until at last the child could neither breathe nor chew.

"Get it down," cried Dick, pushing with a fork handle, "get it down."

The struggling Loo was rapidly becoming black in the face.

"She's choking! Don't you see she's choking?" cried Jenny, her countenance wrung with terror. "Dick, Dick, don't you see she's choking?"

"Hold off," exclaimed Dick—"hold off! Got to go down."

"But she's choking, Dick. Oh! my baby's choking."

"Got to go down," repeated Dick, pressing harder. "A hundred times ye've told me she was starvin'. She ain't starvin' now. It's got to go down."

Here the sounds of choking became so desperate that Jenny attempted a rescue. That was the last touch to Dick's drunken frenzy. Jerking Loo under his left arm, which closed on her like a vice, he struck out with his right, and Jenny went crashing among broken utensils in a corner. Hearing the noise, the people below remarked that the Goodmans were at it again; but they never thought of interfering. They would hardly have interfered had red murder been done. But something in the rigid outline of his prostrate wife caused Dick himself to look at

her curiously. Dropping Loo, he went to see why
she was not rising, prepared to remonstrate in a
convincing manner. The child, finding herself free,
dug out the fried fish with her fingers, and then lay
down, crying, beside her mother.

CHAPTER IV

THE natural impulse was to boot the perverse woman, but something in the motionless form made Dick think hurriedly of water, and he flung out a pitcherful, mostly on the head of Loo, who started up, shrieking. At that Jenny opened her eyes very wide, and looked at him in a vacant, uncomprehending stare. Thereupon he administered a brisk shaking, telling her to get on her pins, and look lively about it. With some assistance she rose, tottering, for her head whirled as if on a swivel. Then, recovering herself a little, she sat on the edge of the bed to comfort the sobbing Loo. As she quieted the child she pressed a hand to her heart; but no word of reproach passed her lips. It was Dick who was reproachful.

"Wot made ye go off like that?" he demanded angrily. "Purtendin' ye were goin' to die out'n hand! Don't you try that dodge on again, 'cos I don't like it, an' I ain't got no money to spend on bloomin' fun'rils."

He was almost sober now, and sitting down by the well-scrubbed deal table, finished his supper. The eating done, he smoked one of Tapley's cigars, watching Jenny out of the wreathing blue spirals, in which he was an artist. The sight of her face exasperated him. What a confounded dumb parade of affliction, all for the trifle of being knocked down! Weren't other women knocked down? and though they scratched like cats, and even landed their husbands in the police courts, did they draw these long, woeful, accusing, imposed-on, aggravating faces? What Jenny needed was a little more knocking down, and she had better not work on his feelings lest she should have it—and suddenly.

Throwing away the cigar stub, it pleased him presently to "turn in," and a minute later he was snoring royally. Having tidied the room and put things in order for the morning, Jenny lay down beside him, weeping silently and pressing Loo to her bosom. But when the child fell asleep she was obliged to loosen her hold and lie off a little, because of a suffocating pain at her heart. This was the second time that pain had come upon her. Was it death? Was she to be taken away? If so, would the good God, the Father of the miserable and the motherless, take care of little Loo? She scarcely dared to think so. In the old days, now so remote and wonderful, viewed across the intervening gulf of time, she had been taught that God was everywhere, and that His love was even about the falling sparrow. But alas! alas! how much to the contrary had she not learned since! She had seen men and women die, not the death of beasts, for beasts die decently, but the death of fiends, raging and obscene. And she had seen them live. O God! how had she not seen them live! She shuddered at the thought of what was before her girl. Better speedy death, a thousand times better, than such a future; a future of nameless guilt and shame, and an end one durst not think of. God everywhere! Impossible. There were places which God had forsaken, given over to the devil and his angels. It was easy enough to imagine a beneficent God in the flowers and sunshine and peaceful white clouds of the country; but here, in the reeking hell of slums, here, where foulness and cruelty and crime were rampant, violating all laws, human and divine, it was the bitterest mockery to say God ruled.

"Oh! my Loo, my Loo," she sobbed piteously, "why were we ever born?"

Putting her arm round the sleeping child, she tried to repeat the prayer of her own girlhood; but the words stifled in her throat. She could not even pray then. The arms that held Loo fell limp, and turning her face helplessly to the pillow, she drenched it in a storm of self-pity.

As the rush of tears exhausted itself she became calmer. Below, the drunken, riotous noises continued. There was a fierce scuffle on the stair, a stamping of heavy boots on the stones, obscene oaths, a scream, a thud, a wailing moan, and then gruesome silence. It might be murder for aught she knew. Life was nothing in Paradise Court and its precincts.

Being high up, the din of the street, that weary, sleepless street, reached her in all its variations. She could hear the hoarse shouts of sluts and ruffians quarrelling, the snatches of unclean song which violated the darkness, and that multitudinous murmur of busy life which ceases not day nor night. Once she held her breath at the furious blowing of a policeman's whistle.

"Somebody's hurt," she thought as she listened, quivering, to the yells and muffled cries which followed.

Towards morning the noises died away in a general drowsiness; but a dull pain at her heart kept her painfully awake. At last light began to glimmer through the little window on which, as by instinct, her eyes were fastened. There is a moment even in East London when, by a miracle little heeded, poisonous dens and crime-blotched tenements are turned to fairy palaces; when the glittering city, radiant and smokeless, lies open to the springs of dawn. Whosoever has seen that first splendour of the sun on roof and dome and steeple will not readily forget the magic vision.

Jenny rose softly, though not without pain, and looked forth upon a sea of shining ridges. Opening the cracked window very cautiously, lest the frame should tumble out, she drank deep of the fresh, crisp air, sweet, she fancied, with the breath of dew-drenched woods. But the chill breeze making her eyes smart, she turned quietly back into the room to bathe them. Dick might beat her if he discovered she had been crying.

Glancing at the bed, she was arrested by the contrast of the faces on the pillow—one so grievously pinched with hunger, the other drink-inflamed. She shivered, partly with cold, for she had lain through the long, sleepless night scantily clothed, partly with horror. She was very stiff and sore now that she moved, but it was not of her own pains and discomforts she was thinking.

Glad of the diversion, she kindled the fire from the half-hundredweight of coal in the corner and set about preparing the breakfast. The warmth, the odour, the brisk crackling of the sausages, and the knowledge that Dick would be pleased, heartened her to a fresh interest in life. When all was ready she spoke insinuatingly in her husband's ear, and he roused himself, asking resentfully, " Wot the bother was about now."

" It's the sausages, Dick," answered Jenny. " Come, dear, while they're hot.

In the same instant his nostrils tasted the delectable aroma of fried meat, and he was up with the eager valiancy of a knight of the trencher challenged to prove his mettle. Loo, too, was awakened; and Jenny, chivalrously invited to " wade in," found her appetite suprisingly good. Indeed, such was the success of the repast that when the dishes were empty

Mr. Goodman wiped his mouth in a gratification which was almost gratitude.

"Jen," he said, looking blandly at his wife, "there ain't nothin' like sosiges, an' you do cook 'em to a turn ; I'll say that, you do cook 'em to a turn."

"I'm glad you like 'em, Dick," she returned, a smile breaking on her wan face.

"Like 'em," echoed Dick. "Lor', I loves 'em, that's wot I do. Give me a sosige as big's a boar constrictor, an' I could just sit down at one end an' suck it out'n sight, that's wot I could do. An' as for Loo, lor, she do tuck 'em in."

He thrust a forefinger into Loo's ribs, and thus encouraged, she clambered on his knee and tried to smother him with caresses.

"Ah! there ye go," he cried delightedly. "A-cuddlin' daddy cos he brings ye sosiges. Yer dead on sosiges, ain't ye, Loo ? Licks yer fingers arter eatin' 'em, an' wishes ye had more, eh ? "

Loo laughed merrily ; and that moment Jenny would have taken it as an honour to be kicked by her husband. How she made haste to "tidy and wash up," so that Dick might enjoy his own fire-side, and how, with tears trembling among her smiles, she furtively watched father and daughter playing, need not be told. He was in good humour ; her sun shone, and she was happy.

Presently Dick rose, and looking at himself in the cracked mirror, remarked facetiously, "Too much booze, old man. If Tommy Binks was to light on ye now he'd be mighty likely to have fust blood."

The mention of Mr. Binks swung his mind to the coming fight. He must call at once on Velvet Chick. Velvet Chick was a friend of Tapley and of a score more noblemen and gentlemen, whose mission is to keep the British muscle in condition. Therefore Chick was the man above all others "to work the orickle" as Mr. Goodman desired to see it worked. Then, with a spasm of irritation, he remembered that, the day being Sunday, the beer-houses were shut "till the respectabilities concluded their rubric mummeries—a much more audacious feat than beer." Mr. Goodman took the thing as an affront to conviviality and a wanton torturing of the thirsty. Velvet Chick, too, would be still in bed. "Better get back there," said Dick; and forthwith composed himself to slumber.

As Jenny watched him sleeping she could have sung for joy, despite the pain at her heart and the wound in the back of her head. They might say what they liked, but Dick was sound at the core. Drink caused all the trouble; if only he'd give up the drink! If—— She fell back from the flaming sword which has barred so many Eden gates.

Dick slept heavily; and Jenny, taking Loo upon her knee, read from a small tattered volume, kept among her sacred possessions, how Jesus loved little children and blessed them.

"And would Desus love me?" enquired Loo eagerly, surrendering to the spell of the sweet old story.

"Yes, darling; He does love you."

"Shoo [sure], shoo, mammy? Dust as I am?" casting a look over her shabby dress.

"Yes, dearie; just as you are."

The child clapped her hands.

"Sh! Don't waken daddy," cautioned her mother.

Loo held her breath, glancing fearfully at the bed.

"Would 'e knock 'oo down again, mammy?" she asked anxiously. "'E knocked 'oo down last night, an' I tied, 'cos 'oo was hurt."

Instead of answering, Jenny went on with her reading. Suddenly Loo broke in, as it were musing aloud.

"I t'ought Desus wouldn't love 'agged little boys an' gels," she said.

"Jesus Himself was poor, darling."

"Dust like us, mammy?"

"Just like us."

The child's imagination was aflame. It was comforting to think that this gracious, beautiful Jesus was poor. But Loo's thoughts became mixed and troubled. She could not understand how, being without money and fine clothes, He could get people into Heaven. In her world the rich alone were able to perform miracles and confer benefits. To Loo, Heaven was a place where people rode on 'buses, or went in carriages attended by flunkeys, and dwelt in fine houses ; a place where little girls had pretty frocks, and plenty to eat, and an occasional penny to spend on sweets, and played with nice, clean, well-dressed little boys till they were tired, and then lay down on soft beds, guarded by angels.

"Oh! mammy," she exclaimed, forgetting her difficulties, "mammy, mammy, if Desus dot us there."

In the sweet, untheological way of mothers, Jenny explained how they might get to Heaven, how Jesus in His love pleaded for men and women and boys and girls, and how sinners should pray to God and they would get all they wanted. This was a great revelation to Loo, who mused a while and then said,—

"Dod listens to 'ittle gels like me?"

"Yes," answered her mother ; "He listens to little girls like you, dearie."

"Den," said Loo triumphantly, "I'll pray to Dod to stop daddy from knockin' 'oo down, mammy."

But to her amazement Jenny changed the subject.

A little later Dick rose, scrubbed his face, dressed with extreme care, consumed what remained of the sausages, and went forth in quest of Velvet Chick.

CHAPTER V

THAT gentleman resided in the Drury Lane region in order to be at the centre of sport. To the land of pantomimes, alleys, and evil smells Dick accordingly made his way, a cigar between his teeth, his step elastic, his chest thrown out, his nose sniffing the clouds. This sort of carriage aerates the blood, and Mr. Goodman was in excellent spirits. Since, like smaller men, he had his vanities, it may be confessed he meant to paralyse Chick with tales of the friendship of lords, and other high patrons of the noblest of the sciences. When, therefore, he reached the residence of Mr. Chick, in a dim, malodorous alley, not a day's journey from Bow Street, he knocked as one who should say, "Look sharp there, a man of consequence waits."

Nevertheless, he had to knock a second and third time before the edge of the crumbling door went slowly back a foot or so, and the puckered, dirty face of a witch-like old woman peered at him suspiciously from the twilight within. Dick would hardly have shone in a Scripture Examination; but in his army days he had heard from the Scotch chaplain of the Witch of Endor. So he greeted the door keeper genially with "Good-day, Mother Hendor. 'Ope I sees ye well."

The compliment was thrown away; she had never heard of Mother Hendor.

"Wot is it?" she asked testily, blinking as she scanned him from head to foot.

He stated the object of his visit, and she snapped, " Wot name? "

" Well, now, ain't that stoopid? " cried Dick, as if vexed with himself. " 'Ere I've gone an' come a-visitin' without my card-case. An' me knowin' as ye'd be particular, too. But it'll be all right, m'm, if you open the door wide enough for me to squeeze through. Gent above knows me."

" Cawn't do that," she retorted, prepared to clap the door in his face at the first sign of aggression. " Must take up the name fust."

" Then you can take Mr. Goodman's compliments, m'm, an' say he's a-callin', an' 'opes it might be conwenient to see him," said Dick, drawing himself up to impress the ill-conditioned hag.

The door banged, and he was left to his reflections.

"Chilly," he thought, lifting his eyes and surveying the dingy house-front. " Wonder where Velvet Chick came acrost that ancient goriller. Turned out'n the Zoo, I should think. Mother Hendor! Lord, she'd scare the bloke as wanted the witch raised out'n his boots ! "

With that he turned and looked about him. Up and down the alley doorsteps were occupied by groups of unwashed, evil-looking men and women engaged in discoursing slander and blasphemy. Half a dozen girls, in bangs and ribbons and faded plush, were chanting the refrain of a music-hall song to the accompaniment of a mouth-organ, blown by a pimply-faced, oily-pated youth at a first-floor window. Spying a stranger with nothing to do, they dropped the song and challenged him to a flirtation. Dick protested his " raspberry tart " was another's. " Married man," he declared—" large family—respeckible—go to church o' Sunday's, besides tea-meetin's.

You really mustn't be makin' up to me, my dears. My missus wouldn't stand it."

Throwing back their heads, the girls laughed the thick, coarse laugh of the slums. They had evidently lighted on a man after their own hearts.

" Pore, innercent lamb ! " they cried. " But don't you be takin' on so 'bout the missus. She's all right ; she's at 'ome with the curate."

Whereupon the alley roared, advising him to mind " them Bible sharps."

In the midst of the merriment the door was again opened very cautiously, but a little wider than before. Mother Endor, duskily visible behind, intimated that he might enter ; and letting fly a Parthian arrow at the girls, Dick plunged into the inner darkness.

The great Chick sat on his bed-edge, in shirt sleeves and unbraced breeches, discoursing to two friends, who shared between them the only chair in the room, and nodded assent to his sentiments while consuming his ale. He held out a mighty paw, which Dick seized and wrung like an athlete, enquiring at the same time after its owner's health.

" A1 at Lloyd's," answered Chick—" A1 at Lloyd's. An' 'ow's yer own feelin's ? "

" A1 at Lloyd's likewise," said Dick cheerily, smiling upon the other guests, whom he knew as brother-sportsmen. " Can't be nothin' better'n A1 at Lloyd's, can there ? "

" Dunno 'bout that," returned Chick. " The *Mariar*, as went down last week, takin' all hands with her, was A1 at Lloyd's. Reckoned the cap'n were drunk when she struck. 'Ave a reviver."

Reaching to the mantelpiece he took down a bottle of ale, which he handed, with a corkscrew and a chipped tumbler, to Dick, inviting him to do " the needful " for himself. Chick had always something sociable for his friends. For the enterprising proprietor of the Spotted Goat, a noted tavern hard by, knowing Chick's standing with the elect, had secured his influence. By the terms of the agreement, Chick was to do the square thing by the Spotted Goat, and the Spotted Goat was to do the square thing by Chick. Therefore he could always satisfy thirsty visitors, or, in his own expressive words, " give 'em a skinful."

As Dick drew the cork, the host made himself comfortable on his matress-throne. Displayed in all his leonine might, he was a man to inspire respect in the brave and terror in the timid. With a black, close-cropped, bullet-head set on the neck of a bull, he had a body on which you would have said the pommelling of mere fists would be as the tapping of drum-sticks. His unbuttoned shirt revealed a great hairy chest, which suggested the lungs of a bison or a brewer's horse. A clean shoulder-blow off that tower of strength was a thing to fell a giant. Early in his career his nose had been flattened and his upper lip split. These facial alterations, in conjunction with an enormous jowl and heavy, rolling eyes, gave him the benign aspect of a bulldog.

Dick instinctively looked up to him, less in love, perhaps, than in jealousy. Tommy Binks could be treated like a common mortal—but Chick, the redoubtable " bruiser," who, but for one or two defects of habit, might dispute honours with Crinch himself! One would not carry a jest too far with Chick. " If he could only be kept six months off the drink," said good judges, " he'd whip any man in England, or out of it." But, unhappily, the Spotted Goat was too much for Mr. Chick.

" 'Ear as you've bin away," he said, looking shrewdly at his visitor.

" Yes," returned Dick, wiping his mouth. " Bin to the country with my family. Not bein' a married man, Chicky, maybe ye don't know as kids needs fresh air."

"Shouldn't 'ave thought as you was the man to take on 'bout kids an' fresh air," laughed Chick. "'Ow's the country? All a-bloomin' an' a-blowin' with roses, a s'pose."

"Sunthin' that way," said Dick.

"An' 'ere," cried Chick, "blest of ye ain't gone an' come back without'n so much as a booky in yer button-'ole. Might a' brought us city blokes, as can't go into the country with our famblies, some of the essence of rose as the nobility bathes in.

Whereat the company laughed uproariously, for Chick, like other great men, was particular as to the reception of his jokes. Encouraged and elated, he jested prodigiously for a full half-hour, and his friends roared with tact and drank with relish and goodwill; for though the jests were bad, the drink was excellent and abundant.

At last Dick got his chance, and swerved to business. Whereupon Chick became a smiling sphinx. He knew all about the forthcoming fight, but untold gold would not tempt him to blab. The time hadn't quite come for particulars; but they might take it from him that the combat was to be "the biggest thing ever known in the hannils of the ring."

"Talk of toffs," cried Mr. Chick, his heart swelling with honest English pride—"talk of toffs, it's nuthin' but princes, an' dooks, an' hearls, an' lords, an' bary-nites of every degree. Bless ye, they're as thick 'bout the Royal Olympian as blue-bottles on fly-paper on an August Sunday arternoon. Hepsom an' the Darby ain't in it."

"They say as Tufty Slogget's a devil with the left," said one of the first comers.

"'An wot's Tom Crinch with the right?" demanded the other. "A bally plaster saint, a 'and-painted

Chiner hangel, a s'pose. When Tufty's a-doin' it with the left, it's my 'pinion Tom'll be attendin' to the right. There ain't no sham Abra'm 'bout 'im, as I've 'eard on."

"I seed Tom last night," said Chick, with the reflected glory of the man who is hand-in-glove with a champion heavy-weight, "an' 'e's as right's a porkerpine, an' as 'ard to get at. The fightin's all right. Wot knocks me senseless is the money. The 'ole bloomin' Bank of Hengland's on."

The three guests wiped their mouths simultaneously over that vision of gold. Then Dick dexterously tried to get the names of the illustrious patrons. Did Chick happen to know if Tapley, the Earl of Wegron's son and heir, was of the number? Chick answered in the affirmative, asking in turn what Goodman knew of Tapley.

"Met him in the country," replied Dick indifferently, as if he were daily in the habit of meeting lords in the country. "Met young Twickham, too," he added. "That's old Bung's son. Don't 'appen to know if he's in it?"

"Yes, 'e's in it," said Chick, opening his eyes. "An' MacTor's in it—that's MacTor's Scotch whiskey. 'E's a beauty. Don't know 'alf the time wot e's tryin' to say—gone on the Scotch haccint; but the money's there. Oh! the oof's all right."

Dick supposed the oracle could be worked so that "friends of the fambly, so ter speak," would be admitted to the show free.

"That orikle ain't no go this twist," returned Chick. "Pay, an' you go in; don't pay, and you stay out. I understand that's the sole an' hexclusive orikle on this hoccasion. An' wot's more, prices is a-goin' up like merkry on a brilin' August day."

Dick took a pull at his glass to compose himself. Then he gently enquired whether his friends might count on Chick's aid to get in at reduced figures. But Chick was powerless. He was, of course, to go in free himself; that was all he could manage. The difficulty, he understood, was to find room for those who were willing to pay any price the committee named. Mr. Goodman emptied another bottle and departed, satisfied that nothing was to be got out of the inflated Chick.

The evening was spent at the Bear and Cubs, where Mr. Wragg was gracious and an admiring audience was liberal with drinks, for it was clear Dick was getting into high quarters.

Next day he wrote a letter to Tapley in his best army hand, recalling their pleasant meeting in the country, and hinting, with that rare delicacy of which he was master, how much a pass to the Olympian for the great night would be appreciated. By return of post came the coveted pass for " Mr. R. Goodman and friend." It was a serious question who the friend should be. After much thought the honour was conferred upon Tommy Binks, Mr. Goodman for the present preferring that form of revenge.

CHAPTER VI

WITH the possible exception of a general fresh from slaughtering her enemies, England loves nothing half so much as a prime, certificated prize-fighter. On that masterpiece she dotes with more than the pride of a parent. The crown and glory of British manhood he is at once a thing of beauty and a trenchant example of the skill, valour, stamina, and fighting ability which have made our beloved country the favourite of Heaven and the despair of the nations. Remembering this, as well as all that was expected of itself, the Royal Olympian rose superbly to the occasion, and Society gave a rousing response. Not since Tom Sayers made putty of the Benicia Boy had the sporting element been touched to such a pitch of excitement and enthusiasm. The " princes, dooks, lords, and barynites," of whom Velvet Chick had spoken with such gusto, gave the event something more than their moral support, while democracy bore down on the committee wild with exultation and a desire for tickets. Chick was right when he said prices were to be raised ; prices were trebled, and when space was exhausted, big premiums tempted lucky holders. But it was in the betting that the choicer spirits revelled. England is rich, America is rich ; and their riches were pitted in a way that made thousands giddy.

Since the days of Adam and Eve human nature has been addicted to forbidden fruit, and of all the morsels that are sweet on the tongue of the sinner,

the sweetest is won by gambling. Nothing else
sends quite the same exquisite thrill through the
members. The oldest hands were readiest to admit
that the betting on Crinch and Slogget was the most
brilliant and thrilling which had ever given them a
vertigo. Tapley and Vincent Twickham were in the
affair prominently and energetically. So was Mr.
Duncan MacTor; not that he cared a jot about
boxing, but the advertisement was good for whiskey.
Therefore the red beard of MacTor shone and waved
an oriflamme in the thick of the excitement. The
Earl of Wegron bestowed his patronage with the
discretion to be expected of that famous amateur,
risking his money with the shrewdness of a veteran.
Viscount Twickham gave the thing his countenance,
partly as a relaxation from more arduous amusements, partly in deference to the spirit of his set.
He liked sport; but the winning or losing of money
was nothing to him. Unlike Wegron and some
others, he was overburdened with gold. So it came
to pass that his friends, appreciating the sacredness
of friendship, flocked about him with tips; and when
the day of reckoning came, pocketed the results with
charming grace. It is a peculiarity of betting that,
given the chance, you cannot help taking in your
bosom friend; and as Viscount Twickham was
blessed with a multitude of the best friends that ever
made a man happy, his disbursements were immense.
He paid with a smiling innocence which touched the
hearts of recipients; for he would have died rather
than divulge the feeling of being victimised. "Poor
devil! he needs it," he would say to himself as a
brother peer went off with his coin.

On the great night Velvet Chick flitted furtively
among the shadows; but by grace of Lord Tapley,
Dick was in open evidence as deputy door-keeper
and chief " chucker-out."

"Fust time in my life," he snickered, "as me an' the police have been on the same side."

It added to the satire of the situation that, in his place of honour, he stood cheek by jowl with a constable who had once assisted in "running him in." Mr. Goodman cherished no grudge.

"You was only a-doin' of yer dooty," he remarked to the astonished constable, on disclosing his identity. "D'ye think as I'd be down on a man for doin' his dooty! That ain't my style. When I was a bloomin' kiltie—that's the Forty-second Royal 'Ighlanders, you understand—I've put two foot of cold steel through 'eaps an' 'eaps of poor devils. D'ye think it was 'cos I hated 'em I made holes in 'em? No, sir. But 'Er Majesty she ses, ' Private Richard Goodman, B Company, Black Watch, your dooty for the time bein' is to stick them blessed niggers, 'cos they 'aven't the sense to behave 'emselves.' An' I stuck 'em, as in dooty bound. When you 'elped to take me up as a D. and D., you was doin' it in dooty bound."

The constable breathed more easily, for it would be an uncomfortable thing to lie under the ill will of one who had the Royal Olympian at his back.

For a week before the fight Dick had his liquor free in all the public-houses within the mile radius. Nay, people lay in wait and disputed for the honour of treating him. At the Spotted Goat he was elevated even above Velvet Chick, a bit of favouritism which made Chick swear revenge. But Mr. Goodman was, in the main, loyal to the Bear and Cubs, Mr. Wragg having dropped a hint it would be worth the hero's while to make that famous pub his head-quarters. There, night after night, he entertained an admiring and thirsty crowd, who made a run on Twickham's ale and MacTor's Scotch hot. The custom of the Spotted Goat, Mr. Wragg told Dick privately, was falling off, in spite of all that Chick could do.

"Well," said Dick, "Chick ain't in with the toffs as I be"—a fact which Mr. Wragg gratefully acknowledged.

His home saw little of Dick. In the small hours of the morning he would tumble in upon Jenny, hiccoughing, but not violent; for to be well filled is, in general, to be amiable, and Dick found the canteen arrangements entirely satisfactory. As tokens of his happiness and affection, he dropped many peace offerings in her lap,—now a sausage, now a chunk of boiled ham, now a pint of winkles, and again a loaf of bread. He even brought her beer, which he obligingly drank himself, since it didn't agree with her; and he remembered Loo's weakness for toffee. In addition, he was able to put a trifle on the fight, and altogether felt that at last virtue was bringing prosperity.

"Jen, old gel," he cried one day, "the best stroke of biz we ever done was that trip into the country. See how things fall out. If I hadn't gone an' got boozed, an' broke that copper's 'ead, an' been run afore the beak, an' him Twickham's ale, an' so got took up by the toffs, we shouldn't be so 'appy now, should we? This is wot ye might call a new hera—rations to yer heart's content, plenty to eat an' drink, an' sunthin' for hextras. Jen, it'll be beaf-steak puddin' for dinner an' plum cake for tea 'fore all's over."

But intense as was Dick's happiness, Jenny was exceedingly ill at ease. Not being in her husband's confidence, she was more alarmed than gratified by this breeze of good fortune. It seemed ominous, unnatural. And, woe of woes! Dick never returned to her sober. Nothing but evil could come of perpetual drunkenness, she told herself. So while Dick soared to the seventh heaven of bliss, Jenny sighed much, and grew so white and thin, that even neighbours, accustomed to pining and drooping noticed it with pity, if also with contempt. Her appetite failed her. The delicacies of ham and sausage stuck in her throat. Her conduct too became erratic. Suddenly, in the midst of her work, she would snatch up Loo and kiss and hug her ; then as suddenly set her down and turn away. Once Loo called out, " Mammy, 'oo tying ; what 'oo tying for, mammy ? " but Jenny, whisking off the tear, turned a laughing face on the child.

" Who's crying ? " she asked, and the next moment she was holding Loo in a smothering embrace.

" You mustn't be sayin' to daddy as mammy was crying," she said, " for you saw that mammy was laughing. Is the toffee very good, dearie ? "

Yes, the toffee was very dood ; but Loo was sure mammy had been tying.

Thus while Dick attended to the affairs of the Royal Olympian, and was the soul of a dozen public-houses, Jenny's heart grew heavier and sorer. And it made bitterness more bitter that there was not one poor soul with whom she could exchange a word in her trouble. Who cared whether she lived or died ? Paradise Court scorned her, scoffed at her. And the great, rich, glittering world outside, the world of decency and happy homes, what was she or her insignificant life to it ? Pleasure passed her by. Religion knew her not. The Church had other things to do than finger the gutter on the chance of picking up a pearl. Missionaries, indeed, there were, whose wry, reproachful faces and tactless ways made redemption sour and excited resentment and ridicule. Dick had fallen foul of one of them, thus frightening the lot from ever climbing the stair again. So Jenny had only the wide-eyed Loo and her own dismal thoughts for company or comfort.

CHAPTER VII

THOSE who expected rousing entertainment from Tom Crinch and Tufty Slogget were not disappointed. Neither were those who devoted their energies to betting. Crinch took the ring with one hundred and twenty thousand pounds on his head ; Slogget almost equally weighted. Having the heavy stakes vividly in mind, knowing also that the grit of two great nations was on trial, and that telegraph wires were held open to thrill the world with the result, the champions exchanged greetings, smiling a deadly intent. Experts, reading their faces, whispered rapturously there was to be no selling of the fight.

They began with the cautious alertness of masters of ring craft. Tufty showed generalship in his use of the left, and Tom was splendidly nimble with the right. The interest was soon of electric intensity. You could hear the soughing excitement rise and fall as one or other got in a telling hit. England gasped and bit her lip when Tom Crinch's left arm swung by his side as if broken ; but it was only momentarily paralysed, and the right peppered so effectively that very soon America had but one eye. The other, as a humorist remarked, was only a dot in the middle of a stale beef-steak. Then the transatlantic brotherhood breathed hard, cursing audibly but unconsciously. But in general honours ran evenly, for the men were excellently matched. On all hands it was owned the Royal Olympian had never witnessed so brilliant an exhibition of manly qualities, which is to say that Tom and Tufty were at once breaking records and making history.

Half an hour after the start the Earl of Wegron leaned towards his neighbour, MacTor, and re-marked,—

" Be Gawd, MacTor, almost as stimulating as Scotch whiskey! Look at 'em, fast getting blind and yet gamer than game-cocks. Combs and eyes may go, but no funk or white feather ! I saw the Benicia Boy done up, and it wasn't a finer sight than that."

" It's grand, it's grand !" responded MacTor, pulling ecstatically at his sheaf of red beard. " I can under-stand now how the Cæsars went daft over gladiators. Did ye see yon ? did ye see yon ? Clean on the point : that's one for Tom ; but God ! there Tufty's made a swashing return. I wonder how many thousand sparks Thomas sees now ? Things are dirlin', I'll bet. It's perfectly wonderful what can be done with four fists, even when they're inside gloves."

" Wonderful, indeed !" put in Lord Twickham, looking hard at the defeatured performers in the ring.

" By Jimminy," cried an American, lifted out of himself by a vehement and damaging passage, " I *do* call that sloggin' ! We'll be going up this minute to prise their eyes open, so's they can see each other. This beats Noo York."

When the champions had been at it an hour wind and stamina were visibly failing. Both men were going down neatly time about, and rising with looks that were more and more dazed. But neither showed any intention of yielding, and the excitement of their backers grew deep and painful. Tufty's terrible left was going wild now, and Tom's decorative right seemed equally irresponsible. Still they grinned out of their gory masks and pounded away, disfigured but invincible.

Backers became furiously impatient. Why couldn't Tom hit out? What was Tufty thinking of? You could see their flanks heaving, you could hear the rattle of their labouring breath. Their legs shook, their arms were limp. But what of that? Why didn't one knock the other senseless? A knock-out blow, a knock-out blow, that was what the spectators wanted.

"Tom Crinch, knock the breath out'n him quick!" yelled a tense voice, rousing pandemonium.

In the tumult Tom, pulling himself together convulsively, got his right fair on his adversary's heart, and Tufty dropped like a brained ox. Ready knees supported him; brandy went down his throat; he was mopped and rubbed and encouraged, and, like the fighter he was, gathered himself valiantly for another round. But the knotted, oaken limbs suddenly bent and twisted as if turned to willow sapling, and the superb battering ram collapsed. Thereupon a shriek like the concentrated scream of a dozen tempests went up. Tom Crinch, staggering and swaying drunkenly, grimaced upon the crowd, trying, as one said, "to wink his blooming bunged-up peepers." The next instant Tapley was wringing the victor's hand, the *élite* of England surging at his back for a like felicity. The full glory of the moment lies chronicled in special editions of sporting and other newspapers and long columns of journals prepared for Sunday reading. Whoso will may read of it in the muscular language of the sporting reporter, who excelled himself on the occasion.

Tom was borne off in noble arms to be doctored, congratulated, and toasted in floods of champagne. Nor was the gallant Tufty neglected. He had failed; but the Royal Olympian loved him the better for the manner of his failure. He had played the man; and Britons are chivalrous to the brave, whether victors or vanquished. So that Tufty, though less in glory than his conqueror, was nevertheless a star of exceeding lustre. The pair shared honours, and went through the ordeal of functions and festivities together. They consorted with the great and the noble; fashionable beauties smiled on them in public, and in private doted on their photographs. They were fêted till the trainers protested; and praised till epithets ran out. But for the jealousy of politicians they would have had Stars and Garters; and more than one influential nobleman declared an intention of having things altered, so that State honours might be more appropriately bestowed. As for the enthusiasm of the populace, when the heroes appeared in public it was past description.

So much Clio deponeth. But that stately dame has a trick of ignoring minor actors in transcendent dramas. When the illustrious sweep on their glorified course, atoms and windlestraws of humanity are caught up like motes in a whirlwind to gyrate unseen or unnoticed. Of the multitude who whirled in the train of Tom Crinch and Tufty Slogget, none was more gleefully in his element than Mr. Richard Goodman. He made "a tidy bit" on Tapley's tips. The genial Tapley also presented him to divers lords and "barynites" who could appreciate a man of his kidney. Finally, he "took the shine" out of Velvet Chick so effectively that Chick insinuated "swelled 'ead." But the chief thing was the renewed connection with Tapley and Vincent Twickham. Dick loved them both, and proclaimed his love nightly in the Ruggler Den, the Bear and Cubs, and other places of social resort. Nor did he hide his sentiments while in their company.

"I say, Tottie," he remarked one day, when the group of friends, including the MacTor, were together in the halls of the Royal Olympian, "'pears to me old Mother Nature's made a mistake for onct with you. She's gone an' put the spirit of a prize-fighter into the body of a jockey, that's wot she's done. Ten stone 'stead of fourteen an' a 'alf. It's 'ard, Tottie, bloomin' 'ard!"

"Have a round," said Tapley, buttoning his coat.

Goodman retorted with a roar of laughter.

"I'll see ye in Jericho fust, Tottie," he cried, "I'll see ye in Jericho fust. I knows my best friend when I sees 'im, an' you bet I ain't going to disfigure him. Hit me if ye like, but hencefor'ard Dick Goodman's fist is for Lord Tapley's enemies, if so be he has any."

Whereupon the company had champagne at Mac-Tor's expense.

Thus absorbed, Dick had little time for the joys of home. He left early and returned—when he could, hiccoughing and unsteady. Sometimes a neighbour obligingly gave him a hand up the black Alpine stair, sometimes he lay down in the darkness and slept, thus causing outbursts of profanity in others of reeling senses who chanced to fall over him. Once or twice Mr. Wragg thoughtfully sent an attendant to soften the zeal of officious policemen by the way; but this attention Mr. Goodman construed as a reflection on his manhood. Accordingly, at two o'clock one foggy Sunday morning, when Paradise Court, for a wonder, slumbered, he tried to mark his resentment on the attendant's countenance. At the first sign of hostility the man bolted, and the practice of sending an escort was discontinued.

To tell the truth, home was Dick's last resort. He preferred the light, the warmth, the manifold odours, and hilarious fellowship of the public-house to the chill and gloom and penury of the garret in Paradise Court. How much pleasanter it was to mingle with convivial groups at the Bear and Cubs than to sit in a miserable room, watching a worn-out woman and a starving child. Yes, the public-house life was the only gay, elevating, enchanting life for a man desiring to taste heaven on earth. In the tavern alone could he taste that spirit which soothes the nerve, and exhilarates the brain, and makes the blood bound, and confers the gift of eloquence, and wins everlasting friends. Dick worshipped devoutly in his temple.

CHAPTER VIII

CHANCING to return to Paradise Court one afternoon at the unusual hour of three o'clock, Dick was astonished to find a carriage drawn up at the entrance, not a donkey-chaise, nor a pony-chaise, nor a hospital van, nor a huckster's waggon, nor a nondescript vehicle of any sort, but a real, spick-and-span West End carriage, with crest and coat-of-arms on the panel, a solemn, overfed coachman on the box, and on the curb a supercilious footman, sniffing disdainfully. Dick quickened his step, a lively interest stirring his heart at this vision of grandeur. Coming up, he paused, casting a critical eye over the sleek men and horses, and the shining, silver-laden harness. That done, he brought his eyes back to the smug red face of the coachman.

"Wot's up, guv'nor?" he asked, meaning to be friendly.

The dignitary of the whip gazed down severely, as if rebuking impudence and measuring off social distance at a look.

"'Ad no hidear as anythink was hup," he said at length.

"Oh!" cried Dick, as if a great mystery had been solved for him, "I see. You drive into these 'ere breezy, open spaces for fresh air ; an' I must say as the exercise 'pears to 'gree with ye. Ye look pretty 'ealthy on it, bloomin' like a potted rose."

"'Bout as bloomin' as you," retorted the coachman.

" You're a putty, 'igh-coloured donjohn, you are, an' no mistake." Whereupon he snickered, winking privily at his comrade on the curb. That engaging youth, slipping behind Dick, squared so scientifically in dumb show that the coachman couldn't keep his broad face straight. Dick was innocently obtuse.

"'Igh colour's expensive, ain't it?" he remarked, looking up very seriously. "Now your face must 'a' cost a fortin. The kind o' paint as you puts on ain't to be got in every paint-shop. 'Tain't every one as can afford to lay on port wine an' old ale, is it? You're a interestin' curiosity ; mind steppin' down till I 'ave a proper look at you ?"

At this a varied and merry crowd, which had collected in expectation of fun, burst into satirical laughter, calling on the coachman to jump down and let the "gennleman" have a look at him. The pantomimic footman, too, increased his antics at Dick's back, thus enhancing the gaiety. All at once Dick turned with an adroit, accidental backhander, which sent the performer skipping to the accompaniment of a running fire of derision.

" I like you, sonny," said Dick gravely. " But wot was you a-hidin' for, an' you so 'andsome ? 'Ave a little sport ?" And he cleared for action.

" It's a policeman 'e wants," suggested the coachman from above ; "'e'll ketch cold if 'e ain't moved on. 'Arry, see if ye cawn't accomidite 'im ; 'e'll do as much for you another time."

'Arry started at a run to fetch a constable, but the next instant swung back, his face suddenly grave and deferential.

"'Er ladyship," he said quickly, springing to the carriage door. Whereupon the coachman drew himself up rigidly, looking as if his eyes were for ever fixed in front, and would not on any consideration defile or demean themselves by so much as a glance at plebs on the pavement. The crowd melted on its several ways, with parting comments on the looks of the men in livery and injunctions to Dick to "let 'em have it."

But Dick's interest had been as suddenly diverted as the footman's. Looking up the court he beheld two ladies of aristocratic mien coming towards him, one elderly, the other also past her first youth, but still young, and very dainty and attractive in her bearing. The elder was leaning affectionately on the arm of the younger, and beside them, curtseying and smiling and furtively wiping her eyes, was—of all people in the world—Jenny. In the dim perspective beyond stood Loo, gazing wistfully with a finger in her mouth. Feeling instinctively that a crucial moment in his life had arrived, Dick stepped briskly forward, giving the military salute.

Her ladyship drew up with a perceptible flutter. Though in her anxiety about souls she ventured into slums, it was with the feelings of one entering a cage of wild beasts on a wager ; and this questionable apparition startled her.

"Who is the man ?" she asked, keeping her eye on Dick, as if at any moment he might spring.

Jenny's white face turned crimson.

"My 'usband, my lady," she faltered, struggling with the hot swirl in her brain—" my 'usband, just coming 'ome."

"Yes, 'm," put in Dick blithely ; "'er 'usband just comin' 'ome—Jenny's 'usband," and he beamed convivially on the visitors.

"Dear, oh dear !" murmured her ladyship ; "and this is the desperate character we have heard so much of! I hope," she whispered nervously to her companion, "I hope he's sober. It would be dreadful——"

Dick's quick ear caught the word.

"Sober!" he cried. "Bless you, m'm, sober's a harchbishop at a hordination, an' tight on his pins as a colour-sergeant day arter promotion. Yes, 'm."

Jenny, who had unconsciously moved to his side, looked anxiously from face to face, her own tense with fear of what the volatile Dick would do or say next. It relieved her to find that, interpreting the word liberally, he might really be called sober. She yearned to give his sleeve a warning tug, but that was impossible. She could not even give a hint with her eyes, for his were comically fixed on the lady before him.

"I've heard of you," said her ladyship, levelling her lorgnette the better to meet his gaze.

Dick grinned.

"Yes, 'm," he said blandly. "I ain't without friends to speak of me. Friends be mighty queer at times, m'm, as you may 'ave noticed. Some speaks the trewth, and some tother thing."

"I daresay," responded her ladyship. "I've heard something on both sides."

"An' I 'ope as a little of wot you 'eard was to your mind, m'm," rejoined Dick gallantly.

"I'm afraid evil tongues have had a chance," was the answer. "But that would be too fatiguing to discuss at present. My son has spoken of you."

"If you was to court-martial me on the spot I couldn't name 'im, m'm," said Dick. "But I'll lay two to one he ain't the sort to peach. S'elp me Gawd, m'm!"

"Shocking!" cried her ladyship—"shocking! Suppose you were to be struck down in your blasphemy."

"I don't want to put the parish in for no fun'ril expenses," said Dick, smiling.

"A dreadful man!" sighed her ladyship—"a shocking, dreadful man! quite lost, I'm afraid, to the proprieties of life and religion. I must send Mr. Quince to you," she added, addressing Dick directly.

"Gennleman's name sticks me, m'm," he returned. "Don't 'ang out 'bout 'ere, do he?"

"He's one of the best known clergymen in London," answered her ladyship with some warmth.

"Beggin' pard'n, then," said Dick, "but if it was all the same, 'e'd better not come. Them Gospel touts lose their way an' get 'urt; yes, m'm."

"Gospel touts!" echoed her ladyship. "You must not speak of the clergy like that. It would do you good to be visited by Mr. Quince—very much good indeed, I think. Meantime, you may remember my son's name. It's Twickham—Vincent Twickham."

Dick instinctively saluted again, eyes and mouth opening in amazement.

"Well! I'm——" He clapped on the curb just in time. "Lord! 'tain't 'alf an hour since I left 'im. Forgive me, my lady, but you 'ave one of the best sons in England; an' that's honest. 'E's one to be proud on, 'e is. Wot did I say, my lady? 'E wouldn't peach, not 'e."

Since Eve first looked into her baby's eyes and saw perfection, no mother was ever offended by a compliment to her child.

"Perhaps you are right," said Lady Twickham. "And since you have adopted the complimentary strain, let me say you have one of the best wives in England."

She glanced at Jenny, who stood in dumb, burning confusion, and with a look in her eyes as if pleading to be spared. Dick turned deliberately and surveyed his wife.

"Yes, my lady," he said, "Jenny be A1; an' it ain't no joke bein' wife to a workin' man as has served 'is country in the army an' can't get a job in consequence."

"A struggle, I daresay," observed her ladyship sympathetically.

"A rough sea an' a lee shore, my lady, that's wot it is."

"Well—well, you look after her and be kind to her, and—and perhaps the rough sea and the lee shore wouldn't be so terrible if the captain remembered to keep sober."

Dick laughed heartily at the jest.

"I dunno, my lady," he cried; "but if Twickham's ale wasn't so good capn's wouldn't drink so much."

"Let us get to the carriage, my dear," said Lady Twickham to her companion, and beat what to Dick seemed an unaccountably precipitate retreat.

When the back of the fat coachman was lost in the surge of the street, Dick turned into Paradise Court, feeling as if the place really merited its name. To his intense joy it was full of people, and he strutted to his own stair-foot gloriously exalted. During the ceremonial interview with the great lady, Paradise Court had flocked to doors and windows, all eyes and ears. When the vision of wealth vanished, it trooped into the open, cellar and garret and all between contributing their sluts and frowsy lords, who simmered about Dick and Jenny, questioning, exclaiming, and exhaling baleful odours. Jenny crept through the press of leering night-birds, anxious to escape to to her own room. But Dick tarried to be lionised. He let it be known that the great lady, who was richer than the Bank of England, represented Twickham's ale, and there were cries about his luck. He would remember them when free samples arrived wouldn't he? He knew they loved him. A few were disposed to be satirical; and to them Dick intimated his perfect willingness to fight then or later, the beaten man to treat all round.

"Me an' Lady Twickham's son is friends," he said trenchantly; "an' the man as rubs the wrong way will fight, or my name ain't Dick Goodman." With which intimation he passed to his eyry. In the twilight of the stair he came upon little Loo, her cheeks monstrously tattooed, and her mouth so full of chocolate she could not speak. Snatching her up, he carried her aloft to Jenny, who was waiting timidly and rather doubtfully.

"Say, Jen," he cried, depositing the child on the bed, "fortin's a-flowin'. 'Ope you milked the old cow proper. How much ? "

"A little, Dick, for Loo. She says the child's starvin' for want of clothes."

A swift change of expression came into Dick's face.

"Come, that ain't good enough," he said. "A little—small silver, so to speak. I'll lay it's gold ; come, plank out."

"She said it was to get Loo clothes, Dick, and was very particular in sayin' that if Loo didn't get clothes, we needn't expect nothing more from her."

"Is she your 'usband, or am I ? " demanded Dick. "When I married you, the bargain was that you was to love an' obey. This is how ye do it. It'll save trouble if you fork out just as lively as you know 'ow."

She looked in his eyes, and saw they meant obedience, instant and absolute. So turning to a shelf in the corner, she took half a sovereign from a broken cup and handed it to him. Once she would have shed tears over the compulsion, but now she only compressed her lips as she contemplated the ragged Loo. Something had come to pass, something so audacious and terrible that the first thought of it froze her. But she had grown accustomed to it, and, after a hot and agitating debate with herself, had resolved upon measures of which Dick little dreamed. For the first time in her life she was playing the hypocrite, resolutely and with malice prepense. Lady Twickham had bestowed two half-sovereigns ; and come of it what might, Jenny was resolved to keep one of them for Loo. For she had been driven to the point when a child's hunger is harder to endure than a husband's wrath. Dick might, indeed, get the half-sovereign; but it would only be by trampling on her dead body, she told herself. So she handed him the coin, not with tears, but with tight lips and a look which might have warned Dick not to rely too much on a woman's docility when fighting for her child. But he did not notice, so eager was he to clutch the gold.

"There ye are," he said, beaming like the sun after thunder. "Didn't I say it was a yellow 'un?"

In the joy of handling it, he forgot Jenny's reluctance to deliver it up, and was disposed to be generous.

"Jen," he continued, the last note of harshness dropping from his voice, "I said you was to obey; that was the bargain, old gel—that was the bargain; but I goes a step for'ard an' says we're partners, you an' me—partners, Jen, in this 'ere concern called life. You 'ave yer good points; an' though an angel was to say contrariwise, I ain't without'n bad uns. There, that's straight. But we're partners. Only I'm the senior partner, boss, 'usband; an' wot I says is, divide fair. You ain't a nagger; you loves Loo—nat'ril; so do I. Partners again. An' you don't nag—that's your chief wirtue, you ain't a nagger. If you was to nag like some wives——"

He thrust his hand into his pocket and brought out some silver.

"There's five bob, 'alf an' 'alf, fair and square. Now kiss yer 'usband, Jen."

Women, says a sage, are the most puzzlingly inconsistent of all God's creations. The tears, which would not come when Dick was hard, came when he was kind.

And he never knew what a victory he had won.

DICK was no less disappointed than astonished by the suddenness of Lady Twickham's retreat. The charm, as he told himself, was just beginning to work; they were just beginning to understand each other; when lo! she turned tail and fled. An artist and man of the world he perfectly understood the value of first impressions, and he fancied that, when negotiations were so abruptly broken off, he was in a fair way to conquest. Nor was he wholly mistaken. The shock of encountering him was, indeed, to Lady Twickham's sensitive nerves, like the shock of meeting a lion on the prowl. For a moment it was impossible to imagine what the appalling apparition would do. But when she recovered herself, she did not find Mr. Goodman quite the desperate creature her imagination had painted him from nods, hints, and shakings of the head. In fact, the scamp grew upon her while she studied him, as he grew upon so many others, who felt that their abhorrence of so dire a character ought to be bitter and uncompromising.

True, he bore upon him the unmistakable signs of depravity. Wastrel and prodigal were writ large on his countenance; and the expression of the whole man told as plainly as could be that he held her dearest creeds in ridicule. It was hard to believe he was destined for her Heaven; but it was almost equally hard to imagine him consigned to penal fires.

Her judgment, in a word, was on the balance ; so that, but for a trifling slip on his part, the interview might have been prolonged with the happiest consequences. Unluckily for himself, he stumbled upon a word which was rigorously excluded from Lady Twickham's vocabulary. She never allowed beer to be mentioned in her presence. Even an oblique reference by the privileged MacTor to the cause of Twickham's greatness nearly cost him her friendship. It was not likely, therefore, that Dick's transgression would be tolerated.

She went off with a compressed mouth, and a feeling of resentment tingling in her gentle heart. Why should this creature of the slums throw beer in her face ?

" A lost character, I'm afraid," she remarked to her companion—" I greatly fear, a lost character. What a face, my dear—what a face ! "

" Yes, there's a deal of Twickham in that face," was the companion's thought ; but, being politic, she said : " To vary the words of Antony to his Serpent of Old Nile,—

'I am sure,
Though he may guess what temperance should be,
He knows not what it is.'

Don't you think, Lady Twickham," she pursued, " he's a fair epitome of the mass that is dragging down our social fabric ? "

" I fear," answered Lady Twickham—" I fear you are right. You have a wonderful gift, my dear—quite a wonderful gift of hitting the nail on the head. But what's to be done ? "

" What you are doing, Lady Twickham. It's the sole hope of redemption. If the rich do not save the poor, then the poor will certainly destroy the rich. Morality, beneficence, knowledge must take pity, active pity, on immorality, cruelty, ignorance, or we are lost."

She smiled piquantly, in relish of her own magniloquence.

"There's the Church," said Lady Twickham, with a musing air.

"The Church, Lady Twickham—the Church! How can you be satirical?"

"Satirical?" echoed Lady Twickham, arching her eyebrows—"satirical? My dear, I don't understand you."

Her companion could not suppress a smile of amusement.

"When you threatened to bring the Rev. Bartemeus Quince down on Goodman's head, I really thought you were jesting."

"Jesting!" cried Lady Twickham, raising herself and facing round on her companion—"jesting! My dear Miss Lush, what do you mean?"

"Only this, Lady Twickham—that in the work of regeneration I fancied we had got beyond the Church. It seems to me the Church, which never learned to lead, has forgotten how to drive. It's no longer the bogey it was frightening sinners to repentance."

"I am sorry to hear it—very sorry indeed."

"The world advances, dear Lady Twickham. Will you bear with a personal reminiscence? As a little girl I stood in mortal terror of the parson. To my infantile mind he was a sort of spiritual police-man, whose office it was to bag sinners, especially little sinners, for that place of torment which theolo-gians have since happily done away with."

"Done away with?" struck in Lady Twickham— "done away with?"

"Yes; abolished, you know, as a barbarism unworthy of a refined age and an enlightened race."

"Eternal punishment a barbarism," cried Lady

Twickham. "What next? I am sure the Bishop of Blockley would never countenance such a frivolous idea. Depend upon it, those who meddle with such matters will get burnt fingers for their pains. Well, Hades is gone ; is Heaven to follow, may I ask ? "

"That remains to be seen. One can only say that, speaking generally, the parson seems to be much more concerned about the present than the future. The other evening, at one of dear Lady Belmore's Gospel meetings, a downy curate socially laid himself out for a flirtation, poor boy."

" With you ? "

" He designed to honour me."

"Shocking !" cried Lady Twickham, so vigorously that the lackey in front swung round like a mechanical toy to see what was wrong, and at sight of her ladyship's face instantly swung back again, kicking his companion's shin to apprise him of the state of affairs— " shocking ! Abominable ! The wretch !—I hope you punished him."

" Indeed, he was too pathetic for punishment. He seemed such a novice among the vortices of London, and so touchingly anxious to be in the fashion, that I thought of the poor fellow's mother, and forgot to be angry. Besides, he was really very amusing."

"A curate amusing !" said Lady Twickham in disgust—" a curate amusing ! The abandoned wretch —he ought to be a low comedian, not a clergyman. Mark me, there's dire retribution in store for him. See if he doesn't come to grief."

" I understand the odds are the other way at present," returned Miss Lush, with one of her meaning smiles. " He's well thought of by his superiors. I heard him called a very good fellow, whatever the significance of that may be. Oh ! he'll have a fat living one of these days. If he plays his cards well, who knows but he'll be on the Bench yet? The Church feeds such lambs choicely and with care."

"I am astonished!" said Lady Twickham, falling back into her place. "You both amaze and grieve me, Miss Lush. I hope I shall not live to see the desecrations you appear to predict. We don't want amusing curates who try to get up flirtations with handsome and clever young ladies." She inclined her head towards Miss Lush. "Pleasantries of that sort, however pardonable among laymen, are scandalous in clergymen—scandalous, nothing less. As for Goodman, I shall certainly send Mr. Quince to him. Mr. Quince, at least, is not amusing, and does not flirt with popular lady novelists."

Miss Lush remembered that Mr. Quince had a wife and thirteen young Quinces.

"I am afraid to picture his reception," she said. "Goodman seemed to resent the notion of a visit."

"The more reason for putting the Church on his track. What else is to be done? Unless," she pursued, as if on a sudden inspiration—"unless, my dear, you were to take up the mission yourself, and use your great influence for him and his kindred. I heard just the other day from Dr. Tinkle, who knows everything, that fiction is fast superseding the pulpit. He didn't like it; but as he said, there it is. In my young days we read stories for recreation, dear,—Sir Walter, Dickens, and the rest. Now, I understand, novels are read for edification. Suppose you devote your next novel to Goodman and his class. What a sermon you could preach, my dear Miss Lush. You would have us all at your feet, as usual."

Miss Lush smiled, unabashed by the flattery; for, as the most popular novelist of England, the darling of boudoir and boarding-school, she was accustomed to strong incense. It came to her every morning in piles of perfumed letters, in newspaper cuttings, and cheques of competitive publishers. As a commercial speculation she was quoted at a fabulous premium; that is to say, she was reckoned to be worth any six of her competitors. The publisher who secured Laura Lush, author of half a score colossal successes, for a title page, could rub his hands in the sweet assurance of the envy of all rivals.

It was feared the brilliant creature would presently dissolve in the blaze of her own glory; but the fear was founded on ignorance of her character. Adulation was to Miss Lush the most delectable and potent tonic; and advertisement the very breath of life. She was a marvellous manager. Even enemies, who poured contempt on her writings, were compelled to admit her genius for business. Those who scoffed most were readiest to read of the scented paper and particular pens she used in producing her masterpieces, the hours at which she wrote, her style of penmanship, her tastes in meat, drink, dress, amusements, and religion, what she admired, what she detested, what she believed, what she refused to believe, and above and beyond all— what she earned. Sober business men, dazzled by Miss Lush's thousands, vowed to abandon stock-broking and pawnbroking and money-lending and grocery and haberdashery and company-promoting and "take up" literature. Even the professions were tempted and fell. Clergymen, physicians, barristers, soldiers, sailors, scrambled for the flesh-pots of fiction, only to find there was but one Laura Lush. Hers alone was the magic which beguiles to the unloosing of purse strings.

If she did not adorn all she touched, she made it instantly popular. She took up theology, and lo! it was a fashionable hobby; she glanced at transcendentalism, and England was all soul; she turned to matrimony, and the ascendency of woman became the passion of all the tough, masterful spinsters in the land; she depicted love's young dream, and all the youths were Romeos and all the maidens Juliets. In a word, she played upon the people as upon a many-stringed instrument, evoking boundless emotion and piles of coin of the realm.

The means by which she achieved this stupendous vogue had all the simplicity of genius. As a woman of the world she affected sprightly ways; but as an author she could have taught an owl gravity. "Not poppy, nor mandragora, not all the drowsy syrups of the world," could medicine the reader to better effect than Miss Lush's books. A frivolous critic professed to find in her success proof of the Hebrew origin of the English people. "For," said he, "they love unleavened bread." In truth, Miss Lush's lucrative romances were a trifle doughy and hard to digest. And precisely for that reason she gained immense credit with the solemn, serious-minded persons who are gratified by a mental indigestion, who dote on the insoluble, and honour economy of wit and a limitless lack of humour.

The pulpit, in spite of Miss Lush's private gibes, was captivated. The great Tinkle himself preached on her works, extolling them in a sermon which was printed and given away gratis by her enterprising publisher. The Rev. Bartemeus Quince, too, emulating the good bishop, called her "divine" and "inspired"; and counselled his hearers to give their days and nights to her writings. In fine, the Lush fever raged like an epidemic, the cynical, satirical, and depraved only escaping it. Is it any wonder that Lady Twickham, who was not cynical, nor satirical, nor depraved, caught the infection? In spite of some early misgivings she adored Miss Lush; partly because it is the right thing to associate oneself with genius, when that is possible ; partly because the gifted novelist was a popular idol ; and partly for reasons which she did not herself understand. It was Miss Lush who piloted her to Paradise Court and to other courts and alleys which the two visited that afternoon. For it all meant copy for the colossal work which, all unsuspected by Lady Twickham, seethed in Miss Lush's mighty brain. Dick was instantly singled out for honour. The rascal had a touch of originality ; and rascals with a touch of originality are much too rare not to be seized upon by the novelist in search of material. There were also possibilities in Jenny and little Loo, and the stench and slime and slang and wickedness in which they and thousands like them existed. How she would splash the grim, abandoned figures on the canvas. Dante painted his Inferno on a narrow canvas with a camel's hair brush ; she would use a window-mop and paint in flaming strokes on the sky itself, so that all men should see and shudder. When, therefore, Lady Twickham, by a chance of telepathy, suggested the slums, Miss Lush answered cooingly, " I think I will." She did not add that already a dozen notebooks and half as many disused bonnet-boxes were full of material to be dumped into the book. This omission, however, may have been due to the fact that the pair were hurrying up arrears of slumming in order to prepare for other and higher events which were at hand.

Book III

CHAPTER I

VINCENT TWICKHAM was about to play two parts, either of which is enough to make a common head light—the part of parliamentary candidate, and the part of bridegroom. From the instant of his birth he was intended for the honour and glory of public life; and from the moment he cast eyes on Lady Gwendoline at a ball in London his fate as a bachelor was sealed. Twelve months he sighed and burned, pleading with tongue and eye for the consummation of his bliss. Then Lady Gwendoline consented to make his felicity perfect. Whereupon trustees talked settlements, in which the Earl of Wegron, as parent and guardian, took the closest personal interest, while attorneys looked to legal deeds and documents. For when blood and money are to be mingled for a long perspective of generations, the union of two cooing souls becomes something more than a sacrament; it is a momentous financial operation.

But before being admitted to Paradise, Vincent must win political laurels. That was Lord Twickham's edict; and compared with Lord Twickham's edicts the laws of the Medes and Persians were lax. Vincent was to go into the House of Commons to protect beer. Not that the English people were in the least likely to give up the national beverage; but it was high time that certain frothy fanatics, who were screeching that beer was of the devil, should be castigated and silenced. Moreover, it was rumoured that a venial Chancellor of the Exchequer had in his mind's eye a scheme for squeezing yet more revenue out of the over-taxed brewer. Therefore, a champion must be ready for the dragons; and it was fitting he should bear the name of Twickham. Nor did the prospect of a tilt with chancellors and faddists displease Vincent. He liked excitement; he had a talent for publicity. At the University Union he plucked the laurel from the brow of pride. Later on, he figured on the hustings in a way which drew compliments from ministers and party managers. In a word, he was master of that deadliest of weapons, the tongue, and took a master's delight in its use.

A metropolitan constituency was selected by his friends, a prior candidate, at a hint from headquarters, promptly effacing himself. The Twickhams, the Wegrons, the MacTors, the Wraggs, and, let it be added, the Goodmans, marshalled and fought with the ardour which means victory. At stormy meetings Dick was worth ten policemen. Wherever there was sign of hostility, there he was, collaring his man, and he gave no time for argument. When the fight was won, Vincent thanked him in the presence of a distinguished company; and Tapley taught him to appreciate champagne. MacTor, too, tried him successfully with Scotch whiskey, calling him a man and brother for the catholicity of his taste in liquors, and quoting Burns to clinch the sentiment.

"You don't know Burns, you God-forsaken bodies of the south," cried MacTor, being exceedingly jubilant, "and couldn't understand him if you did. Man, listen to this,—

'Lees me on drink, it gies us mair than either school or college,
It kindles wit, it waukens lear, it pangs us fou o' knowledge.'

God ! I'd give Robbie ten thousand a year to write my advertisements—just to get merry once a week on my whiskey and sing his feelings. The whiskey trade lost a friend when Robbie died. Isn't he just grand ? But it'll be lost on you."

"Lor'," cried Dick in return, "when I was a Black Watch 'Ighlander ain't I laid down in barrack an' camp a-listenin' to the blooming lingo ? "

"Have ye though," rejoined MacTor, beaming— "have ye now ? Robbie was fashed with two of the most amiable virtues that can warm the breast of man : he loved the lasses—God bless them for all the mischief they work !—and he loved a glass of good whiskey. What is more, he made the grandest poetry that ever came out of human head on lasses and whiskey. And in camp and barrack, my friend, you lay listening to the bloomin' lingo."

"Yes," said Dick ; " Bob McCrae—'im that's serjeant-major now—'e carried Burns as others would carry the Bible. Not as the army crowds its knapsacks with Bibles ; but the 'Ighlanders they do go luney on Burns."

"My man," said MacTor, with sudden solemnity, " there's one thing that turns a Scotch stomach—and that's taking sacred things in vain."

"I never seed the Scotch stomach as turned at anything as 'appened to be going," retorted Dick. " An', I tell ye, they fair worshipped Burns."

"That's better," said MacTor.

"Lor'," continued Dick, "I shall never forget one night, when Bob an' me was new to the business, that we was lyin' on the sands of old Egypt, an' the moon was shinin', so's you'd think it was a great sea that was ripplin' an' sparklin' away an' away right into the sky itself, an' the hot smell of the dust was in our noses an' the thing itself in our throats, an' we could 'ear the gruntin' of the camels on the other side

of the Zareba, an' see the bayonets of the sentries—
English steel in Pharaoh-land, flashin' and gleamin'.
Well, Bob he lays down on his back an' looks up
at the stars kind of 'ome-sick, same stars as Job an'
Abra'm an' them other ancient chaps used to gaze
at, he said, when Moses was wallopin' the Egyptians
same as us, an' he began to say private, like, to 'imself,
Burns's ' Soldier's Return.'   An' 'longside 'im was
stretched an old 'Ighlander, Donald MacDonald, as
'ad killed men of most colours under 'Eaven in 'Er
Majesty's interest, an' slep' on worse beds than the
sands of Egypt—'eaps of 'em.   An' when Bob 'ad
finished his poetry, he says in a sickish kind of voice,
as if he wanted to see his mother, ' Donald,' says 'e,
' think of the thousands away beyond the seas who's
thinkin' of us this night.'   An' Donald, never turnin'
an eye, says back, ' An' think of the millions who don't
care a damn.   Sleep, ye fool.'"

"Capital!" cried MacTor—"capital!   I honour
both men.   And, let me tell you, your friend Bob
would be none the worse soldier for his bit of sentiment.   Laugh as you like," to the company at large,
"but I can't go back on sentiment.   It's the one point
on which my friend, Lord Twickham, and I don't
agree.   He simply won't admit the thing at all.
I say it rules the world.   What, I ask, would become
of whiskey if sentiment were dead?   Tapley," in a
significant aside, "your *protégé's* decidedly interesting.   We must see what can be done for him."

Having got into Parliament, Vincent proceeded to
the more serious business of taking a wife.   His legs
had not reposed a month on the classic benches of
the House when the social event of the season was
celebrated with the *éclat* due to the son and heir
of the Cæsar of the brewing trade and the daughter
of the Earl of Wegron.   The Bishop of Blockley
made the twain one, being assisted in the operation

by the Rev. Bartemeus Quince and the Rev. Dichory Bird. Society, under the auspices of Royalty itself, glorified the proceedings with its presence; then retired to discuss and criticise. For a motherless girl with no dowry but her blood (and that getting thin), Lady Gwendoline, it was admitted, had done exceedingly well—had, in fact, landed a prize. Speculative mammas with the best girls in England to dispose of, forthwith began to look round the peerage and baronetage for similar prizes. The fact that they are rare and hard to capture made Lady Gwendoline's achievement all the more striking.

While the envied pair made Heaven of a castle by the sea, lent for the honeymoon by a friend of the bride's family, Lord Twickham made over the title-deeds of a furnished house in Berkeley Square against their return to London and every-day existence. Lady Twickham saw that it was fit for her son's wife, spending a fortnight in daily examinations and harassings of tradesmen; then turned to her arrears of charity—with the aid of the indispensable Lush.

All this time Dick lived and moved and had his being in an element of which he had dreamed in his more imaginative moments, but dared not hope for as a reality. Now that he was actually in a Canaan flowing with infinitely better things than milk and honey, he could scarcely credit his own luck, though he felt the enjoyment was too deep for doubt. The liquor was excellent in quality and overwhelming in quantity. He need never be thirsty or go to bed sober—which, to tell the truth, he seldom did. Sometimes, in face of expert warning, he mixed drinks, and then it required all Tapley's *finesse* and innumerable half-crowns to keep him out of the police-courts. He was himself dimly conscious of the risks.

"Tottie," he said one day, "if anything 'appens, you're solid, ain't you?"

" As granite," answered Tapley.

" Then," said Dick, " I may drink with an easy mind. Only remember, Tottie, that when I'm proper boozed I ain't no kid to put to bed. For Gawd's sake, look out I don't hit you. Once I nearly did for my best friend in that way. As for you hittin' me—fire away, it don't matter."

There was but a single small cloud in the sky—but it was very black. One day his patron was surprised to find Dick gloomy and resentful.

Why, what's the matter?" asked Tapley, scrutinising Dick's sour face.

" Wot's the matter?" echoed Dick. " Why, ain't Lady Twickham gone an' sent one of them Bible sharps to spy on me? 'E's been at my snoozin'-box with the lady as puts us blokes in 'er bloomin' books to be laughed at. I say it ain't fair on a cove."

" I commiserate you," said Tapley feelingly. " I do, upon my soul. A parson and a woman-novelist—too bad, too bad! They didn't catch you."

" Wish they 'ad," returned Dick. " For wot does the snipes go an' do? They slings such nonsense at my missus's 'ead 'bout 'Eaven, an' 'Ell, an' the kid, an' the risks we was runnin', an' that kind o' muck that she cried fit to bust. She throwed herself round my neck, blubberin' ' Oh Dick! this, an' oh Dick! that; an' passon says as we're goin' straight to perdition 'cept you mend your 'abits,' says she. ' An' oh! will you?' says she, ' an' give up that drink that's a-ruinin' us?' That's the comfort passon brings on a cold day, peltin' to perdition like an igspress train. I ain't goin' to stand it. If 'e comes back there'll be an inquest."

He didn't mention that he took prompt and vigorous measures to disabuse Jenny's mind of the parson's heresies, and that in consequence her head was in bandages.

" Pooh ! " said Tapley, " not so serious—not so serious. If you only knew what I have suffered from parsons. The best parson ever made isn't worth a drubbing. Besides, you know, the poor devils must earn their bread somehow. If they frighten women and children—well, the harm's not great. Don't you worry ; I'll speak to Twickham when he's over the honeymoon. Meantime, I want a little practice with the gloves, and you'll give wrinkles, won't you ? And some of my friends would like similar exercise."

Thereupon Dick was presented to some of the choicer spirits of the Royal Olympian as a modest but accomplished and very worthy professor of the great art.

On hearing this, Velvet Chick swore he'd be eternally lost if he could make out what the world was coming to when a chump-'ead like Goodman was made the tutor and bosom friend " of lords an' gentle-men as calls themselves sportsmen." It was time for decent people to put up the shutters and retire from business. That night he got drunk in mortal disgust, and was put to bed muttering a vow to " bash " Dick " so's his mother wouldn't know 'im." All the same, Dick continued his course of gaiety undisturbed by threats. He patronised Mr. Wragg and Mr. Wragg's friends at the Bear and Cubs, receiving in return the honours he most appreciated. He went to the Ruggler Den, and Tommy Binks and his brother Rugglers joyously did the hospitable. He gave his countenance to music-halls and theatres of variety, sometimes alone, sometimes as aide-de-camp to Tapley, who liked the livelier forms of drama when the per-formers were attractive and agreeable. With Tapley, too, he went to some of MacTor's balls to barmaids, the pair practically taking the frolic *incog.* For the rest, he kept to himself such secrets as might trouble his wife if she knew them, attended loyally on Tapley took his liquor like the prince of good fellows he was, and looked to MacTor for the fulfilment of his promise.

For the present, however, that gentleman had other business in hand. MacTor's Scotch whiskey had reached the company point ; that is to say, it had been boomed and pushed as high and as far as puffing and advertising of various ingenious kinds would send it. Profits had been whipped up with magnificent results. Mr. MacTor, in fact, found the time ripe for securing to himself the full benefit of his shrewdness, enterprise, and foresight. The public was, therefore, to be invited to secure an interest in the finest whiskey that ever made man merry. So one morning, towards the close of his honeymoon, Vincent learned that long floating rumours had at last crystallised to fact. The MacTor was converting himself into a limited liability company, with a capital of a million sterling.

The board was attractively aristocratic, for titles on boards pay. Lord Twickham was chairman, and associated with him were the Earl of Wegron and other nobles of illustrious name and lineage. Mr. MacTor himself appeared modestly at the bottom as managing director. It was not without diplomacy and a considerable expenditure in hard cash that he managed to adorn the front page of his prospectus with so many peers of the realm. One of the hardest to secure was the Earl of Wegron. It was not suggested that he knew anything whatever of the spirit trade, nor that he had the least knowledge of commerce in general ; but his name was invaluable. When the subject of directorship was first mooted, his lordship cast a very meaning look at MacTor. "You wish to have me?" he said ; and on receiving a reply in the affirmative, "Then, by Heaven! MacTor, you must pay for me—that's all."

"Of course—of course, my lord," chirped MacTor, and the bargain was struck.

Lord Twickham was a heavy purchaser, because he had in mind a great scheme—a scheme by which beer and whiskey should be under one control. When Vincent returned, his father presented him with a quarter of a million MacTor shares, remarking, " I have done my fair share of work. Your turn comes now. Consolidate the businesses ; control beer and whiskey ; and you may dictate to kings and ministers."

And that night Vincent dreamed of the greatest conbination of its kind the world had ever seen ; for he too, was, ambitious.

CHAPTER II

THE gods, as wise men know, make no mistakes. In singling out the Earl of Wegron's lovely and high-spirited daughter to be the wife of the richest young man in England, they understood very well, the shrewd humorists, what they were about. They were aware that, endowed with youth, beauty, talent, ambition, the charms of blood, the bewitchment of gold, and a worshipping husband, a woman is irresistible ; and Lady Gwendoline was nothing less. To say she kept her " booth in Mayfair with the rest, to happy issues," is to state a great fact weakly. On wakening from the trance of the honeymoon, she returned to Society resolved on conquest, Vincent following enchanted at the heels of his fate. She glided into action, a vision of radiant fortune, turning many heads. It is a delectable experience, after the rigours of fashionable poverty, to find oneself in possession of a Fortunatus' purse. Lady Gwendoline, forced all her life to practise secret and shameful economy and self-denial, found it deliciously intoxicating. Nevertheless, she kept her head, rising to her opportunities as superbly as a young queen rises to a throne.

In spirit, enterprise, and the priceless gift of pomp, she had, perhaps, but one serious rival—the brilliant Lady Tonkley, wife of Lord Tonkley, the gouty hanger-on of diplomacy. Lady Tonkley was the only child of a greasy-fisted oil-boss in Illinois ; but there was no oil on the daughter's almond hands. That had been well washed off before she crossed the Atlantic to conquer England with her dollars, her wit, her vivacity, and her wonderful eyes. No one had ever discerned a heart in her, perhaps because it was so richly encrusted with gold and gems. Nor was it pretended that she loved the rather dilapidated Tonkley; but she and the oil-boss of Illinois thought he might be a family adornment, and she married him. The Earl of Wegron himself had once his eye on her; but while he was making enquiries on the financial side, Tonkley sailed in and won. The thing was settled in Paris; and Lord Wegron, who was fast coming to the scratch, was both amazed and disgusted.

"Who'd have expected it of Tonkley?" he said to a brother peer, who was also on the look out for an heiress. "A confounded, worn-out old scrub like that walking off with two millions sterling from under your very nose—two millions, if a farthing, the lucky beggar! The taste of a woman is the most incomprehensible thing ever created to vex man. What she saw in him, I can't imagine, seeing what she might have had."

"Just so," said the other, looking in the withered face of Wegron.

"Well," pursued the discomfited lover, "it would be a devilishly risky thing to marry first and look to the finances afterwards. I lost the trick; but damme! I played according to Hoyle."

"I think I'd have reneged," replied the other thoughtfully. "I wish I had had your chance."

"I wish I had it over again," said Wegron ruefully.

The two ladies, who had made casual acquaintance in the course of a London season, after marriage became bosom friends—and rivals. But, in spite of Lady Tonkley's dash, it was Lady Gwendoline who set the pace. She entertained magnificently, gamed a little, travelled, shot, hunted, was a peerless whip, and an unfailing attraction at charitable and religious bazaars. Parsons blessed her publicly and effusively; all other men adored her, jostling each other for a smile, or a token from those dark eyes, which could be so significantly merry and so thrillingly soft. In the art of cajolery the whole stage could have taught Lady Gwendoline nothing. Many a verdant youth got fatuous on her glances. Nor were older heads exempt from her witchery. Lord Cheribink, who was fifty if a day, and in a hot career of pleasure was supposed to have exhausted himself and half the capitals of Europe, came near causing a scandal. Happily, Lady Gwendoline herself was the first to perceive the danger, and switched the gallant off.

" If he'd been younger, my dear," she laughed to a confidante, " or better preserved. But remnants or things on crutches—no, thank you. These are for Americans," and she smiled wickedly.

Many wondered how she came to marry Vincent Twickham, who was " a good, sterling fellow, and all that," but hardly the mate, it was surmised, for one of Lady Gwendoline's adventurous disposition.

The ladies were reserved and critical. It shall not be hinted they were jealous or envious. But they certainly were soberer in their eulogies of the new divinity than their lords and brothers. Lady Twickham sighed softly as she watched her daughter-in-law practising magic. *That* had never been her own way; and in her heart the mother pitied the son a little. He, poor boy, was blindly happy, proud of his brilliant wife, whose face the winds of heaven must not visit roughly. Her wishes were mandates; her very whims were sacred. Lady Twickham, pondering as a mother will when her son is concerned, prayed the happiness might continue.

"Perhaps," she thought—"perhaps, as she gets used to money she'll learn repose, sedateness."

Perhaps, meantime, the card was filled with other things.

Lady Gwendoline was not long in command of the Twickham millions when she marched intrepidly on Twickham Towers, attended by a glittering escort. The family seat, she privately owned, lacked brightness, smacked mustily of defunct custom, owing, doubtless, to dear Lady Twickham's delicate health. But under a capable substitute a swing with the tide would exhilarate them all. Admiral Gwen hoisted her flag, and immediately guests were gladdened by the innovations of the new spirit.

The gaieties began at Christmas. Under Lady Twickham's rule, the Christian festival had always been sacred to family gatherings. Lady Gwendoline introduced a variation. Consequently, her first Christmas as a wife saw a large and distinguished party gathered at Twickham Towers for such entertainment as ready brain and limitless purse can provide. Lady Twickham, looking on with folded hands, supposed young people must be young; but was not without qualms and inward protests. Lord Twickham, who had a robuster taste in pleasure, thought it refreshing to watch youth having an innocent fling.

"They'll be old soon enough, God knows!" he said—"they'll be old soon enough."

"Yes, dear!" sighed Lady Twickham, and made for her own quarters to nurse a nervous headache and imbibe the balmy, healing thoughts of her dear Bishop of Blockley. That saintly divine and writer was ever a blessed refuge from the world and its follies.

Among the amusements planned by Lady Gwendoline was a picturesque pastoral, in which she herself impersonated with bewitching charm the character of a lovely young shepherdess. A gay cavalier (the young Lord Sickle, once Vincent's rival), happening to set eyes on her, was smitten, and instantly laid siege in the gallant manner of his order. Vowing there did not breathe on earth another being with half her loveliness, he proceeded to explain the use love makes—of cruppers. He was holding her hand; and she, blushing coyly and very prettily, with eyes on the ground, was murmuring questions about the faith of men, when there entered her shepherd swain, Reginald Twickham, not over ardent in his part. Immediately she forsook the honeyed cavalier, and running to her own true love, threw herself in his arms with caresses meant to wring the heart of the other. To her amazement she felt him shudder. She caressed him more tenderly, whispering sweet things in his ear; but the shepherd, who had a heavy and troubled brow, shuddered again. The next moment they were in the wings.

"Why, you naughty boy," she exclaimed, "what is the matter with you? Has the love scene upset you, dear?"

Reginald bluntly told her not to be a donkey, and involuntarily put his hand to his head. As he did so, she saw him shiver violently.

"My poor Reggy, you are ill!" she cried.

"Beastly queer," he answered vaguely. "Gwen, I thought you'd never have done messing in there. I can't go on again."

He was sent to his mother, and another shepherd was improvised, for Lady Gwendoline was not to be cheated out of the splendid scene at the end, which showed her torn between love and duty. When it came, a long round of applause, ringing along corridor and hall, testified the delight of the audience.

CHAPTER III

THE sound of cheering fell discordantly on the ear of Dr. Freeson, the family physician, hastily summoned from St. Edmund, as he passed swiftly to Lady Twickham's private room. There he found her ladyship, crouched on a sofa, with Reginald's head in her lap. She greeted him quietly, but he, who knew her better than she knew herself, noted the trouble of the drawn mouth and anxious eyes. Reginald breathed quickly and uneasily, complained of his head, and shivered, in spite of himself.

" This is sudden, doctor," said his mother softly.

The doctor answered with some of the cheering words which the profession gets off by heart, asked a few questions, and proceeded to examine the patient. The disease, however, was not ripe for diagnosis. For the present, therefore, they were justified in concluding the ailment was simply a chill, which would pass off under proper treatment ; but in his own mind the doctor said " typhus."

" You brought him through measles and scarlet fever, Dr. Freeson," said her ladyship plaintively.

The doctor admitted that honour had been his.

" It cannot be a recurrence of either of those diseases, then," continued Lady Twickham. " I am afraid this may be serious—inflammation of the lungs or something of that sort. Reginald was always so careless of himself."

The doctor assured her there was no sign of lung trouble, and got Reginald off to bed, at the same time despatching a messenger for medicines, with orders not to spare his horse. When the patient had had his first dose, the doctor, looking in Lady Twickham's face, said very kindly,—

"There is no cause for alarm; but as I am old-fashioned enough to desire all my errors to be on the safe side, I am going to send at once for a nurse from London. It is best to have a skilled person in attendance."

"Is he feverish?" asked Lady Twickham, the first real note of alarm in her voice.

"Just a little," answered the doctor.

Lady Twickham's nervous headache was gone, and with it her long prevailing languor. She would herself be nurse. Yes; she would attend her boy. She would think he was really ill if a nurse appeared. A physician who means to shine must study diplomacy as well as medicine. With the tact of an expert in feminine humours, Dr. Freeson made an appeal for one patient at a time. On no consideration must her ladyship be fatigued or deprived of sleep. She would forgive him for being stringent on that point, and relieving her of the direct care of Reginald. Lord Twickham, being called in to counsel, sided emphatically with the doctor. So a nurse was procured from London; and privately the doctor warned her to send for him instantly, at any hour of the day or night, should a suspicious change be noticed in the patient.

Next day he was early at Twickham Towers, and the diagnosis said "typhus" with added clearness. Yet for twenty-four hours more he kept the secret, hoping against hope that science might be mistaken. Then facts, becoming indisputable, were discreetly divulged.

Lady Twickham, being extremely nervous, and therefore capable of amazing heroism, astonished them all by her fortitude. Typhus; people died of typhus.

Their duty was to see that Reginald didn't die of it. She relied on Dr. Freeson, and composed her mind for waiting and watching. It was then that Lady Gwendoline showed her mettle. Though keenly regretting the sudden scattering of guests and consequent cessation of gaieties, she stepped quietly beside Lady Twickham, saying they would see to "dear Reggy together." Nor was she a whit less noble than her word, though assailed by vehement protests against running foolish risks.

"I am foolish at best," she laughed, with the candour that wins hearts. "Let me for once be foolish in a good cause, and see what comes of it."

There and then Lady Twickham took her to a mother's heart.

Day by day for a week Dr. Freeson reported that the fever was taking a normal course. Then, one evening, he looked grave and anxious, questioned the nurse closely, and in the end advised calling in the family's London physician. Lord Twickham asked for particulars. Was Reginald's condition worse? Not quite so well as could be wished. Was he delirious? All fever patients get more or less delirious. But was the delirium of an alarming character? There were signs it might so develop.

"Dr. Freeson," said Lord Twickham, "there's no plucking at the counterpane, or grasping of imaginary objects," and the look which came into the good doctor's face sent the blood from Lord Twickham's.

"Wire for Dr. Houghton at once," said his lordship, with difficulty keeping a steady voice—"at once—at once. Do not lose a moment, and—and for the present, keep it from the boy's mother."

That night Dr. Houghton made his diagnosis and held a consultation with his colleague, the outcome of which was a telegraphic summons to Sir William Berkley, the famous specialist in zymotic diseases.

When the telegram was written, Lady Gwendoline discovered there would be no train for two hours.

"A special!" cried Lord Twickham—"a special! Haste—haste." And a special conveyed the great man as fast as express engine dared travel.

With his arrival a dread silence fell on the house, as if its pulses paused in awe. After a word with Lord and Lady Twickham (she would not be denied an appeal for his best aid), he passed into the sick chamber with the other doctors, and the door was shut. Then it seemed the universe held its breath. How still it was—how awfully still! What was going on behind that closed door? What desperate fight was the young life waging in the mists which enshrouded and were choking it? It could not be that death would conquer, Lady Twickham told herself; the good God would not permit that. Yet a deadly fear and sickness were at her heart. Her face was piteously white; her twining fingers were trembling. Oh! what was going on beyond that door, through which they would not let her pass? Rachel weeping for her children has moved the generations with pity. But there is an agony more poignant than Rachel's— the agony of waiting for the word which means life or death.

To Lady Twickham that waiting was anguish un- bearable. Hardly knowing what she did she ran for- ward to demand admittance to the patient. Was she not his mother? But the hands of husband and daughter-in-law were lovingly upon her. No; she could not go in. Her presence might upset the wavering balance. Then she would sit where she could see the doctors as they came forth, and read her boy's fate in their faces. So a chair was set for her within view of the bed-room door, on which she kept her eyes fastened.

Presently Sir William walked out, but his face was

inscrutable. Familiar with death and the alternations of human hope and despair, he knew how to keep a blank countenance. There was another agony of suspense while the physicians consulted. It was well for Lady Twickham she did not hear, or hearing, could not understand, the first word of the great specialist on being alone with his colleagues.

"*Floccitatio*," he said quietly, and the others sorrowfully nodded.

What science could do should be done, but a higher Power was intervening.

Meantime, how tell Lord and Lady Twickham of the thickening mists and the swiftly ebbing strength? It is the daily business of physicians to speak of closing records, and a plan was soon devised—a little hope and comfort to the mother; to the father the stern truth. So Sir William Berkley administered a soothing draught to Lady Twickham, inducing her to retire to her own apartment for needed rest. Then Lord Twickham was taken aside. Softly, very softly and tenderly, the verdict of science was delivered; but under the quiet accents the strong Lord Twickham reeled. It was as if his ears were confounded by the noise of a mighty explosion, and though nothing but the composed face of the physician was visible in the sudden chaos, he felt the world was crashing about him. In that brain, which had been calm in the maddest excitement, there arose a tumult of whirring and beating as of machinery driven beyond power of endurance. The long and ghastly face twitched irresponsibly, and the nails were tearing the palms of the hands. The whole world spun and heaved in a desolating fog.

The specialist understood and waited. He knew all the varied ways in which men take the death sentence. So he watched for the recoil which comes to the strong of will. It came suddenly.

"I will not—cannot accept this as final," said Lord
. Twickham, struggling to compose himself. "You
will forgive me if I suggest another doctor from
London."

He named a man, like Sir William himself, of
European reputation.

"And Sir William," he proceeded, getting better
control of his voice, "see that you do not let any
consideration of expense stand in the way. Anything, you understand—anything or anybody, but
save the boy."

Instinctively he fell back on the idea that to him
who can pay all things are possible. Couldn't
money command science, and science defeat death?
It must be done—must, that was the only word to
be used.

The second specialist came, saw, and owned the
futility of medicine. Science had done its utmost;
the case was now in other hands. The good Dr.
Freeson wept, and Dr. Houghton excused himself
from being present at the next interview with Lord
Twickham.

So the specialists, taking his lordship into a room
and setting him in a chair, told him what was come
upon him. On hearing their judgment, he looked at
them curiously, as though dazed, then all at once
bent forward, face in hands, groaning; and to hear a
strong man groan shakes the heart of even a medical
specialist. The first spasm past, he sat silent, save
for one dry sob which would not be repressed, his
hands on his temples like the jaws of a vice. He
asked no questions; but presently he rose, and
looking at the physicians, said almost in his ordinary
tones,—

"You'll stay, please, and see the end."

With that he left them, going straight to the sick
chamber, from which they made no attempt to

exclude him. Nor had the startled nurse heart to make any protest. Greeting her very quietly, he stepped to the bedside, took Reginald's limp hand, and bending low, spoke caressingly in his ear. Twice—thrice the words of endearment were repeated ; but Reginald did not hear. The nurse watching awe-struck, saw the strong face writhe in pain and the resolute mouth quiver. But Lord Twickham seemed perfectly composed when, raising himself, he turned and asked her,—

" Is he quite comfortable, nurse ? "

" Ye-s, my lord," she faltered.

" Then leave him for a little to me ; and see that we are not disturbed."

With a cold thrill she went, and he locked the door behind her.

When he appeared again, the doctors, stealthily playing sentry, had no need to ask what ordeal he had just gone through. There is a language of the face more tragic than any words of the tongue ; and Lord Twickham's face told he had lost something precious, something that should not be restored within " our bourne of time and place "—never while seasons rolled and suns rose and set. But his manner was serene.

" I am afraid," he said apologetically, " I have been keeping you from your patient. But I don't think I have disturbed him—I don't think I have."

With the step of one suddenly grown old he passed along richly carpeted corridors to his own room. There he changed his clothes for fear of carrying infection, and that done, sought his wife to tell her what was happening to them.

Next morning the darkened windows told the world what had befallen Twickham Towers. It was hard to believe that the great rich viscount, whose word was as the mandate of a god, was subject to the common lot. But there were the desolate blinds, wrapping the place in the awful, if familiar, gloom and hush. St. Edmund gazed, speculating how the proud man would take it, and if his poor lady were heart-broken. The proud man took it in characteristic manner. When the end came, and the specialists, having failed, were preparing to hurry off, he took them into the library and there, in a hand without a tremor, wrote each of them his cheque. He was self-possessed and courteous ; but scarcely grateful. They had let his boy go ; and he knew their hearts were not bleeding because his was cruelly bruised.

CHAPTER IV

VINCENT had little time to waste in grief for the loss of a brother, very deeply, if also very quietly, loved. From the family vault in St. Edmund cemetery he went straight to the defence of his order in Westminster. The occasion was felt to be urgent. Covetous neighbours, fired to emulation by Albion's trick of conquest, were insolently intriguing to slice up the world against all sense of decorum or British prerogative. The country, therefore, wanted more warships to promote that wholesome fear of destruction diplomatically called the comity of nations ; and the Treasury, asked for an extra ten millions, bethought itself of the possibilities of beer. The brewing trade rose against the outrage ; and Vincent, as a conspicuous knight of the threatened industry, was called to leadership. Primed and inspired by the astute general, his father, he stood valiantly by the ancestral guns, fighting with a rousing dash and ardour. But, being young and excited, and righteously angry to boot, he made the tactical mistake of trying to rush the enemy.

While he was exposed, other foes fell upon him suddenly and with disconcerting vigour, not because they loved the Government, but because they hated beer. The water-drinkers, a pale but combative and vigilant sect, perceiving their chance, gathered for an attack on the Twickham and allied interests. Against the Treasury the issue was plain. Brewers were already overtaxed; wherefore, as Vincent easily proved, it would be nothing less than monstrous to make them pay for the new warships. But it was quite another matter dealing with assailants who introduced the element of morality, who asserted, apparently with conviction, that drink is the mother curse, and charged its makers and vendors with debauching the people, tarnishing the national honour, ruining homes, and sending souls to perdition. The debate was adjourned in some excitement; and Vincent, tingling with indignation, retired to consider the charge—a pretty comprehensive one, it must be admitted.

In the lobby his friends clustered about him with congratulations and encouragement. Tapley wrung his hand, praying fervently for a chance to aid in "bowling over the blue-nosed votaries of the water-bottle." The Earl of Wegron poured scorn upon them, and Lord Twickham advised a judicious in-difference.

"I have always made it a rule myself," he said to his son, "to ignore faddists of every description. I am content with the verdict of the people, and I counsel you to take the same course. When you hear wild talk about the iniquity of the drink traffic, consult your ledgers and be consoled. Don't believe off hand that the greatest nation the world has ever seen is composed of fools. After a lifetime spent in business, I found that, for all the babble of fanatics, we sell never a gallon of beer the less."

"Pooh!" exclaimed the Earl of Wegron. "It's all the other way—all the other way. Isn't it, MacTor?"

"All the other way," repeated MacTor, contentedly stroking his red beard. "Never so much beer and whiskey sold as now—never. It's very consoling privately, besides being right—from the national point of view. Destroy the wine and spirit trade, and what

becomes of your navy? Let the navy run down, and
what becomes of your empire? That's the crusher.
To expect England to prosper without breweries and
distilleries would be like expecting a man to stand
erect without a back bone. If you want the French
in command at Portsmouth drown the miller, as we
say in Scotland. A course of Adam's ale and
Samson's on his back."

" Well put, by Jove!" cried the Earl of Wegron,
feeling he must justify his directorship. " If you
want the French at Portsmouth, and the Russians in
Calcutta, and the Germans in Hong Kong and Cape
Town, then by all means remove the curse which
contributes some forty millions a year to the
Exchequer. That's how to kill the goose that lays
the golden egg. If you want to put England—the
England of Drake and Nelson and old Oliver—into
a grandmother's spectacles and nightcap, raze the
breweries, smash the distilleries, and tell the Excise
they may go for an indefinite holiday, because the
British flag is no longer to be kept floating wherever
you turn, an eye-sore to the nations. Ask the mind
of the Government on that matter. Do they, as
guardians of the nation, desire less drinking? Did
Gladstone want less when he called beer the divinest
beverage invented by man since the gods gave up
tippling nectar? You've got your choice: keep your
drink, or haul down your flag."

So the champion was refreshed and heartened. In
the mellow, golden atmosphere of his own circle it
was so easy to heap ridicule on his opponents and
their bleak, unpatriotic cause. Assuredly his counsellors were right, sound economists and patriots, as
well as shrewd men of business. Rarely did private
interest jump so harmoniously with public policy.
As Lord Twickham said, the people were with them ;
they had, indeed, the nation solidly at their back.

The brewery on the banks of the Stare grew prodigiously. Its day-books and ledgers told fairy tales of prosperity, and on the Stock Exchange Twickham shares were prized above rubies. In whatever light viewed, the brewery was unquestionably a colossal success.

"A colossal iniquity!" cried his opponents, and added soothingly he did not understand the enormity he defended. One congratulated him on his consummate ignorance; another on his skill in preserving it amid abounding knowledge; yet another blandly advised him not to be elated, since even ignorance grows stale. He replied hotly to taunts and allegations which his father would not have noticed with so much as a smile of disdain. They pelted him with statistics, and he retaliated with rhetoric. His eloquence gave promise for the future; but for the present, its sole effect was to entangle him more and more deeply in the toils of the enemy. Lord Twickham, perceiving the danger, warned him.

"You have made a good enough start," said the ancient general; "but don't, as you value your reputation, be lured into those jungles they call statistics—that way lie ambushes."

Had Vincent remembered that advice in the moment of provocation, the whole course of this history were different. Being young and sensitive and chivalrous, he forgot to be prudent, though Experience pointedly cautioned him against the folly of heeding empty babble.

"If you let such things worry you," said his father, "thorns and briars will be soft in comparison with your bed. So long as people drink my ale, I eat and sleep not a whit the worse for idle abuse. If you court failure and contempt, try to please everybody: the plan is infallible."

"But, father, all these abominable charges have

been made in the most public place in the world," answered Vincent, the glow of indignation in his face. "The House grinned and gloated; and now, thanks to a free Press, the country is grinning and gloating."

"And you would make it grin and gloat more."

"No; I would refute."

"Refute!" echoed Lord Twickham. "Vin, have you lost your judgment? Add idiocy to idiocy, and tell me the nett result. Refute! Pooh! no more of that, pray. You might as profitably reply to the braying of a jackass. Besides, the world's memory is short; the sermons of to-day are forgotten to-morrow—on the whole, a merciful dispensation. Dismiss the whole thing from your mind."

But Vincent was not as his father. The great gift of impassibility was denied him; which is to say, that he could not at will forget what he did not wish to remember, and proceed as if Heaven itself smiled on his projects. That secret of success Lord Twickham had long ago mastered; it was still dark to Vincent, so that the persecutors easily put him to exquisite torture. Their calumnies made him blaze secretly and furiously. For the first time in his life a burning wrath possessed him, making the thought of vengeance sweet.

CHAPTER V

THE reader will scarcely be astonished to hear that Tapley was of those who scoffed loudest at the "tommy-rot" of the water-drinkers. But he cherished warm regard for his brother-in-law, the financial transactions between them being of a kind to cement friendship; and now, as usual, he was practical in counsel. Vincent had a secret desire to behold with his own eyes some of the reeking horrors of den and rookery attributed to beer—behold, and explode the fallacies in the agitators' faces. Privily he consulted Tapley, and Tapley gave an Englishman's answer—that is to say, the answer of a born man of action.

"Leave it to me," he said blithely, "and you shall have your heart's desire, with some fun into the bargain."

"On one condition," returned Vincent : "that not a soul but ourselves knows of it. I wouldn't have the thing leak out for worlds."

"You're the pearl of discretion," rejoined Tapley cheerfully.

"Well, only one other soul or so—a necessary soul in the enterprise. You're not going to Scotland Yard ? "

"Scotland Yard ? " echoed Tapley. "I know a trick worth several of that."

So Tapley set to work, for the scheme chimed wonderfully with his humour. Within a few hours he called upon MacTor, and learned, as an item of business news, there was very shortly to be a barmaids' ball, the biggest and grandest ever given, " in acknowledgment of the efforts of the young ladies of the trade in getting people to drink MacTor's whiskey."

" They've done a lot for us," explained MacTor ; " and it's but fair we should give them a fling now and again with their sweethearts. Will you come ? The girls are worth squeezing, and not too easily scared."

Tapley admitted some personal knowledge on these points.

" Where's it to be ? " he asked.

" Where would you think, now ? Shoreditch or Bethnal Green, maybe. As it happens, it's to be quite convenient to you. I'll tell you something, though you mustn't be speaking of it. I have been in rooms in your locality for a fortnight, making ready. Never suspected we did business in that way, eh ? " He gripped his red beard, chuckling softly. " Man, there's a lot more in heaven and earth than clever folk suspect—God bless their ignorance ! It's not everybody knows that a trim, tight, good-looking little devil of a barmaid who is up to the game is worth her weight in gold to the like o' me. Now I'll whisper in your ear, as between friend and friend, and neither of us burdened with saintliness, that according to my lights I reward for services rendered."

He opened a private drawer in his desk and brought out a small, brazen-clasped book, fitted with lock and key."

" This is my private ledger," he explained, unlocking it. " You see, I draw so much for business expenses—balls, presents, outings, dinners, and what not, and here are the particulars to a sixpence.

What would our teetotal censors say to this, think ye? If they got their hands on it we'd have fine talk of bribery and immorality in business. Well, I crack my thumb at that. What interests me is that after a little judicious expenditure of this sort, there's an appreciable increase in the sale of my whiskey. That's what concerns me." He touched an electric button by his desk side. "A friend has just sent me a case of champagne for office use," he said. "You're a judge, so you'll just give me your opinion of it "—a suggestion to which Tapley raised not the shadow of an objection. "You see," pursued MacTor, when they had pledged each other, "I can talk freely to you; you're one of ourselves like, otherwise——" He shut his lips to prove how fast he could hold a secret.

"Yours is really one of the most interesting and romantic trades in the world," said Tapley, taking a sip.

"So," responded MacTor, also taking a sip. "Well, you see, most things are just as you make them. We put most of the romance into it."

"I infer it's no longer true good wine needs no bush."

"And you infer rightly," said MacTor, with emphasis. "God bless my soul! it needs a whole forest of bushes—most seductively arranged. Tell me now, how it is you hear more of MacTor's whiskey than anybody else's?"

"Why, because it's best, of course."

MacTor's broad shoulders heaved.

"Man, man," he said, gurgling and rubbing his eyes, "that's a touching bit of faith, and in a time of general unbelief, too. Take off your glass; the stuff's not bad. We can talk quite confidentially; the Earl's on my board."

"Thank you; quite."

"Well, then, my friend, the plain truth is that a score of first-rate whiskeys are on the market this minute. In quality one's just as good's another."

"I thought there was probably some secret in the making."

"Tuts! Water's water, and grain's grain, and a distillery is just a distillery. The secret has nothing to do with distilling, and the funny thing is it's open to all the world."

"Is it fair to ask what it is ?

"Perfectly fair.   It goes by the name of advertising. And you're not to understand by that what's paid for in the newspapers ; that's the most expensive and the least effective way of advertising. It's what's down in this little book that tells."   He tapped the brazen-clasped volume of confidences. "Eh—Lord ! if this book could only speak, what tales it might tell ; but, thank God ! it's dumb. Is it not wonderful that in this age of advertising not one man in ten thousand understands the A. B. C. of the thing ? "

"Then it is all a matter of getting at the public," said Tapley, emptying his glass.

"Mostly," replied MacTor—"mostly, as you say, and yet not altogether, either. It's necessary, for example, to have the stuff."

"As to that, you've only to make the more."

"True," admitted MacTor, his eyes twinkling—"true, as far as it goes ; but it doesn't go far enough.   Tell me, for instance, how you would make ten-year-old whiskey between sunset and dawn."

"I haven't the secret of compressing a decade into a night."

"Then you'd be lost in the whiskey trade. The man who can't work miracles is no use nowadays. You see, we have two kinds of customers. The East End and the Colonies are all right for the raw stuff ; they'd swallow anything. But your silk-hatted West End chappies, and the Scotch—who are rare judges and great consumers of whiskey, I'm proud to say—they must have the real Simon Pure, mellowed and matured. Well, you get a big order for ten-year-old, and you happen to be out of it. What are you to do?"

"Say you're out of it, I should think."

"Man, man, that would be a plan. Well, we supply."

"Supply what you haven't got?" cried Tapley.

"*Revenons à nos moutons*," said MacTor, laughing quietly. "You'll come to the hop, won't you? And I'd like if Mr. Twickham could be induced to come, too. It would do him no harm to see something of his own business."

For himself, Tapley accepted on the spot. For Vincent, he could not of course promise; but he would use his influence, on condition the attendance should be strictly *incog.* Returning to Vincent, he therefore suggested they might begin tentatively with the barmaids' ball, as a thing likely to afford incidental enlightenment. When Vincent begged for particulars, Tapley replied,—

"For one thing, you'll see the trade, as Mac calls it, enjoying itself in its own way. Differently expressed, you'll see the charmers of the public-house blooming in all the glory of fresh paint and cut-away dresses, and the publicans' fat wives fanning their tawny immensities with ivory and ostrich feathers. You might make a worse start, you know."

"Possibly," said Vincent; and consented to join the glittering throng, and dance a turn or two with the enchantresses whose wiles and subtle witcheries so momentously affected brewery and distillery shares.

The scope and brilliancy of the assembly amazed him. Circes of the charmed cup were there from all over London, but chiefly from the West End, where style and spirit enhance the delights of liquor. In the East End, where men drink in a plain, straight-forward way mostly for drink's sake, stodginess may suffice ; but in the cultured West, where motives are mixed even more than liquors, it needs beauty and art combined to make good sales. Matrons of tropic luxuriance were also there, ablaze with gems and busy with costly fans, according to Tapley's prediction. The atmosphere was as heavy with perfumes of a pungent kind as were cheeks with rouge ; and that was heavy indeed, for time and pleasure and stale air, frequently heated, play havoc with the complexion. For an hour or two feminine faces had the brilliant freshness of nature at her rarest. By midnight they were oddly variegated ; but then, hardly any one was in a condition to be critical, save here and there a sober, withering wall-flower, present by mistake and wholly unheeded.

In grace and sumptuousness of hospitality MacTor surpassed himself. Wine abounded, and the brands were picked. Moreover, there were snug little rooms for the gamblers, and cunningly devised nooks and corners for couples hankering, in MacTor's considerate words, " to kittle on the sly," Etiquette there was none.

" We didn't come 'ere to be starched, did we ? " remarked one lively damsel, summing up the general sentiment.

Beside Tapley's, Vincent's zest was cold. Nevertheless, he played the gallant to bold-eyed, under-clad Eves, who asked pertinently if he did not think enjoyment the chief end of man, and ingenuously cleared the way for sultry flirtations. Most of them had spicy vocabularies ; all of them understood the use of the *double entendre*, and could look without wavering into a man's face. Sometimes their enigmatic familiarities embarrassed Vincent. Nor was he wholly at ease with the gross, high-bosomed dames who formed a ceaseless procession to and from the refreshment counter. Being heavy of limb and scant of wind, they devoted themselves to gossip and, relaxed with wine, showed how to talk scandal. To Vincent, whom they took for an innocent outsider, they imparted some interesting particulars of the trade, interspersed with piquant opinions of his own firm. The Twickhams, it seemed, did not unbend sufficiently.

"Now the likes o' this," said one dame, looking round the sweltering scene, " do be good for business. Mr. MacTor's a very kind, liberal gentleman—very. 'E don't mind a extry quid—not 'e, cos 'e knows that if 'e makes the stuff it takes us to sell it. The Twickhams is different. Not that they be 'ard on their friends—oh dear ! no ; but they do be 'igh an' proud. An' they say as young Twickham, 'im as married the Earl's darter, ain't never been seen inside a public-'ouse. 'E's making a mistake, sir, depend upon it—'e's makin' a mistake. It's the public-'ouse as keeps 'em up, an' they should remember that—same as Mr. MacTor does. 'E don't forget who butters his bread for 'im, 'e don't."

Turning abruptly, Vincent went up to Tapley.

"Come," he said, " I'm going ; I've had enough."

"WELL!" said Tapley, as the two went off in a hansom. "Gay little carousal, wasn't it! By Jove! Mac knows the way to the affections of the trade."

" Evidently," returned Vincent.

"Shrewd old fox, Duncan of the burr," continued Tapley. " None understands better that revelry's dashed good business at times."

Tapley was elevated to the pitch of hilarity. His hat rode giddily far back on his head, his eye glittered, his face was flushed. Vincent, on the other hand, showed signs of weariness.

" Oh, I say!" cried Tapley, catching him yawning, " that's a reflection on Mac's hospitality. If you ask me, the thing was capitally done."

" Capitally," admitted Vincent.

" A little more enthusiasm, Vin—a little more enthusiasm. Any wrinkles?"

"Oh yes! I have added considerably to my stock of knowledge."

" I'll be hanged if you seem much elated. Is there any need to be so solemn in leaving such merriment.

" Solemn! Am I solemn?"

" As a mute at a funeral," laughed Tapley.

" I have heard that mutes are at heart very jolly fellows," said Vincent. " But it's a grave business— learning, you know."

"Grave!" repeated Tapley. "Wait a bit, my dear Vin—wait a bit. You're only in the infant school. If the kindergarten makes you grave, what'll you be in the sixth form? This has just been a nip before dinner to tickle the appetite. There you go again! One would imagine you were a *blasé* old reprobate, instead of being taking a first delicious sip. You'll never learn unless you're interested."

Vincent promised to lay the Socratic axiom to heart; and Tapley, reverting to the entertainment, remarked he had had very much worse fun in his time.

"Some of the girls weren't by any means bad looking," he said; "and they know the time of day, too, by Jove! I forget the number of my appointments, sworn to by the glow of wanton eyes. A mere mortal isn't equal to the chances of a night like this. But heavens! the rustling porpoises of wives,—think of them trying to be improper."

He threw himself back with a roar of laughter, knocking his hat rakishly over one eye.

"On your honour, Vin, could you imagine them guilty of an impropriety in anything but manners? Could you imagine anyone breaking the commandments on their account? No. Yet the sly old Mac has sent every one of them home thinking she's a sort of Helen of Troy. He's the 'cutest man in his gallantries I ever met. It would be so easy, you know, to fall into partialities, and there's considerable risk of letting your feelings run away with you in the critical moment; but Mac's as cool and level-headed as a brass nail. Old Joe of Egyptian fame couldn't have been more discreet. Hullo! here we are."

The hansom pulled up and they got out, Tapley merrily chaffing the cabman, and doubling the fare for the privilege.

"Jolly little covey," chuckled cabby to the policeman on the beat, jerking head and thumb at the two men as they disappeared into the house.

"You'd be jolly, too, if you was 'im," responded the policeman. "Know who e' is? 'E's Twickham's ale—that's who 'e is. Could buy up all the kebs in London out'n 'is loose change."

"An' 'e's a friend of yours," smirked cabby; "an' you ain't proud. Gawd! Must 'ave a lotion to wash that down. Ta-ta."

Inside, Tapley led the way to the library for something (not literary) "to sleep on," and while sipping the ruby narcotic, informed Vincent that the plans for the future were made.

"But you're not fit to discuss them to-night, Vin," he said. "After a sleep you'll criticise and amend."

Next morning his first business was to despatch a note by special messenger to Mr. Richard Goodman, desiring that gentleman to meet him at the Royal Olympian at three in the afternoon.

"If you happen to have other engagements," he wrote, "it may be worth your while to put them off."

The messenger caught Dick as he was leaving Paradise Court for the day, in exceeding ill-humour because of the state of the exchequer. For some weeks fortune had been distinctly hostile. His income had suddenly dropped, because of the fickleness of friends on whom he had relied, and his demands on Jenny were becoming more and more peremptory. They were not satisfactorily met; and he had just been remonstrating in his own telling fashion for her failure "to milk the old cow proper." That morning his arguments had produced one and ninepence ha'penny. The day before the amount had been two shillings, and he wanted that figure repeated, for a man of pleasure cannot well maintain appearances on one and ninepence ha'penny a day. Jenny was twopence ha'penny short, and he descended the stair with a resentful tread and a flaming face,—to come upon Tapley's messenger in a jaundiced fog in the court. He answered gruffly to his name, asking trenchantly who was after him now. For answer the startled messenger put the note into his hand. Suspecting treachery, Dick's first impulse was to knock the man down and read the document afterwards. But glancing at the address and signature, he suddenly broke into cries of joy.

"Tottie, that's Lord Tapley," he said excitedly. "Why didn't you say so, matey?"

Tapley's penmanship not being of the kind which he who runs may read, Mr. Goodman smoothed the letter against a wall, and set himself with great deliberation to master its contents.

"Say, mate," he called over his shoulder, after a strenuous effort, "these 'ere 'Gyptian 'ieroglyphics ain't copperplate exactly. Mind 'avin' a go at 'em?"

On the co-operative principle the note was at last deciphered, and Dick could not help slapping his leg in glee.

"That's all right," he cried, for the benefit of a group of watchers. "Tell Lord Tapley I'll see to it. I'm sorry," fumbling in his pocket, "I ain't got no loose change 'bout me. Mind ye next time."

With that he turned on his heel, and next moment bounded in on Jenny and Loo, who gasped together.

"Didn't expect me back so soon," he cried, smiling in their scared faces. "Well, I couldn't keep away, an' that's the truth. I ain't velvet-made, Jen. Rile me an' I cut up rough; but there's worse goin'; an' I'll make yer fortin yet, 'ear that?—I'll make yer fortin yet. Guess where I'm goin' this arternoon."

"To the public-house," was the natural reply; but it was one which Jenny would not venture to frame in words.

" Read that," added Dick gaily, tossing her the letter, " an' tell me wot ye think of it."

" What does it mean, Dick ? " asked Jenny, when she had finished reading, her eyes very wide and her face very serious.

" Never could tell wot I didn't 'appen to know," replied Dick airily. " Don't 'e say ' Three o'clock, Royal 'Lymp. Other engagements off.' That's 'bout good enough, ain't it ? "

If Dick said so, then it was so. Like a dutiful wife Jenny polished his boots with great animation ; then she helped him to tie the striped neckerchief which completed his holiday attire, and brushed him all over carefully with her bare hand. Finally, when he went off, she stood at the top of the stair calling endearing words after him so that all might hear. For it was this infatuated little woman's fondest wish to impress upon all and sundry that, despite appearances, she had really the best husband in the world. As he disappeared below, she turned back to work and think and pray God he might come to no harm.

BY a cunning deflection on the way to the Royal Olympian, Dick managed to fall in quite accidentally with Velvet Chick; and in the course of a brief conversation almost succeeded in turning that gentleman's complexion from flaming red to green, Lord Tapley's name being the poison used. Dick deeply regretted that he was not at liberty to give a bosom friend particulars of the great events ahead, " lords and such like swells being odd in their ideas "; but by skilful nods and hints Chick was made to understand he might expect a sensation.

They parted, Chick, who had a pressing engagement elsewhere, doubling back to watch the boaster in order to put him to confusion later on. He was sure there was no appointment with Tapley; it was just more of Dick's brag : but when he witnessed the meeting he was ready, in his own words, to drop with disgust. A little later he enquired of Tommy Binks "wot the world was a-comin' to ? " in such a tone of ferocity that Tommy thrilled through all his heroic fibres. To enable them to discern what the world was coming to, they resorted to the Spotted Goat, where they cordially invoked the landlord's aid.

" 'E don't amount to much, 'e don't," said the man of liquors, referring to Dick's presumption. " Chick, you'll 'ave to give him a dressing down."

" 'E'll better take care," growled Chick, " that's all I say—'e'll better take care."

Meanwhile, Tapley and Dick were busy and happy in a corner of the smoking-room of the Olympian. Over cigars and brandy-and-soda Dick swore by all the gods he knew to keep eternal silence about the business which brought them together ; then Tapley divulged as much of it as he thought prudent. Dick knew how Twickham's ale overflowed the land. Yes ; Dick knew. The Twickham ale was everywhere.

"You can't get away from Twickham," he said oracularly.

Well, as a young director laudably anxious to master his business in detail, Vincent wished to make certain private and experimental studies for himself— wanted, in fact, to see something of the retail trade.

"Wants to see his ale goin' down men's throats," said Dick, his face a midsummer sun for radiance.

"Exactly," said Tapley. "Curious whim."

"An' where do I come in ? " asked Dick, pushing to the central point.

"Well, how's Mr. Twickham to gratify his whim ? " was the answer.

"No how, as I knows on, 'cept by doin' a public-'ouse crawl," said Dick thoughtfully.

"Public-house crawl ? " echoed Tapley.

"Yes ; round of pubs, ye know. No other way of seein' the stuff disappear as I can think on."

"Hit the nail on the head, by Jove ! " responded Tapley. "Goodman, yours is the plan—the only plan of obtaining first-hand knowledge. But he can't go alone, and he can't go as Twickham. Tumble ? "

Dick could have poked Tapley in the ribs as the deepest-dyed, most delightful rascal in the world, but the place was public. So he merely leaned forward, with a meaning light in his eye, and whispered, "Disguise ? "

Tapley nodded.

"Then," said Dick, his pulses bounding wildly, "I'm his man. You'll go. Yes; that's proper. Tottie, this is goin' to be a big game—the biggest game we've ever played."

They proceeded swiftly to detail, lest too long a conference might provoke comment. Tapley passed a sovereign, which Dick accepted as an earnest of what was to follow.

"You'll have to get a new rig-out," said Tapley, looking over his fellow-conspirator.

"'Shamed of me?" asked Dick.

"Quite the reverse, my boy—quite the reverse, I assure you," was the prompt response. "But if one goes *incog.*, all must go *incog.* In your present clothes you'd be a walking declaration of our imposture."

Thereupon he hastily indicated what the common disguise was to be. They were all to be as horsey and doggy as tailor could make them. Amateurs of sport they would go about, dropping in here and there, as the humour seized them, to make merry with other men of pleasure about town ; they were to observe unobserved ; to drink without getting drunk—a feat which Mr. Goodman thought possible, but exceedingly difficult.

"An' 'ow much d'ye reckon this 'ere new rig-out will cost?" asked Dick.

"Depends on where you buy. Petticoat Lane on a Sunday morning ought to give abundant choice."

"So, so," said Dick. "West End cast-offs come East for a polish. Reckon it'll be all right if the chink's there."

Tapley tabled another sovereign.

"On your honour, now, Goodman, you'll keep sober," he said.

"Oh, Tottie!" cried Dick upbraidingly, "how can you an' me on the strict tee-tote? Just been asked to give my experience at a temp'rince meetin'."

"I apologise," returned Tapley. "And let me see, give me your measurements, and never mind Petticoat Lane. On second thoughts I'll look after the toggery."

"An' wot 'bout the coin?" asked Dick quietly, fearing he might have to refund.

"Oh!" laughed Tapley, "we never demand repayment. Let's call it household expenses. Mrs. G. must not be forgotten."

"Then," said Dick, feeling mightily relieved, "all we've got to do is to get ready."

"That's all," answered Tapley; "and to see we've got sand for prying eyes. You understand?"

Dick nodded, smiling as one who knew how to deal with impertinence and curiosity.

REVERSING the order of the sun, they began in the west, making the eastward descent into Avernus gently, to spare Vincent the shock of a plunge. To attune their spirits to the adventure, they dropped into a West End theatre, mingling jovially with the gay bloods at the bar, and passing thence with the throng of *jeunesse dorée* to the enticing fields where wild oats are sown.

They took experiences and discoveries in diverse ways. Tapley moved from scene to scene, blithe, tactful, jocular, familiar of manner, and ready of tongue; Vincent feigning his character well, but preferring the reserve of a student; Dick for once abashed—abashed by the pure glory of the thing. Mr. Goodman had understood vaguely that as the heavens are higher than the earth, so the West End exceeds the East in life's felicities; but the reality was so much beyond his imagination that he was dumb from joy and amazement—save for intermittent exclamations necessary to relieve the feelings. It may be that Tapley's injunction not to " give the show away " by talking curtailed his speech, though it is likelier he promptly forgot the command. In any case, his mood was one of ecstasy too deep for words. So, like Belshazzar, in the giddiness of good fortune he drank wine, and in his heart praised the gods of gold and silver and crystal, and, happier than the Babylonian monarch, saw no writing on the wall.

Hitherto, it had been his custom to worship his

chosen god with a devotion wholly blind to the style or ornaments of the temple. Now the temple was in itself a thing of voluptuous delight. Craftily and with childish pleasure Dick glanced in the gorgeous mirrors, Narcissus-like in love with the decked-out figure of the sportsman who smirked fraternally back at him. With a fine simulation of effeteness he lolled on sofas which might have given the august legs of princes a sense of luxurious ease. He gazed at painted nymphs and graces and satyrs on wall and ceiling, vaguely conscious of the fascinations of art ; the music of fountains and stringed instruments, mysteriously softened, soothed and charmed him. He laid his elbows on cool marble and looked in the seductive, falsified faces of the handmaids of Bacchus, and studied the " get-up " of the sybarites who came to flatter and drink, wondering within himself at the toleration of Providence.

He would fain have pitched his tent in that warm, dazzling, spendthrift world, where everyone talked folly and acted folly, and the drinks were rare and expensive. O Lord ! that he had money to waste as those gilded apes wasted it. Spying disparity between rewards and merits, Mr. Goodman absently took off a MacTor hot. The moment after he caught Tapley's rebuking eye ; but a simultaneous diversion saved him. A highly gilt youth with a pelican beak and no chin, mistaking the trio for " green uns from the country," essayed to be humorous at their expense. Dick itched to correct his error and mend his manners ; but scenting danger, Vincent and Tapley turned to go. With a smiling " good night " to the chinless one and his friends they passed out, Dick pausing just a moment to intimate that, as an artist in facial decoration, he would joyfully titivate their countenances at any time, and though he did not like to boast, he felt safe in saying their looks could be greatly improved.

"If you go on like that," said Tapley, when they were outside, "I'll bundle you home in a growler."

Dick laughed so uproariously that a constable pulled up to look him over, remarking he seemed to be "took very bad."

"As bad's a copper at an area-gate when the cook's about," returned Dick ; and then to Tapley, "Better insure cabby's life, then ; might 'ave kids dependin' on 'im."

"Well," said Tapley, in a tone of vexation, "we shall all be run in if you don't take care. That'll be the end of it."

Whereupon Vincent chimed in with the statement that if they were running such risks the whole project was abandoned on the spot. Finding his companions serious, Dick contritely promised on his honour to take insults meekly for the future ; but he could not help giving them an account of "Tottie afore the beak," and his friends lying zealously on his behalf.

"Never 'ad yer chin above the dock rail, wonderin' wot would come out 'gainst ye next," said Dick. "Well, there's something ye don't know till ye've worn the darbies an' 'ad yer testimonials read out in court an' put in the papers."

They were passing a lamp-post, and he stopped abruptly.

"See there," baring his right wrist and revealing an ugly scar. "Nearly tore the bloomin' irons apart. Took four coppers to put 'em on, Tottie, not countin' the two as began the row an' wasn't in at the finish. For that little frolic—

> 'The once a week made me go ta-ta
> For a month on the can't keep still.'

But if you was took up ye'd fork out the fine."

"Avaunt, Satan," answered Tapley ; "we're losing time."

Seven nights were devoted to the glittering palaces where rank and wealth drown their *ennui*, Dick religiously keeping his vow. Vincent made vast and curious additions to his knowledge of the beer trade ; Tapley enjoyed himself without thought of instruction ; and Dick was content to take toothfuls of liquor and keep his fists in his pockets and his tongue standing at ease, save when seduced into gentle flirtations with the temptresses who make brewery shares boom on 'Change. In general, however, Tapley was ladies' man, his gifts for the part being pre-eminent. Dick's method was to take by storm ; Tapley won by strategy.

"You mean well, Goodman," remarked his friend ; " but with girls you're the bull in the china shop."

Anyone else indulging in such candour would have endangered his head ; but there were many reasons why Tapley should be forgiven. For one thing, his favour was bread and wine ("peck and lush," were Mr. Goodman's words), with pocket-money and the envy of rivals to boot. While his kindnesses continued he was, therefore, free to chaff. What gave Dick concern, as he lay in bed at mid-day staring reflectively at the ceiling, was not Tapley's acid humour, but a possible change of luck : that was the special contingency from which he prayed heart and soul to be delivered.

On one point his conscience protested. To a thirsty man, whose creed was to—

> "Grasp the goblet with both hands,
> And drink while he had breath."

Tapley's restrictions in the matter of liquor were trying. A full week Dick held out against a sense of lost opportunities. Then his creed proved too strong for him. He had solemnly sworn to Tapley to avoid his old haunts, as if by an oath a leopard might change its spots or an Ethiopian his skin. One day he tumbled out of bed meditative and surly of manner. He repulsed Loo, whose prattlings and caresses he had lately encouraged ; and Jenny's breakfast failed to satisfy, though it included a rasher of bacon, sausages, and an egg. The thought of Tapley's absurdities vexed him to exasperation. He had been round a hundred flash public-houses without once getting properly exhilarated—a thing not to be contemplated with a cool face. Had anyone told him a fortnight before that such an omission was possible, he would have laughed in scorn. Yet,—ach ! he could not bear to think of what he had missed.

A sharp pang of remorse made him curse bitterly. Then a mighty yearning for social joys came upon him. A dispute with Jenny furnished a pretext for seeking them abroad, and hastening forth, he turned as by instinct to the Bear and Cubs, where Mr. Wragg beamed a welcome and rallied him on forgetting old friends.

"Let me see," said Boniface, pretending to jog his memory, "must be considerable more'n a week since you was 'ere last. Didn't think you was the sort to get swelled 'ead along o' toffs. 'Ave the kindness to give it a name."

Laughing contentedly, Dick gave "it a name"; and the pair settled down to an hour's sociality, for it chanced that Wragg wanted news.

At the appointed time Dick met his friends at the rendezvous in Leicester Square, with his hat at an exaggerated military cock, and the old Adam rampant in his eye. Divining what had happened, Tapley suggested "something to eat." So Goodman was taken into a restaurant and fed on grilled beef-steak to enable him " to carry his cargo." The intention was to dispense with liquids, but there the reckoning was without the guest.

"Heh! Tottie—no lotion?" remarked Dick; and before any one could answer, he had ordered the German waiter to bring "three glasses of Twickham's number one at Lloyd's, and look skinny about it."

On returning, the waiter was asked tersely if he had brewed the ale on the premises.

"I vas quick," retorted the Teuton. "Boot Gott in Himmel! I can nod vly."

Dick exploded.

"You can nod vly," he cried—"you can nod vly. Old sourkrowt, wot can ye do?"

The Teuton bristled up, and would have retaliated according to his rights, but for an opportune transfer of silver on the part of Tapley. Feeling his palm magically tickled, he laughed in turn, remarking on the English proclivity for pleasantries.

From the restaurant they went to a billiard-saloon, on the misconception that the rebel might be toned down with a game. Dick stated frankly he "didn't know nothin' 'bout the bloomin' sticks an' balls," and at the third stroke proved it by sending the point of his cue ripping through the cloth.

"There ye are," he said, laughing in the marker's face; "wot d'ye think of that?"

The marker ran his hand along the rent, and answered succinctly with a statement of damages. Dick rejoined with a defiant guffaw. Did the marker imagine he was just cutting his teeth? Wasn't the stuff green baize, and couldn't acres of green baize be bought for the figure named? The marker observed it wasn't his duty to argue, and was going off in quest of the landlord when Vincent interposed by paying the debt.

With that they shifted quarters again. The principals would have suspended investigations for the night, had it been possible to get Dick home without a demonstration; but as he kept informing them he was " fit to face the devil," and meant to do it, they were obliged to go on, despite forebodings to disaster.

It was to be a Piccadilly night, and of all nocturnal carnivals, Piccadilly nights are the rarest. Other delights cloy the appetites they feed ; but, like Egypt's Queen, these miracles of civilisation make hungry where most they satisfy. Summer or winter, under the clear stars or in muffling fog, the nightly revel fails not ; for Clubland has much money and unmeasured desires, with matchless ingenuity in gratifying them. So the witching hour is turned into high noon, and the tides of pleasure surge between the Circus and the Park Corner, roaring like a roost and carrying frail or ill navigated craft to ruin. Only Cleopatra barges ride to and fro with triumphant prow, rustling their silken tackle and diffusing strange perfumes.

In that familiar region Vincent and Tapley were oppressed by fears of detection, for at any moment they might be hailed by " friends on the frolic " ; and though Goodman's exuberance added to the risk, he declined to listen to the voice of reason.

" I thought we come out for a lark," was his answer to Tapley's remonstrance. " Tottie ain't gettin' afraid, is 'e ? "

As they joined the throng pressing westward from the deserted theatres, it was clear Dick meant to make the most of his opportuuities. How to keep him out of the clutches of the law was a problem which troubled his companions, for he flung jests at night-hawks and bantered policemen with equal zest. Visons of dock and magistrate began to haunt Vincent ; and he whispered his fears into Tapley's ear.

" For Heaven's sake get him out of this," he said, indicating the figure ahead.

Almost as he spoke there arose about that figure the rustle of excitement which in a London street denotes a parley with the police. Tapley sprang forward.

"All right, officer," he said smilingly. "Here's a cab; give him a hand in."

The constable growled undecidedly, being new to his office; and Dick was bundled headlong into a four-wheeler, Vincent and Tapley getting in quickly after him.

"You confounded idiot!" said his lordship from between set teeth. "I've a dashed good mind to pepper you."

Dick looked hard at him for a moment, then lay back and roared.

"Tottie, don't you be talkin' to me 'bout no game bantam cocks," he cried—"don't you be doin' it." And he slapped his leg and roared again.

NEXT day Tapley took occasion to inform Dick in rousing Anglo-Saxon what was thought of his behaviour, and how narrowly he missed landing them all in the police-court.

"Just think of the figure we should cut," said his lordship, hotly and honestly indignant; "and all because it was your insane pleasure to act the idiot."

Goodman thought and smiled; but the next instant he confessed his backsliding with abject contrition. "Never 'ad a good thing on," he owned dolefully, "that I didn't go 'ot-foot an' make a bloomin' fool of myself. Seems as if the devil was always at my elbow whisperin'. If you was to go an' wash yer 'ands of me, Tottie, it 'ud just be my luck, an' I ain't sayin' as I shouldn't deserve it. An' yet," he went on, scratching his head and looking comically at his judge, "some people can make no end of fools of themselves without bein' a bit the worse."

It was a case of him who was without sin casting the first stone, and Tapley took it as such. He considered a moment, his face relaxing precisely as the astute Dick expected. It was plain he was not the man to throw a brother sinner overboard.

"Well," he said presently, looking Dick squarely in the eyes, "I don't want to lay any more broken vows on your head. I don't want you to swear by all that's holy you'll never act the fool again, because that would only be another chance for the devil that whispers at your elbow. But I want to tell you that, devil or no devil, the next time you indulge in drunken antics you shall be left to your fate; we go our way and you go yours. We don't go out for such diversions as we had last night. We're not eager to engage in street brawls; and I want you to understand that it's perilous to badger German waiters, rip up billiard cloths, and insult markers, and that we're distinctly averse to the idea of having police-court caricaturists do our portraits for the evening papers."

"It's impossible to mistake wot you want me to understand," returned Dick, the corners of his mouth twitching comically. "Ye've got a gift of plain words, Tottie, I'll say that for ye."

"And a gift of plainer deeds if I'm tried too much," was the rejoinder. "I don't want to be harsh, Goodman, my boy, but just think a moment of the risks. We're doing this strictly on the sly—want to hide it from our dearest friends; and damme, you'd have it blazing in every newspaper in the land."

"You'd be a sweet morsel for the newspapers," admitted Dick. 'A lord in the dock. How a hearl's son goes the pace. Amoosin' hevidence.' I can see the bloomin' bills starin' at me, an' people runnin' to buy."

"And the vision pleases you?"

"It don't," answered Dick quickly—"it don't, s'elp me Gawd! an' that's honest. You've stood by me better'n any man ever done afore, Tottie, 'cept Bob McCrae—'im that's sergeant-major now—an' I ain't goin' to cut my own throat. I ain't goin' back on ye. When ye see me gettin' frolicky again, shunt me, chuck me. I can scrape through where you'd be stuck, an' a time or two more or less afore the beak won't do me no 'arm. But don't you run no risks.

When I get breezy atop I'd let drive at my own shadow. In the Forty-second I lost my stripes for thinkin' as a belt-buckle was meant for a chum's 'ead, an' all along o' bad whiskey."

They were sitting, and he suddenly leaped to his feet, his eyes flashing, and his breath coming quick and hard.

"Lost my stripes!" he cried. "Think wot that is to an army man. Oh! you needn't tell me 'ow it feels to be took an' kicked an' tramped on. Gawd! I should be a non-com. now, colour-serjeant likely, if they could 'a' kept me out'n clink. For I liked the army, Tottie—liked the fightin', too, by gum! Got my officer's praise an' two medals. 'Where are they now?' says you. Where men sell their souls—that's where they are."

He laughed the dry, rasping laugh which comes of the utterness of folly.

"I've thought it all out, more'n once," he pursued, with the conviction of a fatalist. "The army trainin' an' my 'abits, they don't combine to make wot you call a fust-class citizen. Oh no, they don't. That ain't the way saints is made. But the tiger must live till 'is time comes. Some day the newspaper nippers will be hollerin' 'Orful tragedy,' an' you'll read an' find Dick Goodman's name, an' you'll say ' Poor beggar! I told 'im wot would 'appen ; but 'e wouldn't be warned, 'e wouldn't take no advice.' No ; 'e was never good at takin' advice, though it's dirt cheap. 'Eavens ! if grub an' drink was as cheap as advice, wot a rippin' world this'd be. But I beg your pardon, Tottie. We're on for the East End, aint we ?

"On the condition I have named," replied Tapley.

"It's my native 'eath," cried Dick ; "I'd know the smell of it anywhere. Just name the spot, an' leave the rest to me. I'm your's, Tottie, an' Mr. Twickham's. 'E don't talk free an' easy an' pal like, same as you do; but I like 'im—I like im.' I can see 'e does a deal o' thinkin', an' I know 'e ain't the man to quarrel with. I know that kind o' man the minute I lay eyes on 'im. Minds me o' my cap'n—no tongue in barrick, couldn't be bothered jabberin'; but show 'im where there's fightin', an' its who's there fust. Got 'is V.C.; an' Mr. Twickham's 'is breathin' image."

Hearing of the compliment, Mr. Twickham modestly hoped he was worthy of the comparison; and Dick rejoined gallantly all he wanted was the chance to face death to have his V.C. also.

"It's a chance we all get," said Vincent quietly.

"Yes, sir," rejoined Dick. "But most of us don't stay to wear the bronze and laurel."

"Now you moralise," put in Tapley. "May I beg of you to turn off the tap?"

But Vincent nodded sympathetically.

THERE was to be a fresh disguise in conformity to East End fashion. Dick, of course, relapsed naturally into the attire of Paradise Court, and Vincent and Tapley were to assume as close an imitation as ready-made clothes could effect. The scene of transformation was the back room of a Hebrew outfitter, in a malodorous alley on the edge of a great slum. On learning their business, the greasy son of Abraham looked suspiciously at the three; but as no objection was made to the hundred per cent. premium he put on to cover risks, no questions were asked.

The change was taken as an excellent jest till Tapley, chancing to glance in a mirror, nearly had a fit.

"Heavens!" he cried, tearing off the furbished ready-mades and flinging them into a corner. "Death rather than disfigurement. And ugh! I itch as if all the fleas in Jewry were feasting on me."

At that Vincent also felt crawling sensations of the skin, and he, too, began to strip with desperate haste. It was less easy than they imagined to discard the feelings of civilisation.

"Here, Goodman," said Tapley, kicking the new acquisitions, "resell these to your friend the Jew, and express to him the uncircumcised Philistines' extreme regret for declining to wear them. Holy Jerusalem! how the place smells. An ounce of

civet, good apothecary, to sweeten the imagination.
If we could get new noses—patent trap-noses—and
feelings impervious to the itch, we might do business;
but ugh! these Israelitish perfumes are too robust.
Come, Vin! Goodman will follow when he has resold
the fleas."

Dick's wrangle with the Jew, who had little English,
but a profound comprehension of his own interest,
was stiff and prolonged. Mr. Goodman argued
with force and point that if the clothes were worth so
much half an hour before, their value could not have
been greatly depreciated by a little handling. The
Jew raised his hands and shrugged his shoulders. He
was a stranger; he did nod know English coosdoms.
The clothes had been worn—they were now second-
hand; and as Jacob was a holy man and a just, he
could nod bossibly sell them again as new. He
would dake his oath they were now worth so mooch—
so mooch and nod a varding more; and he thoughtfully added, that in case of police enquiries he would
know nodthing—nodthing whatever. He knew
gentlemen get into drouble sometime.

"Ole man, I wish I was a Jew," said Dick, laughing
ironically.

He yearned to teach the snuffy foreigner some
English coosdoms, among them common English
honesty; but thinking discretion the better part of
wisdom, pocketed the coin, expressed his opinion of
the giver, and departed, by no means so ill satisfied
with the transaction as he pretended.

Rejoining his friends he suggested "grub."

"A peckish business, this trampin' o' streets an'
rummagin' of ole clo' shops," he declared, gaily leading
the way to an eating-house with a chunk of fly-blown
beef in the window for advertisement.

"Wot's it to be?" he asked politely. "There ain't
no scarcity, as ye can see."

He showed them great tureens of yellowish stew, in which pieces of fat floated like dead jelly-fish, and huge tins, in which sausages bubbled in boiling grease and onions. There were also smoking dishes of sauerkraut, each with its portion of sickly white pork in the midst. He recommended the sausages, and was allowed to order for three. His guests sniffed, tasted, looked at each other, and by a common impulse pushed their plates from them. Dick ate alone and ate with relish, murmuring it was impossible to account for tastes.

From the eating-house they went to a tavern, where there was a round of beer. Though it was still early, in the evening the bar-room was thronged. Many of those who babbled and drank were women: some so old and palsied that they could hardly raise the glass to their oozy mouths; others were young mothers who shared the gin and beer with their babes, "to give the kids the proper taste"; others, again, were mere girls, whose brazen looks, as they nodded to their "young men" over liquor, denoted a knowledge of forbidden fruit. Vincent was glad to get out, and said so.

"Lor' bless you! that ain't nuthin'," Dick assured him. "You just wait."

It was again Saturday night. The main thoroughfares were lined with stalls, naphtha lamps flared and flickered in the wind, casting grotesque shadows, nameless odours floated in the air, and over all was the ceaseless, strident cry which rose or fell according to the urgency or lung power of the criers. Costerdom was exerting itself mightily, and costerdom has demonic energy.

Here and there the explorers paused, mingling with the groups about stalls, asking prices, and pretending they couldn't afford to buy.

"Here, honey," cried an old woman, flourishing two

red herrings in Vincent's face, "a penny, an' fit to make a king's mouth wather, be the powers they are! No! There ye are, then," clapping on another. "A penny the lot—a penny for three beautiful red herrin'—only a penny. Och! sor, won't ye buy now? an' me owld man an his back wid the rheumatiz? Buy, me jewel; an' when yer atin' the tastiest mouthful in London, think av poor owld Judy O'Grady that ye made glad. There, I'll make it four—four av the best red herrin' as ever wuz kippered at a farthin' a head. What are ye made av, any way?"

Vincent did not buy the herrings, but he bestowed a silver piece.

"Och! be the howly s'ints," cried Judy, "an angel in the form of a purty young man. May the blissin' av S'int Patrick rest on ye, sor! Here, Sally Ann," to a girl of ten on the opposite side of the stall, "what are ye afther hidin' there for? Off to the Two Drovers wid ye, an' fetch me a mug o' Doublin stout for to dhrink the gintleman's health."

Forthwith Vincent was besieged, some offering to join Mrs. O'Grady in drinking his health, if he provided the needful; some pressing him to invest in articles of food, or ornaments for his "gel"; and others gently chaffing after the manner of Alsatia. From the banter and the importunity he was fain to take refuge in a tavern into which Dick dexterously whipped him out of sight.

"If ye go on doin' that, sir," said Dick, "ye'll 'ave the whole bloomin' East End arter ye."

Vincent drew a long breath and coughed. The place was full, hot, and reeking with divers fumes. The landlord, a cask fitted with limbs and a red knob for head, came up, spread out his fat hands on the counter, and said, "Well?"

"Got Twickham?" asked Dick.

The red knob nodded.

" Three glasses, please."

But when Vincent tasted the beer, he spat it out.

"That's never our—that's never Twickham," he said, loud enough to be heard.

"Heh!" shouted a pimply youth, gesticulating gleefully in anticipation of sport. "Cove 'ere says it ain't Twickham."

The landlord turned from the far end of the bar, whither he had gone to serve other customers, the look of an angry bulldog in his eye.

"Oo says wot ain't Twickham?" he demanded.

"'Im," answered the pimply youth, jerking a thumb at Vincent.

A black shadow deepened to purple the red of the landlord's visage.

"We don't stand no monkey tricks 'ere," he said fiercely, planting himself opposite Vincent. "You asked for Twickham ; you've got Twickham. Wot the 'ell 'ave ye to say?"

He was a man with enormous ears and the jowl of the ideal bully of the British public-house—a superb "chucker-out."

Dick was stepping nimbly forward to take the matter in hand, but Vincent prevented him.

"It's all right, landlord," said the offender apologetically.

"All right," repeated the landlord—" no, tain't all right, not by a long chalk. Serve ye jolly well right to be pitched on yer 'ead, comin' in 'ere hinsultin' honest men. Come, take yer bloomin' carkis out'n this if ye want to get it away whole."

"A bit 'ot, ain't it?" remarked Dick, as the three got into the coolness of the night.

"What came we out for to see?" asked Vincent, making the best of a forced retreat. "But I'll take my oath that wasn't Twickham."

"I wish you'd let me tell 'im so," said Dick, " sweet

an pretty, so's he'd be tempted. Wot a side o' bacon he'd make."

"You forget we're not out for the scientific use of our fists," responded Vincent. "Let's proceed."

They turned into a music-hall, and Vincent had time to reflect. He felt that his education was proceeding apace, and the curriculum certainly included unforeseen subjects. The variety of life comprised within the four mile radius was sometimes perplexing and sometimes appalling. In the past he had heard much of the tastes and diversions of the masses, listening with indifferent heart and ear as to missionary tales which did not concern him. Now heart and ear were tremblingly sensitive. In this strange, new university he learned at lightning speed and with nerves on the tingle.

An hour of the music-hall sufficed. When they came forth again the Saturday night pandemonium was at its shrillest and loudest. A sort of yellow glare, as of a conflagration struggling in fog, was upon the seething streets. By their greater brilliancy the thickly studded public-houses stood out like white spots of light, hospitable beacons to all who would be merry in a world too much given to sadness; and everywhere Twickham's ale and MacTor's Scotch whiskey were thrust on the attention. Vincent owned he was a shrewd man who invented the tavern, a philosopher whose system, grounded on human nature, would outlast the fame of kings and conquerors. Empires might rise and fall, Churches grow and decay—nay, religions themselves come and go, but the tavern would flourish while men were thirsty or jolly or wretched. In all seasons and weathers there were the public-houses flaming their invitations to the happy to come and be happier still, and to the miserable to make haste to drown their misery.

Nor did they flame in vain. Wherever Vincent

and his companions turned, the public-houses were full to overflowing. From several they turned away from lack of room. Vincent noted once again that woman, the domestic angel, everywhere shed her benign influence on the convivial scene. She drank, now morosely and with wrathful mutterings, now with liquorish laughter and ribaldry, and anon with cursings which made the hardened cold. Occasionally she was young and good-looking ; oftener she was fat, and sodden, and watery of eye, and dishevelled, and disputatious, or scraggy, and old, and bleared, and rheumy. And it appeared that the older and more bleared she was, the better she loved her gin. Grandmothers taught granddaughters not to be afraid of drink ; and in gratitude granddaughters " treated," or got sweethearts to treat for them, till old knees bent, and old tongues wagged blasphemously, sometimes till old heads rolled in the dust, and there were cries of, " Hey ! ole gel, must carry yer licker better'n that," and bursts of merriment over the plight of dishonourable age.

At times the rough hand of the " chucker-out " was seen. Once, as the three were passing a splendidly illuminated palace, ornamented by a change-light advertisement of MacTor's whiskey, the door opened, and a woman was pitched head foremost into the gutter. She scrambled up, dripping filth, and lurching back, retorted upon those within. The next minute she was in the gutter again.

Vincent's blood boiled. Running forward he assisted her to her feet, asking if she were hurt.

" Hurt," she repeated, gazing unsteadily at him— hurt : look at me. Do I look hurt ? 'E knows I aint got no more coppers—'e knows 'e's got 'em all ; an' when I aint got no more I'm chucked. Gawd blast 'is soul !" And with that she made back once more, to be delivered to the police.

"Is this a common spectacle?" asked Vincent grimly.

"Come along any Saturday night an' see," was the answer from Dick. "'Tain't till near closin' time as ye see the chuckin' out, not proper. 'Ullo! there goes another."

This time it was a man, and he was reflective rather than noisy.

"I aint s' drunk," he said, sitting up and scratching his head. "'Sault 'n battery. I ain't s' drunk, 'pon m' 'onour."

Dick gave him a hand up.

"Eh! Johnny, time to go 'ome to yer 'ole woman," said Mr. Goodman cheerfully.

"Mush 'bliged," said the man, trying to steady himself—"mush 'bliged," and moved on, feeling the wall as he went.

"TOM, had you any idea all this existed next door?" asked Vincent, as they, too, moved off.

"A vague idea," answered Tapley. "One tastes the thing in the precincts of the Royal Olympian, you know. But I must say my knowledge is wondrously increased and clarified. You don't look happy, Vin."

"My ignorance is being dispelled somewhat roughly. But we've begun and we'll go on, though the finish should involve a walk along the sewers. Eh! Goodman?"

Goodman responded that a knowledge of the beer-shop should form part of every gentleman's education.

"Milk's good an' honey's good," said Dick, thinking reminiscently of the army chaplain's accounts of Canaan, "an' there's worse things nor water in the desert. But ye can 'ave 'em all, so long's ye give me beer—an let it be Twickham, please."

Twickham it was, in a Twickham tied house which chanced to be handy. On entering Vincent was gratified by an air of decency and order not common to East End public-houses. The house was clean, well fitted out, well managed, and obviously prosperous, being, indeed, at that moment so crammed the new comers could hardly edge their way in. The landlord bore the regulation trade mark—the flash studs, rings, and chain, the red face, and Falstaff waist. Nevertheless, his appearance suggested a humanity and an intelligence rare among dispensers of the magic cup. For the Twickhams took extreme pains to secure the right men for their houses—men who had the art of popularity, yet did not endanger a licence. The landlord, noticing the trio, smiled blandly, though he did not know them from Adam. It was his habit to smile a welcome upon all respectable customers, for, as he said, the practice paid and cost nothing.

"Appear to be pretty busy, sir," remarked Tapley, acknowledging the salutation.

"Well," responded the landlord, looking round with a complacent grin, "don't take much to coax 'em to drink, do it?"

"No, indeed," rejoined Tapley; "one sees they tumble it off with great gusto. I take it the chief thing for a roaring trade is the right stuff."

"An' I reckon we give 'em *that*," said the landlord, cocking his head as one who knows—"yes, I reckon we give 'em *that*. You'd travel a bit before beatin' Twickham—a longish bit."

"Join us in a glass of it?" said Tapley, with a wink at Vincent.

"Gettin' kind of 'ot—don't mind if I do," came affably from the landlord; and a smart barmaid, flushed with heat and flattery, pumped them four glasses.

It was almost impossible to keep pace with the demand. The ivory handles went up and down unceasingly; unceasingly the till-bell rang, and the empty glasses went to the wash-basin. Vincent looked round the thirsty crowd feeling a glow of pride. This was appreciation indeed; here was the popularity which made the Twickham coffers overflow.

"How long have you been in this house, sir?" he asked, turning to the landlord.

"This 'ouse, let me see. Three year exactly—three

year nigh a day. When we took the place over it was a East End 'ovel. What does Lord Twickham do? 'No go for me,' says 'e; an' down comes the 'ovel an' up goes this, as you see it. The 'ovel does ten barrels a week o' bad beer; we does more'n a 'undred of the best that is brewed. An' I tell you, it's rising steady. If you was to say to me, sir, that there's anythink better'n Twickham in the market, I should take the liberty of replyin' as it ain't true."

"Competition keen?" asked Tapley.

"Competition?" repeated the landlord, a withering scorn in his tone—"competition? Yus, wot some calls competition." He leaned forward, one eye closed, and his voice lowered confidentially. "There ain't no competition when Twickham's about. 'Andy 'ere there's a place—I won't name no names, but ye wouldn't be done up travellin' to get to it. Well, the 'ouse I mean be a tied 'ouse, rival o' Twickham's —though, bless you! there ain't no rival, not proper. An' wot 'appens?" He put his hand to the side of his mouth, bending still more confidentially. "They uses their beer to flush their sewers. Yus, sir, pours it down the drains."

"The idiots!" ejaculated Tapley. "What do they do that for?"

"Ye ain't in our trade, sir, I can see. There be such a thing as keepin' up appearances; may 'ave 'eard that. They wants good returns, so many barrels a month; people don't want the stuff. Wot are they to do? Why, put it down the sink. They say as the rats do lie about drunk."

He drew himself up chuckling.

"You don't find it necessary to flush with Twickham," remarked Tapley.

"Wot d'ye think? Look round you; why, they takes it like mother's milk."

"A little more for yerself, then," suggested Dick,

who was always put out by the sight of empty glasses.

But the landlord thought he'd better not have any more beer.

"Drop of port wine, if you please," he said, and fiiled himself a glass from a large decanter.

"'Old 'ard there!" cried Dick. "None o' yer cold tea tricks."

"In our business arter all?" said the landlord, turning sharply.

"Never mind," returned Dick. "Tain't friendly to swill cold tea when gen'lemen asks ye to 'ave good ale with 'em."

Not wishing to understand too much, Vincent looked round on the crowd. It was becoming every minute more and more closely packed, the women being almost as numerous and jovial as the men ; and he was surprised to see many of them taking whiskey.

"Duncan should be here," whispered Tapley, who had also noted the run on whiskey. "I tell you his throat-scorcher is going."

Before Vincent could answer, the door opened and a white face was thrust in. It was a woman's face, wasted pitifully, but in that moment tense with the fury of the tigress. The blazing eyes fastened on a man convivially engaged in a corner.

"Jim, you come 'ome out of that," said their owner, in a voice shrill with passion.

"You go to ——" retorted Jim, the scowl of the insulted lord on his brow, adding he would indulge himself in a general holocaust if her persecutions did not cease.

The landlord was instantly on his majesty. He knew husbands and wives must have differences—it was so ordained by nature ; but he pointed out that a public-house was hardly a suitable place of settlement.

"Can't 'ave no rowin' 'ere," he said, with the jerk of the head which was law.

The woman turned on him vehemently.

"No," she cried, "ye can't 'ave no rowin', ye grinnin' pot o' ale; but ye can take my man's last copper, an' leave me an' the kids to starve—ye can do that."

Next moment a man had taken the transgressor firmly by the arm.

"Can't 'ave no 'owlin' dervishes 'ere, missis," he remarked, leading her forth. "There!" and the door closed behind her.

Jim emptied his glass without budging.

"Women are like mills, always wanting something," said a thin, shaky voice. "My friend, your marital felicity's at a discount to-night. The lady will comb your hair."

The speaker was a young man, and evidently as much out of favour with fortune as Jim with his wife. Though the place was suffocatingly warm, his frayed coat was buttoned tight to the throat. His face was mottled, and his eye beery and bloodshot. There were men about him with tightly buttoned coats and beery, bloodshot eyes, but they were as congruous as a chromo on a cobbler's wall. A child could have told that this man, with the tremulous voice and the elegant accent, was a foreigner in Alsatia. A tumbler, with a piece of lemon-peel in the bottom stood before him. The liquid was already a reminiscence.

Having uttered his jest, he fumbled in his vest pocket, and producing a few coppers, which he counted with miserly care, asked a barmaid to be good enough to repeat the dose.

As he raised his glass to drink, he caught Tapley's eye and bowed ceremoniously. The next minute he was crossing the room, a hundred amused eyes following him.

"I hope I do not intrude," he said, bowing again.

" Not at all," replied Tapley. " We're in a public place ; it's free to all."

" We're in a tavern, sir," rejoined the stranger gravely, " and theoretically a tavern is free to all. But, sir, you needn't be as old as Methuselah to discover that practice and theory conflict—ay, conflict grievously. Somebody proved this by a very pretty syllogism, which, unfortunately, I've forgotten. My memory is not what it was ; perhaps, sir, you'll sympathise and excuse. As to the tavern you may, it is true, enter— if you are sober enough (though you witnessed the repulse of the lady just now), but you shall not accomplish the main purpose minus the wherewithal— which is to say, you shall not drink unless you pay. *Ergo*, a tavern is not free. I trust, sir," addressing Dick, whose expression was scornful—" I trust my presence is not disagreeable to you."

" Welcome's a fightin' cock," answered Dick. " Only kind o' rummy."

" Kind o' rummy," repeated the stranger, as if weighing the words. " Perhaps so, yet—but never mind that. For ought I know you may be a philosopher, one of the catholic sect who make a temple of the tavern, believing human nature can best be studied in its cups. If so, will you favour me with light on one or two simple questions—as, for example, why men drink."

" Because they likes it, old fellow."

The stranger's gravity deepened.

" They like it," he said, as if pondering deeply. " It has been proved, I believe, that one and one make two. The crux, my dear sir, is, who implanted the liking ? "

" God A'mighty, I should think," replied Dick, with a roar of laughter.

" Yes, must have been God Almighty," assented the stranger, "unless the devil had a finger in that pie also. One never knows. However, let us assume you are right ; then comes the why, the wherefore."

Dick looked puzzled.

"Ah!" cried the stranger, in sudden animation, " I thought you couldn't take that wall. I've seen a right reverend bishop come a cropper on it. The why and the wherefore—the wherefore and the why. Can you," raising his glass, " explain philosophically why I find this delectable ? "

" Because it's good," said Dick, with emphasis.

" As near absolute truth as possible," rejoined the stranger. " It is good. I have proved it, and it was a special Scotch hot—that is to say, a hot MacTor, with the eighth of an inch of lemon paring to flavour it. Some people prefer MacTor neat. It matters not : it is good ; and MacTor is a public benefactor. So sir," bowing to the landlord, " is he who keeps a tavern and dispenses universal consolation.

> ' I wonder often what the vintners buy
> One half so precious as the stuff they sell.'

That, sir, is Omar, a lover of the tavern.

" 'Omer ? " said the landlord.

" No, sir—not Homer, though he, too, sang of the wine cup like a lover. As a Greek scholar your mind naturally ran on Greece. My nightingale sang in Persia, a most wise, sweet song, and desired for his monument an empty glass."

He looked ruefully at his own. Then fumbling once more in his vest pocket he produced fivepence ha'penny. His face fell as over a cruel disappointment. Again he searched his pocket, as a starving man might search a wallet, feeling in every corner through the tattered lining for an extra copper. Dick watched with deep sympathy and appreciation. How often had he, too, hunted for that odd penny which meant another drink. Yet again the stranger counted his coppers; but he could make the sum no more than fivepence ha'-penny. Convinced of that, he returned fourpence to his pocket.

"Price of a bed in a doss-house," said Dick to himself; and he knew how the man was torn between a passion for liquor and the desire to sleep on straw instead of a doorstep or under an archway.

"If I were not for the moment at odds with Lady Fortune," said the stranger suavely, holding three ha'-pennies between finger and thumb, "I should certainly do myself the honour of inviting you to drink with me."

"Let the honour be with us," responded Tapley.

"Sir," said the stranger, bowing profoundly, "you are exceedingly polite. It will gratify one to pledge you."

It was in MacTor hot he did it; and as in the warmth of a new friendship he chanced to empty his glass at a gulp, he accepted another, his eye visibly moistening. Dick studied him with mingled pity and amusement.

"Down on yer luck, eh, matey?" asked the man of the world.

"You have divined an unfortunate fact," returned the stranger, blinking curiously. "The Lady Fortune has used me abominably—abominably.

> 'Oh! many a cup of this forbidden wine
>   Must drown the memory of that insolence.'

Gentlemen, your health!"

There was such ardent drinking of healths, that presently the stranger began to exhibit signs of overdone conviviality. He mixed up his phrases, his politeness became mere travesty, and he dwelt with maudlin pathos on the evils endured by the righteous in an unfeeling world. All at once he called attention to the fact that the glasses were empty; but at that the landlord bent over the counter, asking quietly,—

"Ain't you 'bout 'ad enough, guv'nor?"

"Shir," retorted the stranger, "a gen'man can besh judge of sush things for 'mshelf."

"I'd go 'ome if I was you," said the landlord.

The stranger looked him over, swaying unsteadily.

"If you tell me the way I shall be s'bliged," was the response.

But Vincent whispered in Tapley's ear; and Tapley, turning with a smile, said,—

"Come, old fellow, time we were off."

"Yesh," answered the stranger meekly, and followed them.

CHAPTER XII

OUTSIDE there was a sudden change of weather. It had rained a little deluge, and the long perspectives of liquid mud had the dismal effect for which miry London streets, glimmering in gaslight, are unrivalled. It was cold, too. Even such as had dined well and could button thick coats over warm blood felt the wind nip ; unfortunates who never dined at all, or whose blood and clothes were thin, felt it at their marrow. The stranger looked along the muddy desolation and shivered.

"Ugh !" he said, "cold, wet, nashty. I'll go back." And before the others could raise a protest he had wheeled and re-passed the swing-door.

"Seems to me I know that man," said Vincent, turning to Tapley.

"Know him," cried Tapley, in astonishment.

"Yes ; and if I'm right, though he's fearfully changed, his name is Herbert Ingledew. We were college chums for a while."

"Great Scot ! and what made him a public-house sponge ?"

"Precisely what I should like to find out. He was always a man of pleasure—set the pace with wine-parties and all that. Let's follow him."

As they entered the stranger was deep in argument with the landlord.

"We can't 'ave no drunk men 'ere a-causin' a distu'bince," the landlord was saying.

"Drunk!" echoed the other, drawing himself up to the best of his ability. "Shir, you're inshulting."

With a nod of intelligence to the landlord, Vincent stepped forward and touched the hypothetical Ingledew on the arm.

"Mr. Ingledew, I think," he said softly.

In spite of the stupor of drink Ingledew started.

"Shir," he responded, swaying like a scarecrow in a tempest, "my name's Johnson; and thish beast's inshulted me," bobbing his head at the landlord.

"Come, old fellow," whispered Vincent, taking his arm, "I want to speak to you."

"Want shomething to drink first," was the dogged reply. "Thesh the coin; MacTor hot, pleash."

"Not if you was to lay down gold for it," said the landlord.

"Not s'much's a heel tap?"

"Not so much's a heel tap."

In that instant a man laid a beer-glass on the counter, with half a teaspoonful of dregs in the bottom. Quick as thought the stranger clutched it and drained it dry.

"Not heel tap," he muttered—"not heel tap. He, he! Beashtly shame," and he raked in his coppers.

"Come, out'n this," thundered the landlord.

And Vincent, tightening his grip, repeated, "Come!"

"Whatsh you want me for, eh?" asked the man, leering helplessly. "Whatsh been up to now, eh? Pleesh-court?"

"A month 'ard an' yer 'air cut," put in a bystander, whereupon there was a roar.

"Ta-ta, mate. 'Ope as you'll 'ave a good time," added another; and to the sound of ironical laughter the stranger marched out between Vincent and Tapley, Dick following as rear guard.

" Where do you live ? " asked Vincent, when they were beyond the range of satire.

" Eh ? " came deliberately and a trifle defiantly.

" Where do you live ? "

" Where do I live ? Anywhere ; not particular. Doss-house—cellar—anywhere," and he blinked at Vincent in a kind of inane triumph.

" And your name is Ingledew—Herbert Ingledew."

" 'Tec., eh ? " inquired the supposed Ingledew, retiring a step.

" Buck up ! " put in Dick impatiently. " Can't ye see, ye bloomin' goose, as the gentleman wants to be friendly."

" Wantsh to be friendly," repeated the other, with extreme gravity. " Thatsh odd."

" I assure you our motives are indeed of the friendliest," said Vincent. " Now forgive my asking a well meant question. You're Herbert Ingledew, aren't you ? "

The man took an involuntary step backward, swayed perilously, drew himself together, and advanced to his old position, keeping a solemn eye on his questioner.

" No," he answered with great deliberation—" no."

" Ten years ago were you not at ——? " naming a famous college at a famous university.

" Yesh."

" And you're not Herbert Ingledew ? "

" No."

He staggered, spun mysteriously on his heels, tilted suddenly, recovered in defiance of gravitation, and repeated, " No."

" Shatisfied ? " he demanded, after a pause.

" This is very odd," rejoined Vincent good-humouredly. " Ten years ago you were at ——, and yet you're not Herbert Ingledew."

" No."

It was then Dick had an inspiration born of a profound knowledge of drunkenness.

"Wot was you ten years ago, mate?" he asked insinuatingly.

"Undergrad. at —— "

"Quite so ; but the name—no 'tec. business. Wot did they call ye?"

"Herbert Ingledew."

"An' wot are ye now?"

"Dr. Samuel Johnson."

Tapley roared.

"Making dictionaries?" he cried.

"No," replied Dr. Johnson seriously. "Odd scholarly jobs—reciting, inditing, write letters shometimes ; make a little."

As he said this he lurched forward, and would have fallen but for the timely aid of Dick.

"Bit rocky on yer pins," remarked Mr. Goodman sympathetically. "Come, buck up ; don't want to be leavin' our cards on ye at police court fust thing Monday mornin'."

"Shertainly not," rejoined Ingledew, lurching again.

"Good God!" ejaculated Vincent, musing aloud. His thought was, " And this is Ingledew—Herbert Ingledew, of the flash wine-parties and the fancy horses."

It would have been incredible, but for the palpable evidence of the wreck, helplessly rocking there in the wind and rain.

"Where d'ye 'old out?" asked Dick, pursuing his investigations—"where's yer snoozin' box?"

"Friendliesht motives," murmured Mr. Ingledew— "friendliesht motives." Then he gave the name and number of a street in Spitalfields.

Dick whistled.

"Bad?" enquired Vincent.

"If Ole Nick has wus, I pity 'im, that's all," was the answer.

"Then he'd better not go there in his present condition," suggested Vincent.

Ingledew, whose chin was deep in his breast as if he were lost in thought, instantly lifted his head.

"Oh yesh, he'll go," he put in—"musht go."

If he were thwarted there might be a scene, and Saturday night scenes in the open street are things to be avoided by all who have characters to lose. Besides, they knew no other lodging to which Ingledew could be taken. So Dick hailed a battered growler on the prowl for a drunken fare, and the four were driven to the address named.

To visitors from the world of respectability one doss-house differs from another just as widely as differ two peas in a pod. You enter an ever open door, make your way along a darksome passage, like the corridor of a jail out of love with sanitation, until you are brought up sharp by the deputy. Sometimes this deputy is a man, sometimes a woman. If a man, you instantly recognise a master of trip-hammer fists ; even in the woman you are confronted by an athlete, trained to deliver the shoulder-blow as part of the nightly routine. Materialising suddenly out of nothingness, he or she blocks the way, scrutinising you as if to discover to what particular branch of crime you devote yourself. Occasionally this portentous figure surveys you in grim silence, and, at most, its speech is generally confined to a monosyllabic statement of prices. These vary according to taste and means. If you are down on your luck and therefore economic, fourpence is the figure ; if flush and "going the pace," sixpence ; in the Grand Hotels and Carltons it may rise to a shilling. The coin transferred, you are turned loose into the great common room or kitchen, in which vice, crime, disease, deformity, and misfortune herd.

Innocence getting a glimpse of these chosen resorts

imagines that one refuge is precisely like another. Therein innocence errs. For this subterranean world, no less than the upper sphere of sun and air and decency, has its *bon ton*, its class distinctions, which are as nicely observed as in Mayfair itself. The common thief, having a professional status, scorns the tramp or petty huckster ; in turn, the thriving burglar disdains the common thief ; the gentleman who has risked his neck and got off by " doing time " flouts the man of jemmies who resigns " swag " because it would cost blood ; and with one accord they all contemn the nondescript who exists at starvation point, no one knows how. The Ingledews, being without art or craft, swarm to the lowest doss-houses, and endure the grossest abuse of Alsatia.

At this particular establishment it was clear Mr. Ingledew was well known. The deputy, a solid block of brawn, five feet eight and forty-three round the chest, eyed him severely as he shuffled in.

" 'Ere again, and drunk as usual," said the official testily. " Allus on the batter. You are a beauty, you are."

Ingledew affected to smile.

" Yesh," he answered meekly, presenting the essential coppers. " Ther'sh the cash."

He was passing on, but remembering his benefactors, wheeled, struck the wall, and rebounded against the deputy.

" Now then, wot are you a-shovin' about ? " demanded the man gruffly. " Want to light on yer bloomin' nut outside, p'r'aps."

" Friendliesht motives," mumbled Mr. Ingledew, gaping at his friends. " Shaw me home."

With that, he turned abruptly, entering the room at a run. His plain intention was to make for a bench on the far side ; but taking no note of obstacles, he crashed broadside into a woman retiring from the fire with a black, smoking tin can. Being knocked out of her hand, its contents poured on the head of a child, who started up screeching. The next moment Mr. Ingledew was stretched on the floor with the amazon dancing about him.

"Spilt the coker and burned the kid," she cried, letting him have her boot toe in the ribs. "Get up, ye swine, till I dekirate yer face."

As she spoke a man leaped to her side with a blistering curse. The next instant the deputy was among them.

"Now then," he roared, "if it's smashin' ye want, just say so. Come," he added, grabbing Ingledew by the coat-collar and lifting him to his feet, "you tumble off to bed, if ye ain't 'itchin' to be made into putty. There, steady! Wots them bloomin' legs of yours made of, anyway?"

"An' wot 'bout my coker, as I ain't got a cent to buy more wif?" demanded the woman, dodging as for a crack at Ingledew.

"Yes," put in the man, "wot 'bout 'er coker? an' wot 'bout the kid as'll 'ave to be took to 'orspital?"

Ingledew was bundled out of sight; and then, as Vincent's agent, Dick poured oil on the troubled waters. As a friend of the man who had so unluckily caused the damage, he begged the woman to accept sixpence for her lost cocoa, and would the "kid" accept another sixpence, and perhaps it needn't go to 'orspital after all. The woman accepted the proffered coin in discharge of all claims for spilt cocoa; but the father of the child declared he couldn't think of squaring for less than a bob.

"An' bloomin' cheap at that, too," he said, casting an eye over his offspring.

Negotiations satisfactorily closed, Vincent took the

deputy aside, and there was heard the pleasant chink of silver.

"Yes, sir," came immediately afterwards from the deputy. "You may depend, sir, I'll look arter 'im. 'E do booze beyond all reason, 'e do. Glad to see you again. Good-night, sir ; good-night, gentlemen." And he bowed them into the street.

Book IV

WHILE Vincent and his friends were deep in their studies of East End sociality, England had the misfortune to lose a prized political idol. On the next Sunday, as a felicitous Providence ordained, the Bishop of Blockley preached in Westminster Abbey, and it was felt he could not possibly get out of a panegyric on the man to whom he owed his bishopric. When Dr. Tinkle consented to expound the Gospel in town, the throng which invaded the favoured church was as that which buzzes in a West End theatre on a first night. In this instance, the press was denser·and the congregation even more fashionable than usual. Lady Twickham occupied a position near the pulpit, whence she could observe the chief performer with ease ; and she brought with her Lord Twickham, whose admiration for the fashionable divine fell just a trifle short of a burning desire to hear him sermonise. Lady Gwendoline and Vincent were likewise present ; and Miss Lush worshipped between the pale face of Tapley and the red beard of MacTor. Indeed, half Mayfair contrived to squeeze itself into the Abbey ; for Mayfair has a taste for things funereal when the accessories are dramatic and appropriate. It was understood the Recording Angel had a busy halfhour of it when the Bishop of Blockley preached.

On the virtues of the political idol lately taken

away he surpassed himself. Let none imagine that politicians are always eminent according to their skill in trimming or in swallowing principles. The great man, whose translation to Paradise Dr. Tinkle so touchingly deplored, strove for place out of pure benevolence. A political saint (especially happy in his ecclesiastical appointments), his one aim was to aid in the upward progress of the race. And he had the uncommon felicity of seeing his aspirations fulfilled. The preacher drew an enchanting picture of a world turning its back on all manner of wickedness—ay, even of pleasure—from a desire to rise to the height of noble ideals ; and he dwelt with melting unction on the—

> " One far-off divine event
> To which the whole creation moves ";

an event, the bishop ventured to think, which might not be so far off as the prophet-poet imagined.

Such of the congregation as had not their sensibilities well in hand breathed excitedly. The unregenerate Tapley yawned ; then all at once he grinned, thinking of Saturday night's experiences, of Dick, and Herbert Ingledew, alias Dr. Samuel Johnson, of flaring dramshops, of dishevelled, fighting, red-eyed men and women, of alcoholic laughter and language which would give the Bishop a fit ; and while he thought there fell on his ears the honeyed accents in which Dr. Tinkle described mankind striving in competitive enterprises of godliness.

" Poor old Tinkle ! " he said to himself. " Is it possible he believes all that stuff ? "

With that he leaned towards Miss Lush, whispering in her little pink ear,—

" Put in your next book that the devil's sick and dying."

Miss Lush replied with an arch glance which said

he was exceedingly naughty to mention such a thing in such a place, but, being a man, was forgiven.

The service over, she coyly rebuked him, declaring Dr. Tinkle was "a dear, good soul," and appealing to Lady Twickham for confirmation.

"Yes," said her ladyship, looking significantly at Tapley; "it would be well for the world if we had more Tinkles."

Tapley gallantly agreed; but within an hour he was remarking to his brother-in-law,—

"I say, Vin, are bishops paid for concealing the truth? Think of what we saw last night and heard to-day."

"You musn't be unreasonable," returned Vincent, a strange light in his eye. "Hasn't a wise man declared that a discarded mistress isn't half so dangerous as truth? You wouldn't have the clergy wantonly getting into trouble, would you?"

"Certainly not," rejoined Tapley, scratching his head. "But what boggles me is this, if bishops are afraid of the truth, how's a poor, misdirected devil to get to Heaven?"

"There's the old-fashioned way," said Vincent. "I'm not sure what the latest routes are. I say, are we Christians?"

"Supposed to be. Why?"

"Don't know exactly. The Sermon on the Mount came into my head. You can't account for coincidences of thought."

"The Sermon on the Mount! Can't say I remember much of it. 'Blessed are the poor, for they shall——' I forget precisely what was to happen. Might be described as slightly Utopian, mightn't it?"

"Daresay. The idea that occurred to me was, what would be the effect if things were managed on the principles of the Sermon on the Mount?"

"Chaos, my boy—chaos," returned Tapley emphatically. "Couldn't be done. Why, bless my soul! imagine MacTor running his whiskey show on such lines. Wouldn't hold out a week. But Duncan's much too 'cute to try that method."

"You think it would mean ruin?"

"Instant and complete, my boy—instant and complete. And as for the St. Edmund Brewery, why——" He raised his hands and laughed.

"Well, what of the St. Edmund Brewery?" asked Vincent, feeling as if an exposed nerve had been touched.

"You might shut up shop, knock the bungs out of the barrels, and let the stuff run. Vin, we're not afraid of the truth, whatever right reverends may be; and, between ourselves, beer doesn't make for righteousness. Try to imagine a man, bung full of Twickham, thumbing the golden harp. Don't be disquieted; but the thing's impossible."

And though Vincent laughed, it was as a man laughs under an icy douche unexpectedly turned on.

A little later Lady Gwendoline was rallying him on his depressing seriousness. By chance, that afternoon husband and wife had an hour to themselves between engagements, and Lady Gwendoline hinted there was business to transact affecting her happiness. "And what is the business?" enquired Vincent playfully.

She took a gorgeously embroidered hassock, and sitting on it at his feet, looked up in her most entrancing manner.

"Is it very wicked to talk business on Sunday?" she asked, the prettiest fear of doing wrong expressed in her face. For answer, he bent down and kissed her.

"You're so serious, Vin, I didn't know whether I might speak," she went on sweetly. "Indeed—indeed, Vin, you did look grave."

He expressed contrition, and promised to keep a brighter countenance.

"I have noticed you several times looking serious of late, dear. Vin, are you unhappy? Is anything troubling you?"

"Unhappy!" he cried, looking in her eyes with the ecstasy of a lover—"unhappy, Gwen, beside you!"

"And yet," she said, the suggestion of a pout in the corners of her mouth, "you go away night after night with Tom, and never tell me where you've been."

"You are always so much engaged, I haven't the chance. You shall know presently. Meantime, my little Gwen has something to ask."

They had gone more directly to the point than she intended, but the most dexterous manœuvering could scarcely have accomplished her purpose more happily. For half a second she hung her head, toying with a lace handkerchief; then she looked up, a resistless smile lighting her face. She had a confession to make; she had been a naughty girl of late. Vincent warmly denied it. He was good—very good; but let him wait and hear. No; he wouldn't wait and hear—that is to say, he wouldn't listen to any self-blame. How good he was, the dear boy! Well, he knew what was expected of her as his wife. She found to her dismay, and her dismay was ravishing to look upon—she found she had inadvertently been exceeding her allowance. She had been spending too freely, because she was his wife. He laughed and kissed her again. Money—why, wasn't money made to be spent? Yes, doubtless. All the same, she had been spending too freely.

"You know, Vin, dear, you have been so good," she said, holding up her face to his. "And I'm such a duffer at accounts and reckoning that—that I've got a little into debt."

"Is that all?" he asked, taking the upturned face rapturously between his hands.

Yes, that was all.

"You foolish little woman!" he cooed, bending over her—"you foolish, foolish little woman!"

"Kiss me, Vin," she said; and he kissed her yet again.

Then he said that on the morrow her bank account should be put right.

"I'll be more careful for the future," she promised demurely.

"If you are I shall not love you half so much," was the response.

"Dear, good boy!" she murmured, smuggling closer to him. "Everybody envies me," she went on, after a pause of perfect bliss. "It's nice to be rich, isn't it, Vin?"

"Do they say we are rich?" he asked, fondling her hair.

"In every way, except directly by words. The other day, for instance, Lady Tupton was admiring my chestnuts and wishing she could afford prize horses. Her manner said I could afford anything."

·Well, thank God, you can," said Vincent— "mostly anything."

Never before had the Twickham millions been so sweet as they were in that moment of enchantment.

"We are very rich," murmured the enchantress at his feet.

"We are," he answered.

A delicious thrill ran through Lady Gwendoline. Her heaven was realised. She had more money than any other young wife in England. "More money," she thought, sighing out of pure happiness. But she must take an interest in her husband's affairs, so she asked when he meant to make his next speech in the House. "I am going to be very proud of you," she added radiantly.

"You are *going* to be proud of me?"

"Well, you know what I mean, you perverse boy. I *am* proud of you, only, you see, it's private pride. Sir Richard," meaning a famous political leader, "said lots of nice things about you at Lady Rumbury's reception the other evening. Ever so many people are waiting for your next speech. When is it to come?"

"I don't know," he answered. "Perhaps never."

"Never," she echoed—"never. Why, the battle isn't over, is it?"

"No; I think it's just beginning, little woman."

He was stroking her cheek unconsciously. All at once she drew herself up, turned and looked him squarely in the eyes.

"Why, Vin, you have the tone of one talking in riddles," she said.

"You have a quick imagination," was the answer.

Finding himself free he rose and strode round the room.

"Vin," she cried, leaping up and going to him, "something's the matter. Tell me what it is."

"The matter, sweetheart?"

"Oh yes! I'm sure there's something wrong."

He turned and paced the room again, his head bent, his fingers working nervously. Suddenly he pulled up, facing his wife.

"Gwen," he said, "I am going to tell you something of which you mustn't speak."

"Yes, dear."

"You remember how they twitted me in the House with ignorance of my own business. Well, they were right."

"Right?"

"Yes, I was grossly ignorant. You said just now

I went out without telling you where. I'll tell you now. I went to gather facts, so that I might refute the slanders of my opponents. Clerks and ledgers will give quantities, but I wanted to see the people drinking. So Tom and I went out Haroun Alraschid style."

"And you have seen?"

"The effects of drink."

"Yes," said Lady Gwendoline, startled by his tone. "But that was a mere frolic."

"A very serious frolic, Gwen. I have seen what I shall not forget."

"Vin, you did not allow yourself to be shocked. The other side must not be allowed to triumph."

"Gwen—Gwen," cried Vincent, and it seemed the words were torn from his heart, "I would give fifty thousand pounds to have my old ignorance restored."

THE call came in the House of Commons, and Vincent sat still, sat chin in breast, knowing what that dereliction of duty meant. Lord Twickham chanced to be at Twickham Towers, but hurried up to town, and in the evening dined quietly with his son. They rose early from the wine, conversation having failed, and turned into the library, Vincent's heart beating an agonising quick step. Noticing his son's agitation, Lord Twickham slowly lighted a cigar and passed his case, which Vincent took as one about to be executed might take a glass of brandy. For perhaps two minutes there was silence; then Fate began to speak.

"I have taken the first opportunity, Vin," said Lord Twickham, "to find out what your silence in the House means. Brewers attacked in the Commons, a Twickham present, and not a word in defence. I am puzzled, and have come for an explanation."

A feeling of suffocation came upon Vincent. The rigours of cramp were in his throat; he could hardly articulate.

"The fact is, sir," he gasped, "I don't think I'm fit for the House of Commons."

"Not fit for the House of Commons," repeated Lord Twickham, dwelling on the words in a tone equally expressive of irritation and astonishment. "What nonsense is this? Have the goodness to tell me what's behind. I expect my son to be quite frank with me."

Again there came upon Vincent that cruel constriction of the throat. Body and mind seemed paralysed.

"I have been studying the question a little," he managed to get out at last; "and—and, if you'll forgive me, sir, I'd rather not make any more speeches upholding beer."

For half a minute Lord Twickham looked at his son without so much as winking.

"A case of sick conscience?" he asked then, in a tone of ineffable contempt.

"I don't want to give my convictions any high-sounding names," gasped the wretched Vincent.

"Ah! it is sick conscience, then," said his father yet more witheringly. "Might I ask what has alarmed that sensitive monitor? Has there been any thing at the Brewery to shock it?"

"Nothing, sir—nothing whatever," answered Vincent, squirming like the worm on the hook.

"Ah! I am glad of that," rejoined Lord Twickham deliberately; "I was afraid that the greatest Brewery in the world, the work to which your father has devoted the energy of a lifetime, might be conducted on wrong principles—what self-righteous people would call immoral principles. It's not the brewery that's gone against the gorge, then. Will you tell me what has?"

Vincent pulled desperately at a dead cigar, his face as grey as the ash at its end.

"I don't think that hesitation will make things easier, Vin," added his father. "I fancy it will be best to take me into your confidence at once by telling me what has gone wrong."

"I don't know that anything has gone wrong, sir," said Vincent, proving by his manner that the whole world was wrong. "It's only this. In order to refute those who accused me of ignorance, I have been studying the drink traffic."

Lord Twickham's brows gathered darkly.

"Studying the drink traffic," he said; "perhaps you will tell me from what point of view you approached the study."

"I wished to be perfectly impartial, to get information at first-hand."

"My own rule," said Lord Twickham. "Was it at the Brewery you prosecuted your investigations? In first-hand study of beer I take it you'd begin with brewing."

"When I said first-hand I meant in regard to consumption," explained Vincent, with a parched mouth.

"As to that, our ledgers would enlighten you. In fifteen minutes a clerk would give you a tabulated statement. I have one every week."

"I am not making myself clear," stammered Vincent, whose head buzzed as if with whirling machinery. "I wanted to see the people drinking; to learn something of the retail trade."

"That's interesting. Well?"

"And Tom and I went round to find out for ourselves."

"Upon my word!" cried Lord Twickham. "The Arabian Nights over again. Did you go as the Hon. Vincent Twickham and Viscount Tapley, or did you affect a disguise?"

"We were disguised," replied Vincent, feeling helpless in the grip of this inquisitor.

"Arabian Nights for a certainty! Did Tom and you venture by yourselves?"

"No; a man named Goodman accompanied us. You may remember him."

"Oh yes! I remember him very well. A choice

guide and protector, I should think. He must know the beauty spots of the metropolis. And under his guidance you played the spy. I should have left the office to my subordinates."

" No, sir—not spy. We only wished to learn."

" That's all spies usually do—wish. Doubtless you have learned."

Vincent felt he must cry out or collapse.

" We have learned things unspeakable," he said desperately. " Oh ! father, if you only saw the horror, the hideousness of drink among the people."

" I have been forty years in business," returned Lord Twickham freezingly. " During every day of those two score years I have been studying the drink question. Believe me, my interest in it is old, and at least as close and personal as yours can possibly be after a casual ramble round the public-houses. And I am reminded that it is to drink you owe the position to which you were born. It may be distasteful, though I confess its unpleasantness had not occurred to me. But, agreeable or the reverse, the plain fact is that drink, or, to be precise, beer has made you possibly, I will even say probably, the richest man of your years in England. That, you may tell me, is your misfortune. I can see you have suffered a kind of nausea, such as, it is said, overcomes young surgeons when they first take to practical surgery. But the surgeon's knife is one of the most beneficent instruments of science ; and you may take it that dissecting and operating rooms will not be abolished because young gentlemen of delicate stomachs occasionally find them offensive. Nor will breweries and public-houses be done away with, though ten thousand times ten thousand fanatics should cry ' horrible ! ' Speaking for myself, I ask no man to drink more of my beer than is good for him. At the same time I decline to be responsible for the actions of fools. My business is conducted with a constant regard to decency and order. I am misinformed if our tied houses are not even better than the law requires. Might I ask how my son found them?"

"A striking contrast to some others," answered Vincent eagerly. "It was gratifying to see them so well managed."

"That's as it should be. We have never lost a licence; never had a difficulty in obtaining or renewing one. If you understood the liquor traffic, these facts would speak for themselves. I find, moreover, that the consumption of our ale is increasing year by year, and I tell you frankly that continuous growth is one of the deepest gratifications of my life."

He threw his half-smoked cigar into the fire.

"You have told me of your discoveries, Vin," he went on. "Listen, and I will tell you something. My father, your grandfather, was one of the ablest men of business into whom God ever put the breath of life. Considering his opportunities, he did wonders for the Brewery. I don't boast if my opportunities exceeded his. He made that possible, and his ideals were my inspiration. When I came of age, I resolved that the Twickham Brewery should be without a rival. I kept the intention to myself, for the world rightly discounts boasters. But I worked, I planned, I made this experiment and that, failing often where I counted on success, but learning something from every mistake. Our errors are our best teachers. Well, I pushed at home and abroad. Time passed. I went my way, sometimes over obstacles, sometimes round them; and at the end of twenty years I heard people say the Twickhams were forging to the front; at the end of thirty years they were without rival.

My youthful dream was realised. Now, at the end of forty years, when I am an old man, my son sits in judgment and tells me I have been a fool."

Vincent's head swam. He was crushed, and to the crushing were added the stings of conscious disloyalty. The horrors which had tortured him like a nightmare suddenly grew insignificant and vanished in presence of the outraged father.

"You do me injustice," he cried, in piteous self-defence. "I did not sit in judgment; I had no intention of imputing blame. You will believe I did not presume to judge."

"I am anxious to believe as much of my only son," answered Lord Twickham, relenting; "and let the credit of good intention be mutual. You, in turn, will believe that I have looked at questions affecting the consumption of beer at least as closely as the keenest of my critics. You don't imagine that I have been all these years at the head of a brewery producing two million barrels a year without hearing a great deal of the horror and hideousness of drink. That report has been my daily portion. Had I been told of futile wills and gluttonous, bestial appetites it would have been more to the purpose. I make no parade of morality; and I believe the counting-house was never meant to be a church. But if, in these days of sickly consciences, it is necessary to be ethical in business, then I say emphatically that ale is a blessing. If the incontinent find it a curse, who is to blame? To indulge in sweeping condemnation of drink because there are drunkards is just as logical and reasonable as to condemn religion because it makes fanatics and maniacs. I will mention a fact you may have forgotten—a hundred thousand shares of the St. Edmund Brewery are held by clergymen, and five times as many would be held by the Churches had the allotments equalled the applications. We might have a board of bishops and deans. Is the Church, therefore, engaged in sending people to perdition ?"

He rose, drew himself up to his full height, which was six feet two, walked to the window, wheeled quickly, and came back. As he advanced Vincent also rose, and their eyes met in a close, confiding gaze. Looking into the strong face above him, there came upon the son a swift feeling of adoration for the father who had triumphed so magnificently and so magnificently justified his way. To oppose him was like opposing a law of nature.

"Has your mother heard of this ?" asked Lord Twickham, after a moment's silence.

"No, father."

"Then it is my wish that nothing be said to her touching it ; and we'll keep this conversation to ourselves. Take my advice, and blow the cobwebs to destruction. I shall expect to hear no more of them. Now, I fancy, they will be expecting us in the drawing-room."

CHAPTER III

THE tussle which Vincent dreaded was over.
Lord Twickham won handsomely ; and the
feeling of the vanquished was one of exceeding joy,
because defeat eased him of many torments. For
the moment his sole regret was that the past was gone
irrevocably—in other words, that the House could
not now listen to the undelivered speech. Partial
amends might, however, be made by a greater devotion to the interests of the Brewery ; and forthwith
Vincent devoted himself to business with the zeal of
a convert imbibing a new religion.

It had always been part of his creed that in the
case of Twickham's beer it was eclipse first and
the rest nowhere. But only now did he begin to
understand what the tenet meant, to realise the
scope of that odorous hive on the banks of the Stare,
and appreciate the genius which made it the marvel
of the age. In the perfection of its working it seemed
the vast machine was automatic, until one pierced
to the centre and discovered the directing brain. Even
in an age when obedient Nature suffers herself to be
turned into a manifold driving-wheel, there must still
be a man behind the machine ; and behind this
stupendous engine, acting with the force of destiny
itself, the man was Lord Twickham. He had his
managers and deputies by the score, experts all, and
all unsuspecting puppets of one ruling, organising
intelligence. The St. Edmund Brewery was merely
an alias of Viscount Twickham.

With a quickened admiration Vincent went his way, seeking opportunity to prove his loyalty and finding it at every turn. He was thrown much into the society of McTor, and McTor's methods and manners were bracing to the blackslider. For although the Shorter Catechism had once been thoroughly birched into Duncan, never, since reaching years of discretion, had he allowed it to hamper his conscience. Moreover, his scorn for the water-drinkers was more potent than compound logic.

"It's a funny thing," he said to Vincent once, after covering them with ridicule, "that our hottest fanatics should be reformed drunkards."

"Not the least," put in the Earl of Wegron, who had listened, chuckling—"not the least funny. Take the man who's been scared a time or two by the d. t.'s. He's afraid to drink, because his constitution's like a tinder-box soaked in paraffin—the least touch of fire and off it goes. Now it happens that the natural man is not an angel. What the *ci-devant* boozer can no longer enjoy himself he can't bear to see others enjoying. That's the secret of half the reforming zeal with which a much enduring world is vexed."

"Reforming zeal," said MacTor. "Yes! There's not an old wife of either sex but must babble about reform, as if the devil were to be caught by putting salt on his tail. Now, wipe the public-houses off the face of the earth, and what do you think would happen?"

"I have never troubled myself to think what would happen," returned the Earl. "What would be the consequence if we reformed you out of existence?"

"Why, red hot anarchy. Have you ever pictured a sober, respectable, determined East End awakened to a sense of its wrongs, rising *en masse*, and marching upon Park Lane and Berkeley Square, pillaging as it went, and trampling coronets under foot?"

"If they were perfectly sober they'd have the sense to preserve the coronets," remarked the Earl.

"In any case they'd have them. Do you know, I always think of that seething East End as a menagerie of wild beasts, kept under, partly by art, partly by fear. Some day, as sure's God's in Heaven, they'll rise before their masters have time to catch the first train for safety; and then, my noble friend, you'll have Carlyle's roaring hell-porch of a Hôtel de Ville over again, with grim Saxon determination to keep the fun going. When British sansculottism realises its right, it'll be high time for some of us to pack. Moscow conflagrations are nothing to what will happen."

"Pleasant prophet!" said the Earl. "When do you expect these things to come upon us?"

"When drinking is abolished," was the answer. "Let the under world get perfectly sober, recover its wits, and take stock, and by Jove! the Wegron title-deeds will help the bonfire. I'm talking seriously."

"Faith, and that's precisely what you're doing," admitted the Earl. "But this new Bartholomew rout is not to come off while distilleries remain?"

"I think not."

"I breathe again," said the Earl, "though your meaning is a little cryptic,—is that the word?"

"My meaning is perfectly plain to all who know the slums," replied MacTor. "Drink is the universal drug which takes the edge off calamity, and makes misery bearable. The enemies of your order growl when you roll by in your carriage; oh yes, they do. They'd like to pluck you out and wrench your head off. But at the corner stands a public-house; in they turn, and straightway forget their enmity. Close the public-houses, deprive socialism, anarchism, or whatever else you like to call it, of its anodyne, and presto!

you are perched on a powder-magazine with a lighted
fuse at the base."

"Keep 'em drunk, MacTor—keep 'em drunk," cried
the Earl; whereupon there was a peal of laughter.

Somehow Vincent could not laugh.   His face was
hot, his nerves were quivering.   He made no comment ;
but he thought much, and as he thought his sky
darkened again.   There was a conspiracy, then, to
keep the victims of fate in their misery.   Had he or
his any part in that conspiracy ?   If so, what was to
be done ?   Should he, Alexander like, cut the gordian
knot, or should he try to untie ?

CHAPTER IV

FOR the present the plan of letting it alone was easiest. Considering the genius of things for self-adjustment, there might be no need either to cut or untie ; and, in any case, precipitancy was the special folly to be avoided. Happily, there was plenty of diversion. Ingledew, for instance, silently appealed for charity, and, indeed, pledges had been given concerning him. Wherefore Vincent and Tapley, attended by Dick, returned to the lodging-house in Spitalfields, according to appointment with the deputy.

When they arrived that gentleman chanced to be expediting the departure of a guest whose time was up. The ejected had picked himself out of the gutter, re-entered the passage, and expressed an unbiassed opinion of the ruling power. He was just going out head foremost a second time as the visitors came up. At sight of them the deputy apologised profusely, smoothed his irate quills, pulled down the shirt-sleeves tucked for action, and smiled as benignly as was possible to a professional " chucker-out " taken unawares.

Ingledew sat on a bench in the great common room, nursing a gross wrong. Spying his friends, he rose to meet them, smiling sadly from the depths of a profound dejection. The fact is, he was perfectly sober, and perfectly sober, Mr. Ingledew's mood was one of silent despair.

"'E ain't 'appy 'cept when 'e's drunk," explained the deputy, in a bass whisper.

Mr. Ingledew heard and nodded. It was the simple truth.

"This minute my tongue's on fire," he said dolefully.

"Feels kind o' blistery, eh!" put in Dick, who had experienced similar sensations.

Mr. Ingledew shook his head.

"Blistery doesn't express it," he croaked. "Grilling and roasting would be nearer the mark. Brazier inside."

"Would be out to drink," said the deputy, "till I told 'im 'e'd be eternally chucked if 'e did. Then he sits down, mumblin' 'bout 'avin a fire inside an' not allowed to put it out."

"Ah God! what it is to be burning alive," broke in Mr. Ingledew. "I have made a little study of theology, sir," addressing Vincent, "and if this isn't Hell I cannot imagine what is. I feel like a red hot furnace."

"Reckon 'a mother-in-law' would 'bout suit you," suggested Dick, looking at him compassionately. "Wot you wants is a drop of old an' bitter."

Ingledew smacked his torrid lips.

"Old and bitter," he repeated. "Dear friend, is it possible? I've got three ha'-pence—three half-pence. There they are ; is 'a mother-in-law' possible?"

Considering the urgency of the case, it was agreed he might have one drink—just one, to cool his fiery tongue. So Dick was deputed to take him to a public-house and bring him back in ten minutes. In their absence the essential business with the deputy was transacted—that is to say, a certain sum of money changed hands for Ingledew's benefit, with the accompaniment of that palm oil which makes the life of deputies sweet.

Ten minutes passed and the drinkers had not returned. They were still absent at the end of half an hour. At the end of an hour Vincent was accusing Dick of default; but the deputy reminded him it was easy enough to get a man of Mr. Ingledew's kidney into a public-house, but "the devil's work" to get him out again.

"Well," said Vincent impatiently, "we cannot wait here all day."

"Suppose we go in search of them," suggested Tapley. "No one will know us hereabouts."

So they left, the deputy directing them to the One-eyed Stag, a favourite resort of Ingledew when he possessed the price of a glass. Thither they went, and found their birds, according to expectation, seated jovially on high stools and deep in talk with the land-lord. It was evident at a glance that the limit of a single glass had been exceeded. Ingledew was chirpy, and Dick fairly radiated happiness. The entry of his friends, indeed, cut him short in a graphic account of themselves, their wealth, position, social qualities, and particularly his own "chummy" place in their regard. The tale was not half told; but enough had been said to enlighten Ingledew. As they entered, he raised his glass and bowed genially; then dismounting from his stool, advanced to meet them.

"I had not dared to dream of this," he said, with a sweeping genuflexion. "I thought—but how could I be sure? Yet another proof, sir," beaming upon Vincent, "that truth is stranger than fiction."

Vincent looked puzzled.

"I don't quite understand you," he responded.

"Ah! but I understand you," cried Ingledew glee-fully. "The same good heart, the same good fellow as of yore."

Vincent cast a reproachful look at Dick; he had been blabbing then.

"Just to think of it," continued Ingledew, stepping back that he might the better admire. "I cannot describe the emotions which stir in my breast. I could—but there, all philosophers agree that regrets are vain. You honoured me in the past; you honour me now. I wish I could show my appreciation as I should like."

"In good MacTor?" laughed Tapley.

"In good MacTor, my lord," rejoined Ingledew.

Vincent felt uncomfortably warm, and proposed a return to fresh air. Ingledew protested. What! go away without drinking his friend's health? Never.

Tapley and Vincent exchanged glances; they were in for it, and might as well look pleasant. Ingledew was, therefore, asked to name his beverage.

"I'm loyal to old friends," he answered. "Make it MacTor, and," to the landlord, "Mr. Crump, let it be hot."

Hot it was, and "special" to boot, and Ingledew had the deepest pleasure in drinking it "on so auspicious an occasion." Dick took equal delight in a foaming glass of Twickham, the landlord graciously accepting another. Vincent and Tapley were content with sherry. Seeing they dallied with it, Mr. Crump desired to know if it wasn't good, and on being assured of its excellence invited them to "toss off, then." They modestly reminded him it was early in the day for repetitions; whereupon he retorted it was never too early or too late to be sociable, and he should take it as a mortal offence if they refused to drink with him. Ingledew applauded the sentiment; and Dick was of opinion it did one's heart good to hear a man "as is a man, an' not a bloomin' ole woman," discuss the liquor question.

The second round disposed of in a glow of good fellowship, Mr. Goodman put in his claim as entertainer. He, too, had his feelings; wherefore he had his way. But at the proposal of a fourth round Vincent grew obdurate. They therefore took leave of Mr. Crump, Dick and Ingledew effusively expressing their affection.

They were hardly fifty yards from the door when there swung round the nearest corner an open carriage, drawn by a pair of gleaming black horses.

"Heavens!" ejaculated Vincent, gripping Tapley's arm. "The mater's blacks."

Tapley whistled.

"No use running," he said; "may escape notice. Hullo! Lush is there; slumming, by Jove!"

The carriage came up and was passing, when Miss Lush's quick eye lighted on the group on the pavement. The next instant the carriage had stopped, and Lady Twickham, erect and amazed, was examining them. Tapley ran to her side, hat in hand, his face wreathed in propitiative smiles. Vincent followed more leisurely, conning explanations.

"Well, upon my word!" cried Miss Lush airily. "*You* slumming. Wonders will never cease."

"Never, while men and women last to keep them going," responded Tapley, with a glance at Lady Twickham. But her eyes were fixed on a figure standing rigidly at the salute some ten paces off.

"Our old friend of Paradise Court," whispered Miss Lush.

"So I see;" returned Lady Twickham, "and the other?" she queried, indicating Ingledew, who seemed torn between a desire to hide behind Dick and a wish to rush forward and embrace some one.

"A discovery," answered Tapley. "A natural history curiosity who has lost his reckoning, and finds himself in the east when he ought to be in the west."

"Another case of tumbling down the ladder?" enquired her ladyship.

Tapley nodded; Lady Twickham sighed.

" Now that you've caught him, what do you intend to do with him ? " asked Miss Lush.

" Depends on his constitution," replied Tapley. " Might be worth putting in a book, Miss Lush. That sort of thing's all the go now, isn't it ? "

" Is it ? " she answered, smiling ravishingly ; but she was not thinking of books. Once she dreamed a dream of a Countess of Wegron, looked in the mirror, and behold ! the rapt face of Miss Laura Lush. And why not ? If the stage leads to a coronet, why not the novel ?

" Constitution," she added, keeping her eyes on Tapley's face. " Is it to be a case of Spartan treatment, then ? "

" With your shield or on it, my son," laughed Tapley. " Pardon me, Miss Lush, these relics of a lost classical education will turn up. As to our friend, he is really worth your attention. Gentleman— admires Solomon, though denied the gift of wisdom— bits of innocent jollity, you understand, here a little and there a little, quite on Scriptural lines. You'd have us all wild over the romance you could make out of him."

" Thank you, I shall remember that," she said radiantly, busy with a more personal romance.

" His companion appears to have constitution enough for two," remarked Lady Twickham, bringing the attention back to Dick. " Pity he couldn't impart some of it to his wife and child."

" Understand he tries, like a good husband," said Tapley. " Bestows periodical black eyes on his wife. Treatment considered highly tonic in the East End."

" Deserves to be put in irons and flogged," rejoined Lady Twickham severely. " But how comes it you have him in tow ? *Protégé* of yours, Vin ? Ah well ! he does you credit."

She beckoned, and Dick advanced briskly, struggling with a grin. At two yards' distance he drew up, saluting again. Lady Twickham adjusted her lorgnette and scrutinised him. She noted his air of prosperity had increased since their former meeting ; but looked in vain for any corresponding mark of respectability. Being still an amateur in East End ways, she made the mistake of assuming that respectability was among Dick's ideals.

" Well," she said, in her severest manner, " I didn't expect to meet you."

Dick delicately hinted that the surprise was mutual, and insinuated a hope that her pleasure was equal to his.

" Ever since you was at Paradise Court been thinkin' of you, m' lady," he said, intrepidly taking the fence. " An' as for Jenny, why, I ain't got no words fit to tell 'ow she do go on—no, m' lady."

He grinned ; Lady Twickham puckered her brows. This man was spoiling for want of a chastening, whatever the other might be.

" I regret to find my advice so little heeded," she retorted. " Jenny has not her troubles to seek. What are you doing now for a living ? "

Dick glanced slyly at Vincent for a cue. Would it be right to " peach " ? No cue being vouchsafed, he was obliged to cough in order to gain time. Then he wiped his eyes, apologising for the state of his bronchial tubes, and chancing to look round, caught sight of Ingledew. Heaven had provided a scapegoat.

" 'Elpin' to look arter 'im, m' lady," said Dick, jerking his head at the figure behind.

" Is he a friend of yours ? "

" Sorter, m' lady. Fell across 'im in a pub—I mean one o' them 'ere snoozin' boxes where they lays 'em out at fourpence a 'ead."

Again he glanced at Vincent, as much as to say,

"Why don't you 'elp a bloke? I'll peach, if you don't look out."

"It's quite true, mother," interpolated Vincent, coming to Dick's relief. "I have just discovered that the gentleman behind is an old friend of mine."

Lady Twickham's eyes expressed deep horror.

"A friend of yours," she cried, keeping to well-bred amazement. "Have you been slumming?"

"A little, mother."

"And you have been aiding and abetting him, Tom?"

Tapley admitted the offence.

"Why, this grows romantic. But there, the police think we're blocking the street. We are just going round by Paradise Court. This evening you will tell me all about it." And she gave the order to drive on.

THE four stood watching till the coachman's spacious back and Miss Lush's feathered head passed out of sight. Then, by a common impulse, Vincent and Tapley looked at each other, Tapley bursting into laughter.

"No use trying to do good by stealth, Vin," he said. "Right hand wants to be charitable ; left immediately on its track ; and the fat's in the fire before you know where you are."

Vincent was grave. He was thinking of the promise to his father, and the probable consequence of his mother's discovery.

"I wish they had stayed at home," he said, in a tone of irritation.

"Is the age of chivalry really gone then?" responded Tapley. "Think of the charms of Lush."

"She seemed very sweet," said Vincent.

"Sweet," echoed Tapley. "The dear creature exudes sweetness like a sugar cask in the sun. Can't help it. Clever, too, by Jove ! I hear everybody reads her books. They say she makes anything up to twenty thousand pounds a year. Wish to Heaven I could scribble. If one could only wind her up, say, for five years, and turn her into a joint-stock company, what a hit she'd make on 'Change."

"You'd take shares ?"

"Rather—as a spec, you know, not an investment. Hanged if I believe she'll hold out. Takes old chaps like Shakespeare and Scott and Dickens to do that. The new stuff's all froth. But she's coining now. Clean upset all my notions about authors. I used to think of them as a set of raw-boned, lean-faced beggars, who had the secret of existing on nothing at all, or dined casually like a Constantinople cur. I only wish my bank account were half as healthy as Miss Lush's."

"I understand she does a lot of good," said Vincent.

"Providence chooses strange agents," returned Tapley. "Dabbles in religion and philanthropy and all that sort of thing, doesn't she? Tried a book of hers once; fell asleep and forgot what it was all about. Seemed a kind of sermon. Hullo! Mr. Ingledew has a remark to make."

Ingledew, whose courage was now restored, stepped forward, apologising for his inability to vanish into thin air when the occasion called for sudden disappearance. He could not forgive himself for retaining a bodily shape that might compromise his benefactors in the eyes of ladies.

"But you know it wasn't my fault," he pleaded. "I'd gladly have stayed a while longer with Mr. Crump."

"Assurances are needless," said Tapley. "You'd stay with Mr. Crump till the Day of Judgment, supposing the liquor held out so long."

Three pairs of eyes were upon Ingledew, and they pierced, for he was unspeakably dilapidated and full of holes. Looking at him, his friends understood that if charity were to rescue she must begin at once, and repudiate half measures. From the crown of the head to the sole of the foot the man urgently needed renovation; and most he needed to be shorn and washed—washed with all the power of soap and water and disinfectants. So he was taken to a barber, who operated gingerly, not without signs of revolt and a double fee ; thence he passed to an outfitter, who was bribed to destroy the old clothes ; then he was gently led to a public bath and made clean—a fearful hygienic process. Shining like the ransomed, he returned to the den in Spitalfields, and every one, from the deputy down, disclosed the long held secret—that they had always known he was a toff in disguise.

Dick, who had hitherto regarded Ingledew with the tolerant contempt of a superior intellect, all at once experienced acute twinges of jealousy ; but like a good husband, he reserved the expression of his feelings for the privacy of home. The Ingledew parade, as he named it to himself, well over, he hurried to Paradise Court, and found Jenny still agitated over Lady Twickham's visit. Her agitation was the more prolonged, because she had lately been undergoing a special course of marital discipline, the visible effects of which had excited the wrath of Lady Twickham and the dire denunciation of Miss Lush. Her ladyship, indeed, vowed she would call Goodman to account ; but Jenny prayed her to forbear, well knowing that lectures out of furs and laces would be the sheerest waste of time and effort.

What particularly interested Dick, as he hastened home, thinking of Lady Twickham, was not her opinion on this or that subject, least of all on his behaviour, but the amount of her latest benefaction.

"'Ear as you've 'ad visitors," he cried, as he bounced in upon his wife. "'Ow much is it this time ? "

A look of mingled fear and pain came into Jenny's face.

"Lady Twickham says as it's all for Loo," she answered hesitatingly. "Says as the child looks starvin'."

"Oh! does she?" said Dick. "Very good on 'er, an' very complimentary, I must say. But I didn't 'appen to ask wot she said, but wot she did. 'Ow much is it?"

"Not much, Dick."

"Not much, eh!" he growled, his face darkening ominously—"not much; an' 'er so good at makin' remarks, besides not knowin' 'ow to get through 'er chink. Let me 'ave it."

"You won't take it from me, Dick," pleaded Jenny. "There's Loo; look at her. Let me keep it this once, do, Dick dear. Lady Twickham made me promise to get things for Loo. She'll never give me more if I don't."

At this insolence Dick lost his patience. If Lady Twickham bestowed her charity on such terms, she might keep it; and she'd better not be coming to his house to dictate. By Heaven! he'd be master, in spite of all the lace petticoats in the land.

"An' the she-moke wot writes books," he cried, "was she 'ere, too?"

Yes, she had been with Lady Twickham.

"A-spyin'," he went on furiously. "She'll put us in 'er bloomin' books, that's wot she's arter, an' 'ave people laughin' at us, an' maybe wipin' their eyes over you, as ain't blessed with a 'usband you can dance on. Gawd! ain't it fine? Damn all women wot don't work for a livin'."

He spoke as one who was not to be appeased; but though his wrath was kindled against womankind, he was sober enough to be politic. Therefore he would not lay hands on Jenny lest "the ole cow," hearing of it, might withhold her benefactions entirely. But he warned his wife that if she persisted in thwarting him she might send cards to Lady Twickham and "the she-moke wot writes books" for the most glorious row in the annals of married life.

" And you'll let me keep it, Dick, won't you ? " said Jenny, whose mind ran on the money.

" I ain't got nuthin' to do with it," he answered, in disgust. " You keeps on yer own 'ook. Lady Twickham comes 'ere an' says wot's to be done an' wot's not to be done, an' yer 'usband dussn't squeak. Go an' buy Loo silks and satings and yerself the same."

With which he banged the door, so that a shower of dry-rot fell, stamped down stairs, and made for the Bear and Cubs.

" It is quite true," he said to himself hotly as he strode along—" quite true as it's the women wot drives the men to drink."

CHAPTER VI

WHILE Wragg entertained Dick with his best liquor, Lady Twickham was gently putting Vincent to inquisitorial torture. Bountifully endowed with the virtue of curiosity, her ladyship was not to be denied a detailed and explicit account of her son's explorations in Alsatia, nor of the accident or motive which led him thither. Unluckily, she had time and opportunity to examine and cross-examine, to suggest, pause, turn back, requestion and probe, till the heart, which she regarded as her own, lay bare before her. Lady Gwendoline was absent on one of her many missions of pleasure—a hastily arranged run to a race-meeting with friends devoted, like herself, to sport. Vincent, indifferent at the moment to the triumph of jockeys, remained behind, as it chanced, to become the prey of the inquisitor.

It was remarked, not without significant nods, that, having captured the prize, Lady Gwendoline "made the pace" as if marriage were an act of emancipation and husbands were created to provide establishments.

"You don't wish to be tied to my apron-strings," she had said laughingly to Vincent before the honeymoon was well over. "As little, I am sure, do you wish me to be dragging at your belt. I think we both believe in rational freedom. We can trust each other."

"Of course—of course," answered Vincent, hurt

because a woman cannot belong exclusively to the man who loves her.

And from that moment Lady Gwendoline allowed no marriage tie to impede her movements. This had not escaped the notice of Lady Twickham, who was old-fashioned in her notions of wifely duty, and had a mother's eyes besides. Sometimes she pitied Vincent a little—a very little; for she would not admit, even to herself, that her son was neglected by the woman whom he honoured with his name. But Gwen might think less of the pursuit of pleasure, be less eager to lead the giddy throng.

Vincent had many touching proofs of his mother's solicitude. Nevertheless, he devoutly wished she were less curious about his doings. For if he refused information, her affection would be wounded; if he gave it, he should be a traitor to his father. Unhappily, he had not the diplomatic gift of saying convincingly the opposite of what he meant. But remembering the wisdom of reticence, he made a handy compromise with his conscience—that is to say, like many a good man in a fix, he told the truth, but not the whole truth. He had gone to the slums, he told his mother, for arguments to confound his assailants in the House of Commons, and in the course of investigation fell in with Ingledew.

Now nothing engaged Lady Twickham's sympathy so readily as a real concrete case of misery and misfortune. To square accounts with Heaven for the blessings showered upon her she did her best for the wretched; and her charity was catholic. Vincent adroitly made the most of Ingledew. The man might be to blame, but he was exceedingly miserable, his misery being the keener because he had known better times and associations.

" You must bring him to me," said Lady Twickham, instantly busy with schemes of regeneration.

"Certainly, mother," replied Vincent, glad to get her off the main track. "But you'll give him time to draw breath first. The poor fellow could hardly bear an interview yet."

"Very well. Do you want money?"

Vincent thought he had enough for the present.

"Well, well! Should you want any, you know! And what about the man Goodman? I gather he accompanied you in your explorations!"

Vincent answered in the affirmative.

"A pretty Christian!" she remarked.

"A muscular Christian, mother."

"More muscular than Christian, I'm afraid. Did you bring him sober through it all?"

"Almost," laughed Vincent.

"Says a good deal for your management. Miss Lush calls him the most consummate piece of ruffianism she has ever known."

"A novelist ought to have more discernment," rejoined Vincent, feeling an oblique personal aspersion in this compendious estimate of Dick.

"My dear, Miss Lush has wonderful discernment; I can vouch for that," said Lady Twickham.

"Then she ought to put it to better use. By the way, is she in love with Tom?"

"In love with Tom!" cried Lady Twickham, in a scandalised tone—"Miss Lush in love with Tom! Vin, what do you mean?"

"What I say, mother. The radiance she shed on him to-day was quite dazzling."

"You silly boy! Miss Lush is wedded to her art; I have had it a thousand times from her own lips."

"My impression is she'd like to be wedded to something else," said Vincent.

"How dare you, Vin?" demanded Lady Twickham. "Miss Lush's heart is in her writing. She could never do what she's doing if she were married."

" Does marrying spoil a novelist ? " asked Vincent quizzically. " I thought writers of fiction might rather like to experiment in the real thing. The fictitious must grow tiresome. Tom's practical. For instance, he thought that by converting her into a limited liability company, a pretty penny might be realised."

" I will not permit such talk," returned Lady Twickham decisively. " It's very improper in Tom to make·such remarks, and in you to repeat them. Miss Lush does a great deal of good ; and is my friend."

" I beg your pardon, mother," said Vincent penitently. " I am sorry to do Miss Lush wrong ; but she does Goodman wrong. With all his faults I believe there's the making of a man in him."

" As there's the making of a statue in a quarry," retorted Lady Twickham. " Needs a deal of shaping ; and I must say Mr. Goodman shows rare resource in concealing his high possibilities. I'm afraid he's not a saint, Vin."

" The British Empire doesn't owe its existence to saints, mother. Goodman has fought for his country. His misfortune is to be a born fighter."

" Evidently ; and he keeps his hand in. The manner in which he maltreats his poor wife is shameful. I find it hard to believe in a man who beats his wife."

Vincent was responding with something about use and wont in the East End, when the door opened and his father walked in. Taking advantage of the interruption, he left to keep an engagement elsewhere, happy in having kept his secret.

" Vin has just been telling me of his adventures in the slums," Lady Twickham remarked to her husband.

" Oh ! " he responded, in a tone which made her look curiously at him.

" Didn't you know he had been in the East End ? " she asked.

" Oh yes ! I heard he'd been slumming," replied Lord Twickham. " How did you come to hear of it ? Did he volunteer the information ? "

" On the contrary, I had to pick it out of him. The first inkling came quite by chance."

" Chance plays a big part in the world. Tell me about it."

" Well, this afternoon I was on a charitable round with Miss Lush, and in turning a corner whom should we come upon but Vin, Tom, that man Goodman, and another, whose name, I learn, is Ingledew."

" That's interesting. Caught them red-handed, so to speak. Who or what is Ingledew ? "

" As to the who, he's an old college friend of Vin's ; as to the what, I judge him to be a particularly miserable child of misfortune."

" Ah ! " said Lord Twickham, " a philanthropic discovery."

" Something of that sort," admitted his wife.

" We have philanthropy in the blood," remarked Lord Twickham. " Vin, of course, couldn't help taking this Ingledew in tow. Did he till you what else he found in the East End ? "

" No ; practically nothing beyond Ingledew. He talked some nonsense about Miss Lush being in love with Tom, and Tom turning her into a company."

" That's worthy of Tom," said Lord Twickham, with a dry laugh. " Floating her on the Stock Exchange : the idea's good. For the rest, why shouldn't Miss Lush be in love with him ? Falling in love is not reckoned a crime. Besides, Tom's got qualities which tell with women, and though he's poorer than a church mouse, he's got a title. Even Lady Bareacres enjoys the privileges of position. Vin didn't tell you of his discoveries in detail, or of the impressions they left ? "

"No; the talk was almost wholly about Ingledew
and Goodman."

"He said nothing about drink?"

"Nothing."

"Didn't he mention what took him to the slums?"

"Oh yes; now I remember he told me he went for
arguments to overwhelm opponents in the House.
But why are you so mysterious about it, Vincent?
Has anything happened?"

Lord Twickham looked at his wife for some
seconds without speaking.

"Much—very much has happened," he answered
then. "Vin went out denying, and returned believing."

"Believing what?" asked Lady Twickham, a note
of real alarm in her voice.

"I'm glad he didn't tell you," said her husband
slowly. "It's best I should do that; and, since
the matter has come up, do it now, lest distorted
versions should reach you. Vin, my dear, has been
taking a leaf out of the book of Balaam, when that
good man disappointed his friend Balak; or more
correctly, perhaps, has undergone the experience of
Saul of Tarsus on the expedition to Damascus."

"You startle me," cried Lady Twickham, her eyes
amply confirming her words. "Tell me all quickly.
Saul of Tarsus underwent sudden conversion. To
what is Vin converted?"

"To an abhorrence of all his father's work,"
answered Lord Twickham deliberately. "Not to
speak in riddles, he is overwhelmed by the horrors
of the drink traffic; thinks it the greatest curse on
earth, and all that, and holds it responsible for most
of the vice and folly of mankind. I am not sure
whether we are to tear down the Brewery and
cultivate leeks and cabbages among the ruins, or
abandon it to the owls and foxes as a sign of the
curse that is upon it. You see, I have reared a judge

to condemn my actions—a comforting thought at sixty-five, when one is too old to begin over again. It seems I am engaged in a huge conspiracy to ruin my fellow-men—a soothing verdict from one's son and heir."

Lady Twickham's face was pallid with horror.

"You make me ill," she said—"really, I shall be ill."

"Oh no, don't be ill," returned her husband quietly. "It is a mistake to take anything in this life too seriously, and especially a fit of fanaticism. It will probably pass, after the manner of fits. Meantime, I am not the least ashamed of myself. I have made what I could of the gifts God gave me. It's a pity Vin should be offended ; but I declined to go into the pathology of a sick conscience, and asked him not to tell you. The fact that he kept his promise is an encouraging augury. I think he will soon be quite well again."

"But what can have led him to reflect on you ?" said Lady Twickham, her face a study in perplexity.

"To do him justice, the reflection was only indirect, and not intended to be personal," was the answer. "As to the cause, he went among unpleasant scenes, and being green, got a touch of nausea. He found that men sin, and is surprised they should suffer. In his amazement he rushes off, as so many good people rush, to lay blame and responsibility on the wrong shoulders. It seems the drunkard is to be forgiven ; but the brewer and the publican are to be condemned beyond hope of salvation. That's vicarious responsibility with a vengeance. Presently we shall have the wise man clapped in jail for the delinquencies of the fool. We live in the most logical of worlds. But don't you worry ; we've probably heard the first and the last of Vin's disapproval."

IN times of trouble it was Lady Twickham's custom to seek (and find) consolation in the works of the Bishop of Blockley. Upset by the revelations about Vincent, she had recourse to the usual medicine; but for once the soothing mixture was without efficacy. Finding no comfort in Tinkle she shut the book, and for half an hour lay back in her chair, her hands folded in her lap, and her eyes on the ceiling, thinking intensely. What would be the consequence were Vincent to turn against his father? On which side should she range herself? The question made her thrill eerily, and in sheer fear of the answer she rose hurriedly and went to the library, where Miss Lush happened to be working. The novelist looked up in surprise.

"Dear Lady Twickham, I thought you were resting," she said. "You ought to be resting"; and her expression seemed to ask what was wrong.

"One cannot always rest when one would," replied Lady Twickham. "What have you been reading, my dear?"

"Only a volume of statistics, and I feel as if I had been regaling on chaff. Statistics are like an anatomical statement of the number of bones in a skeleton: you have the information, but the living organism remains vague. It is hard to conjure living reality out of dry bones."

"I thought your imagination could conjure up

anything—as, indeed, I know it can. What particular statistics have you been studying?"

Now the question was a delicate one, and the discreet Lush hesitated just an instant in her reply. Would it be prudent to tell the truth?

"Very oddly, statistics of the drink traffic," she said, taking risks.

Lady Twickham's eyelids quivered a little.

"And what do you find?" she asked.

"The usual rows of figures, of course," answered Miss Lush, smiling as if to say, "What could you expect from a mere work of reference?"

"No deduction, no moral?" inquired Lady Twickham.

"Oh yes; we live in an age of deductions and morals. The compiler is quite in the fashion; he's a bit of a preacher."

"Let me see," said Lady Twickham, stretching out her hand for the book. "You know my weakness for sermons."

Miss Lush passed the book, indicating with a forefinger where the sermon began. Her ladyship read the passage, silently and with perfect composure.

"A very trenchant sermon," she remarked pleasantly, laying down the volume. "My only criticism is that the preacher falls into violence, smites hip and thigh, so to speak, when a flick in the face might suffice."

"A Samson among the Philistines with the jawbone of an ass," suggested Miss Lush archly.

"Always apt, my dear, always pat," responded Lady Twickham, nodding assent. "Well, Samson overdid things in the end, poor fellow! But pray," glancing at a bundle of papers on which Miss Lush had been busy, "if it's not impertinent, what are you doing? Another new novel, my dear? Ah!

you novelists are so sly ; alway watching, detective like, the foibles of your fellows."

Thus trapped Miss Lush had to own she was, indeed, engaged on a new work of fiction, planned on a colossal scale.

"And these are jottings," said Lady Twickham, fingering the papers with the emotion natural in one permitted to handle the tools of genius.

"Yes ; I am frightfully conscientious," admitted Miss Lush, blushing prettily. " You can have no idea, dear Lady Twickham, of the labour and pains of novel writing. For my last work, ' The Purblind ; or, the Fool and his Folly,' I had no less than a dozen discarded bonnet-boxes full of notes."

"Good gracious ! " ejaculated Lady Twickham, surprised out of her well-bred reserve. " A dozen boxes full of notes ? "

"Crammed," said Miss Lush ; "in truth, over-flowing, like the measure of Scripture. Oh ! I assure you it's no fun amusing the public nowadays. Time was when you could put anything into a story, so long as it was amusing, or sensational, or—or savoured of scandal. But that's all changed. You've got to grind like a specialist now."

"And even then, I suppose, the critics disparage."

" Disparage ! " repeated Miss Lush, with a tinkling laugh. " They'd disparage the angel Gabriel. They disparaged my twelve boxes of notes ; talked of having raw material thrown at their heads, as if wood could be hurt."

" Well, you had a very gratifying revenge. The whole world knows the sensation made by ' The Purblind.' How many copies were sold, my dear ? "

" A hundred and fifty thousand in the first month," answered Miss Lush modestly ; " two hundred and fifty thousand within three months."

" A quarter of a million ! I wonder your head

wasn't turned. I should think such figures stopped the critics' mouths effectually."

"Only made them gibe the more," said Miss Lush merrily.

"Well, it is the fate of all great and original souls to be misunderstood," rejoined Lady Twickham consolingly. "I have read that when one of your works appears rivals are crushed."

Miss Lush could only confess the fact, and vow that the fault wasn't hers. She really couldn't help it if the public bought two hundred and fifty thousand copies of her book in three months, and left her rivals to starve. She pitied those rivals, some of whom were really worthy and industrious people, though they hadn't her knack of success.

"And the new novel? What is it about?" asked Lady Twickham.

"Speaking generally, the East End. The social conditions are picturesque and dramatic."

The sermon in the book of reference bore on the evils of drink, and the question whether Miss Lush meant to deal with that problem trembled upon Lady Twickham's lips, but she held it back. Her poignant interest in the liquor question must be locked in her heart. Distrusting her own power to keep it secret, she turned abruptly and left the room. Miss Lush gazed after her in astonishment.

"Something's troubling her," said the shrewd Lush to herself—"I'm sure something's troubling her."

A FTER two hours with Mr. Wragg, Dick left the Bear and Cubs in a state of glorious exhilaration. He was flushed and high voiced, but tolerably sober, until the fresh air began to stir the fumes in his brain. Then he saw strange sights—to wit, streets heaving like a sea, and houses and people deliriously performing leap-frog. Setting down his feet very firmly, he did his best to face the madness with composure.

"The 'ole bloomin' place is tight," he muttered, looking round. "That's wot comes of mixin' drinks."

He stood for a little as if considering, his eyes fixed on his boot-toes. Eastward lay Paradise Court and Jenny—his wife, Jenny, who no longer ago than that very afternoon dared to have an opinion of her own when his wishes were concerned.

"An' tain't the fust time, neither, by a long chalk," he thought. "Serve her jolly well right if I was to scoot." He threw up his head defiantly. "Wonder 'ow she'd feel if I was to scoot, leaving 'er without no bloke of 'er own to wallop 'er ?" he asked himself.

Again he glanced eastward ; then wheeled, facing to the west. Towards the sunset was the open road for husbands with grievances. Westward he would go, taking the Ruggler Den on his way. It seemed years since he had been in that hall of divinity, and Tommy Binks and the rest of them would be spoiling for want of a stirring up.

" I'll let 'em 'ave it 'ot," he said, wagging his head and lurching off—" I'll let 'em 'ave it 'ot."

At a particularly congested spot he dived among the traffic in the roadway, bringing down on himself curdling speeches from a dozen drivers and the spume of horses suddenly reined up. Growling defiance, he proceeded miraculously among wheels and forelegs to come plump upon a constable who had watched the performance, wondering whether an ambulance would be necessary for the mangled man.

" 'Bout as bad as gettin' 'mong the dervishes," remarked Dick pleasantly, and turned to sing after abusive drivers of drays and cabs.

" Been drinkin'? " said the constable, looking as if he meditated an arrest.

" Qui' right," answered Dick, closing one eye. " Only a man not fit to stand could ever crosh there." And he went his way, reflecting audibly on the intelligence of the metropolitan police.

At the Baited Bull he refreshed himself with a " mother-in-law," and made enquiries as to the recent course of events in the neighbourhood. That done, he turned into the darksome court, the scene of many a grisly tragedy, climbed the black, familiar stair, and safely navigated the intricate passages in which a soberer man would infallibly have lost himself. Before the inner sanctuary he paused one moment to draw breath. The next, pushing open the door, he entered the dusky holy of holies, where sat the high-priests shrouded in pungent tobacco smoke. Through the murkiness he discerned half a dozen upturned faces, and had no difficulty in recognising those of Tommy Binks and Velvet Chick.

" Ho, ho ! " cried Dick, drawing himself up to the best of his ability. " 'Ows the bloomin' lot o' ye? Got a seat for a cove ? "

Some one kicked an empty whiskey case towards him.

" Nice easy-chair," said Dick, setting it against the wall. " Didn't expect to see me, eh ? " grinning on the company when he was seated. " Reckon ye thought I was a bloomin' 'tec. comin' to drink yer 'ealth. Well, give the lotion a name," clinking half a crown on the table. When it was named and procured he was asked what he had been doing with himself lately.

" Doing ! " cried Dick, waving his glass in the air— " doing ! " and he launched into a tale of public-house joys and social honours nicely calculated to make the mouths of listeners water. He was soaring beautifully in the regions of imagination, when all at once Velvet Chick let off a satirical shaft. Dick was just sober enough to discern that the insult was deliberate, and to express his resentment in suitable terms. Instead of apologising, Velvet Chick was at pains to drive the insult home ; and Dick's pulses began to beat up for retaliation. Had he been in his right senses he would have remembered that the man sitting opposite, with the bulldog jowl and the rolling, red eye was Chick of the iron fists—Chick, who took " sauce " from no one under the dimensions of a champion heavy-weight. Being three parts drunk and on his honour, he leaned forward and addressed the offender in the language in which Paradise Court frames declarations of war. At that Velvet Chick rose and shook himself, an unholy joy beaming in his purple face. Tommy Binks, who understood without explanation, remarked it would be inconvenient to have " a mess in the place " ; moreover, damage done to furniture would have to be paid for in cash. Chick said the point was important, and if Dick were agreeable they would retire for a little by themselves. So they went out together.

Ten minutes later Velvet Chick popped in his head to say he must be off now ; and an hour afterwards Dick was found, limp and gory, in a corner of the black court. As he was unable to give any account of himself, he was taken on a police ambulance to the nearest hospital, where the surgeon-in-charge remarked succinctly he had got something he shouldn't forget, supposing he recovered his wits, which was doubtful.

Now that surgeon was a good surgeon, as was proved by the fact that he was entitled to append half the alphabet to his name; but he made the mistake of taking his patient's recuperative power at the human average. So judged, Dick ought to have died at least a dozen times in various quarters of the globe; and he had no present intention of putting the hospital authorities to the expense of a funeral.

Next morning found him in full possession of his faculties; but when asked for the fragment of biography which would explain his misfortune, he absolutely declined to be pumped. There he was, to be treated for wounds and bruises if they liked; if they didn't like, he presumed they were free to chuck him—a form of hospitality with which he was not unacquainted. After some dubitation, however, he gave his address; and Jenny, tearful and trembling, hastened to discover the extent of her trouble.

"Thought you was a widow, maybe," said Dick, blinking up at her from among his bandages. "'Ow'd you like to be a widow? Nice piece of luck that 'ud be, eh!"

"Oh Dick! don't talk like that," cried Jenny, dropping on her knees beside his cot. "Who done it, Dick? tell me who done it."

Dick studied her wet face with evident satisfaction. He was not above vanity, and those tears were a tribute to his worth.

"Chum o' mine," he answered; "done it well, too, I must say. Only 'e don't want no talk 'bout it, 'cos 'e's so bloomin' modest."

She had been warned not to excite the patient, and had to leave without the knowledge she desired. But she could not help asking if he were much hurt. Dick replied he was merely having a rest, and expected to be home for dinner.

"Some of yer extry spiced sosiges," he said ; and meanwhile she might let Vincent Twickham know where he was detained. "P'r'aps want to see me on business," he explained gravely. "Besides, Lord Tapley an' 'ims good company ; an' they ain't none too lively in 'ere, 'cept when they're takin' away the corpses."

"Don't, Dick—don't," cried Jenny, hiding her face in her apron. "It makes me feel creepy and sick."

"That's wot comes of 'ome training," rejoined Dick. "If ye'd seen 'em 'eaped in Gov'mint trenches same's me, a stray corpse more or less wouldn't take away yer appetite."

Here the nurse in charge of the ward interfered. The patient was feverish and must not be exhausted ; and certainly all that was visible of Dick looked extremely feverish indeed. So, having bestowed a furtive kiss on the end of a bandage, Jenny left, drying her eyes as she went.

Some hours later a cab drove up to the hospital entrance, and out of it stepped Vincent and Tapley. Hearing them as they entered his ward, Dick rose to his elbow, and they could see he was trying to smile. Much talk being forbidden, they briefly expressed their sorrow at finding him on his back, hoped he would soon be well again, and asked how it had all happened. Dick glanced round cautiously to see there were no uninvited listeners.

"Fact is," he said, with a meaning twinkle in his eye, "I looked in at the Ruggler Den last night. Don't want to peach or nothin' like that, but me an' Velvet Chick 'ad a difference, an' I got this 'cos

I was boozed. A man's a fool to fight when 'e's boozed; though it's then 'e wants to fight most, the bloomin' silly!"

"Are you very much hurt?" asked Vincent, bending over him.

"A bit bashed, that's all," replied Dick. "Ye see, sir, I hadn't no chance, bein' boozed, an' 'im sober. But a man deserves wot 'e gets for not bein' able to take care of 'imself."

"Did Velvet Chick attack you?" put in Tapley.

"T'other way about," answered Dick, not without a note of pride. "Bein' boozed, I nat'rilly went for 'im."

"And how the devil did you manage to get boozed?" demanded Tapley. "Didn't you promise on your honour to keep sober?"

"It was all along o' Mr. Wragg," explained Dick meekly. "Bein' a bit in the blues towards evenin', owin' to the fog, I turns in there, an' 'e was mighty sociable, was Mr. Wragg. 'E's an honour to a public-'ouse, is that man. An' 'is missis, too, she wanted to know 'ow you was, both of you, an' she asked so pretty, I told 'em you was rippin'. An' Wragg up an' says we must drink your 'ealth, both of you, which we did; an' then we drank 'is 'ealth, and then 'is missis', an' then mine; an' the next thing was the kick up with Velvet Chick. Chick can use 'is fists."

"Evidently," said Tapley, looking hard at the wreck before him.

"I ain't never denied it, Tottie," rejoined Dick. "But you leave 'im to me, an' see wot 'appens."

"If you meddle with him again we shall be attending your funeral. But there, you're breaking the rules by getting excited. Lie quiet, or you'll be seeing black dogs."

"Yes," said Vincent pleasantly; "and we'll be

back to see you. Is there anything we could do for you?"

"Nothin', sir, as I can think on," responded Dick, as if considering. "The ole woman's a bit broke up 'bout seein' 'er 'usband lyin' 'ere an' not understandin' 'ow. If you was to come acrost 'er by accident, you won't say nothin' 'bout Velvet Chick. That sort of information don't do a woman no good."

Interpreting this speech aright, Vincent and Tapley took a hansom to Paradise Court, where Jenny was pricking her fingers (her eyes being dim and sore) on work for a Jewish tailor in the cellars below. Loo, who chanced to be scouting on the stair, retreated precipitately, sounding an alarm, a circumstance which guided the visitors to the right door. Jenny had just time to thrust her sewing under a corner of the bed and hastily brush the thread ends from her dress before the knock sounded. That knock made her heart stop; for she was certain they came to tell her Dick was dead. Vincent's hearty greeting and Tapley's cheery face reassured her, though she fluttered like a captured bird as she curtseyed and bowed them in.

Loo, meanwhile, had taken up a position behind the bed, whence she could observe the enemy, who were, of course, bent on mischief. Well meaning ladies she occasionally saw in that room; but men never came except to make "mammy" cry. So she watched narrowly as her mother set the only chairs for the visitors, wondering at the folly. But presently she became aware of a singular thing in her experience—namely, that the enemy spoke in a friendly and affable way about "daddy," saying he would soon be with them again, and, contrary to all expectation, seemed to have come for the express purpose of diffusing happiness. Taking heart of grace, Loo ventured out of her entrenchment. Then her astonishment received the finishing touch when, on rising to go, one of the gentlemen slipped a gold piece into her hand with no more ado than if it were a lollipop. Loo could only stare in bewilderment; such things were unaccountable. It was unaccountable, too, that her mother should be more put about by the kindness of these visitors than she usually was by the bullying of others.

NO folly in the world is more easily accomplished than that of assuming vicarious responsibility ; none has less expected consequences. At breakfast next morning Vincent became aware that the failings of two highly fallible men were on his shoulders, and that the burden might be troublesome. For the present, one lay safely in hospital ; the other was quarantined in a Spitalfields lodging-house ; but he knew they depended on him with child-like confidence for succour. There was no mistaking Dick's tone and look at the last interview; and from the first Ingledew exhibited a faith worthy of higher things. The situation was discussed with Tapley, who promptly agreed that the pair could not be abandoned after being led to hope.

"We're bound in honour to see them through," he said, "though the landing's dark."

Ingledew would have been removed forthwith to better quarters but for the fact that the deputy, in whose charge he lay, was in league to keep him sober, and could freeze his soul with terror in case of disobedience. But it was necessary to think out some scheme of deliverance, for he could not for ever be kept immured in a Spitalfields lodging-house, even for his own good. So they paid him an early visit, ostensibly to enquire after his health ; in reality to find out whether he wouldn't like to imitate the prodigal son, and return to his family. But at the mere suggestion a shivering terror seized him. For the love of God they would dismiss the idea from their minds. Oh! if they only knew how shamefully he had been treated by his family! No, no—they would not send him home; anything they liked but that.

The shameful treatment, it should be said, consisted of a patient, heart-breaking effort made by long-suffering parents to keep Mr. Ingledew in the paths of rectitude. In this pious enterprise a mint of money was spent. He had been sent to Australia, to America, to South Africa, with costly outfits and prayerful exhortations, which he promised, with tears, to follow. At the same time letters of credit were entrusted to his father's bankers and their agents for his use. Abroad, he was generally happy and prosperous, just as long as the letters of credit held out; then he mysteriously found his way back to England. To hear him relate the adventures of a stowaway was an enthralling experience. But it was with accounts of orgies in other lands that he captivated Alsatia. A tale of riotous festivity under a sensuous foreign moon was a trump which Ingledew played with unfailing success. How many glasses of MacTor it procured him it would be hazardous to state; for Alsatia treats generously in return for being amused.

" It was out there I got the taste for the stuff," he would say. " You find it everywhere—like bugs and Bibles. But I must say that what MacTor sends abroad is abominably crude." And with a " Here's to you," he would toss off his glass to prove his appreciation of the home stuff.

Once, and the last time, he returned home—it was a dramatic, never-to-be-forgotten moment—to find his mother's funeral train leaving the door.

" You did this," said his father hoarsely, staggering at sight of him—" this is your devil's work. You may come to see the last of her you have killed, but never let me see your face again."

Room was silently made for him in a mourning carriage. He was dishevelled by travel and reeking with brandy, drunk an hour before to fortify him against the meeting; but he went as he was, his father sitting by his side, bowed in grief and shame. When the final scene was over, he was taken firmly by the arm, thrust into a carriage, and driven home to the desolation he had made. In the evening his father took him to the station, put him in the London train, and bade him go—for ever. He went, and London swallowed him, as it swallows so many of his kind. Disappearing from the eyes of all who knew him, he went down and ever down in the vortex that sucks insatiably, till he reached the nethermost circle of hell.

How he lived is a mystery known to God alone, as it is a mystery beyond guessing to drawing-room moralists how multitudes of the children of folly and misfortune contrive to exist. It is to be presumed that every man who attains eminence in wrongdoing starts with a good spice of the old Adam; and that spice is the salt which preserves. But one day the salt loses its savour. Time and the devil, working insidiously, at last bring down their quarry, and one more soul goes to the Ancient of Days for judgment, leaving the preacher a moral. The toils were closing about Ingledew when Vincent came upon him.

" 'E won't last much longer, 'e won't, poor devil ! " Alsatia said, giving him something to speed him on his way. And once or twice it had occurred to himself, on awakening, ill and exhausted, from a debauched sleep, that the game he called life was nearly over, that the time was at hand when he would lie down in the dark like a stricken beast, and be thrust into a pauper's coffin, and dumped in a parish

pit with a dozen wastrels packed on the top of him.
Then he would rave for drink, crying out that he was
burning alive. When drunk he had the happiness
of the sot ; when sober he was utterly and unspeakably miserable ; for it was his misfortune to have the
remnants of a conscience, and a faculty of reflection
which was an instrument of torture. In that respect
he was at a bitter disadvantage compared with those
about him.

To prove that the new regimen disagreed with him,
he fell desperately ill.

" E'll die if 'e don't 'ave liquor," said the deputy,
a man deeply versed in the eccentricities of the toper—
" 'e'll die, that's wot 'e'll do, an' there'll be a hinquest
an' all the rest of the blessed mess."

So he was authorised to prevent the catastrophe ;
and Tapley was able to tell MacTor how his whiskey
saved the life of a fellow creature.

" There's worse medicine than whiskey," responded
MacTor, rubbing his hands. " I have more faith in
it than in drugs, and that's honest."

It took a protracted course of MacTor, as well as
some drugs, prescribed by Dr. Brinkley, a local
practitioner called in by Vincent, to get Ingledew
over the crisis. The same physician was put in charge
of Dick, who was removed to Paradise Court as soon
as the hospital people could be induced to part with
him. He had received more than he suspected
from Velvet Chick ; and the Twickham tonic was
pronounced rank poison. Dick protested vigorously.
He had been " bashed " before, and had never given
up his glass ; for the life of him he couldn't see
why he should give it up now, when he most needed
the cup that cheers.

" It's for your life you're doing it, my man," said the
doctor. " If you drink, you die ; take your choice.
There's a great deal too much alcohol in his system

already," added the man of science privately. "He's just ripe for a finishing inflammation. A man lives hard for twenty years, and in the twenty-first is aggrieved because nature so much as hints at rendering her account. Now while she is marvellously generous in giving credit, she positively declines to tolerate a bankrupt. In the end she is pitiless in exacting her own. Give our friend a quart of whiskey now, and you may send for the undertaker."

"I think you've frightened him, doctor," laughed Vincent.

"I have been thirty years in practice," returned the doctor gravely, "and I've never yet seen the man in his senses who, if it was put to him in the moment of danger, wasn't afraid of death."

"Isn't religion supposed to get one over that fear?" asked Tapley.

"I'm not a priest," answered Dr. Brinkley; "I only know that medicine doesn't."

"Not even in the case of doctors?"

"The man," rejoined the doctor, "who has put his hundreds under ground quakes none the less when his own time comes. But if physicians were sentimental they'd go mad."

"Well, well, doctor," put in Vincent, "you'll pull Goodman through."

"If you keep him sober," replied the doctor. "I don't undertake to heal wounds and fight the devil at the same time."

"A pretty pickle we've got into, Vin," remarked Tapley.

"Never mind," was the cheerful response; "we've got a new amusement."

For a while the new amusement took the form of daily visits to Spitalfields and Paradise Court, with a smuggling of such delicacies as the masculine mind and a knowledge of the patients' tastes suggested.

The incarnation of meekness, Ingledew took what he got with proper gratitude. Dick, on the other hand, cursed his fate and called the doctor names. To comfort him they brought newspapers, which Tapley, sitting on the edge of the bed, read aloud in defiance of orders. It chanced that the Black Watch was doing gory work in India, and Dick followed the course of events breathlessly.

"The Red 'eckle to the front, as usual," he would cry. "Tottie, let's 'ave the fightin'."

And when, in the account of the storming of a position, Tapley read how a certain major led the left wing through a devastating fire, Dick nearly leaped from his bed.

"My ole cap'n," he shouted—"my ole cap'n ; the man as is like you, sir ; the man as would lead through 'Ell if the colonel said so. Lor', lor', them there stickin' the blessed 'eathen, an' we 'ere ! " And Dick fell back in disgust.

Going to and fro about Spitalfields and the purlieus of Paradise Court, Vincent saw yet more of the horrors which appalled and yet fascinated him. At Tapley's suggestion, experimental rounds were made with Dr. Brinkley.

"Where I go, you cannot always follow," he told them. "I live and move and have my being in an element of perpetual epidemics. But where there's no infection, and you think your stomach's strong enough, you're welcome."

So they went where the shilling doctor goes, into the warrens of crime and vice and festering misery ; among the fetid dens, where the outlaw hides, and the outcast lies down to die ; through the black alleys, where the thief rests for a little from his labours, chuckling over his own exploits as described by an enterprising Press, and men talk robbery and murder as brokers talk per centages ; down to the cellars, where the famished can scarce guard against the rats ; up to the garrets, where the wail of misused infancy never ceases ; into pest-holes, where the living and the dead lie side by side, and the dead are stripped that the living may drink ; up and down regions in which the people, from the child of three to the old man of sixty, give their days and nights to infamy, and take their wages in defiance of law.

"My God ! if they were to rise !" was Vincent's thought.   But what he did was to enquire of the doctor if the rich, respectable sections of the community had any idea that all this existed by their side.

" None whatever," answered the doctor.   " The police, the hospitals, the slum doctors, the publicans, and a few philanthropists know.   The rest don't know and don't care.   They think that the heathen lives somewhere abroad, and has a black or a brown face, and dines on his next-door neighbour.   Now it happens that I've been abroad in my day, among blacks and browns in their chosen haunts, and I tell you the real heathens are in the heart of the capital of our country."

" Well, doctor, they don't kill and eat each other," said Tapley.

" True," returned the doctor ; " we just manage to keep them from that.   But I'm not sure they don't do as bad, or worse.   What you have seen may suggest what you haven't seen, what you daren't see, what you could not look on, though God in His infinite forbearance tolerates it.   Oh, the fools we are ! "

" Fools ? " repeated Vincent.

" Fools, sir, blazing idiots," rejoined the doctor. " We go wiping out frontier tribes and leave the slums to fester, frantically extending the empire,

while the heart of that empire rots—ay, sir, rots—
polluting the whole body politic. All the foreign
enemies in the world are not half so dangerous as
the inhabitants of our own slums. We subscribe
millions a year for the good of the heathen abroad,
who doesn't want us, and ignore the heathen at
home, who appeals for help. One of these days
we shall have our reward—ay, and God in heaven
will declare a just reward."

"And what would you suggest, doctor?" asked
Vincent, tingling strangely at hearing his own
thoughts from another.

"Suggest!" echoed the doctor. "Why, nothing, of
course. I know the value of snubs and sneers."

"You are the very man who ought to make
suggestions," said Vincent warmly.

"I'm a plain man," replied the doctor, "and have
enough to do in getting bread for my wife and
children, without meddling in affairs of government.
Still, I'll admit that ugly thoughts have been forced
upon me."

"As, for instance?"

"Since you ask, as, for instance, that if we don't
control the traffic in certain things, it will presently
control us."

"You refer to drink, I presume," said Vincent.

"I'm a candid man," returned the doctor; "I
refer to drink."

"And what would happen, doctor, if the drink
traffic controlled us?" asked Vincent.

"I am not here to draw harrowing pictures, but
to minister to the sick," was the answer. "But I
can imagine an outraged people rising in the might
of wrath."

"Well, thank Heaven! we've a standing army,"
put in Tapley.

"May God spare me the sight of rifle barrels

levelled at people contending for their rights!" said the doctor.

"Rights!" repeated Tapley quickly. "Pray, what rights have criminals and drunkards?"

"The right to protest against the system which makes them criminals and drunkards. But there, we're getting into an argument, and an argument never yet did any human being good. I shall be at the dispensary this evening from eight to ten. If you care to look in you shall see a little more of your fellow citizens."

"Just one word more, doctor," said Vincent. "You have referred to the drink traffic. Am I to infer you attribute what we have seen to drink?"

"Drink and misfortune, and what these entail."

"But why, in Heaven's name! do the people make such fools of themselves?" cried Tapley. "Nobody forces them to drink."

Dr. Brinkley shrugged his shoulders.

"A complete answer to your question would involve an enquiry into the causes of original sin," he said.

"And have you no cure?" asked Vincent, trying hard to curb his eagerness.

"Each of us, I suppose, has his own ideals," replied the doctor. "Mine is to alleviate suffering by the aid of science. Then I've sometimes thought I should like to be a millionaire."

"A very common wish," laughed Tapley.

The doctor bowed.

"A very common wish," he admitted.

"And if you were a millionaire, doctor?" said Vincent.

"Then, sir, I suppose I should be as ignorant or as indifferent as other millionaires. But if, by any chance, I obtained the knowledge I possess now, I should do something to feed the starving, to clothe

the naked, and, if possible, to hang the low publican and the Hebrew landlord. Believe me, even criminals and drunkards would be wonderfully improved if they could count on something to eat when they're hungry and an overcoat when they're cold. The first law of nature is to live ; these people live as they can. If they can't live one way, they'll live another ; and I can't help thinking it's to our interest they should live decently. And, let me add, it's no use tinkering their souls when their bodies are, so to speak, falling to pieces. A starving man doesn't care a red cent about hopes of salvation. But I can't expound. Am I to expect you at the dispensary ? "

The hour was awkward ; but Vincent was urged by a desire for knowledge, and Tapley was not yet tired of adventure. Therefore, while the West End dined, they studied a procession of the diseased and the deformed and the tortured.

" Well, what do you think of it ? " asked the doctor, when the procession ended.

" Horrible ! " said Vincent—" horrible ! "

And he went his way pondering many things, but chiefly what Dr. Brinkley would do were he a millionaire.

Book V

CHAPTER I

A T the end of three weeks Ingledew left Spitalfields for airier quarters, chosen by Dr. Brinkley,
Vincent and Tapley personally superintending the
removal. Having settled him in decency, and
warned him against intoxicants, they returned in a
righteous glow to Berkeley Square, to find Lady
Twickham, Lady Gwendoline, and Miss Lush together.
For interesting domestic reasons Lady Gwendoline
was at present avoiding society ; and Lady Twickham,
being tenderly solicitous, thought it her bounden duty
to devote her spare hours to her daughter-in-law. As
often as Miss Lush could be torn from her work, that
woman of genius made one of the company, and
vastly entertained the prisoner. So the three were
now in conclave, sipping tea and administering the
social universe. The intruders had, of course, to give
an account of themselves ; and Ingledew's name came
up by accident.

"Oh, by the way, Vin," remarked Lady Twickham,
" you promised to bring that unfortunate creature to
me. Why haven't you done it ? "

" He's been very ill."

" Where ? "

" In Spitalfields."

" In Spitalfields ! " cried Lady Gwendoline, pucker-
ing her brows.

" In Spitalfields ! " echoed Miss Lush, promptly
taking the cue.

"You are surprised," said Tapley; "but I assure you it is no uncommon thing for a man to fall ill in Spitalfields. It's the chief place in London for funerals—on the wholesale parish principle."

"Tom!" ejaculated Lady Gwendoline, in severe reproof. "And you've been there?" looking from her brother to her husband.

"And why not?" demanded Tom. "It's a variation on the usual amusements, and a jolly picturesque one, too."

Vincent looked anxiously at his wife, fearful of ugly impressions; but she was evidently receiving no impression whatever.

"I don't understand the taste," she responded, fluttering her laces, as if to shake off contamination.

"You wouldn't care to study the picturesque East Ender?" enquired Miss Lush.

"I should as soon think of studying beetles and toads," was the answer. "I've always been taught, and I believe in the teaching with all my heart, that it's best to let the poor and vicious alone. To go staring at them as if they were reptiles in the Zoo would only irritate them, I should think."

"Bless you, they don't mind," said Tapley.

"In any case, it would be unkind," rejoined Lady Gwendoline; "and as for doing them good, why, that would be like expecting soap and water to make a nigger white. The pater says they're incapable of improvement, and that, besides, they're necessary. I'm treading on delicate ground," smiling upon her mother-in-law, "but my firm conviction is that Providence has fixed a great gulf between the rich and the poor, the nobles and the proletariat—isn't that the word?—and that each should keep their own side."

"By Jove! Gwen," cried her brother, "if you haven't gone and got hold of a whole system of sociology."

"Naughty boy," murmured Miss Lush, chiding with her most bewitching smile—"naughty boy, to make sport of great problems."

"I beg your pardon, Miss Lush," he said; "I ought to be more careful in your presence, because you write books, and that sort of thing would boggle me completely. Shouldn't know how to begin, you know. All the same, I can't help thinking that men and women have a quite superfluous gift for devising problems. Now the only problem which bothers me is how to get the best out of life, and I can tell you," he added, with a wag of the head, "I find it deuced hard. It's not so easy as it seems, getting just what you want in this world."

"Except in fiction," suggested Vincent. "There all things are for the best in the best of all possible worlds."

"I don't know," said Miss Lush modestly. "Fiction tries to follow fact, though its shameful how fact sometimes plagiarises from fiction. The poor novelist invents a sensation, to find it forthwith repeated in actual life."

"Isn't imitation the sincerest form of flattery?" asked Lady Gwendoline sweetly.

"I should think Nature must welcome a tip," interpolated Tapley. "After all these measureless æons we hear so much about, she must be getting a trifle stale, poor thing! It's no joke, carrying on the world for a million years or so, all by oneself, so to speak."

"It's kind of the novelist to come to the rescue," cooed Lady Gwendoline. "Well, if I were a novelist, all the good characters left at the end of a book should be happy."

"Wedding bells," said Miss Lush, with the faintest of blushes.

"Yes; only I shouldn't have the course of love run

too smoothly, you know. To prevent insipidity I'd have plenty of obstacles, and despair, and tears, and sighs, and passionate vows, by people who could keep them."

"And at last general embracing," remarked her brother. "Very interesting, isn't it, Miss Lush?"

"Very interesting," admitted Miss Lush, smiling divinely.

"Only, you know, it's never the least like that in real life," pursued Tapley. "Nobody that I know has gone through a course of agonised affection to reach the altar. The romantic stuff we get in books is just so much tommy-rot; don't you think so?"

"When I see young men becoming cynical," interposed Lady Twickham, "then I know their turn has come. Who is it, Tom, dear?"

Whereupon the company laughed, Miss Lush feeling she would give half the revenue from her next book to have the correct answer to the question.

"The talk of novels, my dear Miss Lush, reminds me of your new book," her ladyship went on. "How is it progressing? Miss Lush," looking round impressively, "is deep in a new novel, and you won't guess what it's about."

"Love, of course," ventured Tapley, who knew as much of the bent of Miss Lush's genius as of Assyrian inscriptions.

"May I divulge, my dear?" asked Lady Twickham. "Thank you. Well, it's about the East End."

As she expected, there were cries of wonder and demands to be informed "how ever" Miss Lush came to choose such a subject.

"Miss Lush may choose her subject anywhere," Lady Twickham told them. "It's the art that signifies."

Miss Lush, with the light of joy dancing in her face, bowed to the dictum.

"By Jove! I'll read that book," declared Tapley, with emphasis.

"So shall we all," said Lady Twickham—"so shall we all. I mustn't be telling tales out of school. Wait, and you shall have a sensation."

Thereupon they blithely returned to Spitalfields and Paradise Court, whither, for the present, we need not follow them.

Another week's doctoring and general renovation in the matter of dress made Ingledew, it was thought, fit to be presented to Lady Twickham. At the appointed hour she studied him as she might have studied a natural history specimen exhibiting a rare and interesting disease, Vincent watching intently.

" Pathetic !" was the verdict when he was dismissed, with an expression of sympathy and an exhortation to shun strong drink—"pathetic ! What are you going to do with him ?"

"A hard question, mother," laughed Vincent. "The natural thing would be to send him home; but he says they won't have him."

"Renounced him in despair, I suppose," sighed Lady Twickham. "The Ingledews, I find, are well-known county people. Would it be any use my interceding ?"

"I don't think I should make intercession just yet," returned Vincent. "His father is, or was, very angry with him, and might decline reconciliation We must try to find out."

Lady Twickham looked pensively at her son. They were alone ; and many thoughts surged in her breast.

"It's a terrible thing when father and son are divided," she remarked plaintively—"very terrible. I fancy young Ingledew has exhausted his father's patience. By the way, how does your other *protégé* progress ?"

"He's out of hospital. Goodman's exceptionally tough. I think he must have as many lives as a cat."

"And he'll lose them all suddenly, if he doesn't take care. His wife informed me she hadn't the least idea how he got hurt. Do you know?"

"Oh yes; he told me quite frankly. It seems he fell out with a sort of professor of pugilism, ironically called Velvet Chick, and got the worst of it."

"Tipsy, I fancy," said Lady Twickham. "What is to become of him?"

"What is to become of them all, mother?" asked Vincent, smiling sadly.

She gave a little start, a question which she durst not put trembling on her lips. She knew what was in his mind; he guessed what was in hers; and each strove after an elaborate indifference, their thoughts surging and beating about the same hidden point. Accidentally Vincent mentioned Dr. Brinkley, repeating some of his statements.

"Does he know the East End well?" asked Lady Twickham, a strange sensation at her heart.

"He's been thirty years in the slums, mother."

"Then he knows. Does he ascribe any cause for the degradation and general wretchedness?"

"Yes," answered Vincent quietly. "He ascribes drink."

Lady Twickham's pulses beat painfully. She could hardly trust herself to speak; but she must say something.

"And do you agree with him?" she asked, and waited for the answer as for a death sentence.

Vincent looked at her, love and pity blended in his face.

"Any one who is honest must agree with him, mother," he said slowly.

A reeling sensation came upon Lady Twickham.

Though seated, she felt as if she were falling down a bottomless pit, and her face grew deadly white.

Vincent leaped to her side.

"Mother," he cried, "what is the matter? Are you ill? Have I agitated you?"

She put out a trembling hand to him.

"No, dear," she gasped; "it's nothing. I shall be well instantly."

THE secret was out. From Vincent's own lips Lady Twickham heard how he regarded the traffic which brought him his wealth ; and there fell on her a dark and horrible sense of a world suddenly gone wrong. With a beating and confused mind she sat down to think, her son's fateful admission and her husband's scornful comments ringing alternately in her ears. Alone amid the grandeur of Mayfair she bowed the head, pressing throbbing brows with her fingers. Her mother's insight told her they had not heard the last of Vincent's disapproval ; and picturing the shock of conflict between father and son, she quivered as one touched in the quick. What would Lord Twickham say? What would Vincent do? What would the world think?

Had Miss Lush been near she would have gone to that fountain of consolation ; Miss Lush being too far off, she went to Lady Gwendoline. Nothing could be more natural than that in any matter touching a man's honour or interest, his mother should take counsel with his wife. But in her commotion it had not occurred to the mother that the wife might not be as well informed as herself. So she plunged into the subject, like a fugitive hard pressed, taking the flood at a bound ; and instantly drew back in sharp self-reproach for the rashness. Lady Gwendoline laughed at Lady Twickham's delusion. Vincent would never be so foolish as to fly in the face of his own interests. They must really give him credit for some common sense ; the thing was too absurd to be discussed—quite too absurd.

A little later she rallied him on his "attack of conscience," and was amazed to find him look grave.

"I didn't wish to have you bothered just now," he said ; "but what mother has told you is true."

"True!" cried Lady Gwendoline. "You don't mean that, Vin—you can't mean it."

"I wish to God you were right, Gwen," was the reply—"I wish you were right."

"Why, of course I'm right," she said, affecting a gaiety she did not feel, for there was a disconcerting look in her husband's face. "What can have put the silly idea into your head ?"

"What speaks nothing but truth. But there, *you're* looking serious, and that's absurd. We ought to be thinking of other things, little duck."

She nestled close to him, and he caught her in his arms.

"Oh ! you're too violent," she panted. "No—not that, Vin," she corrected quickly ; "but you are so dreadfully in earnest."

"Even in loving my wife," he said, smiling in her face. "Well, she'll forgive me. Her gown is not the least crushed. Upon my honour."

"You ridiculous boy," she said, daintily tapping on the bridge of his nose—"you very ridiculous boy."

What is whispered in the closet in the morning may in the evening be shouted from the house-top. Quite naturally, news of Vincent's vagaries reached Tapley. Then it percolated through the Earl of Wegron to MacTor ; and in due course Miss Lush flew to Lady Twickham for contradiction of the evil report. But none durst speak of it to Lord Twickham ;

so the co-partner of destiny went on his way, masterfully planning for the coming generations.

Apart from Lady Twickham, MacTor took Vincent's apostasy most deeply to heart. For a whole day he went about muttering to himself, "I won't believe it ; I can't believe it ; it's absurd."

He consulted the books of the MacTor Distillery Company, and found the delinquent the registered proprietor of a quarter of a million of the capital. MacTor trembled, thinking what might happen.

"Godsake, if he was to kick up ! " he said to himself. " I wish fools weren't created to vex man in business. But Vincent can never mean what is attributed to him ; I won't believe it."

And, indeed, it was not until Tapley had been closeted a full hour with his brother-in-law, and reported Vincent's ugly frame of mind, that the gravity of the situation was realised.

For the first time in his life Tapley gave way to excitement.

"Hang it, you know, Vin," he protested, in the private interview, "you really mustn't be going off the rails like this ; it's preposterous."

"Going off the rails ! " repeated Vincent. " I'm trying with all my might to keep on the rails, and it's the hardest work I've ever had. You know what we've seen."

"Great Heavens ! " cried Tapley, his amazement not wholly smothering his disgust, " you don't mean to say you're dwelling on that ! We have seen a lot of fools whom all the powers in the world could not wean from their folly."

" We've seen more, Tom."

" What, pray ? "

" Respectable people pressing the folly on the fools ; that's the rub."

" Upon my honour, I don't understand you, Vin."

"If I must be explicit, we have seen great and powerful organisations, in which some of us are interested, engaged with all the resources of civilisation in sending people post-haste to Hell. There, the truth's out!"

"Oh! I say, that's getting sulphurous. I'm no theologian; but I understood Hell was abolished."

"We won't quibble. So far as I can see, ruin is Hell and Hell is ruin. Take your choice of words. If you have come through our late experiences without being forced to the conclusion I have named, then I envy you."

"Vin," said Tapley solemnly, "if I had for a moment guessed this possibility, I'd have seen you hanged before going to the slums with you, ay, and Goodman shot for his sins. He's at the bottom of it all. Confound him! if he had kept away from St. Edmund, or been left to his deserts——"

"I should still be in a state of happy ignorance," broke in Vincent.

"Anyway, this wouldn't have happened," said Tapley.

"If the end were seen from the beginning, I daresay many of us would steer a different course," rejoined Vincent quietly. "But you mustn't blame Goodman. I am sure the promulgation of the truth would be the very last thing he would think of. You may take it he had no evangelical designs on me."

"Vin, I don't like to hear you talk like that—upon my soul, I don't," said Tapley, with fervour.

"Then let's talk of something else," replied Vincent. "Goodman and Ingledew are on our hands. You'll help me to see them through."

Tapley departed in a perturbed and anxious state of mind. Nor had the Earl of Wegron and MacTor happier thoughts when Vincent's extraordinary ideas were repeated to them.

"This will never do," said the Earl decisively.

"Never," repeated MacTor—"never. Can't you bring him back to reason, my lord?"

"Gad! I don't like the job," said the Earl. "It's a delicate enterprise, you know, teaching your son-in-law sense. You're the very man yourself, MacTor."

"H'm," said MacTor, "and how am I to set about the thing?"

"Must feel our way gingerly," rejoined the Earl. "Suppose, now, you were to get him quite informally to luncheon, in your private room, and my son and I would drop in accidentally, you know. If the three of us can't bring him round, he's lost."

"Capital!" cried MacTor—"first-rate! See what the diplomatic mind does."

So Vincent casually visited the MacTor offices, and was casually invited to luncheon ; and the Earl and Viscount Tapley dropped in accidentally according to arrangement, and were included in the luncheon party. It was a merry luncheon ; the talk sparkling as gaily as the wine they drank. The meal was nearly over when the Earl put a simple question about business.

"You'll excuse me," he said apologetically, "but you know, MacTor, I'm on the Board, and the law's getting deuced strict about the duties and responsibilities of directors."

"Quite right, too," replied MacTor promptly. "Directors are for directing, not merely for pocketing fees as a reward for amusing themselves with other people's money. What amazes one is the leniency of the law. If all had their due, half the Boards in England would be serving their country under the sign of the Broad Arrow. But so far as we're concerned, if our accounts were to be investigated to-morrow I think you might sleep with an easy mind to-night. I have just been looking into things a little, and since we're all in the same boat, I'll confess sales were never so satisfactory as they are now. That's what comes of dealing in an article that the public want and the public must have."

"Good!" said the Earl ecstatically. "You'd raise the spirits of Job himself."

"If I had the proper spirit to ply him with," answered MacTor playfully. "Don't you think, now, that if Eliphaz the Temanite and his friends had brought a drop of good whiskey to that famous conference, it would be worth all their misapplied wisdom?"

"Probably," admitted the Earl. "Might have taken the edge of Job's sarcasms—softened the old chap's tongue, so to speak."

"It softens tongues to-day," said MacTor.

"And I drink yet higher success to it," added the Earl, raising his glass.

While the Earl and MacTor ran on thus, they watched the effect on Vincent; but for all their jocularity his face remained immitigably grave.

"I wish I had more of your shares," pursued the Earl, with a meaning look at MacTor. "But I suppose they're not to be picked up?"

"Not exactly picked up," answered MacTor. "They're rising, you know—constantly rising; and shares that are going up are not to be had in the bucket shops. With the next dividend I think you may expect a brisk little spurt. Lord Twickham thinks we can go at least two and a half per cent. better than in our first year, and you know how mouths watered over what we paid then. I know we can, and add to the reserve, besides carrying forward a pretty little tit-bit. Oh! the shares are healthy—perfectly healthy, thank you. I wish I were as lucky in my holding as some of my friends."

At that moment Vincent looked up, and MacTor

smiled congratulations upon him. Remarking that the room was uncomfortably warm, Vincent rose, and made a pretence of looking out of the window. Then he examined pictures of the MacTor Distilleries with which the walls were adorned, Tapley joining him in the study; and all the while the Earl and MacTor exchanged nods and signs.

"Why the deuce doesn't he talk?" the Earl seemed to say; and MacTor seemed to respond, "Why the deuce doesn't he?"

"By the way," remarked Duncan carelessly, looking over his shoulder at Vincent, "when the next Liquor Bill comes up in the Commons, I hope you'll scorch the teetotalers. I daresay you forget there's no trade on earth has to cope with so many prejudices as ours."

Swinging half round, Vincent looked down into the rubicund face turned towards him, a sudden glow in his eyes.

"From what you have just been telling us of the prosperity of the Distilleries, my championship is not in the least likely to be necessary," he said.

Something in the tone made MacTor spring to his feet.

"Godsake! what's this?" he cried, plucking at his red beard.

"A thing not worth discussing, Mr. MacTor," answered Vincent. "Only I'm glad your shares are going up, as I may possibly realise."

"Realise!" gasped MacTor.

"Realise!" repeated the Earl. "Why, Vin, what on earth does this mean?"

"A man may wish to realise on a rising market," said Vincent, and deftly dismissed the matter.

CHAPTER III

ONE thing the interview put beyond doubt to the Earl and MacTor, that however foolish or fantastic Vincent's notions might be, his defection was a fact which could not be laughed away. Both felt he had devised a crisis, and was sweeping others with him.

"It's an ugly business," remarked MacTor, when Vincent and Tapley had gone off, leaving their elders together.

"A very ugly business," admitted the Earl gloomily.

"What's to be done about those shares?" said MacTor. "If he throws them on the market, it'll give us a nasty shake."

"What's to be done with the whole blessed business?" demanded the Earl. "It's a strange thing, MacTor, that those who have everything mortal can wish won't be content, but must for ever be after something else, worrying themselves and others."

"Yes," said MacTor. "But—

> "'Human bodies are sic fools,
> For a' their colleges and schools,
> That when nae real ills perplex them,
> They make enow themselves to vex them.'

It's Bible truth. Robbie never hit the bull's-eye cleaner in the centre. Now, here's Vincent Twickham has all that a man can covet: wealth, health, youth, position, the loveliest wife in creation—oh, yes, she is! although she's your daughter—in short, the most glorious possessions and prospects, public and private; and he goes on like a disappointed old maid preparing to make the best of the next world because she's lost her chances in this. I'm dumbfounded—tut! I'm disgusted,—that's what I am! I thought better things of Vincent. I wonder if his father knows? Don't you think we ought to find out? Lord Twickham's the man to nip these eccentricities in the bud."

"Um!" said the Earl, pursing his mouth. "We must be cautious how we rouse Rhadamanthus. I might mention the thing to him incidentally, as an absurd and incredible rumour which had reached me."

"Do; and, for God's sake, be quick," urged Mac-Tor. "I'm not at ease about those shares. You never know what a man that's daft on principle may do. I wouldn't have the Distilleries upset just now for all the principles in the world."

Scarcely had he done speaking when Tapley returned to them, excited and gesticulative, saying that Vincent had gone to his father, and there would be the deuce of a tempest.

"I tried to prevent him," explained Tapley,—"to reason with him. But he was as stubborn as ten mules; couldn't have believed it of him. 'I owe it to my father to tell him all, and at once,' was all I could get out of him. They're together at the office now."

The Earl whistled; MacTor stared with a blank face for a minute, then smiled inanely.

"Well, perhaps on the whole it's best," said the Earl.

"Perhaps it is," added MacTor dubiously. "I hope they'll take care of those shares between them. It would be devilish to have them thrown on the market just when we're getting ready a ripping balance-sheet."

Thrice a week Lord Twickham gave some hours to the city. Knowing it was "city day" with him, Vincent went straight to the Twickham offices to unburden; but, finding his father engaged with people of importance, he proceeded to his own room. Opening his desk, he drew out some papers; but the idea of work was the bitterest self-satire. He rang for *The Times*, but could not fix his mind even on the report of a rival brewery; so he lay back in his chair staring blindly at the ceiling. What was this that was wrenching his life so suddenly and so cruelly? It seemed that a thousand electric needles were setting his brain on fire. He could not think, and might have fled in terror of madness, had not the head clerk appeared opportunely to say his lordship was disengaged. The man would have shown the coming chief in; but Vincent preferred to go to judgment alone.

"Thank you, Binns," he said. "You are busy. Don't trouble."

On entering the presence, he noted instinctively that his father's face wore an expression of lively satisfaction. Lord Twickham, who was bending closely over some papers, greeted his son cheerily, without looking up. Vincent thanked Heaven for the chance to collect himself. All at once Lord Twickham pushed the papers from him, and swung round. He was smiling, for he had just brought a great scheme to a successful issue, and his heart was beating pæans of joy; but at sight of his son's face, his smile gave place to a look of startled astonishment.

"Good gracious, Vin! what's the matter?" he cried. "Are you ill?"

If a man about whom the universe is falling in pieces be ill, then Vincent was very ill indeed, though he strove to appear at ease.

"No, not at all," he faltered; "but, if you are

not busy, I have something important to say to you."

" Important ! " repeated his lordship. " Portentous, rather, to judge by that face, Vin. Have a glass of wine."

Vincent gulped the wine, and felt better.

" Now," said his father, " we will talk. What have you to tell me ? "

" I hardly know how to begin, sir," returned Vincent, in a voice he scarcely knew as his own. " It's about the subject on which we had some conversation once before."

Lord Twickham pressed an electric button at his desk-side.

" We are to be engaged for some time," he told the clerk who appeared. " See that no one is admitted."

Then, turning back to Vincent, " Now tell me all, and don't be flurried."

" Yes," said Vincent, bracing himself desperately. " I preferred you should hear it from myself, rather than from any one else."

" Has any one else heard of it, then ? "

" Well, Gwen and Tom know a little, and I think Wegron and MacTor. That's why I have come direct to you."

" That's what I should expect of you, though I should prefer no one else in the secret."

Secret ! the word made Vincent shiver. Great Heavens ! did his father not understand that it was no secret, but a fact, that was already setting tongues wagging ? A secret ! rather a thing to be borne abroad on tempests.

" You may remember the talk we once had," said Vincent, feeling as if the floor were collapsing.

Lord Twickham brought the tips of his fingers together, and raised his eyebrows a little as he answered :

"Yes, I remember that my son disapproved of my life-work."

"Not that, father," cried Vincent, with a sudden pang. "Not that."

"Not disapproval? Well, then shall I say my son didn't relish the position to which he had the misfortune to be born, though millions envy him? Let me put it like that. Now I hope he comes to tell me he has changed his mind."

Vincent's heart thumped so high in his throat that he gasped for breath, and a giddy, sickening sensation came upon him.

"On that occasion," he managed to get out, "I left you, determined to see with your eyes, and—and I cannot."

For a moment his lordship stared without winking.

"You cannot," he said then, "you cannot, and you have come to tell me of your failure? I will not ask whether the effort was seriously made; but it is necessary I should know what the confession portends."

"Father," cried Vincent piteously, "will you force me to go through it all again? Since that talk with you, I have suffered indescribable agony. God is my witness how I tried to follow your wishes—to blot the thing that displeased you from my mind. But it would not go—or, rather, it went for a little, to return with fourfold force. What I have seen haunts me like a horrible nightmare!"

"There are many disagreeable things in a world not specially designed for fastidious people. What have you seen?"

"Havoc and misery unmentionable," replied Vincent, becoming fluent from sheer desperation. "Homes ruined, children forsaken, and filthy or beaten because they would not take quickly enough to crime; men and women wallowing in foulness;

good living made impossible ; the sick and dying laid where you would not put your dog,—the whole an inferno past imagination, and, worst of all, father, worst of all, was the conviction that three-fourths of the appalling tragedies were due to strong drink ! "

" Did you go in search of all those things ? "

" On the contrary, I tried to shut my eyes to them ; but they were forced upon me."

" Ah !—by whom or what ? "

" By what I have told you and a great deal more that I couldn't tell you,—by what goes on daily and nightly in the hells of London. I had no idea such things existed ; I could not conceive that our riches were the harvest of ruin and shame and misery."

" Vin," answered his father slowly, " you have done what none before you ever succeeded in doing : you have made me sorry for myself. Think of that in time to come. When you were announced, I had just put the last touch to one of the biggest schemes ever devised in connection with the Brewery. Not dreaming of the results of my evil deeds, I saw my son and my son's son in the far future carrying out my plans, and I fancied them praising my foresight. Now mark the fitness and timeliness of the reproof. In the moment of my triumph the son who was all my hope steps in to rap me over the knuckles and shiver my fool's paradise to atoms. If a man wants to lay up disappointment for himself, he will give his days and nights to schemes and plans for others. Ironic fortune will see he is requited."

Vincent was dumb. There swept upon him a tingling shame for himself—a thrilling pity for the strong man suffering so acutely. He was sorry, not so much because of what his father said, as what he looked and what he was. In all such contests the personality's the thing ; and Lord Twickham's personality bore all before it. Had Vincent obeyed his feelings he would have yielded unconditionally, begged to be forgiven, and promised never to speak of the subject again. But a fire had been kindled in his heart which would not be quenched; it burned even in that moment of trial and rebuke. Lord Twickham did not understand a quickened conscience, and could not therefore appreciate the scruples of his son. He would never have allowed his honour to be impugned; but he would have trampled mercilessly on the quixotism which hesitated in matters upheld by law and approved by all the codes of honourable men. Vincent, on the other hand, told himself his father did not know, could not know, the havoc, worse than pestilence or death, wrought by drink.

"Oh, sir! you don't know what it is as I do," he cried, recovering his speech.

Lord Twickham laughed bitterly.

"No," he admitted, "probably not. I'm sixty-five and you're not yet half that age. I devoted my life to the rearing of a fabric which has moved some men to envy and many to admiration. Coming to it with a discernment and knowledge beyond experience, you are able to condemn offhand. For forty years I have been aware that multitudes drink more than is good for them; but it never occurred to me I was responsible for their folly. You, studying the matter for forty weeks, open my eyes and correct my error. I congratulate you on your acuteness, even if it be displayed at the cost of filial feeling."

Vincent shrank as if the lash were upon his bare shoulders; and, indeed, lash never cut so keenly through quivering flesh as his father's words through Vincent's soul.

"I beg of you not to take that view," he pleaded.

"I don't see how I am to avoid it," returned his father. "You see, I make and sell more beer than any other man living. You tell me beer is a great destroyer ; therefore I am the most reprehensible of the many monsters engaged in the ruin and degradation of the people. But we shall gain nothing by going over that ground. The question is, What are you to do ? "

To that question Vincent had no coherent answer. He had thought vaguely of legislation, that most futile of expedients for benefiting a people, and, suddenly pressed, blurted out his crude thoughts.

" Induce Parliament to abolish public-houses ! " said Lord Twickham, his voice rising and his face hardening. " Go to your party leaders and ask their minds on it. Bah ! the Government would not last a week that so much as proposed to tamper with the public-houses ! I think you have overlooked one element in the case, that the supply of beer merely answers the demand. The people want beer, and get it. If you don't supply it, somebody else will ; and where's the benefit ? "

" A reasonable supply rationally used," Vincent was saying, when his father broke in impatiently.

" You talk of reason where men's tastes and appetites are concerned. That implies gross ignorance of the world."

" What fills me with horror," rejoined Vincent, " is the manner in which drink is pressed upon people who would be better without it. You know better than I the thousand and one devices employed in tempting drinkers to their ruin. At every corner stands the public-house flaring the latest lure. You tell me the foolish have themselves to blame ; but, father, are we right in taking advantage of their folly to enrich ourselves by ruining them ? "

He spoke quickly and excitedly, drops of sweat standing on his forehead.

" I was not bred a casuist," answered Lord Twickham shortly. " But suppose you throw me

overboard and take the drink traffic in hand, have
you calculated the cost?"

"I have been too perturbed to go into particulars,"
replied Vincent.

"I would count the cost if I were you," said his
lordship. "It is always well to see whether the
game is worth the candle, to observe some proportion
between effort and aim."

He unlocked a private drawer in his desk, and
drew forth a note-book.

"Your share in the evil is more than nominal,"
he remarked, consulting it. "And the cost might
surprise you. In addition to the shares in the
Brewery, I find you hold a quarter of a million in
the MacTor Distilleries Company."

"And those I intend to sell," said Vincent.

Lord Twickham put the book back in its place
and locked the drawer. Then he rose, the look of
the angry Titan in his face.

"It's out of my power to prevent you from being
foolish," he said, looking down on Vincent. "But
I will not permit you to destroy or impair any concern in which I am interested. If you were fifteen
years younger, I would cane this nonsense out of
you, if the hide came with it. As you're a man,
I cannot well do that. But there is something I
can do, and that is to keep you from tampering
with properties which you never helped to create,
and apparently are unable to appreciate. Mark
me! you are to hold your hand at that. I began
my work when I was young; and now that I am
old, so long as it pleases God to spare me, I will
go on. If you will not help me (and I think I can
do without you), all I ask is that you do not wantonly
raise your hand against me, not because I fear it, but
for the sake of decency. I am ignorant of your plans,
for you do not honour me with your confidence."

"Oh, father!" cried Vincent, his face streaming, "I have no plans beyond a wish to refrain from violating my conscience."

"That means you cannot take any active part in the work of the Brewery. Very well. I will see that your name is erased from the list of directors. And I may add that when you want to sell your shares, a buyer will be ready for them."

CHAPTER IV

SCARCELY was the interview ended, and Vincent once more shut in his own room trying to reconstruct his universe, when Lord Twickham telephoned for his broker. Promptly as responds the world to the call of the great, the man of speculation arrived.

A person of fashion and figure, the first impression he produced was that of being an exceeding credit to his tailor. But nothing could be more egregiously wrong than to mistake him for a common dandy. He dressed well, partly because he liked dress, but chiefly because millionaires, who alone can afford to neglect fashion, like to see a distinction made between themselves and their agents. Even in his attire he had an eye to business. His name on 'Change was great, for it was said that what he did not know about speculative finance was certainly not worth knowing ; and he was the confidant, which is much more than being the friend, of lords and plutocrats. Therefore what was confided to his ear lodged there. He was the very last man to whom, under vows of secrecy, one would impart the secret that was to be blazed abroad. He had Lord Twickham's entire confidence, which was worth thousands a year.

"I wanted to see you at once on rather important business," explained his lordship ; "that is why I sent for you instead of writing. I must tell you that my son has got some inexplicable idea into his head about the evils of drink."

" A temporary delusion, my lord," suggested the broker softly. " The young and ardent are subject to such things."

" Yes, exactly. They come like teething and the measles ; but until Vincent gets over the trouble, one can't be sure what may or may not happen. At present he speaks of relinquishing his part in the Brewery and the MacTor Distilleries Company."

The broker gently hinted that such folly was indeed inexplicable.

" That, you know," continued Lord Twickham, " may mean some shuffling of the cards. A man suffering from a fit of conscience is like a man in the delirium of fever—hardly responsible for his actions. My son, as you may remember, holds a considerable number of both Brewery and Distillery shares. Now, what I wished to see you about was to instruct you to buy instantly on my account any shares which may be offered in either company, in blocks of two hundred or over—less will not matter."

" Will your lordship give me written instructions ? " asked the broker.

" Certainly."

And thereupon the order was written.

The broker dismissed, Lord Twickham sent for MacTor, disappointing several callers who were waiting for a word in his ear. MacTor responded with the alacrity to which financial considerations inspire saint and sinner alike. The Earl of Wegron accompanied him, and for family reasons was admitted. On entering, they instantly divined from Lord Twickham's set face that a battle had been fought. How the issue went they could only guess.

" Well," said Lord Twickham, when the hasty, constrained greetings were over, " this is a pretty business, isn't it ? "

" You refer to Vincent," said the Earl, feeling

almost for the first time in his life what nerves and emotion meant.

"Yes, I refer to Vincent. You know, of course, what has happened?"

"Dimly," rejoined the Earl—"very dimly and imperfectly. He had luncheon with us to-day, and the subject came up; but he declined to discuss it."

"Ah!" said Lord Twickham, secretly pleased that Vincent had not babbled; "I suppose he thought it best to bowl me over first. There are many things besides charity which begin at home. Well, it devolves on me to announce my son's decision. I regret to say he is dissatisfied with us."

MacTor turned as pale as was possible for one with so much old port in the blood.

"God bless my soul! what can possess him?" he cried.

"I think you can guess," answered Lord Twickham.

"That little devil of perversity men call conscience," put in the Earl—"that's what possesses him. It's a little devil that grows insolent with pampering—insolent and censorious. When men's conscience hangs about the neck of their heart, as the saying is, they're in a bad way. By Heaven! I think the play-actor was right when he said it makes cowards of us all."

"The play-actor's truths don't help us much at present," remarked MacTor ruefully. "What I can't make out is how Vincent has gone astray."

"It's my fault," said Lord Twickham.

"Your fault!" cried the others together.

"Yes. You may remember that one day at luncheon in the country the doings of that rake Goodman formed the topic of conversation. His wife was an old servant of ours, and Lady Twickham pitied her. For her sake Tom and Vin were despatched to play the Good Samaritan, and all the rest flowed from the incident. It looks," addressing MacTor, "as if destiny were catching us in our own gin."

" Destiny's the cruellest thing in existence, as I know to my cost," said the Earl emphatically. " But I fail to see why Vin should turn sentimental in matters of business,—the world would soon go to smash on that basis."

" I would not have you judge him too harshly," returned Lord Twickham, smiling faintly. " I see the reason, though I cannot admit its validity. Without consulting me, he went to the slums, poor boy, for weapons to overthrow our assailants. Had I suspected such a thing he should never have paid them the compliment. But he went, and he saw more than was good for him. We all know there are elements in the drink traffic which must shock a sensitive mind. MacTor and I must shut our eyes and drive ahead, regardless of the unpleasant things by the way. We cannot afford to stay because our wheels happen to be deep in mud. But even we feel sometimes that the mud is very deep and very dirty and slimy. It was too deep and dirty for Vincent, because he came to it in his green state. He has not yet realised that such things must be ; his instincts are fresh. Let's be just, and own his motives are pure. His fault is to harbour a conventional morality, a morality which would make earth an Eden if all men were wise and strong and pure and continent. They are not, and never will be ; consequently mere conventional morality is like water in a sieve. Other duties are put upon men, and my own plan has been to pursue my own ends in my own way on my own responsibility. I take the risks. Vincent needs hardening,—that is all."

"It's unfortunate his scruples should get the upper hand just at this juncture," said MacTor, thinking tremulously of the shares. "They may do substantial harm."

"Don't be disturbed on that account," returned Lord Twickham; "I have taken the necessary steps to protect our interests. I may tell you that every share which Vincent sells (supposing he sells any) shall be bought at market price; therefore you need not fear a slump."

MacTor could have embraced his lordship. So long as the Distilleries were safe fools might practise folly to their hearts' content.

"Our material interests are secure, I think," pursued Lord Twickham. "What will suffer are a father's feelings, and they are not quoted on 'Change. Well, let them take such doctoring as events prescribe. Meantime, you will do me the favour to keep this matter as quiet as may be."

"Certainly," said the Earl.

"Certainly," echoed MacTor. "Vincent's probably not beyond reason yet, and the Brewery and Distilleries are safe."

Lord Twickham bowed.

"Absolutely," he said—"absolutely!"

Almost as these words were spoken, Vincent passed with an uncertain step through the main office to the street door.

"His lordship has the Earl of Wegron and Mr. MacTor with him, sir," explained the faithful Binns. "Perhaps you would like to go in, sir?"

Vincent paused a moment, a fierce desire to rush in and overwhelm them in their sophistries rising within him; but he crushed it down.

"Not now, Binns, thank you," he answered, moving on.

At the door he hailed a hansom, and next

moment was swallowed in the stream of London's traffic.

" I don't know what's up," said Binns confidentially to his assistant ; " but something's the matter. You should have seen his face as he went out. Take my word for it, something's happened."

CHAPTER V

ISTORY records but a single instance of conscience undeviatingly followed, and the straight line ends in a cross. Common men waver and deflect, beat about and tack, often foundering in the clashing currents of the world. Vincent was only human, with all the human weakness of divided love and defective vision and frailty of purpose. In paining his father he lacerated himself, and his anguish was a kind of frenzy. As he whirled along, neither seeing nor hearing the surge and din of London's traffic, a raging remorse burned in his heart. What was he to set himself against his father, the man whom the whole world honoured for probity, admired for energy and fixity of purpose? Nothing, less than nothing. Certainly vanity or self-sufficiency had no part in Vincent's thoughts. If by some great deed, some unheard-of sacrifice, it were possible to prove his loyalty, he would have leaped at the chance; but mere renunciation, misunderstood and contemned—what was it? In that moment of distraction the most pitiful of all pitiful things.

And yet, so complex is man, he had before him, in that very instant, harrowing pictures of pollution and squalor and iniquity; and there sounded in his ears, in sullen undertones of thunder, the hoarse, stifled cries of the wretches out of whose ruin, moral and material, he made his wealth. Great God! was it so? Could it be that he, or any one dear to him, could be the devil's instrument in this wholesale destruction of humanity? He shrank, gasping, as if his gold poured upon him in a molten stream.

All at once the cab stopped, and he was startled by a voice from above. Looking up, he saw a pair of bloodshot eyes in a bloated countenance peering intently at him. The purple face, set in the black frame, appeared menacing and malignant, though its owner was politely, if huskily, asking for further directions. On engaging the cab, Vincent had said "Charing Cross," with no reason for going there. Recovering himself, he now said "Piccadilly." The face disappeared, and the cab went on. At Piccadilly Circus he dismissed it, and walked to his club—the experiences of that midnight when Tapley and Goodman and he were gaily in quest of knowledge rising to his mind. How much had happened since then! They had got knowledge, at least he had, and never had he found anything half so bitter.

In the club he ran through the comic papers, flinging one after another aside in disgust. The jokes were meaningless; the pictures silly or blasphemous. Life was not an idle jest, in spite of the buffoon and the caricaturist. The Master of Life never jests, and though His tolerance is unexampled, it is not quite inexhaustible; and the poor little Merry Andrew, the grinning ape of quips and cranks, is quietly snuffed out at last. Though blessed with a native relish of humour, Vincent turned from the woeful pleasantries as from sickening sweetmeats.

With the serious papers he fared no better. Of what interest or concern, to one tortured by eternal realities, were those canting party "leaders," those long, frothy columns about the nothings of to-day, which would so speedily give place to the nothings of to-morrow, and these in turn to the endless nothings which would follow?

To-morrow, and to-morrow, and to-morrow ; brief candle lighting the way to dusty death ; walking shadow ; poor player strutting and fretting his hour— and then heard no more. Strange thoughts for a fashionable club-room !

Rising like a man from distempered dreams, Vincent strode out, exchanging absent-minded salutations with friends, who looked a second time at his white face. He would have a game of billiards. To billiards he must give an undivided attention, and so snatch a moment's ease from his torment. But he handled the cue as he read the newspapers, with dancing nerves and a mind distraught.

His opponent, being greatly his inferior in skill, expected to lose, and, amazed at winning by long odds, wanted to know " what was up." The greenest tyro, indeed, might have beaten Vincent ; for his hand trembled so that he missed unmissable strokes, sometimes missed the balls entirely. That made him reckless, and he signalised his inability by tearing the cloth.

" No use," he said, trying to laugh. " The gods of billiards have forsaken me " ; and paid the reckoning.

Finding no rest in the club, he turned once more into the street, with no idea whither to go. Standing irresolute at the door, he was assailed by cries of " Keb, sir, keb ? "

" All right," he said to the nearest crier ; and gave Ingledew's address, with instructions to drive fast. If only he had wings, or were like the lightning, he might get away from his troubles. Twice he remonstrated with the driver for crawling, though more than one zealous constable thought of a summons for furious driving.

" Gent looks as if 'e'd bin 'avin' a drop extry at arternoon tea," chuckled the cabman, in expectation of being able to extort a double fare.

Ingledew was found, poring in a chastened spirit over a battered classic, retained none knew how.

"These old chaps are so serene and restful," he explained apologetically ; "they present so complete and refreshing a contrast to our flurried existence."

"Do they? Oh yes, of course they do," returned Vincent, who would at that moment have paid any price for serenity and restfulness.

"Yes, indeed," pursued Ingledew, glad that the subject interested his patron. "You see it's Plato," holding up the book. "It may surprise you to hear I once showed an aptitude for philosophy, and Plato's the king—fallen at present on strange company, you'll think. I have just been reading a passage about the pleasures of memory, and a seraphic account of the loveliness of wisdom. It almost makes one long to be wise. It is very sweet."

"I daresay," said Vincent, with a dry mouth.

"Yes, very sweet," added Ingledew. "Yet let none imagine that Plato is all honey and sunshine. May I read you this—as a sort of penance? Thank you. I assure you it cuts like a Damascus blade."

And he read :—

"'*This is the justice of Heaven, which neither you nor any unfortunate will ever glory in escaping, and which the ordaining powers have specially ordained. Take heed therefore, for it will be sure to take heed of you. If you say I am small and will creep into the depths of the Earth, or I am high and will fly to Heaven, you are not so small or so high but that you shall pay the penalty.*'

"That gave me a nasty sensation. Oh dear me, Mr. Twickham, how pale you are!"

"Am I?" replied Vincent, feeling that his pallor was deathly. "I have been warm, and have perhaps cooled rather quickly. It's nothing."

"You are really very pale," persisted Ingledew.

"I have just a drop of what the doctor allows me. Permit me to share it with you."

Running to a cupboard, he produced a small bottle.

"You see it's but a drop," he said, holding it up to the light.

"Like Mercutio's wound, 'tis enough," replied Vincent, smiling. "If you please, I will help myself." He poured out the third of a glass of MacTor's best, and drank it. "There, that will bring the blood back," he said, with a wry mouth.

"It's not worth putting back," said Ingledew wistfully, again holding the bottle against the light. "Mr. Twickham, I drink to your happiness."

"Well, I must be off," was the abrupt response. "I'm glad to find we're getting along so nicely, as the doctors say. Accept that for current expenses," laying two sovereigns on the mantelpiece.

"As a loan," returned Ingledew, an expression of pain in his face. "A loan, mind you, Mr. Twickham, and nothing more. I have demeaned myself in numberless ways ; but, please God, I will pull together and repay. It's a loan."

"A loan, of course, old fellow," said Vincent. "God knows when the best of us may be in a strait. You would help me at a pinch, wouldn't you ? "

"With my life," answered Ingledew quickly, "with my very life. Mr. Twickham, I think I could pray you might one day need help."

"That were unkind of you," was the rejoinder.

"Don't misunderstand me," said Ingledew impressively. "I am wretched, but I am not ungrateful. No one ever thought of doing what you have done except my poor mother, and, may the Great Judge pardon me, I broke her heart—killed her ! Oh ! her death is on my head as clearly as if I actually shed her blood."

"We won't talk of that," said Vincent. "It's useless recalling unpleasant memories."

"Ah!" cried Ingledew tragically, "they recall themselves. They are like vipers which secretly coil about the heart, and sting and sting in the dead of night till you think you must go mad. As we make our bed, so we must lie on it, says the proverb. Pah! that is nothing. The Greeks were right about Nemesis. That grisly huntress of souls dogs the steps of every man, watching to see him trip or commit himself. When he does she is upon him, and down he goes to Hell. I have been there—and Dante hasn't."

"You believe in Nemesis?" said Vincent quietly.

"Shall a man doubt when his hand is burned or his heart torn?" was the response. "As we sow, so shall we reap. My God! it is terrible, terrible!"

Vincent bowed his head.

"Terrible!" he repeated, almost inaudibly. But the next moment his head was erect and his face alight.

"You forget the compensations," he cried, "you forget the compensations. What would you have but to reap as you sow? Would you sow wheat and reap tares? God does not disappoint in that way."

Ingledew was prepared for an argument, but Vincent was not to be detained. With the great text ringing in his head he went off:

"*Whatsoever a man soweth, that also shall he reap.*"

"Thank God for that," he said in his heart. "Thank God for that."

CHAPTER VI

FROM Ingledew's quarters he went direct to Paradise Court, again instructing his cabman to drive fast. But the pendulum had swung back, and the tumult within was now a madness of exaltation.

"Whatsoever a man soweth, that also shall he reap," he repeated, his heart rising in a kind of lyric ecstasy, so that streets and people became phantasmally unreal, or rather, vanished from his consciousness altogether. The stoppage of the cab recalled him to earth.

"How much?" he asked, on stepping out.

To the experienced eye regarding him from above, he seemed a pliant, agreeable person, so the owner added a hundred and fifty per cent. to the legal fare, and grinned benignly on being paid without a murmur.

"Wish I 'ad more of the same sort," thought cabby, turning to go.

As he groped his way up the dark stair to Dick's aerial chamber, Vincent's nostrils were tickled by a savoury odour of cooking meat. On a landing half-way up a boy stood sniffing enviously, and far in the dusky remoteness there was a glint of white, as Loo darted to alarm the garrison. Jenny, curtseying profoundly, welcomed Vincent at the threshold. If Jenny possessed cloth of gold, she would have spread it every inch for him as a carpet.

"Are you alone, sir?" she asked, looking into the twilight dimness below for Tapley.

"Quite alone, Mrs. Goodman," he answered. "I have come to see your husband by myself."

Entering, he found Dick vigorously engaged upon an underdone beef-steak—the doctor having that morning rescinded the injunction against high living—and congratulated him on his prosperous condition.

"Thank 'e, sir," said Dick, wiping his mouth and drawing his sleeve across the swollen veins of his forehead. "Doctor's orders do make a cove peckish. Don't mind, sir, my attendin' to business?"

"Business by all means," returned Vincent, smiling. "Go ahead."

Jenny, who but half an hour before came in with the steak, was still "tidied up," as if for an errand; and, indeed, she presently went out again, taking Loo with her, to visit a sick woman somewhere in the lower regions. It was, in fact, the crone who had once cursed her with all the curses of Paradise Court, and now lay dying in dire hardship. Jenny referred feelingly to the old woman's plight, and would have given an account of the case from the feminine point of view, had not a glance from her husband warned her of the bad taste of such a thing. So she curtseyed and went.

"You mustn't mind 'er, sir," said Dick, when the sound of her descending footsteps died away. "I never did see 'er ekil for takin' on 'bout things. Seems to me she could do the worryin' for a whole bloomin' street. There's allus sunthin' a-troublin' 'er. Now she goes off to see if she can't keep an ole woman from dyin'—yes, sir, an ole mug as once went for 'er till she cried. I ain't like that. Them as kicks me 'ad better look out for their shins. That's my plan."

Vincent reminded him of the Scriptural injunction to return good for evil, and love our enemies.

"Love our enemies," said Dick, with a vicious cut at the steak. "Mighty fine, when ye ain't got nuthin' to forgive. Wonder 'ow many does it when their toes is tramped on? 'Minds me of our ole Scotch chaplain. One night 'e'd be tellin' us to love our enemies same as you, an' next mornin' we'd be off to fight 'em, with 'im prayin' Gawd to 'elp us to smash 'em up. Queer kind o' religion, sir."

Vincent owned the fairness of the deduction; but persisted in thinking Jenny deserved praise, not blame, for her efforts to ease the last moments of a departing sinner.

"I believe it's one of the things she'll never regret," he said.

"P'r'aps not," responded Dick dubiously. "But I once let a man go without a wallopin' when 'e deserved it, an' I ain't forgiven myself yet. There's some things as it's a man's dooty to do, an' when 'e don't do 'em 'e's sorry for ever arter. I'm sorry 'cos that man's twelve foot under ground, an' I can never 'ave another chance. I'll tell you something, sir."

And with a comical look he imparted a secret which made Vincent stare. The half-raw beef-steak, it appeared, marked the initiation of a plan for the total and ignominious discomfiture of Velvet Chick and his satellites of the Ruggler Den.

"Just give me three weeks of this," said Dick, nodding over his plate, "an' see wot 'appens."

"But you're not going to fight again," protested Vincent.

"P'r'aps not," returned Dick. "Likely I'm goin' to take Velvet Chick's sauce lyin' down. It's to be 'Please walk over me, Mr. Chick, an' never mind my feelin's; I'm the meekest cuss you ever seed.'"

He laughed satirically.

"Listen, sir. With enough beef-steak an' a bit practice o' nights, if I don't pepper that crew blind the doctor can draw my teeth an' feed me on pap."

"You remember what Lord Tapley said."

"Wot did 'e say, sir?"

"Why, that if you fought Velvet Chick again he'd be attending your funeral."

"That was boozed," said Dick, giving his mouth a wipe and pushing away the empty plate. "That was if I was boozed. I reckon Tottie ain't just the man to whoop if t'other thing 'appened. I ain't afraid of Chick, though I once was. I've faced the guns o' that 'ere enemy as we should love, walked right up to 'em when they were blazin' away 'otter than ever Velvet Chick's fists could go. Sometimes I wonder 'ow I've lasted so long, an' death gettin' so many chances at me. Gawd alive," he cried, his mind aflame as it reverted to the past, "the 'eaps an' 'eaps of men I've seen dyin', good men too, an' me left to dance the bally out!"

"It must be a terrible thing to see men dying," said Vincent, shrinking gruesomely at the thought.

"Don't know as it is particular," answered Dick. "It makes you feel a bit queer at first, p'r'aps, to see yer chums spin on their 'eel an' throw up their 'ands an' drop groanin' an' 'ollerin'; but ye see you want to get at them as does the shootin', an' that saves the feelin's. As to the actool dyin', why, that's done quiet enough."

"I suppose so," said Vincent, feeling his flesh creep. "Goodman, have you ever thought what comes after?"

"Arter wot, sir?"

"After death."

"The Scotch chaplain uster bum about it, not as I could ever foller 'im quite. It's wot comes before death that gets me on toast. 'Ullo, Loo!"

The child, lighter of foot than her mother, had

bounded in upon them ; Jenny followed presently, her face very white.

" 'Ow's the ole woman ? " asked Dick.

" Dead," replied Jenny, turning away. " Dead."

" Drunk last night," said the philosophic Dick, " dead this mornin', dumped in the black 'ole to-morrow ; that's 'ow the world goes, sir. A suppose our time's comin'."

Vincent rose suddenly to go.

" Pray we be ready," he said, and hurried away.

CHAPTER VII

AT dinner that evening Vincent talked with resolute gaiety; but when he left the table, having eaten little and scarcely touched wine, he was glad to escape alone to the library. Throwing himself limply into a chair, he looked unseeingly round the book-lined walls, the forced mirth passing in a tragic sigh.

Save for the solemn ticking of a clock on the mantelpiece the hush of death was on the room. But the sweet influences of the sanctuary were not upon Vincent. The subject which would not give him peace burned, an incandescent point in his mind. He thought of his father's sore disappointment, of his mother's startled eyes, of the amazement of his friends, then of the tragedies he had seen; and he buried his face in his hands, groaning aloud. While he was thus bent, the door opened noiselessly, and his mother stole in on tip-toe. Hearing the slight rustle of her dress, he looked up, and rose to meet her, trying his best to smile. Without a word of greeting she ran forward, and kissed him passionately on the cheek.

" I have heard," she whispered. " I have heard."

The room and all that was in it seemed to reel about him.

" You have heard ? " he responded hoarsely.

" Yes, dear, I have heard."

His dry mouth crackled, and it appeared to himself he was suffocating.

"What does father say?" he managed to get out.

"Sit down, dear, and I will tell you. You are troubled. There!"

He obeyed, and she sat on the arm of the low easy-chair beside him, her hand on his shoulder.

"Tell me, is he very angry?" he said, looking up pitifully.

"Not angry, dear," she answered softly; "only sorry."

An exquisite anguish wrung Vincent's features.

"And you, mother, are you sorry too? Don't hide the truth, whatever you do."

For answer she took his head in both her hands, pressing gently on the temples, which she could feel throbbing.

"My poor boy, how hot your head is!" she said. "You are working yourself into a fever."

"It burns like a furnace," he replied. "But that's nothing. Mother, are you sorry?"

He gripped her hand as in a vice, crushing the rings so that they cut; but she shut her lips to stifle the gasp of pain. She would hardly have protested had her fingers been cut to the bone.

"Are you sorry, mother?" he repeated. "Tell me that."

"I cannot but be sorry when anything divides my son and his father," she answered in a low voice.

"Yes, yes! But the cause," he cried, "the cause!"

He was looking into her eyes as if his eternal salvation depended on her reply. They were filling with tears, and the sight maddened him.

"You understand," he went on, his voice rising in supplication. "Oh, mother, tell me you at least understand."

Will not the mother who bore him understand a

man? Yes, she understood, and sympathised, and pitied.

" I understand, darling," she murmured, clasping him round the neck, " I understand."

" Thank God ! " he gasped, " thank God ! " and fell back, as one relieved of great pain.

" I wish I could help distressing you in this way," he went on presently, unconsciously patting her cheek. " Mother dear, you know I would give my life for you ? "

" Yes, dear, I know."

" And for father, though I vex him so much. I know he is deeply pained."

" He has only one son left, dear," came from trembling lips. " He has only you, Vin."

The tears which she tried to keep back, gushed in spite of her ; but she held up bravely. " Think what it is, dear, to have but one son, and he disappointing the hopes built on him. Fate could scarcely wound with a keener arrow than that."

" It's keenest for me," he cried, leaping to his feet. " It's keenest for me. I would do anything to please my father, or to save him an instant's pain. God knows I would. I have tried with all my might to drive what I saw and heard from my mind. But I cannot, I cannot. Oh, mother, think what it is to be growing rich upon the crime and misery of blinded victims ! We call them foolish, and use their folly in sending them to ruin and destruction—because it pays. Such things must carry a curse. I wish it were not so ; but I feel, and the feeling grows stronger, the more I see, that the drink traffic is a traffic in souls. Mother, it is awful ! "

Going up to him, she gently took his arm.

" Don't agitate yourself so, dear," she said ; " we will talk of it again. Perhaps we may find a way out. There, some one is coming."

As the words were spoken the door opened, and Lady Gwendoline walked in. She understood the situation at a glance.

"What!" she cried, in a tone of bantering rebuke, "worrying about that horrid old subject again? Really and truly, Vin, you mustn't be such a donkey."

Vincent affected to laugh playfully.

"Nothing like a downright compliment to shake the foolishness out of a man," he responded. "But we weren't worrying, Gwennie."

"Glad to hear it," she rejoined. "Mightn't we have some music or cards or something? This place"—glancing round—"always oppresses me. The spirits of the great dead are not gay company. Come!"

CHAPTER VIII

ALL the pressure of which a roused and scandalised Society is capable—and it is immense—was forthwith put upon Vincent. Of his friends, a few, the Earl of Wegron, Tapley, and MacTor among them, condescended to reason with him. Of the rest, some cajoled, some censured, and others ridiculed. At Lady Gwendoline's instigation, duchesses, countesses, and other dazzling dames fluttered about the backslider, delicately wheedling, pooh-poohing, and burning the incense which stifles apostasy. When that feminine mode of argument comes into play, logic, we know, retires abashed. Since Adam set the example of graceful surrender, no man has ever quite successfully withstood the wiles of coaxing Eves.

Vincent had the defect of being intensely human. It was certainly very sweet to find so many fair and noble creatures concerned about his social redemption. Had they taken him in time, had the iron not been allowed to get so deep into his soul, he might have been enticed back among the lotus-flowers. As he showed a disposition to go his own way, after the manner of the Twickhams, Fashion, altering its tone, asked cynically if it were really a case of conscience, or merely of lunacy, and decided by an overwhelming majority for lunacy—at all events, for delusion of an almost incredible kind.

The folly, however, they might have overlooked;

the bad taste they could not forgive. There are many methods of going astray, said the men of knowledge, and Vincent's was surely the most idiotic of them all. With his resources he ought to have hit upon something picturesque, something which would really titillate the Epicurean imagination. If he aimed at sensation, then his invention was assuredly a very lame dog. Faugh! he had no ingenuity in his obliquities. Gilded youths, with great talents and slender purses, wished to Heaven they had his chances. Eh, Lord! millions to go to the devil on, and to sneak thither by a back alley! It was a stain upon the whole order of the elect.

Guilty Vincent was, and obstinately guilty. When one of the censors, growing bold, derided with more insolence than was becoming, he remarked incisively on the wisdom of attending to one's own business. The retort was taken as proof that his malady was incurable. So the apostles of pleasure turned away, grimacing, to give place to other counsellors.

Of these, the chief, and by far the most impressive, was the Right Rev. Josiah Tinkle, D.D., Lord Bishop of Blockley. Vincent had escaped to Twickham Towers in hope of peace, and thither, by grace of Lady Twickham, Dr. Tinkle followed him. The bishop was sorely distressed over Vincent's aberration (revolt he had first called it, but the word was harsh), and, as spiritual adviser to the family, felt it his duty to speak a word in season. He was able to do it soothingly and convincingly, because his creed had long harmonised the principles of profit and loss and of the Sermon on the Mount. Though zealous for religion, he never forgot the beneficent influence of Consols. You cannot have a strong Church without a full treasury; nor a full treasury without a prosperous commerce. In England's commerce beer represents many millions sterling. Ergo beer is one of the most potent of spiritual agents. You perceive how perfectly he was armed for the encounter ; and, indeed, the great Blougram himself was not better equipped for " argumentory purposes," when, radiant with wine, he and Mr. Gigadibs pushed back chairs, and watched to " see truth dawn together "—an experience for philosophers.

What's your reward, self-abnegating friend ? That was Blougram's pill ; it was Tinkle's also, only he hid it deftly in ecclesiastical jam. He honoured the man of tender scruples—none more ; but, with all the authority of a prelate, justified the ways of honourable merchants and traders in suiting the world which " gives us the good things." Blougram again, you see. Vincent had had an unpleasant experience, had witnessed scenes too harrowing, perhaps, for untried nerves. Well, the bishop was able to assure him that, in the mysterious dispensation of Providence, such things must be. Who's to blame ? The question was asked, so that the answer was already given in the tone.

The enthusiasms of youth are beautiful, beautiful, repeated the bishop, dwelling unctuously on the word. Youth is the period of fervour, of heaven-high aspirations, and noble if impossible ideals. It is in youth we rapturously build castles in the air, and resolve to create new Edens out of trampled, weed-choked gardens of the world. Dr. Tinkle rolled his eyes ; all that was very beautiful. But alas ! change comes with the years. Time damps and saps fervid hearts, and with accumulating knowledge, men, very reasonably, come to accept what is, and cease to yearn idly for what might be. Thus they are fitted for the practical affairs of life.

But did the early flame burn for nothing ? By no means, exclaimed the bishop, by no means. God has so arranged the world that there is good in everything—in the fire of youth, no less than in the hard common sense of middle age. Unless wilfully quenched, a subdued light continues to illumine—the inside of a bushel, thought Vincent.

The problem is not perfection. An inscrutable Wisdom has ordained men shall not see perfection on earth, so that they may long for Heaven. Therefore, to avoid shipwreck here below men tack and turn—in other words, proceed by fair and reasonable compromise. There's a great instinct which guides mankind. Even the Church, admitted the bishop, cannot afford to be wholly spiritual. To maintain her place and influence she has to cultivate a certain worldliness. As for the drink traffic, said Dr. Tinkle, touching the tender spot with his most sympathetic finger, doubtless it is open to gross abuse—like religion, and liberty, and wealth, and power, and other priceless things. Nevertheless, we ought to be grateful for all God's gifts ; and for himself, he was much too thankful for the general good to condemn the whole for a part.

Vincent felt the blood beginning to tingle in his veins ; for he had the Twickham aversion to sophistry.

" I think, my lord, you are a shareholder in the Brewery," he said, his eyelids contracting as he watched the effect.

The bishop bowed, smiling. Yes, Lord Twickham had been good enough to allot him some shares, and he had never had cause to regret the investment. Vincent shut his lips hard, because it is unseemly to put a bishop to confusion with ill-bred truths about love of dividends. But his private thought was, " If the Church talks like this, who is to blame the tavern ? "

Contriving to turn Dr. Tinkle over to his mother, Vincent slipped out unperceived for a whiff of fresh air to purify the vitiated atmosphere. It was a golden autumn evening. The fragrance of ripe fruit and cut corn mellowed the air, and the far-off music of reaping charmed the ear. Quitting the shrubbery, in which he wandered at random, Vincent entered a park, whence he had wide views of wood and field, and men and women idyllically engaged in harvestry. Almost as far as he could see, on every side spread the Twickham lands, and below the gigantic Brewery sent up its pillar of smoke, black against banks of rose-red cloud.

For a while Vincent stood gazing wistfully upon the fair rich country over which people said he should one day be lord, and at the clustered town, lying, as it were, in the hollow of his hand. But he had no thought of lordship. As he gazed, a strange, new sensation came upon him. It was as if his heart became suddenly aware of unsuspected sentiment in the familiar scene, as if impassive nature, melting sympathetically, were surprising him with her confidences.

What did it mean? Walking a little farther, he spied a moss-grown stone at a tree-foot and sat on it. The sound of the reaping machines ceased, and he saw the workers slowly disappear hither and thither. How many harvests had been gathered upon those plains! A thousand years the bountiful fields had smiled to the autumn sun ; and should smile at the end of a thousand more. His heart leaped. How would the world look after another ten hundred years? If he could but see what the centuries had in store ! Perhaps he should see. Giving his imagination flight, he lost himself in reverie. The west flamed blood-red ; but he did not see the miracle of colour. Dusk fell, and he was still dreaming ; but presently in the dim light he was startled by the noise of footsteps. Springing up, he met his father.

"Oh!" he said, his heart very near his mouth.

"Oh, Vin, is that you?" asked his father, with well-feigned lightness. "Don't you think it's getting rather chilly to be admiring the scenery? Besides, the night's upon us. A particularly fine sunset, wasn't it?"

He did not tell that, having missed him, he came out in search of Vincent.

They returned to the house, talking indifferently. At the great door Vincent lingered a moment, looking into the soft glow which suffused the western sky.

"How peaceful it is!" he said, turning with a sigh.

His father's quick ear heard.

"What makes you sigh, Vin?" he asked.

"Oh! did I sigh? I'm sure I can't tell why; but it's nothing."

Yet in the silence of midnight Lord Twickham was thinking of that sigh. Taken in conjunction with the look on Vincent's face, there was something in it which haunted him like a premonition.

NEXT day the family returned to London. Lord and Lady Twickham would have prolonged their stay in the country, but Vincent suddenly announced his intention of getting back to town, and they could not resist the desire to be with him. He was very restless, though striving to be composed, and moody, though trying to be cheerful. Often they would look at him furtively, acute distress in their hearts; but neither referred to the cloud which darkened about them, seeming to blot out the face of Heaven. They would at least refrain from harassing him in the crisis of his disease.

Others were less considerate. Again and again MacTor and Tapley and the Earl of Wegron renewed the attack, sometimes descending upon Vincent singly, sometimes all together. He bore with them good-humouredly, because, unlike Dr. Tinkle, they abstained from saccharine morality. MacTor, indeed, boldly upheld his own practices, and those of the trade generally.

"It's do as we're doing or take a back seat," he said; "and a back seat's much too cold for me, thank you. People go to the devil on drink, you say. Well and good. People go to the devil anyway; if not on drink, then on love or religion, or something else equally excellent. You see, that's the natural destination of the majority; and I tell you quite frankly, Mr. Twickham, the scheme of universal salvation by denying the thirsty is just pure lunacy. You can't so much as make a beginning with it. Besides, man, consider the scandal of the thing. Here's your father, the greatest man of the age in his own line, and you go throwing stones at him. Is that becoming? Tut, tut! have a glass of champagne, and let nonsense cease!"

The Earl of Wegron was cynical according to his habit; but Tapley was guilty of real earnestness; and Lady Gwendoline, offended by her husband's persistent fatuity, was also zealous in opposition, and that hurt Vincent only a little less than the suffering face of his mother. The eloquent and ingenious Lush, too, put forth her rarest art in coaxing him out of his heresies. And he would have given them all the joy of escorting him back to the fold, but for the fact that he had been swept past the turning-point.

The trade heard, and wondered with a feverish, profane wonder. In every bar-room in the kingdom " Young Twickham's revolt " was an absorbing topic of conversation. What was to be the end of it? How did old Twickham, the unlucky beggar, feel? And how was he likely to chastise the offender? These were the questions which roused ten thousand speculative intellects to wild activity. The young scoffed ; but seasoned topers, taking a more serious view, rose unitedly against the presumption of the new generation. What right had Vincent Twickham to give himself virtuous airs? Was he better than the father who had always given them beer? If his conscience was out of order, let him dose it with the family ale ; and let him also beware how he tried to deprive honest folk of their legitimate drink.

These were Mr. Wragg's sentiments ; and, in his utter disgust and dejection, Dick could not help echoing them. For a whole evening the pair debated the matter; and so deeply was Dick affected, that, in the small hours he staggered into Paradise Court, hiccoughing tragically over the insanity of those who don't know when they're in clover.

"Gawd!" he exclaimed to a figure reeling past in the darkness; "Gawd! 'e is a bloomin' fool!"

The figure stopped, swung round, advanced a step, retired erratically, and finally brought up, swaying against the blackness of the wall. By its dress a sober person could have told it was a woman.

"'Oo's a bloomin' fool?" it demanded huskily.

"'Im!" answered Dick, waving his arms. "'Im!"

"Better mind 'oo yer a-insultin' of," said the figure, and reeled on.

"Well, 'e is a fool!" reiterated Dick. "Goin' back on beer (hic); 'e is a blasted fool!" and he too disappeared.

When the Ruggler Den heard, Tommy Binks, though the reverse of demonstrative, danced a gleeful jig, calling for drinks all round. Oh, ho! what had he so often told them? Fate would yet knock the stuffing out of Goodman, for all his insolent snobbery and yarns of aristocratic pals, and they, bless them! they should be present to see the sport!

Meanwhile, Vincent spent days and nights of raging fever in battle with himself. A hundred times he was tempted to give it up, and return penitently to beaten ways. Perhaps he was wrong, perhaps all his friends were right. It might be his brain was breaking down, and that what he called principle was, as MacTor expressed it, mere lunacy. In any case why should he be a martyr? What would it benefit him if every slum in London were sober and decent? And at that craven question would come the swift stinging revulsion. The wronged and the wretched were calling to him for aid. Their wail was ever in his ears, the vision of their misery ever before his eyes. Could he like a selfish coward turn away from them? No: win or lose he would go on; and those who now sneered and condemned would one day understand and appreciate. Rising one morning, ghastly after a sleepless night, he finally acknowledged to himself the impossibility of going back.

Meeting Dr. Brinkley in the course of the day, he stated his decision, and was wrung by the hand

"You understand what it means?" said the doctor.

"I ought if thinking about it helps," answered Vincent.

"Then," cried the doctor, "in God's name go ahead! Go straight ahead. Only avoid rashness. You will need money, much money."

Vincent thought that difficulty could be got over.

"That· is good," said the doctor. "I am not of those who run down money. It's a great blessing: in your scheme, a necessity as well as a blessing. For what have you to do? Not to make war on public-houses. That would be like dribbling rose-water down a sewer-grating."

"My head rings, doctor," said Vincent. "Put the project into words."

"Yes, I daresay the head rings," replied the doctor feelingly. "Heads must do that if the world is to be kept from going to smash. As to the project, you are to engage in a great process of weaning, and you will often fail and be faint-hearted, for the sot is not easily turned from his sottishness, and the powers arrayed against you are strong."

"And the start, doctor?"

"Well, you must above all things be practical. Food and clothes are always conducive to happiness. Therefore feed and clothe—substantially. Don't imagine that tea and a currant bun, some shop-soiled calico, and a sermon on the beauty of holiness, will make people content and prosperous. Half of them would throw your tea in your face, and roar down your sermon—provided they condescended to notice it. Attend to the body first, and the soul will be the easier of access. Having fed and clothed, you might give a thought to the lodging. Creatures made in God's image should not be expected to thrive in sties where beasts would sicken and die. If you could signalise the start by hanging a thousand cent. per cent. landlords of the seed of Abraham, you would be doing the community a service. The Jew's a fungus that saps slum life. He's there, however, faster than a barnacle to a ship's bottom, and he's not to be dislodged for the present. All you can do is to see he doesn't draw too much blood with his pound of flesh. Then having seen to the lodging, you will come to your central idea—that of providing wholesome rational pleasure. Give the victims of our social and economic systems a chance of indulging in innocent diversions : give them music, give them literature, give them song and dance ; but for Heaven's sake don't give them sermons! And for the rest God bless you! He will understand."

Vincent's heart swelled ; tears of joy came into his eyes.

"So be it," he said, grasping the doctor's hand. "So be it. Let doubt end ; let action begin."

It began with the stroke which Lord Twickham anticipated. One morning 'Change rang with the news that fifty thousand MacTor shares were offered—and instantly bought, as it was discovered, by Lord Twickham. The intelligence sent a thrill to the uttermost ends of the kingdom.

CHAPTER X

THE evil that was feared had come, and must be faced with what nerve God vouchsafed. Imperiously ignoring the disgrace, Lord Twickham went about with shut lips, disdaining so much as a reference to his son's rebellion. Lady Twickham brooded and wept when she had a chance; and loyally divided her ministrations between the husband she worshipped and the son who was part of herself. And Lady Gwendoline, being straitly forbidden to think of outside concerns, willingly turned inward to matters of more intimate interest.

As for the rebel, he gave to his wife a tenderer attention; to his father and mother a deepened affection. Their way could no longer be his way; ahead he could see wide and ever wider divergences; but that only made the communion of hearts closer. People wondered how the masterful Lord Twickham tolerated a weak-kneed son, forgetting that if the son were weak-kneed there should be no talk of toleration. They expected to see Vincent punished as an example to all rebellious sons and faddists; and lo! in secret he seemed to be cherished with a particular fondness, as if wrong-doing were the golden key to the affections.

The rebel, on his part, was equally puzzling. Though the sensation of his revolt eclipsed all other sensations, he could not be induced to discuss it; nor had he a word of vilification for the camp he forsook. To the water-drinkers his reticence and aloofness were a sore disappointment. When they came, serenading, to claim him as an ally, he told them he had plans of his own which he desired to work out in his own way, according to his own lights. Whereupon they began to surmise he was missing the road to Heaven after all. Their worst suspicions were strengthened when they found him holding stubbornly by old friends. He clung to Dick Goodman as notorious a scamp, they all knew, as any within the four-mile radius, though Dick threatened to kick a missionary sent to demonstrate the evils of beer-drinking; and he coddled Ingledew, a weed that could never be cultivated into a flower. No, he certainly was not to be counted as an ally; rather a paradox come to perplex.

It was soon proved that their ideals were not his. Under counsel of Dr. Brinkley, who knew the slums by heart, he laid his schemes; and wholesome amusement, not deliberate reform, was the guiding principle.

" The glaring defect of nearly all existing systems of temporal salvation," said the doctor, " is that they are tediously and offensively didactic. Too much preaching, sir—too much preaching and too little practice, that's what's the matter with us. If you are to save, avoid the preachy as you would avoid the plague."

Therefore, instead of a new preacher, there arose a new professor of pastime. From a Hebrew landowner he purchased, at not more than twice its value, a site on which to realise his dream—the Metropolitan Hall of Recreation. And intense was his joy in studying plans, in conferring with architects and builders, in ranging the world for suggestions, and in watching the burrowing for foundations for his palace of delight. Here was something tangible with which the practical Twickham spirit could content itself; and the fact braced like mountain air.

It was also the cause of infinite gossip and curiosity. The thirsty and unwashed flocked to see the riven earth, speculating what would come of it all, and wondering whether there was to be free beer. When it became known that beer was excluded, a shock of disgust went through the community.

"Bloomin' reformatory!" said one husky critic.

"If them's 'is lines," said another, his mind running on the exclusion of liquid comforts, "the pubs is safe."

"Ain't there nobody about to teach the bleedin' idjit sense?" enquired a third, sticking out a scornful underlip.

Politer cynics remarked with a snicker, "The millennium's at hand, since a Twickham turns his back on beer."

All the while Vincent went about his business, genially disregarding criticism. If he were on the right lines results would speak for themselves, suggested the Twickham spirit; if he were on the wrong lines, the less said the better. With Dr. Brinkley he went to and fro among the dark places of England's heart, bestowing much in charity, and hiding his benefactions as if they were criminal offences. Dick was commonly of the party, because he was rich in resource, and his right arm was strong where the arm of the law was decidedly weak. Besides, in spite of differences about drink, Vincent had won the fighter's heart.

"'E may have water on the brain a bit," said Mr. Goodman, in explanation of his hero-worship, "but 'e ain't got none on the 'art, an' Lor' pity the mug as says 'e 'as. Nor he don't go talkin' at a cove as takes a drop. I've my beer as usual."

This catholicity of sentiment likewise made a bond-slave of Ingledew, who followed among the black, swirling, underground currents, trembling at his own temerity.

Being well provided with funds, Dick and Ingledew occasionally indulged in surreptitious festivities of their own. It chanced one evening, while near Drury Lane, that, partly from curiosity, partly from sociality, they turned into the Spotted Goat, and behold! Velvet Chick in the seat of honour, with Tommy Binks by his side. Dick greeted them with extravagant cordiality, introduced Ingledew, and asked them to "give it a name." They in turn made the same request of him, and the rounds were many. As the talk grew in ardency past events cropped up ; and Dick, suddenly waxing hot, made certain assertions calculated to excite the listeners. Ingledew implored his friend for God's sake to be careful ; then, finding his appeal of no avail, fled in terror. But Velvet Chick smoked his cigar placidly, regarding Dick with contracted eyes, while Tommy Binks merely spat and grinned. Presently Dick departed, leaving the air palpitating with challenges.

That night his conduct was the subject of an animated discussion at the Ruggler Den, and the Rugglers chuckled joyously. Velvet Chick poured out volumes of smoke as he meditated, and Binks was chiefly engaged in watching the heavy-weight's face. Vincent's assumption of righteousness was also discussed ; and the toast, " May all prigs perish ! " was received with gleaming eyes and ecstatic grunts. When the meeting broke up, Velvet Chick and Tommy Binks conferred half an hour by themselves.

Three weeks later the inseparable four, Vincent, Tapley, Dick, and Ingledew were returning in the dusk after a visit to some of Ingledew's old quarters in Spitalfields. With Vincent it had been a busy and happy day. In the morning he had had a long, con-fidential talk with his father and mother, and Lord

Twickham had expressed gratification in the fact that his son's divagations were not leading to open opposition. In a merry, bantering way he even wished success to the Metropolitan Hall of Recreation.

Thus encouraged, Lady Twickham had in the afternoon permitted Vincent to take her to see the foundations, the architect being present with a picture of the completed building. As they were driven, chatting together, it seemed mother and son had never before come so close to each other. Vincent was in high spirits ; he had a thousand things to tell, and he told them with the gusto of a boy describing a new game. Looking at his eager face, his mother's eyes glistened wistfully as she thought all might yet be well.

Elated by his mother's open interest and his father's implied forgiveness, Vincent went off blithely with Tapley to meet Dick and Ingledew, according to an appointment made the day before. Together the four explored some of the darker caverns of Spitalfields, like Daniel passing scatheless through dens of wild beasts, because silver was strewn plenteously by the way. At the lighting of the lamps they looked in on their old friend, the deputy, and, having cheered him in his pit, turned westward, talking lightly, for Vincent was still exhilarated. It was the hour when factory and workshop pour forth their grimy, medley brigades to aggravate the common tumult ; and the pavements were confused torrents. Wherever the press gave elbow-room, the younger spirits, as yet unbroken by hardship and hard living, lightened the march with rude horse-play. Youths, in token of affection, thumped the damsels of their choice ; and the damsels retaliated with squeals of delight ; or boys and girls chased and ducked in boisterous disregard of the threats of the elders with whom they collided. There were many cross-currents, and jostling, accidental and intentional, went on merrily to the sound of laughter and of cursing. Several times Dick felt the wanton impact, and responded deftly with the stiff elbow or bent shoulder as in days of old. Once the fist came into play, and the crowd, quick to feel the electric thrill, paused, craning its neck and shouting for the fun. But Vincent jerked Dick aside; the instant commotion died as swiftly as it rose, and the torrent rolled on, clamorous as the tide racing over shingle.

"Let us get away," said Vincent, feeling as if the breath were being pressed out of him.

"All right, sir," answered Dick cheerfully; "it do be a bit tight in 'ere. Kind of 'minds me of the shock of the 'Ighlanders takin' niggers on the bayonet."

They were turning into a side street, which promised relief in its emptiness, when all at once Vincent, who had got some yards ahead, was jostled almost off his feet. Seeing him reel, Dick leaped to his aid, hitting out right and left. As he struck he caught a glimpse of the livid face of Tommy Binks, and he rather felt than saw that other livid, familiar faces were behind. At the same time he was conscious of a noise like the soughing of a mighty wind among trees, and he knew the crowd was closing in, panting to see a fight.

Now in a London street tumult anything may happen; and something happened now on which the most sanguine lover of sensation durst not have counted. For perhaps the space of one minute the crowd swayed, uncertain and unseeing. What was going on in that hidden inner ring? What was the scuffling centre knot about? The answer came sharp and startling in the crack of a pistol, followed, quick as trigger could be pulled, by another and another. With the last came the frantic blowing of a police-whistle. Half a moment the multitude stood motionless, holding its breath in awe; then, as rises a tempestuous billow, it heaved and pitched forward, roaring deliriously.

In the first rush Tapley and Ingledew were cut off from their companions; but at that hoarse shout Tapley crushed distractedly in, to find Vincent and Dick stretched side by side on the pavement.

"What's this?" he cried, living terror in his voice. "Vin," bending over his brother-in-law, "you're not hurt. Tell me you're not hit."

Vincent turned on his side, his hand pressed to his chest, and Tapley was horrified to see a dark red stain on the white shirt.

"Oh, my God!" he gasped, dropping on his knees.

At that Dick lifted his head, made as if to rise, wriggled feebly, and fell back, limp.

"Domino, Tottie," he said quietly, looking up, an expression half smile, half pain, in his eyes. "Mind 'im." And lay still.

Tapley bent more closely over Vincent.

"I'm choking," came in a panting, gurgling whisper —"oh! I'm choking."

Tapley ran out the waistcoat buttons, and a constable tore off the collar and ripped open the shirt. Then Tapley, hardly knowing what he did, shouted Dr. Brinkley's address.

"Run," he called frantically—"run!"

Fortunately the messenger had not far to go, and within two minutes the doctor was on the scene.

"Shot through the lungs; Goodman twice," he said, after a swift examination; and he ordered the wounded men to be carried instantly to the hospital. "This," he remarked to Tapley as they followed— "this is the gratitude of the slums."

"Is it serious, doctor?" asked Tapley, his heart stopping for the reply.

"I'm afraid it is," said the doctor—"I'm afraid it is." And proceeded with bent head.

CHAPTER XI

THE hospital surgeons did their work with the calm celerity of experts in tragedy. When first treatment had been given, and the patients, scarcely conscious, were tucked away in care of nurses, Dr. Brinkley took the house-surgeon aside.

"Well!" he said, scanning the face of the other anxiously.

"It's very serious," was the response.

"Not death?" said the doctor, his voice quivering.

"It may be death," answered the surgeon quietly.

A film came before the doctor's eyes.

"Oh no!" he protested, with a short, hard breath. "It must not be death; we cannot let it be death."

"Not if we can help it, Dr. Brinkley. But I needn't tell you of the dangers of internal hemorrhage in such cases. We can't even search for the bullets. For the present we can only try to keep in life. I hope we shall succeed."

The doctor passed a shaking hand across a damp forehead.

"What will Lord and Lady Twickham do?" he said helplessly.

The surgeon did not answer; his business was with the ills of those lying within the hospital walls, not with the probable feelings or doings of· those outside.

To Tapley and Dr. Brinkley it was a racking problem how Vincent's father and mother were to be told of their misfortune. Lady Gwendoline, being in a very delicate condition of health, must for the present be kept in ignorance.

"You'll do it, of course," said Tapley. "You're experienced in imparting bad news."

"On the contrary, you'll do it," returned the doctor.

"I couldn't," protested Tapley—"I really couldn't. I should make a mess of it; I am sure I should. Feel how I am perspiring."

"Perspiring!" repeated Dr. Brinkley. "I'm deadly cold. I've rough-handled death in the slums for thirty years, and never felt chilled like this."

In the end they did it together, scarcely knowing how; and within five minutes the gleaming blacks were racing for the hospital as in all their sleek lives they had never raced before. But their speed was in vain. Lord and Lady Twickham were conducted to the house-surgeon's room, where the impossibility of disturbing their son was gently explained to them. Lady Twickham, whose beseeching, terrified eyes implied that the surgeon held power of life and death, pleaded piteously to be allowed to stay and watch. She would not disturb Vincent by word or act. She would be quiet—absolutely quiet; but she must see and take care of her boy. When that, too, was gently denied her, the strained heart rebelled, and she would have called out upbraidingly but for the dry sobs which choked her. Lord Twickham, himself on the verge of a sob, comforted her brokenly; and the surgeon, versed in the eccentricities of anguish, waited gravely.

"Your ladyship may rest assured that everything possible shall be done," he said softly, when she could listen. "It is because we wish to restore him to you quickly that we guard him so jealously now." He presented a list of the surgical staff to Lord Twickham.

"Your lordship will see," he said, "he shall have the very best skill in London."

Lord Twickham nodded, distrusting his power to speak. There came a call for the surgeon ; and they were bowed out.

As they passed along a corridor a door opened, and Jenny came out weeping convulsively. Mr. Ingledew, it seemed, had burst in upon her, crying out his news. She flew to the hospital, and for ten minutes had been begging ineffectually for a glimpse of Dick. Seeing Lady Twickham, also weeping, she ran forward, her hands out imploringly.

"Oh ! my lady," she cried, taking hold of Lady Twickham's dress, "what's happened ? Tell me what's wrong. They won't let me see my husband."

"They won't let me see my son," returned Lady Twickham, the tears streaming down her face.

Jenny staggered back, her wet eyes fixed in a wild stare.

"Your son !" she panted. "My lady, they're not killed together. Say," clutching at the dress again— "say they're not killed together."

"Not killed," put in Lord Twickham, in an unsteady voice, "only hurt, and they must not be disturbed."

Jenny curtseyed instinctively.

"Thank you, m' lord," she said. "Then we shall see them by-and-by."

"By-and-by," repeated Lord Twickham, turning away.

"Jenny," said Lady Twickham, "give me your arm ; my poor head swims."

And Jenny gave her arm. For a moment social inequalities were obliterated. They were merely women—women, and in trouble for their beloved. In an instant of sunshine the bolt had fallen. The idols of their hearts were swept out of sight, and were lying in the dread silence behind, bleeding, perhaps dying, and they were denied admission. They went out together, wrung as by spasms. Lord Twickham, waiting outside, assisted his wife into the carriage, then turned to her who had no carriage.

"Your husband helped my son," he said hoarsely, putting something into Jenny's hand.

"Thank God for that!" sobbed Jenny—"thank God for that!" and went her way, blind with tears.

For a week the three haunted the temple of woe, with flickering hopes that turned to despairing sickness as the days passed and they were still put off. Then one morning Jenny was taken through corridors so silent that the beating of her own heart made an awesome noise. After many turnings she entered a large, bare, white-washed room, and there, on a bed behind a little screen, with the light falling softly on his face, lay Dick, white and clean and peaceful. But he did not look up at the sound of her approach ; nor did he speak when she bent over him. For an instant her head swirled giddily, and a noise as of tempests was in her ears. Then the gracious tears came, soothing away the tumult.

At dead of night Jenny had often imagined the frenzy of grief and horror which must seize her at the awful moment. She thought she would go mad and rave ; and she had visions of herself led forth shrieking ; and lo ! what she actually experienced was the hush which follows the devastating storm. The nurse was ready with aid, but it was not needed. Kneeling, Jenny kissed the white face again and again, her tears falling on it like a benediction. She could caress now without fear of protest : Dick was her own—her very own.

With a lump in her throat, the nurse walked away ; and Jenny, alone with her dead, bowed in profound thankfulness. For Dick was safe at last.

Never again would he wander amid perils it made her heart ache to think of; never again should she have to sit by a cold hearth waiting for him in fear and trembling. No—never again.

After a while she rose, looking round. Noticing her, the nurse stepped forward; and then Jenny learned that in the end Dick fell asleep as softly as a babe in its mother's arms.

"Did he leave any message?" she asked, her heart hungering for a last word of remembrance.

"All the time he lay he was hardly able to speak," said the nurse. "But I was to tell you he was hit trying to help Mr. Twickham; and you weren't to be sorry, because——"

"Because why?" cried Jenny.

"I think," answered the nurse hesitatingly, "because he hadn't been very good to you."

"Oh! but he was good to me," protested Jenny, her tears gushing afresh—"he was very, very good to me!"

"Well," said the nurse tenderly, putting an arm about her, "he gave his life for another."

"That was Dick," cried Jenny, "saying he was bad and dying for another. That's not bad, is it?"

"No, dear," replied the nurse softly, "that's not bad."

Jenny moved on, drying her eyes.

"May I bring Loo, that's our little girl, to see him?" she asked.

"Bring her, and I will look out for you," was the response.

She brought Loo; and, kneeling together, the woman and the child paid their tribute to the man who had so often wronged them both, yet, as Jenny believed, loved them all the while, and, if put to the test, would have died for them. Perhaps she was right.

At the door, as they were leaving, they met Lord and Lady Twickham.

"Brought your little girl to see her father?" said his lordship kindly. "How is he?"

"Gone, m' lord!" answered Jenny simply—"Dick's gone."

"Gone!" echoed Lord Twickham; and then passing on, "God help you!"

Lady Twickham stayed just a moment to solace the widow and orphan, herself in direr need of comfort.

That day his father and mother came with the promise to see Vincent; but again they were disappointed, and the disappointment seemed even sorer than usual. Lady Twickham pleaded to be allowed to go in to the patient just for a moment—just for one moment, because she had news which would cheer him.

"The fact is," explained Lord Twickham, "an event which he had anticipated with a young husband's eagerness took place this morning. A son was born to him, and he'd like to know."

The physician ventured to congratulate them all. But such good news was exciting. Would they have patience just a little longer? As they would understand, it was necessary to be careful—very careful. In a few days more the patient could probably bear an interview.

So they returned home, sick and heavy at heart, to find an officer awaiting them with the intelligence that two men, arrested on suspicion of having fired the shots, were discharged for want of evidence.

"And this morning one of the victims died," said Lord Twickham, galled by the failure of the law. "In a crowded London street murder is committed, and the murderers go free."

"It's because the street was crowded, my lord,"

rejoined the officer. "In a big crush the chances are no one sees the shots fired, not even those who are hit. So it's been in this case, my lord."

"They ought to be caught!" retorted his lordship impatiently, hot with a sense of grievance against things in general—"they ought to be caught! We're beaten about!" he remarked to his wife a minute later. "Everything's going wrong! We're terribly beaten about!" and sank into a chair.

Nevertheless, hope leaped up again when, on strict promise of keeping quiet and obeying instructions, they were at length permitted to see Vincent. The ghost of his former self, he lay very weak and still; but he smiled up at them, and kissed his mother's hand in token of love and gladness. And as he held it she bent low, whispering the joy which had come to him. A radiance of delight danced in his eyes.

"And Gwen?" he asked, feeling that heaven and earth were whirling about him.

Gwen was doing well.

"Thank God for that!" he sighed.

Had she heard of his accident? Yes, she knew he was slightly hurt.

"Don't make much of it," he said faintly.

No, they would not; and he must compose himself and not worry, because they were all impatient to have him with them again. As they rose to go, he beckoned his father to bend close, and asked how Goodman was. Lord Twickham shuddered, but managed to control himself.

"Goodman is better, dear," was the answer.

"I'm glad of that," came with a faint smile. "I asked, but they won't give me any information in here."

Then his mother kissed him, and they went.

The next time they saw him, he intimated he had a particular favour to ask. He was longing, yearning, to set eyes on his boy. Would they gratify him? The physician shook his head ; but Vincent's look of pain and Lady Twickham's pleading prevailed.

So they came again in the afternoon, and his son was put in Vincent's arms—arms so feeble that, light as the fluffy bundle was, it sank upon the poor wounded breast. Looking into the tiny, sleeping face, Vincent's eyes filled with tears, but he hid them by bending and pressing his lips against the soft, warm check. At that the big blue eyes opened and stared at him in wonder, and he drew the babe closer to his bosom. What his thoughts were in that moment of agonised joy none shall ever know.

As he clasped his son there came a quick, convulsive movement of the shoulders. Noticing it, the physician motioned urgently to have the child taken away, and Lady Twickham was adroitly induced to go home with the nurse. But Lord Twickham was shown into a waiting-room. When the baby was lifted out of his arms Vincent fell back, his eyes strained in frantic appeal, and a gurgling noise in his throat. The next moment the physician was bending over him. A glance showed what had happened. The excitement had reopened the healing wound, and a deadly hemorrhage ensued. Science did what it could to check the flux ; but to the experienced eye it was soon plain what was taking place.

"He's going," said the physician, lifting a pallid face ; "call Lord Twickham."

Lord Twickham came swiftly, a ghastly presentiment at his heart. The physician silently indicated a seat by the bed-side, and he sat down, holding his son's hand. Once he kissed it, but not a word passed his lips. He could not tell how long he had sat when he saw the physician feeling for the pulse.

"Well?" he said hoarsely.

"He's gone," returned the physician softly.

Lord Twickham bowed his head.

"Merciful Heaven!" he groaned, sinking on his knees; and then, "Cover his face—cover his face," and he hid his own.

An age he seemed to crouch in that agony of soul. At length he rose, his face quivering, his eyes bloodshot, and having given some broken instructions, walked out. In the vestibule he met the Bishop of Blockley, come to make enquiries. The bishop looked apprehensively in the ashen face.

"How is he?" he asked, bating his breath.

"At peace," answered Lord Twickham—"at peace." And then, before the other could speak, "I shall go to him; but he shall not return to me."

ON the outskirts of the town of St. Edmund-upon-Stare, of which people had said Vincent Twickham should one day be lord, stands a snug cottage inhabited by a young widow and her little daughter. In all that flows from the virtues of order and cleanliness, it is at once the pattern and the envy of the neighbourhood. Nor does it lack the charm of the softer graces. In summer the roses cluster under its eaves, perfuming the breeze which cools the chamber within; the garden gleams with flowers, and honeysuckle smothers the fences. Even through the bleakness of winter it is distinguished by an air of cosy richness and content.

It is the cottage in which Jenny as a girl dreamed sweet dreams, and whither, her tragic romance over, she returned to glorify the memory of the man who had won and abused her heart. Women are born worshippers. But could Dick have heard the stories which Jenny was so fond of telling Loo, as the pair sat together in the evening twilight, he must have wondered by what stretch of fond or deluded fancy he came to be numbered among the saints.

"You know, dear, it is to daddy we owe all we have," Jenny said once, looking round on a material comfort which sometimes made her sad, because he was not there to share it. "If he hadn't been brave and good we shouldn't be so happy now. For, you see, he died for young Mr. Twickham; and then Lord

Twickham gave us this house, where mammy lived when she was a little girl like you."

"For ever and ever, all to ourselves?" asked the child.

"Yes, dear, for ever and ever, all to ourselves."

"And we sha'n't have to go back to London any more?"

"Not to live; but you would like to go and see daddy's grave, wouldn't you, dear?"

"Yes," answered Loo doubtfully; and then eagerly, "Oh! mammy, isn't it fine? We sha'n't be hungry no more; nor go up and down horrid black stairs, with people callin' nasty things to us; an' you won't cry no more, mammy?"

"Hush, dear, you mustn't say that."

"But I hate London," persisted Loo. "I do—I do hate it."

They were interrupted by the sound of approaching wheels, and Jenny, hurriedly feeling her hair with one hand and brushing her dress with the other, ran to the little gate to welcome Lord and Lady Twickham. Often in their drives they went by the cottage, taking their grandson with them, so that Jenny might comfort herself by kissing his hands and blessing him. And, as time passed, he would sometimes be lifted out of the carriage and taken into the garden, where Loo was privileged to entertain him, the elders looking on. Lord Twickham generally watched in silence, but once he was heard murmuring unconsciously, "We must take better care of him—we must take better care of him."

His son's death, it was remarked, transformed the stern Lord Twickham. He still kept his place at the head of the Brewery, which prospered more and more. The accomplished man of affairs still met the Earl of Wegron, MacTor, and the rest with the old unfailing keenness; but in private his face had often a pensive, wistful look, as if his thoughts were busy with days and scenes now mystically remote. In particular, it was found he had grown tolerant of ways and opinions at which he once scoffed ; and to the amazement of many, who ought to have understood him better, he made Vincent's schemes his own. Once when Jenny thanked him for his goodness, he answered, his eyes moistening, " It is for his sake."

And the motive which made Jenny a pensioner restored Ingledew, tearfully penitent, to his family ; and finished the Metropolitan Hall of Recreation. When certified complete it was presented a free gift to the people. " In memory of my son," said the donor simply.

At the same time certain lawyers were instructed to add a codicil (duly authenticated) to a certain will in their possession, whereby it was provided that so long as name or wealth should remain to the House of Twickham, the Hall was not to be suffered to fall into decay, nor to be perverted from the intentions of its founder. So that the world had good reason for remarking the old lord came to be more solicitous about the fulfilment of his lost son's wishes than about the welfare of the great Brewery.

THE END.

Printed by Hazell, Watson, & Viney, Ld., London and Aylesbury.